LIME TREE HILL

FRANCES COWIE

BLUE BUTTERFLY PRESS

Lime Tree Hill

Published by Blue Butterfly Press.
www.francescowie.com
Copyright © 2020 by Frances Cowie.
The moral right of the author has been asserted.

ISBN: 978-0-473-52178-3 (Paperback)
ISBN: 978-0-473-52179-0 (E-book)

A catalog record of this book is available from the National Library of New Zealand.

This book is a work of fiction. All characters, businesses, and events in this publication, other than those clearly in the public domain, are fictitious. Any resemblance to persons, living or dead, is purely coincidental.

The author acknowledges the trademarked status and trademark owners of various products that have been used without permission. The publication/use of these trademarks is not authorized, associated with or sponsored by the trademark owners.

Cover Design: Steven Novak | www.novakillustration.com
Editor: The Error Eliminator | www.theerroreliminator.wordpress.com
Developmental Editor: Emma Bryson

240616

To Eva, Mimi, and Demi.
What great joy you bring to my life.

LIME TREE HILL

CHERRY GROVE

IF TAYLA WHITMAN had caught an earlier flight to Clifton Falls as planned, she might not have noticed the obscenely large billboard at the intersection of Airport Drive and the Eastern Pacific Highway.

But as the taxi driver stopped and waited to turn left, Mitchel Harrington—all lit up in his half-naked glory, complete with a self-indulgent bulge and a knowing smile—caught her gaze and held it. Tanned to perfection, abs of steel, molded pecs, and wearing the tightest pair of boxer briefs she'd ever seen, did the man have no shame?

Tayla stared for longer than appropriate, given her distrust of him. Sure, physically, he was one of the most mesmerizing men she'd ever met. But good looks meant nothing if a person lacked integrity. And this latest stunt proved her opinion of years before to be true—the guy was a prize jerk.

As they approached her family home, Tayla straightened in her seat, her attention fixed on Lime Tree Hill's southern block. Five hundred yards north, Cherry Grove sat landlocked by acres of citrus trees, and farther along the straight stretch of highway, the main entrance to Lime Tree Hill was barely visible.

"Up there on the left," she said to the driver. "Cherry Grove."

"I hear it's been a bad season for cherries," he replied.

Her father had said as much when she'd talked to him just before his heart attack. At the time, Tayla had asked how they were coping, but he'd brushed her off. Her parents rarely discussed the financial side of the orchard with Tayla and her sisters. "Yes. The last couple of seasons, actually."

The driver pulled to a stop outside the house, and while he unloaded her bags, Tayla looked fondly at the large villa, her eyes misting with tears.

A few moments of composure later, she stood on the veranda and watched the taxi pull away. Tayla wondered if Mitch was at home. Unless the lights were on upstairs, the packing shed where he worked and lived was barely visible from Cherry Grove. But when Tayla looked out over the trees, the place was unusually dark. Maybe he was out on the town, strutting that tight butt around some seedy bar. After all, it was Friday night.

Tayla opened the front door with a shove and switched on the light. The house smelled slightly stale, the result of being closed up for over two weeks, and its stillness unsettled her. But when she trundled her suitcase down the hallway and into the living room, she smiled. A white jug full of sprigs of lavender sat on the sideboard, scenting the air with the aroma of mid-summer. She inhaled deeply.

Home.

Walking from room to room, Tayla opened the windows against the oppressive air. After living in Australia for the past three years, she'd forgotten that Clifton Falls summers could be almost as hot as Sydney's. She headed to the pantry in search of something to eat and opened a half-pint jar of preserved apricots left over from last year's crop. Scooping out the fruit with her fingers, she savored the sweet tang of summer as sugar syrup dripped down her chin.

She was just about to unpack when the phone on the sideboard rang, setting butterflies free in her belly. It was after nine thirty. "Hello. Tayla speaking."

"Tayla. It's Ned. I noticed the lights on. Your mother asked me to keep an eye on the place, so I'm glad it's just you. How's your dad doing?"

"Ned. Hi. He's improving slowly. And sorry, I should have called you. I thought it might be Mitch checking up on Dad." Tayla trundled her suitcase into her bedroom and heaved it onto the bed.

"He's away until tomorrow night."

Good. "Actually, I saw him as I left the airport." The billboard flashed across her mind. "Almost all of him."

Ned chuckled. "You mean the billboard. Can't say I like it much myself. Four grown men posing in their underwear like idiots. Still, the money they raised funded a new defibrillator for the Youth Sports Trust. Every second man in Clifton Falls owns a pair of their boxers now, even an old fella like me."

"And here's me thinking he'd gone into modeling."

Ned chuckled again. "Are you staying long?"

Tayla hesitated. Was she? "I'm not sure yet. Dad has to stay in Auckland for now, so I'm holding the fort in the meantime. Anyway, thanks for your concern. No doubt I'll see you around."

"I look forward to it. Call me if you need anything."

"Thanks. And give my regards to Maggie. Goodnight."

As she hung up the phone, Tayla sighed. How did you pack a large family home full of memories into one a quarter of the size? And what would happen if the sale of the orchard fell through?

She unzipped her suitcase and opened the lid. Neatly aligned packing cells greeted her—bras, panties, jeans—and packed in an alabaster habotai silk garment bag underneath, her wedding dress lay abandoned. Stilling for a moment, she resisted the urge to take one last look before dumping it in a charity clothing bin or drowning it in the river and letting it float out to sea.

But she couldn't bear to drown it. The ocean didn't need any more garbage.

Tayla pulled the bag free and walked down the hallway, out the back door and over to the implement shed where her old Subaru wagon sat—a trusty runabout that her parents had kept 'just in case.' She opened the rear door and lay the bag inside, then turned and walked back into the house, one lone tear tracking down her cheek.

As Tayla reached the kitchen, the muffled sound of her text alert had her searching for her phone. She found it on the counter, next to the empty jar of apricots, and glanced at the screen.

Hayden: Please pick up!!! This has gone on long enough.
Hayden: You have no idea what I've been going through this past couple of weeks. Where the hell are you?
Hayden: Sweetheart don't do this. You're better than that.

Tayla switched it to silent. There'd be no more texts to Hayden. She'd made that decision in the departure lounge at Sydney Airport. Blocking his number would be her next step, but she couldn't deal with that finality right now. How long would it be before he stopped texting her? Before she accepted he was no longer hers. Before she'd packed away her feelings, hiding them from view.

She brought up her contacts and hit Ruby's number, hoping her sister would answer.

"Hi there. How does it feel to be home?" Ruby asked.

Lonely. "A bit strange to be honest. Like time's standing still. Also, we may have a problem."

"Really? What?"

"The lawyer called me while I was waiting for my flight. He couldn't get hold of Dad, and I'm next on the list, apparently. There's a hitch with the sale. They've summoned me to a meeting on Monday."

"Is it serious?"

"I'm not sure. You know what Ian Christie's like. He mumbles

4

away, and I have no idea what he's saying most of the time. Anyway, I'll call you once I know more. But let's keep this under wraps for a bit. I don't want Mum and Dad to worry."

"Good idea. Do you think Mitch will be at the meeting?"

"I hope not. He's the last person I want to see."

"Really? I saw him at Christmas. I swear that man gets hotter every year."

As the billboard flashed through her mind, Tayla couldn't help but smile at the mental image of a half-naked Mitchel Harrington. "I wouldn't know about that."

"Don't try to BS me. Didn't you have a massive crush on him once?"

"As if." Tayla suspected her denial carried little weight. "And if I did, it lasted all of five minutes. The guy accused me of ripping Norman off, remember? He even threatened to call the police."

"I know, but he's still as sexy as chocolate cheesecake." Ruby chuckled. "Time to let it go, Tayla Tilly."

Tayla smiled at her sister's use of her childhood nickname. "Yep. Just one of the many things on my self-improvement bucket list, *Ruby Tuesday.*"

"Anyway, I should get to bed. The girls will be up for breakfast before I know it."

"Goodnight. I'll call you tomorrow."

Tayla ended the call and looked around the room. The photos on the walls, net curtains floating softly in the breeze, and the tiny TV her parents watched every night. How could she pack it all away without their guidance? And how would her mother cope with her father? Her dad, once fit, strong, and proud, now struggled to make conversation, even with those he loved most. And in the two weeks Tayla had sat at his bedside, she'd pondered the frailty of life, love, and commitment until her thoughts were as stripped bare as her ring finger.

2

THE HITCH

MITCHEL HARRINGTON PRIDED himself on being a man of his word. Having to go back on said word tied his stomach in knots. Pulling out of the Cherry Grove deal was bad enough, but after Barry's heart attack, telling him and his wife would be one of the hardest things he'd ever had to do.

Simon Harrow stood as Mitch entered his office. He smoothed his hand over his tie and offered Mitch a chair. "You ready for this?"

"Not even close. Norman's probably looking down on me right now with a huge I-told-you-so grin on his face."

"Crap happens, but we're supposed to walk around it, not through it. Still no movement from your great-uncle?"

"Nope. I thought he might reconsider, but he's not the type to indulge whims. His words, not mine."

While they waited for the Whitman Family Trust representative to arrive, Mitch and Simon talked business until his lawyer's PA knocked and opened the door. "Ms. Whitman's here."

Behind the PA stood one of the Whitman girls, but Mitch wasn't sure if it was Lisa, Ruby, or Tayla. The only one he'd had much to do with was Tayla, and that was before she went to university. She hadn't spoken to him since. Not that he could blame her after he'd accused her of stealing.

According to her mother, she now lived in Sydney. And as he spent most holidays in Tulloch Point with his parents, he rarely saw any of the Whitman siblings.

The men stood to greet her. "Please come in," Simon said. "I'm so sorry to hear about your father. Is he doing okay?"

"Thanks for asking. He's slowly regaining his strength."

Simon looked at Mitch. "You two have met?"

"We have." She offered no pleasantries, not even a smile. "Mitch."

He reached out, shocked at the chill of her skin as they shook hands. With the same hazel eyes as her mother, she looked like an older Tayla, but everything about her was chalk to Tayla's cheese. This Ms. Whitman held herself with a confidence Tayla had never possessed. He thought back to when he'd last seen her, before she'd left for AUT. At that stage, she'd been in full goth mode, with a pixie cut, purple Doc Martens, and a blood-red ring in her nose. Black, on black, on cherry black. Maybe the woman in front of him was Lisa.

"Hi, it's nice to see you again," he said with a smile.

Ignoring his polite greeting, she sat in the offered chair, crossed one long leg over the other, and swung her stiletto-clad foot. Wearing a taupe blazer over a white top and black skinny jeans, she looked casually chic but aloof. With her long slender neck, delicate hands, and full lips, Mitch found it hard to take his eyes off her.

"Can someone please tell me what's going on?" Her tone of superiority caught him off guard. But then, what had he expected?

"I'm afraid we've struck a glitch," Simon said.

"So I gather, but our lawyer was light on the details. What sort of glitch are we talking about? Moving the settlement date?"

Mitch shot Simon a sideways glance. He might as well get

straight to the point. "Unfortunately, I'm unable to settle at this stage."

She stared at him, looking dazed. "I don't understand. You've paid the deposit. And my parents have already purchased a property in a retirement complex."

Now it was Simon's turn to speak. "They've bought elsewhere? Before settlement?"

"I advised them against it, but my father's made some rash decisions lately. If you can't settle on time, they may lose everything."

"I'm sure the bank will supply bridging finance if they need it," Simon offered.

"Not now that Dad's unable to work. And what about the deposit?"

"Under the terms of the agreement," Simon continued, "Mitch will forfeit his deposit. That should help in the interim."

Ms. Whitman kept her gaze on Simon, her dismissal of Mitch clear. "I spoke with their accountant this morning. Cherry Grove is heavily mortgaged. Before the sale, the bank was threatening foreclosure." She turned to Mitch and looked him straight in the eye. "How could you do this to them?"

"I'm sorry. Jean and Barry have been good neighbors. I didn't expect this to happen."

"Expect it to happen? Didn't you crunch your numbers before scribbling your name on the dotted line?"

The hairs lifted on the back of Mitch's neck. The woman could pack a verbal punch, that's for sure.

"Look, Tayla, we're trying to do our best here," Simon said.

Mitch stared in disbelief at the woman sitting in the adjacent chair. Tayla? Surely Simon had made a mistake. But she didn't contradict him.

"Excuse me if I sound cynical," she countered. "But I fail to see what *your best* is at the moment."

"We're willing to do whatever we can to help, but unfortunately, Mitch is right. His offer for Cherry Grove was genuine at the time, however, there will be no settlement in the foreseeable future."

"So, what do you suggest I tell my father?"

"I'll tell him," Mitch offered. He'd planned to talk to Barry and Jean anyway, but Barry's ill health had changed everything.

"No, you won't," she snapped. "You've done enough damage. And, as I hold enduring power of attorney, I insist this conversation be treated as confidential. I don't want to worry my parents until Ruby and I have considered our options."

"Do you think I wanted this?" Mitch kept his cool, but still, he wouldn't let the way she'd spoken to him slide. He'd thought about her a lot over the years. In his imagination she'd exuded sweetness and innocence despite her goth exterior, but the Tayla sitting next to him didn't resemble her younger self one bit. "I understand your parents are the innocent party in all of this, but they aren't the only ones who'll be negatively affected."

She scoffed. "I don't know how you can sit there and turn this around so it's all about poor old you. My father has just had open-heart surgery. He's worked hard all his life for this. Now you come along and pull the pin. Unbelievable."

"Okay, let's take a breather." Simon straightened his tie. "I agree. This is an unfortunate set of circumstances we find ourselves in, but—"

"And what circumstances would they be?" Tayla asked. "If it was all fine months ago, what went wrong?"

Simon shot Mitch a concerned look.

"The reasons are not up for discussion," Mitch said.

Tayla crossed her arms over her chest and looked away. "Of course not."

"Right." Simon cleared his throat and addressed her. "My advice is to consult the trust's lawyer."

"And tell him what? That we've been scammed?"

"No." Simon stretched out the word. "That, unfortunately,

Mitch is unable to proceed with the purchase right now. I understand it will take time to process what this means for your parents. If there's any way we can turn this around, I'll be in touch."

For a moment, Tayla said nothing. She glanced at Mitch with a dismissive flick of her lashes then back at Simon. "Thank you, Simon. I appreciate your concern."

Tayla stood, her chin held high. Mitch did the same, surprised at how tall she was. "I'm sorry we had to meet again under such circumstances." He offered his hand.

She showed him her palm. "Don't. Please…just don't."

Simon cleared his throat again, and Mitch knew how he felt. Still, he'd never expected it to be easy.

"If the situation changes, we'll be in touch," Simon repeated. "In the meantime, I suggest you have a word with a realtor, just in case anyone else is interested. I know you're not in a strong position with the orchard landlocked by Lime Tree Hill, but it only takes one person to want it."

"Thank you." Tayla sighed heavily as she walked toward the door, and when Mitch held it open, she brushed past him without another word.

He turned to Simon once she was out of earshot. "Now I know how a male praying mantis feels." He rubbed the back of his neck. "Shit! As much as I loved my grandfather, he had a warped sense of reality. I wonder if she knows about the other offer."

"If she doesn't, she'll find out as soon as the orchard's back on the market. And even if they have to drop a few hundred K, I reckon she'll take it. What other choice do they have?"

Mitch shook his head. "Imagine having the Stone and Pip Group as neighbors. Chris Stone would love to get his greedy mitts on Cherry Grove, even if it was just to piss me off." He sighed. "Who knew a broken engagement could cause so much shit?"

"Wait a minute." Simon stood and reached for his jacket. "I have an idea. Come on. Shout me lunch and I'll fill you in on the way—strictly off the record though. What does Tayla do for a living?"

"She's a physiotherapist, or at least she was. I haven't seen her in ages."

"That's a plus. There should be plenty of work around here in her field," Simon replied. "I bet those hands give a great massage. Do you think she's single?"

When he caught Simon's drift, Mitch's protest was loud and clear. "Piss off."

3

STRICTLY CONFIDENTIAL

TAYLA PULLED her old Subaru into a parking space outside the Surf Life Saving Club and cut the engine. She sat for a moment, wondering what on earth had just happened. One thing was for sure: Mitchel Harrington with that deep voice—like gravel sprinkled on velvet as Ruby had once described it—was going down. That was the second time he'd messed with her, and he needed to know it wasn't okay.

She swore under her breath. How could he do this to her parents? They'd been so excited. After two years of little interest, the orchard had finally sold to Mr Organics next door—the same man she'd once had an enormous crush on. The man their neighbor Norman had always referred to as 'the boy.'

As a rule, Tayla didn't get angry. Anger was a wasted emotion that chewed you up inside. But if the past couple of weeks had taught her anything, they'd taught her this: It was okay to be angry, especially with men who pissed you off. Men like Mitchel Harrington, with his tight boxer briefs and white-toothed smile, and Hayden Lockhart—all broken promises and wedding bell blues.

Screw men! She was done.

Tayla stared out at the Pacific, longing for a gray day. Why should the sun keep shining when all this turmoil was smothering her? She opened the car door and flicked off her heels before stepping across the boardwalk and down to the shore, where the flat surf mocked her.

Back home in Sydney, Bondi was her beach of choice. She'd stand in the water, with her skirt hitched up around her thighs and the breakers lapping at her knees, willing herself to take one more step. Some people called it grounding. She called it progress. Thinking about it now, she felt suddenly homesick for the full waves and the many hours spent in the Icebergs Pool, swimming away her blues while the surf crashed over the sea wall.

As she walked along the beach, her thoughts turned to Hayden. What was he doing in his role of new father? Did he help with feeding and bath time and bringing up wind? Or was he too busy at the hospital? Had he already found someone else to enjoy an 'intellectual relationship' with? Someone other than her.

The sound of her phone brought her to an abrupt stop. She pulled it out and glanced at the screen before hitting *Accept*. "Hi, how's Dad?"

"Not so good today." Ruby sounded strained, and an image of their father lying in the coronary care unit flashed into Tayla's mind. "Still, the doctor said to expect this. Anyway, how did you get on? Did you see Mitch?"

"Oh, I saw him all right."

"Is he still as handsome as ever? That man's biceps could crush me any day."

What could Tayla say to that? *Of course, the bastard.* "Are you alone?"

"Yes. I gather things didn't go well. You sound stressed."

Tayla stopped walking, wondering how to lessen the blow for her sister. "Mr. 'Organics' Harrington, with those selfsame biceps bulging out of his shirt, can't settle."

"What? You're joking!"

"I wish. The details are sketchy, but he's prepared to forfeit the deposit, so it must be serious."

"No way. He can't do that."

"Apparently, he can. What are we going to do? Even if we scrape together the retirement condo money, we can't let the bank take the orchard. Mum and Dad would be devastated."

"Shit! We can't tell them. Not yet. Mum's a wreck as it is."

Ruby was right. Now would be the worst possible time to tell their mother, especially when Mitch and his lawyer had given her no details. "I might just pay the man a visit tomorrow. See what on earth's going on."

"Good plan. I'm sorry I'm not there to lend a hand, but I can't leave Auckland at the moment. When do you have to be back in Sydney?"

When hell freezes over. "I'm not sure. I've applied for compassionate leave for a few months, just until we find out what's happening with Dad. Anyway, give him a kiss from me. I'll try to fly up next weekend. I need to talk to you about Hayden."

Ruby hesitated. "Okaaay. Are you sure you don't want to talk now?"

"No. It's a face-to-face tale of woe. And, Rubes, best if we don't tell Lisa in the meantime. Just in case she lets something slip."

"You know me. 'Strictly confidential' is my middle name. Call me if you find out anything. Where are you? I can hear seagulls."

"At the beach, clearing my head of cobwebs."

"I forgot to ask you how the surfing lessons went."

Tayla took a deep breath. It had taken her weeks to muster up the courage to book the lessons, and when she finally had, she'd paid straight away so she wouldn't back out. Now would she ever conquer her fear of open water? "They didn't. I came home instead. But one day."

"Just don't push yourself too hard right now. You have a lot on your plate."

"Yeah. Bye, Rubes. Love you."

When she returned to the car, Tayla noticed the garment bag on the back seat and swallowed hard. It was time to visit the Salvation Army Family Store.

The *tish-tish-tish* of oscillating sprinklers woke her at 6 a.m.

A self-confessed city girl of late, Tayla had forgotten how noisy living on an orchard could be. She lay there for a moment, resisting the urge to use the bathroom while trying to go back to sleep. But the more she tried, the more the events of yesterday's meeting crowded her thoughts. Every time Mitchel Harrington appeared in her mind, he stood looking at her, half-naked, with his arms crossed and that sexy grin plastered on his face. Just like the billboard.

Tayla picked up her book and opened it, but after scanning the first few paragraphs, put it down again, her mind racing. Finally admitting defeat, she pushed back the covers and planted her feet on the wooden floorboards.

Shrugging on her robe, she padded through to the kitchen and looked out the window, hoping for a cooler day. But not one cloud floated in the emerging blue.

The evening before, Tayla had pored over the trust's bank statements and accounts, sipping a glass of pinot as she tried to get a handle on her parents' financial position. Like everything her father did, the records were meticulous, but that didn't mean there was any money. Quite the opposite.

While poking around in their affairs didn't seem right, her mother had no clue when it came to the 'money side of the business' as she called it. And Tayla couldn't talk to her father. Not until he was stronger, anyway.

She wondered what had happened to the harvest payment. They harvested the cherries in December. It was now early

February, and the account was in the red by tens of thousands of dollars. There'd been no significant deposits in the past sixty days.

As she turned on the coffee machine, she checked the clock above the kitchen table. Seven fifteen. Too early to call Mr. Billboard, although she considered it. According to her mother, he lived alone in the loft above the packing shed. Tayla wondered why Mitch didn't live in his late grandfather's cottage. Perhaps he didn't want to entertain his conquests in the house where Norman had died.

Thinking about Norman made Tayla's chest pang. She'd had a fondness for him from the first day they met. And through their mutual love of books and movies, they'd bonded like old friends from another time. Apart from Hayden and her closest friend, Tim, she'd never had that connection with a man.

The night before, Hayden had phoned at some ungodly hour. Despite what he'd done, she missed him. The warmth of his hand on her back, his dry wit, and the way he pulled her in with his smile. But what could he say? 'Sorry, sweetheart. I thought I'd mentioned I'd gone back to my ex and we were pregnant.' Had those two important facts completely slipped his mind?

Just like their wedding. The chauffeur-driven limousine, her ivory silk gown, and the engagement ring—now hidden in its box in her underwear drawer. If Ruby hadn't called to tell her about their father, she might still be waiting at the chapel. Dying of thirst and embarrassment.

A knock on the back door startled her. Pulling her robe tighter across her chest, Tayla listened again. On the second knock, she ran her fingers through her hair and cracked open the door. Mr. Billboard himself stood on the step, an adorable pug puppy at his feet.

"It's a little early for callers, don't you think? I'm not even dressed."

He offered no smile. "I'd like a word. Can I take you out for breakfast?"

"Have you had a change of heart?" When Mitch looked puzzled, she continued, "About buying the orchard."

"It's not about having a change of heart. But a change of circumstances could make all the difference."

"Meaning?"

He hesitated. "Look, all I'm asking for is thirty minutes. I have something I'd like to discuss."

The Mitchel Harrington had something to discuss. *Great.* "After yesterday, I can't imagine what more there is to say. So, it's a 'no' to breakfast."

His stare caught her a little off balance. He'd had that effect on her when she was seventeen as well, but she never expected it to be the same nine years later. It was his eyes. Moody blue as the sky on the eve of dusk, and just as mysterious.

"I have an office at the end of the packing shed. Shall we say" —he checked his watch—"nine thirty?"

"This morning doesn't suit. And I don't like being summoned."

"Fine." He huffed out a sigh, his loss of patience on open display. "Between one and two this afternoon, then?"

"I'll see."

"Look, Tayla, be there or not. It's your call." He turned, picked up the pup, and walked off without another word.

Tayla shut the back door with more force than intended, his words bouncing around in her head. And although part of her knew she was being unreasonable, by the time she hit the shower, she was mad as hell.

And yet, despite her better judgment, Tayla knew she'd make the meeting. After all, curiosity has its own agenda.

4

RESERVATION

MITCH WALKED AWAY FROM THE WHITMANS' with some reservation. He wondered if the woman knew how beautiful she was—flaunting an attitude, makeup-free, and fresh from sleep. Would she make the meeting? He wouldn't hold his breath.

As he passed Norman's cottage, he stopped. He still found it hard to go inside. The old man had been Mitch's last remaining link to his late father, and he'd felt his death keenly. Although he'd renovated the villa until all traces of Norman had been scrubbed from its interior, every time Mitch entered the kitchen, his late grandfather's presence lingered. Even after all these years. What would Norman think of his plan? He'd probably be grinning from ear to ear.

Mitch whistled for the pug. "Come on, Mr. Edward. Let's go get some breakfast, boy. I have a feeling we'll need a full stomach for this one."

Ned looked up as Mitch entered the large packing shed with Edward at his heels. After Norman's death, Ned had continued to manage the orchard until Mitch took over the reins. Now in his eightieth year, Ned still helped run the packing shed, despite the operation being substantially larger than it was in Norman's day.

"You been at the Whitman place all night?" Ned chuckled, his hands busy as he sorted lemons into a box.

"Very funny. I'd be in the river weighted down with a concrete slab by now if I had. Tayla Whitman hates me with a passion."

"But she seems so wholesome and sweet. You could do a lot worse if you ask me. Besides, a little love-hate tug can be fun."

"How would you know?"

"I'm old, not dead." He winked. "Maggie and I still spar sometimes. Making up is the best part of marriage."

Mitch chuckled. He enjoyed Ned's sense of humor, always had. The older man had an intuition about him that Mitch admired. "Okay, that's enough of the relationship advice. I'm going upstairs to get something wholesome and sweet of my own—toast and honey. Tayla may be polite to you, but I'm on her search-and-destroy list, especially now."

Ned stopped what he was doing. "So you've told her?"

"Yep. She's coming over after lunch. We'll need some privacy, so keep everyone away while she's here, okay?"

"Will do."

Mitch entered his office and sat at the desk. He leaned back in his seat with a sigh, closing his eyes briefly until he heard a knock on the window overlooking the packing shed.

"Morning." His friend Luka stood in the doorway. "I'm just heading up the Valley. Mum said you have a box of fruit for her."

"Yeah, it's on the bench outside the door."

Luka studied him. "How did the meeting go?"

"Not the best. Do you remember the Whitmans' youngest daughter, Tayla?"

"The goth girl who worked at the supermarket?"

"The very same." Mitch stood and followed Luka out the door. "Turns out, she's their power of attorney."

"Is that a problem?"

"Let's put it this way. While we were in Simon's office, I felt like she had my balls in a vise and was twisting them slowly every time I opened my mouth."

Luka winced as Mitch picked up the box of fruit. "Ouch. She always seemed such a timid thing."

"Not anymore. She's as cold as a hoar frost...but twice as beautiful."

Opening the back door of his truck, Luka flashed his usual shit-eating grin. "You're interested?"

"Maybe. But not in the way you think." He slid the box onto the back seat. "Last week, I might have looked the other way, but this could be bigger than the both of us."

"Meaning?"

"I'm not too sure myself. I'll fill you in on Wednesday."

Back in his office after lunch, Mitch checked his email for orders. Although he'd never expected to enjoy the lifestyle, after a shaky start, he now loved running the orchard with a passion. Having witnessed way too much destruction at the hand of man, he saw organics as a way to do his bit.

He picked up his phone and checked the notifications.

Prue: Hey, I haven't heard from you for a while. Are you okay?

Mitch reread her message. *Was* he okay?

Mitch: Yeah, all good.
Prue: Can we catch up when I'm in CF next? We really need to talk.
Mitch: There's nothing more to say. Is there?
Prue: I still love you. How many times do I have to say I'm sorry?

Mitch: I'm sorry too. But it's over.

As another text came through, Mitch slid his phone across the desk. He sat with his head in his hands, knowing it if he didn't shut down their exchange, he might cave. Tell her that he hadn't been okay for months. That he still loved her too. Still thought about her every other day. Still questioned why she'd cheated like that.

He stood and clicked his fingers. Edward looked up. "Come on, boy. I need some fresh air."

Tayla arrived just after two. Standing before him in a floaty dress and Chucks, her light brown locks caught the afternoon sun that filtered through the open packing shed doors.

He still couldn't get used to her this way. When she was a student, she'd kept her natural features hidden under layers of makeup, and her eyebrows had looked like they'd been tattooed on by some kid with a gun in his garage. But those dark ruby lips had been perfectly applied, the nose ring always in place.

Now everything about her was light. From her hair to her clothes to her barely there makeup. Everything except her mood. Her mood was darker than midnight.

"Tayla. Thanks for coming." Mitch rose from his chair and stepped toward her. "Shall we go upstairs?"

"Here's fine." She took the seat in front of his desk before he'd offered it and shot him a frigid glance. "What's this about?"

Okay!

As Mitch returned to his chair, he thought back several years. After his grandfather died, he'd asked Tayla to have coffee with him so they could reminisce about Norman, the man they'd both loved. But she'd refused, her demeanor similar to now. "I want to discuss the sale."

"Apparently, there is no sale. But please, enlighten me." She paused. "Why make an offer you couldn't deliver on?"

Mitch went to speak, but scarcely pausing to draw breath, Tayla continued, "You have no idea what you've done, do you? You might not think you owe me an explanation, but I disagree."

"That's why we're here, isn't it?" Gathering his thoughts, he stood and walked to the window. He turned. "Norman attached extensive stipulations to my inheritance. Don't get me wrong, I'm extremely grateful for everything he's done for me, but he wanted to make sure I didn't screw it up. I had to be twenty-eight before the orchard was mine, which suited me fine. I was traveling with my job and didn't want to give up that lifestyle when I was younger."

"Yes, I remember him talking about that. What would happen to the orchard when 'the boy' took over."

"I think he'd be happy with how it's turned out. Of course, he never had a passion for organics. Thought it was some hippy fad." He leaned his butt against the front of his desk. Tayla scooted her chair back a fraction, as if his presence unsettled her, but her hazel eyes never left his.

"I was due a substantial payout at the end of last year. But there was a hiccup, and the estate trustees refused to release the funds. I'm still interested in buying Cherry Grove, but I can't raise the money right now without jeopardizing my cash flow."

Her eyes widened. "So you'll let my parents go under instead?"

"I hadn't realized they were in such a dire financial position. Barry acted as if everything was fine. Although I did wonder when he asked me if I wanted to lease the cherries."

"What do you mean, lease the cherries?"

"I've leased Cherry Grove's trees for two seasons now. It's common practice. Fruit trees are leased all over the district. Your father wanted the money early, so I paid him for the crop in advance."

"But that doesn't make sense. Why wouldn't he have mentioned that?"

"I think the dream's turned into a nightmare for him lately.

Cherries need dry conditions with low humidity. Our climate's not ideal, and as a result, Cherry Grove's crop hasn't reached export standard for the past few years. When competing with fruit from Central Otago, they don't stack up."

"So, how do you make them profitable?" Her frown deepened.

"Sell them fresh through the farm gate store. Even then, they can be a loss leader. Any surplus, we pickle in brandy or dry them."

"I didn't know any of this."

"But you hold their power of attorney?"

"Yes, but Dad never discusses his finances with any of us. Not even Mum."

That didn't surprise Mitch. Barry was a proud man with old-school values. A nice guy who'd lost interest in his business. Simon Harrow was right; he'd stumbled upon the solution with a simple comment of jest. "I'm sorry I had to go back on my word, but I have an idea."

At this, Tayla appeared to relax a little. "Go on."

"Are you in a relationship?"

Her cheeks flushed. "Excuse me?"

"Because if you're not, I want to marry you."

5

WEDDED WOE

TAYLA STARED at Mitch in stunned disbelief. If he hadn't looked so serious, she would have laughed in his face. "Is this some sort of sick joke?"

"Do I look like I'm joking? I need a wife. You need a sale. It's a business proposition, nothing more. I'm not looking for a connection. A few months of wedded woe, then we go our separate ways. The sale goes through, and your parents can spend their days playing bridge at the retirement complex. Everyone's happy."

"Except me."

Mitch cocked a brow. "Well, that's your choice."

"And what will our families say when we invite them to our version of *Meet Me at the Altar*? I hate that show."

"Really? I thought you'd be all over reality TV."

She scoffed. "As if. So, let me get this straight. You need to be married to inherit the money?"

He nodded. "That's about the gist."

Tayla moved her chair back a fraction. The guy was living in La-La Land. "You can't be serious. I'm sorry, but the Norman I knew would never make such a stipulation. It sounds like some ridiculous eighties sitcom."

"Maybe, but he always said a man should be married by his early thirties. Even though my great-uncle knows the sale won't go through if I don't get the payout, as executor of the will, he won't budge on Norman's wishes."

"So why make an offer on Cherry Grove if you didn't have the money?"

Mitch frowned. "I made a hasty decision. Now I'm paying the price for my stupidity."

Tayla wanted to walk out of that office, through the tree rows, past Norman's cottage, and never set foot on Lime Tree Hill again. Screw the curiosity rearing its inquisitive head. A man didn't refer to himself as stupid unless he had good reason.

Memories of her own 'bad decision' surfaced. That long wait in the chapel, the sun streaming through the stained glass windows, turning her gown a riot of color. The panicked knot in her chest when she'd realized Hayden was a no-show. The look of pity on the photographer's face when she'd told him to delete all the pictures he'd spent an hour taking. She wondered if Mitch's 'bad decision' was as miserable as hers.

"And you think another bad decision will right all wrongs?"

"I have no delusions on that score. But if we treat it as a business deal, what's the worst that could happen?"

Everything. "No one would believe us."

"Why not? We've known each other for years. We could say you've always carried a crush."

Mitch moved back to his chair behind the desk as she struggled to hold her tongue.

"When we reconnected recently, you couldn't stay away from me." He stopped, his eyes alive with mischief. If he took it a step further by flashing a smirk, she'd be out of his office and on her way home. "With Barry in the hospital, we eloped to keep things simple. It's the perfect scenario."

"My father being in the hospital is a perfect scenario? Unbelievable!"

"That's not what I meant."

Tayla glared at him until he cleared his throat. "How long have you been planning this…this horror pantomime where I'm the co-star with a crush living out my worst nightmare?"

"Since I left Simon's office. He suggested it. I dismissed it at first, but as I drove home, I thought, why not? I could be the one with a crush if that makes it easier."

"How kind. But that's even more of a stretch." His response to that was a knowing smile. *Arrogant bastard.* "So, what happens to the money if you don't marry?"

"It goes to various charities once I turn forty." He paused. "It's Norman's way of pissing me off from beyond the grave. He liked to pull the strings, and he keeps on pulling."

Tayla had plenty more to say, but she didn't know where to start. The simple solution was to shut down this ridiculous conversation. She went to stand but stopped when he continued, "Now I know you're not in a relationship, the only problem—apart from you hating my guts—is what about your life in Sydney?"

She'd asked herself that very question every waking hour for days. What about her life in Sydney? Her job? Her apartment? "Hate may be too strong a word. As for Sydney, my plans are on hold for a few months. Mum and Dad need me here."

He waited for further explanation, but she didn't want to confide in Mitch about her life in the city—her life on pause.

"Okay. That's good." Mitch leaned forward and steepled his hands. "What do you think?"

"Thank you for finally asking my opinion." She didn't bother to mask her sarcasm. "I think you've got rocks in your head."

"But you're keen?"

"What! No. Of course I'm not keen." She stood and walked toward the door. "Have a nice day."

"Tayla?" He picked up his phone. "What's your number? In case I need to contact you."

"Call my lawyer."

6

BUYING TIME

BACK AT HER FAMILY HOME, Tayla flopped onto the bed and buried her head in the pillow. She let out a frustrated scream. He had to be kidding. Marry him? Would he expect her to wash his socks and cook him dinner, or would their arrangement include no level of domesticity? And what about the other? Would they share a bed?

She shuddered at the thought, her breasts tingling for some traitorous reason.

Overwhelmed by the summer heat and Mitch's proposition, she stood and opened the French doors, letting the easterly from the coast waft through the net curtains. Tayla had always loved this room. With its iron bed, monochrome tones, and sanded-back floor and dresser, it represented the very essence of home. She'd moved in after Lisa had shifted to Auckland. Before that, she and Ruby had shared.

Tayla moved to the bookcase and pulled out a copy of *East of Eden,* inhaling the musty scent as she opened it to the title page. It was the last book she and Norman had read together. And even now, she often read random passages aloud. Just as she had with Norman.

Norman. What an impressive human he'd been. Intuitive and

patient—a man who'd spoken so eloquently when they were alone yet couldn't maintain friendships or family ties. And now Mitch thought he had a solution to his grandfather's excessive need for control. And that solution also benefited Tayla's need to play the role of family protector. The youngest child on a mission to make everything right, and the perfect way to let Hayden know she'd moved on. Even if that was the last thing she imagined herself doing.

Dinner that night was a lonely affair of pasta tossed with a jar of her mother's homemade tomato sauce and topped with parmesan and fresh basil. As she ate, the texts from Hayden kept coming. *Please pick up. I miss you. Call me!!!* She knew she'd have to face him at some stage—to separate the domestic details of their lives—but dealing with his demands was no longer high on her list of priorities.

Later, settled on the veranda with a cup of green tea, Tayla opened her laptop and typed 'Clifton Falls horticulture realtors' into the search bar. She scrolled through the results. There didn't appear to be many orchards for sale around the province. So why hadn't Cherry Grove gained more interest?

She looked toward Lime Tree Hill as Mitch's SUV hurried down the drive and onto the Eastern Pacific Highway. For an uneasy moment, Tayla wished she were still in Sydney, dining out or catching a movie. Going somewhere. Anywhere.

Tayla picked up her phone as it vibrated and hit *Accept*. "Hey, Mum, how's Dad?"

"Stable. More to the point, how are you? You okay down there on your own?"

"Course I am."

"We had a call from the realtor today. The settlement date for the retirement complex has moved back a month. That gives you some breathing room with the packing. Have you made a start yet?"

Tayla didn't have the heart to say she hadn't even filled one cardboard box—couldn't face the thought of it. "Kind of."

"Listen to me." Her mum sighed, chastising herself. "I'm not even giving you time to get your feet on the ground. Have you seen Mitch?" Her mother stopped just long enough to take a breath. "If you need anything, give him a call. I know you had no time for him when you were younger, but people change, Tayla. And we'll be forever grateful for his interest in Cherry Grove. The Lord works in mysterious ways, that's for sure."

For once, her mother's use of that particular cliché was spot on. Mitch's interest in Cherry Grove had mystery written all over it, but Tayla was certain 'the Lord' had nothing to do with it. "I saw him this afternoon," she said.

"Did you? I think he's off to visit his sisters soon. They're both pregnant, due a few weeks apart."

Tayla hadn't realized Mitch had siblings. She'd always thought of him as a spoiled only child. Not that all only children were spoiled, but if there was a stereotype to fit, he'd be snug and cozy in that role.

As her mother talked nonstop, Tayla replied when necessary, but couldn't bring herself to raise the sale of the orchard. Or non-sale as was the case now. Still, the later settlement date bought her some time. How she'd use that time, she had no idea.

"I secretly hoped you two might get together once you'd matured."

"Mum!" Tayla chuckled. "How can you even say that after how he treated me?"

"You can't blame him for jumping to the wrong conclusion. He was just trying to look after Norman's interests."

Tayla sipped her tea. She never understood why her parents appeared to be lifetime members of the Mitchel Harrington fan club.

"He's done so well with that business," her mother continued, "even owns a commercial property in town. Anyway, he's engaged now—to a girl from Tulloch Point. Prue someone. Come to think of it, I haven't seen her around lately. She's not really my cup of tea. All made up with false eyelashes and those squared-off nails with different patterns on them. Beautiful, though."

Mitch's comment about bad decisions flashed through her mind. Was 'Prue someone' mixed up in his bad decision? "Hey, Mum. I'd better go. I need an early night. Give Dad a hug from me."

"I will, sweetheart. And, Tayla?" She heard the catch in her mother's voice. "Thank you. It must be difficult for you right now. Is there a chance you and Hayden will get back together?"

Tayla sucked in a breath. She'd forgotten about Hayden for a moment—how she shouldn't be in love with him anymore. Anything she said would be a lie, or at least, part of one. "I don't think so. But I'm fine, so please don't worry."

Her mother went quiet. "Do you still love him?" she eventually asked.

Tayla's breath hitched before she had a chance to catch it. "We've drifted apart over the past few months." *If only that were true.* "You know how it is."

"Look, if you want to return to Sydney, you go. We'll manage somehow."

Tayla rubbed her eyes, eager to end the call before she let something slip that she shouldn't. How many little white lies could she tell in one go? "No, I'm fine. Actually, I'm looking forward to the break. And I have lots of leave owing, so that's not a problem. But those preserved apricots might all be gone by the time you get home."

"You eat them up. That's what they're there for. Talk soon."

"Love you. Say hi to everyone for me."

Tayla strolled through the house, switching off the lights as she went, her thoughts not on Hayden for a change, but on Mitch. Why put in an offer he couldn't settle on? And what had happened to 'Prue someone,' the fiancée?

On her run along the river track the next day, Tayla mulled over her conversation with Mitch. Did the guy really expect her just to lie down and say, 'yes, I'd love to marry you'? Reality TV aside, how could anyone even contemplate a fake marriage? It was stressful enough planning a real one.

And yet, maybe his plan held an iota of merit. It would get her parents out of the red, and at least she wouldn't have to sleep with the guy. Although, when she thought about it, sex with her fake-husband-to-be would scratch the itch she hadn't dared touch in the past. What would Hayden say about that?

She shut down that mental picture. Plotting revenge on Hayden was childish, and she didn't like where her thoughts were going. Sleeping with Mitch would only complicate their agreement—without a doubt. And yet...

Her interest in Mitch had developed the first time she'd laid eyes on him, the day he'd sauntered up to the checkout where she worked, carrying a shopping basket full of snacks, chocolate, and condoms. As much as she'd tried to push away that teenage crush over the years, and despite their history, she still found him one of the sexiest men she'd ever met. With his slightly too long hair, cut-to-perfection body, and that amused smile playing on his full lips, Mitch was a handsome man. But her fascination with him had little to do with his good looks. It was more his presence. A confidence that would seem like arrogance on other men.

As an impressionable seventeen-year-old virgin whose only experience of romance came from chick flicks and novels, she'd once used the word 'dreamy' to describe him. Now, many years later, 'egotistical jerk' seemed a better fit.

By the time she arrived back at her family home, the sun sat above her in a relentless haze of heat. She'd head back down to the river later to test the water and her hesitance. Her swimming coach had continually stressed the 'you can, and you will' approach, but right now, she needed to call Tim.

Tim Benson and Tayla had been close friends since high school —sometimes inseparable, other times linked by nothing but their patchy social media posts. But that bond they'd formed over being different—he gay, she a goth nerd—remained strong. No matter how many years or miles separated them, he still had her back. Always.

Tayla grabbed her phone from her bag and sank onto the sofa. Putting her feet up on the coffee table, she hit Tim's number.

"Hey, you." Tim's voice breezed over the speaker. "How are you settling in?"

"Okay. It's quiet without Mum and Dad here. And what's with the traffic?"

"What do you mean?"

"There is none."

Tim laughed.

"Anyway," Tayla continued, "if you're not busy tonight, can I cook you dinner? But I need you to come alone."

"Just as well Brandon's away, or he'd be devastated."

"I know, but I have a secret, and it can't be shared."

She could almost hear Tim clap his hands. "I love secrets. What time? Half six?"

"Perfect."

As the sun shone in a cloudless sky and the willows along the bank dipped their lower branches into the river, Tayla looked over her shoulder to make sure no one was watching. She removed her dress and slipped into the water, the coolness stealing her breath. And as her breasts adjusted to the cold, her tight nipples peaking just above the waterline, she wondered what Mitch would think if he found her swimming topless in his branch of the river. She smiled at the thought.

Immersing herself to shoulder height, Tayla gripped the smooth stones with her toes and took three slow, steady breaths. Keeping contact with the bottom, she lowered herself to the tip of her chin, her arms swirling across the still surface of the water.

Earlier, she'd rummaged in the vegetable garden, hoping to selvage some salad greens for dinner. But the few rotting lettuces, dried-up cucumber vines in the greenhouse, and trusses of cherry tomatoes—split and decaying on their stalks—proved one thing. The orchard and garden were too much for her parents and probably had been for a while.

Still, she'd visit Lime Tree Hill's farm gate store before dinner to stock up on vegetables and soft cheese and crusty bread. Maybe even a carton of their organic ice cream her father raved about. Once nothing more than a tin shed selling a few odds and ends, the popular stall was now a bustling food market with organic treats to die for.

For now, she lay back, recalling her swimming coach's instructions, her arms keeping her afloat in the shallow stream. She took another deep breath, trying to clear all fears from her mind and stayed that way until her heartbeat stilled. *Bliss. Pure bliss.*

Clambering up the bank later, she glanced toward the packing shed loft window that overlooked the river, certain she'd seen a shadow cross the glass. She grabbed her towel and scampered behind a tree to get dressed, adrenaline rushing through her veins. Had he seen her?

Smiling at the thought, Tayla wrung out her wet panties before walking home, blissfully naked underneath her dress of cotton voile.

It was time to call Ruby.

Tim arrived early, bearing a bottle of wine, a huge bunch of flowers and flashing a grin. Tayla wanted to wait until they'd eaten to tell him about the proposal, but he was having none of it. With a glass of merlot in one hand and a vegetable knife in the other, he insisted on making the salad while she talked. "So, what's this big secret?"

"I might be getting married soon."

Knife poised, he stopped mid-chop. "Shut the front door! Has that Hayden guy finally come to his senses?"

Tayla froze. She hadn't thought of Hayden since lunchtime. "No, we broke up...before I left Sydney. Sorry, I should have told you before now, but life's been crazy lately."

"What? I thought you were solid as. What happened?"

"It's a sorry story I can only share after a second glass. Until then, I have something I want to run past you, but don't interrupt until I've finished. Okay?"

"Sure. Wait—you're pregnant?"

Tayla chuckled as she reached for a slice of cucumber off the chopping board. "Tim! What did I just say? I'm not pregnant. So if you don't mind..."

"Go right ahead," he said with a wide grin.

Tayla chose her words carefully while Tim listened without interruption. By the time she'd finished, his mouth was as wide open as his expression and the salad bowl was still empty.

"What do you think?"

"Let me get this straight. You're going to walk down the aisle with Mr. Limo Tree to save your parents' financial ass?"

"Pretty much. But you can't tell anyone. It has to look legit. But Ruby knows."

"And? What's her take on all of this?"

Snippets of her earlier phone conversation with Ruby surfaced. Her sister had plenty to say about Mitch's proposal, none of it good. "She thinks I'm crazy."

"And she'd be right. But, we're all a little crazy sometimes." He waggled his brows suggestively. "Do you get to sleep with him?"

"What? No, of course not. It's a business arrangement!"

"Pity. I bet he's rocked a world or two in his time."

Tayla tried to fight the mental picture. She failed. "Stop it. As if he'd be interested in rocking *my* world."

"Why do you say that? You're a catch. Maybe that's his plan—to lure you into a life of passion via a fake marriage."

She snatched another slice of cucumber. "That imagination of yours is running wild again."

"Well, real life is just too depressing. And for what it's worth, I think it's a fabulous idea. Mitch gets his bride, your parents get their money, and you have somewhere to live until you return to Sydney. It's a triple win. But…"

"Go on."

"With his rugby coaching and his work in the community, Mitch is a popular guy. Especially with the ladies. My concern is, can you trust him to be discreet? What if it gets back to your folks that their new son-in-law's a randy man-whore? They'd be devastated."

Earlier, Tayla had thought about Mitch and his high profile, wondering how she'd fit into his world. "Yes, you're right. But he's not really a randy man-whore, is he?"

Tim cocked a brow. Grinned. "Clifton Falls may be a small city, but people still gossip as if it's a country town. It's not like living in Sydney."

"So, what do you suggest?"

"Set some ground rules. Expecting Mitch to be celibate is a stretch, but if he wants to play away, he needs to pick his playground carefully. Or, make sexy time one of those ground rules."

A warm blush crept up her neck. "You think we should sleep together?"

"Why not? He's hot as. You may as well take any benefits offered."

"That's a complication I don't need. Anyway, it's not like he was offering, and I can't sleep with someone I don't have an emotional connection with. Besides, he's not my type."

"Brandon and I met on a one-night stand. Now we're solid as. An emotional connection doesn't necessarily have to come before sex."

"Maybe not, but..." Tayla stopped herself before blurting out her virginity status. When it came to her sexuality, she'd never been one for sharing, even with Tim.

"But?"

She took the roast chicken and potatoes out of the oven and placed them on the table. "This is a mess of epic proportions."

"You know what they say. One person's mess is another's opportunity. So, if you need a witness and photographer," Tim continued, "I'm your man. What's the time frame?"

"Thank you. Settlement's due mid-April, so a few weeks yet."

"Just as well it's an elopement." Tim placed the bowl of salad on the table. "Right, let's get this chicken carved, then you can tell me what happened with you and Hayden."

Tayla huffed out a heavy sigh and dropped her shoulders. "Do I have to? I'm starving, and I don't want to ruin my dinner."

Tim held her gaze the way only he could: with love and compassion. "He hurt you, didn't he?"

She opened the fridge to get the dressing and let the cool air soothe her. "Yeah. But hearts mend. The memory may stay with me forever, but I'm slowly stitching myself back together."

7

RUBY'S ON A TUESDAY

Ruby's suburban house was lit up like a Christmas tree when the Uber pulled up outside two weeks later. Tayla had caught the dusk flight from Clifton Falls to Auckland. When she walked in the door, her nieces were already in bed and her brother-in-law at work. Ruby greeted her with a tight hug, a compassionate smile, and the promise of a glass of chardonnay.

As she'd approached Clifton Falls Airport, Tayla had been unable to resist another peek at the billboard. She wished they'd take the darn thing down, so she didn't have to look at his naked torso every time she drove past. It wasn't as if she needed reminding what an annoyingly handsome man Mitchel Harrington was. It had occurred to her, more than once, to either look away or focus on the other men in the shoot. But what was it they said about train wrecks?

As Tayla followed Ruby toward the kitchen, the smell of curry wafting through the house helped her relax. They ate straight away, their conversation focused on their father and Cherry Grove. It wasn't until Ruby served an almond coconut cake for dessert that the discussion turned to Mitch.

"So, what have you decided?" her sister asked.

"Well, as I said on the phone, I've been over the orchard's books with the accountant, and it's not looking good. They even have credit card debt they can't meet the repayments on."

"Really? I had no idea."

"So it's 'say yes to the dress' and a walk on the dark side for Tayla."

"But you don't even like the guy." Ruby served herself another slice of cake and added a dollop of cream.

"And with good reason."

"Maybe, but you can't hold on to that grudge forever. When you look at it from his viewpoint, it was a bit weird, you doing all of Norman's shopping and holding his credit card. And Mitch has apologized for that tiny whoops in judgment."

"Yes, but only after I showed him my book of receipts. Can you imagine how I felt? He was so nice to me straight after Norman died, and then suddenly, I'm 'Tayla the petty thief.' I'd done nothing wrong, but I was scared stiff of the man. My poor little teenage self had her illusions shattered, that's for sure."

Ruby pointed her fork at Tayla and grinned. "I always knew you two had a history. I thought you might have—"

"What? Slept with him? I couldn't even talk to boys back then, let alone men. And I was hardly about to lose my virginity to Norman's hunky grandson at seventeen."

"You never had a sense of sexual adventure. Not like Lisa and me."

"I never had the chance, did I? My sex-ed consisted of dogged-eared pages of mildly erotic fiction, not actual experience."

"What about at AUT?"

Tayla sighed. Her university years had been like all the others. Dry. "I went on a total of five dates, all unfortunate."

"The men or the dates?"

"Both. Some guys just have no idea. One even wore white dress shoes with his jeans."

They both giggled. It was always the same when they were

together. They giggled about everything. "But it happened eventually?"

Apart from Hayden, Tayla had never discussed her non-existent sex life with anyone. And with Hayden, the details had been glossed over to the point where she'd almost slipped on them. Ruby wasn't usually one for questions, but with the wine flowing nicely, their party of two took a sudden turn into Honest Truth Road.

Tayla reached for her wine and gulped down the final mouthful. She stared at her sister.

"No way! You're still a virgin?" Ruby's eyes widened in disbelief. "How is that even possible? What about you and Hayden?"

"He wanted to wait."

"Until when—the freakin' cows came home to roost?"

"Until we were married."

"Hold on. Back up. Married? When was this happening?"

Apart from those first few days at her father's bedside, Tayla hadn't shed many tears since leaving Sydney. Now, as much as she tried to keep the jovial mood of their conversation going, one lone tear trickled down her cheek. "It felt like we were on our way, do you know what I mean? He loved me. I'd never had that romantic love before."

She stopped to blow her nose. "He'd been working long hours at the hospital, or so I thought. When he asked me to marry him, he suggested we elope, then have a small party for our family and close friends later. He'd been married before, so didn't want a big affair. I was reluctant at first, and sad you guys wouldn't be there. But when I thought about the drama Lisa went through with her wedding, I agreed."

"So what happened?"

"We decided to have no contact for a week beforehand, so it would be more exciting when we saw each other again. The day of the wedding was unbearably hot, and even as I slipped into my dress, I couldn't shake the feeling that something was terribly wrong."

Ruby's brow furrowed as she reached for Tayla's hand.

"The ceremony was set for noon…the only time the chapel had available. I arrived early. The photographer wanted to take some shots at the altar, so we shared the limo. When we'd finished, I sat in the front pew as the world rushed by outside. By the time the hour was up, I hardly noticed the noise in the chapel grounds as the guests arrived for the next ceremony."

Tayla's voice cracked as she recounted the events. "The conversation in my head wouldn't hush. He'd had an accident… changed his mind…been called into work and would run in at any minute, still straightening his tie. I found myself second-guessing the time…the day, the date, the address. Even my sanity. I must have checked my phone a hundred times. Called him, texted, left messages. But he never answered. Never showed. It was one of the loneliest times in my life, and I've had my fair share of those. The celebrant ushered me out the back and into a waiting cab just before the next bride arrived."

"You had the wrong day?"

"No, right day…wrong man."

"He left you at the altar? No way!"

"It turns out he *was* at the hospital, but not with a patient. His ex-wife went into early labor, and they welcomed a baby boy on the Monday morning. I'd had no idea they were still a couple."

"Sweetie, no. I'm so sorry."

A sob caught in her throat. "All the time we were together, he'd been seeing her too. No wonder he was hardly ever home. Not that we lived together. That was our next step."

"And was it his baby?"

"According to his PA. She's a chatty little thing. I called her, pretending it was about a patient. She was more than happy to share Hayden's exciting news."

"Have you talked to him since?"

Tayla plucked a tissue from her sleeve and wiped her eyes. "Once, a few days after I landed in Auckland. He offered me every excuse under the sun at first. But in the end, he was too exhausted to keep up the pretense. Of course he apologized…said he loved us both, and still wanted to marry me, but the timing wasn't quite right. Can you believe that? It all came down to timing. If it wasn't for the baby's early arrival, we would have been married by now. How scary is that?"

"I'm so sorry you went through that alone. Why didn't you tell me when you were up here last?"

"I should have. But, you know, Dad was so sick, and I needed time to lick my wounds. As it turns out, I'm packing up our family home, and Hayden's in Sydney dealing with poop explosions and sleepless nights. Meanwhile, we'd started to meld our lives, so I still have stuff at his place. And I need to sort out my apartment. I should do that this week if I can get a cheap flight."

"Do you still love him?"

Tayla chewed her bottom lip while she considered her sister's question. "I've been asking myself that very thing since the moment I boarded the plane to come home. You don't stop loving someone because they've done you wrong. You may love parts of their personality…their behavior less, but that final disconnect takes time. In some ways, marrying Mitch will give me that time. I won't be able to pack up and return to Sydney, knock on his door, and ask him why. I can hide at Lime Tree Hill and take stock."

Ruby looked at Tayla with concern. "Maybe. But what will you have at the end of it? A 'divorced virgin' label to attach to your story. Isn't it all a bit too drastic?"

"Yeah, I've thought about that, but with my history with men, what does it matter? Think of it this way—historically, marriage for purely romantic reasons was never popular. Women married for honor, or necessity, or economic advantage. And my decision to marry Mitch would be purely economic."

"Yes, but that economic advantage is for Mum and Dad, not

you. You're lining yourself up to be the sacrificial lamb, and I'm the only one in the family who even knows about it."

"And that's the way it has to stay. Mind you, I haven't seen Mitch for a couple of weeks. So who knows what's going on in that head of his?"

Ruby picked up their plates and took them to the sink. "You said his lawyer suggested we contact a realtor?"

"He did. I had a look on the net but didn't know where to start. I hoped Mitch would still settle, so I put it in the 'too hard' basket."

"With interest rates being so low right now, you'd think he'd be able to raise the money. Lime Tree Hill's a huge operation. He must be loaded and then some."

Tayla shrugged. "Maybe he doesn't like debt."

"Maybe. Anyway, do you remember Andrew Harper? We went out for a while in high school. Broke my little heart, then wanted me back a year later."

Tayla shook her head. "No. Why?"

"He owns Clifton Falls Realty. I'll give him a call."

8

BONDI BEACH

TAYLA WALKED into her apartment in Bondi Beach and looked around. She'd hesitated before booking the flight, her stomach in knots as the anticipation of returning to Sydney clouded her every thought. Now here she was, back in her cozy home, struggling with a tinge of regret and an unexpected tug of homesickness for Clifton Falls.

She'd leased the apartment furnished, complete with a hammock strung from one balcony support post to the other. Not that the balcony was part of her package. It belonged to the apartment above. Hers was a tiny ground-floor space, three blocks from the beach, with just enough room to park herself and her Vespa.

Tayla opened the windows and listened to the sound of children's chatter and laughter as they ambled home from school. She recalled her life here: weaving her scooter through the crazy traffic, devouring the local sourdough, and early morning boot camps at the beach. Her home for three years, it had been the first time she'd lived alone, and she'd loved it.

Hayden had a three-bedroom terrace in Paddington. She'd been there many times but had seen no sign of a wife. Apart from hers, not even one feminine toiletry lurked in the bathroom. She

43

wondered where else he lived in that double life of his. Probably Darling Point, or somewhere equally as fabulous.

She eyed her treasures: small market finds—paperbacks, jars of shells, and candles. Apart from her beloved Vespa, there wasn't much else to pack, just a few things from the kitchen and her favorite linen sheets. Half a dozen boxes should do it. She'd managed to sublet to the daughter of the couple upstairs for a few months. That should give her enough time to sort out the orchard and remap her journey.

After hours of cleaning and sorting, Tayla walked along Campbell Parade in search of food. She bought a burrito—bursting with beans, rice, and avocado—and sat on the steps by the lifeguard tower, eating slowly as she fought to hold back the tears.

When Tayla moved to Sydney, Bondi had been a deliberate choice. She'd had a dream—to stand in the surf without fear and be lifted gently off her feet by the swell of the Pacific. To carry a surfboard under her arm as she walked home, like many of her neighbors did. Now that dream would never be realized, and the regret threatened to overwhelm her.

When she let herself into Hayden's terrace house the next day, everything looked exactly the same. He liked order. Symmetry. Even their dates, his notes, and his timetable were slotted into neat squares on a calendar. Black pen on white and written with such a precise hand for a doctor, that she wouldn't dream of adding to the script.

His bed was unmade—unusual for him—and on the chair, a shirt and tie lay where he'd left them. She inhaled, but there was no lingering scent to remind her of his touch, his kiss...her longing. Because she had longed for him. Wanted the intimacy others had talked of. And on those rare nights when he'd invited her to stay, she'd imagine what it would be like to make love—to finally experience that physical bond that unites two people—as Hayden slept beside her.

The sound of her phone had her rummaging in her bag, her thoughts snapping back to the present. She glanced at the unknown number before answering. "Hello?"

"Tayla? It's Mitch."

She sat on Hayden's bed, unsure why her stomach flipped at the sound of Mitch's deep voice. "Hi."

"How's Clifton Falls?"

"Actually, I'm in Sydney. Where are you?"

"In London, visiting family."

London? So that's why she hadn't seen him before leaving for Auckland. "Oh, okay. I didn't know that."

"I just called to see how Barry was."

Tayla wanted to ask why he hadn't called her mother instead. But maybe he didn't want to bother her. "He's doing much better, thanks. How long are you away for?"

"Another three weeks."

She removed the phone from her ear and pushed the speaker icon. "I'm glad you called. I've given your proposition some thought, and I'd like to…well, consider your suggestion."

He fell silent. She imagined him lying in bed with the phone in his large hand, naked from the waist up, every muscle on full display and a slight frown on his brow.

"Did you manage to get hold of a realtor?" he finally asked.

"Not yet. We're still working through a few things, but…"

"Okay. I've given it some thought too. It seemed like a good idea at the time, but to be honest, I can't see it working. If you get another offer, you should grab it."

Tayla's heart sank. Just when she'd decided to go ahead, he'd countered with a 'thanks, but no thanks.' "Oh. Okay."

"No one would believe us. Besides, it's obvious you're uncomfortable around me, and I'm too busy to deal with that kind of energy at the moment. I'm not one for confrontation."

Energy? Why didn't he just say 'bullshit'? Because Tayla was certain that's what he meant. "Of course."

Silence stretched between them again.

"Tayla? Are you still there?"

"I'm here," she said, but there was nothing more to add. "We must have a bad line. Anyway, thanks for your call. I have to go." With that, she hung up. If her phone hadn't been brand new, she'd have thrown it against the wall. But no man was worth a broken iPhone.

Tayla hurried over to the closet and looked inside. The few clothes, bathrobe, and gym gear she'd left there were still in the same place. But when she studied Hayden's things with a critical eye, she noticed something she'd paid no attention to before.

Lack.

There were no rows of running shoes—although he owned many pairs—very few casual shirts, not even many shorts and T-shirts in his drawers. And when she looked up, there wasn't even one box of memorabilia on the top shelf.

Tayla stuffed her things into a duffel and picked up her paperback from the nightstand. She didn't want him arriving home after a night in the operating room to find her poking around. But then, he wouldn't come here at the moment, would he? Not with a new baby at his other house.

Downstairs in the kitchen, she placed the keys on the counter then rummaged through her bag, her hand finding the small ring box. Apart from a weekend away in the Blue Mountains, the ring was the only thing he'd ever given her. Tayla smoothed her fingers over the velvet, and after setting the box on the counter next to the keys, she opened the lid.

Fashioned from white gold with a large center stone and square diamonds on either side, it was a beautiful ring. Hayden had picked it himself—told her so after he'd proposed. He hadn't wanted to announce their engagement or their plans for a wedding. It would be more romantic, he'd said, to elope and tell everyone after the fact.

Now there'd be no announcement.

Now that beautiful ring would never be worn. Not by her, anyway.

Resisting the urge to try it on one last time, she closed the lid. And as she stepped out the front door and pulled it shut behind her, an unexpected wave of freedom swelled in her chest.

They'd shared their last kiss, their final goodbye, but at the time, she hadn't realized it.

The following day, Tayla returned to Auckland on the early morning flight, leaving Sydney and Hayden and the excitable waves of Bondi Beach behind. And later that evening, as she sat with her father, she couldn't get over how frail and vacant he seemed.

When Tayla went to bed that night, she cried into her pillow. First, for her dad as he'd been: fit and strong and proud, with a smile that didn't stop. And then, as the enormity of the situation with the orchard hit her, she cried for herself. Things would look better in the morning, but for now, tears seemed the only way forward.

Several days later, Hayden texted his angry demands, pleading for them to meet. *Why this? Why that? Why, why, why?* But by then, Tayla was already back in Clifton Falls.

Already wondering what on earth she should do.

9

HAPPY RETURNS

AS HE STOOD on the small balcony off his bedroom, a movement down by the river caught Mitch's eye. Tayla, running along the track, her athletic upper body barely covered by a bra top, and her hair pulled into a high ponytail. Initially, Simon's suggestion of a wife for hire had seemed to hold merit. But the more Mitch thought about his loved-up sisters in London, the more he questioned his motives. Living a lie was always a bad idea, especially when it affected so many people.

As Mitch watched Tayla jog in and out of view, he recalled the afternoon they'd been officially introduced—the day after Norman passed away. She'd stood in his grandfather's cottage, a string bag of books and groceries in one hand, her expression one of shock and disbelief as Ken broke the news of Norman's passing. At that stage, although he'd known of her visits, he'd had no idea how much his grandfather had meant to Tayla, so the silent tears she'd quickly wiped away with the back of her hand had puzzled him.

He'd noticed her several times before that day—riding her bike through the orchard and standing behind the checkout at the supermarket where he shopped. The first time she'd served him, he'd momentarily lost himself in those hazel eyes before he'd pulled his credit card from his wallet and handed it to her. He remembered thinking, why would this introverted girl, fashioned in goth from head to toe, want to spend time with his ultra-conservative grandfather?

Now, years later, he found Tayla in his thoughts more and more as he pondered her detached nature, the vibrant color of her hair, those tiny freckles across the bridge of her nose, and her delicate jawline.

Mitch turned to grab his sweatshirt off the bed, and when he looked back, Tayla had reached Norman's cottage. She stopped and bent forward to catch her breath. After checking over her shoulder to see if anyone was watching, she opened the gate, climbed the half-dozen steps to the veranda, and peeked through the living room window.

"Time for a walk, boy," Mitch called Edward to heel. The pug sat and refused to budge. "Come on, I'll carry you halfway"—he scooped down and picked him up—"but that's all, you lazy little pooch."

"So, what do you think?"

Tayla's hands flew to her chest. "Shit! You gave me a fright."

"Sorry, I didn't mean to sneak up on you."

She untied the hoodie from around her waist and shrugged it on. "I didn't realize you were back."

"I flew in yesterday." He bent down and unclipped Edward's leash.

"How was London?"

"Great. Cold, but I love it there."

"I've never been, but it's on my bucket list." She tugged up the zipper, covering her exposed midriff, and nodded toward the pup. "What's his name?"

"Mr. Edward." He picked him up.

49

"He's adorable. May I hold him?" She accepted the puppy and snuggled him into her chest, massaging under his ears as Mitch watched. "I'd love a pug."

Mitch reached into his pocket and pulled out a set of keys. "Feel free to pug-sit any time you want."

"Thanks." She put Edward down. "Anyway, I should get going. Mum said you'd refurbished the cottage. I was just curious."

"Yeah, it's a B&B now. Keen for a look?" Mitch unlocked the front door and instructed Edward to sit. "You spent a lot of time here when Norman was alive."

Tayla hesitated. It had been years since she'd been inside, and she had no idea how she'd feel after all that time. The thought of him lying dead in his bed still freaked her out.

Mitch cocked his head in invitation. "Come on."

Following him along the hallway, Tayla trailed her hand along the wood paneling. "I love this, how you've painted the tongue and groove off-white," she said, trying to keep her voice even. "Everything's so much lighter."

"Thanks. The place was a depressing dump before. All that floral wallpaper and dark wood." He opened the door to Norman's bedroom.

She looked from the doorway, reluctant to venture inside but also surprised by her lack of reaction. There were no goosebumps or shivers up her spine. "It's beautiful. The palette reminds me of the silkworm cocoons lying in a straw basket that my biology teacher had on a shelf in her classroom." She glanced over her shoulder and caught his amusement.

"Come see the kitchen."

Apart from the black enamel coal range, the kitchen was new. Tayla couldn't believe how the cabinets and appliances nestled into the space as if they belonged. In the adjoining sunroom—Norman's nook as she'd once called it—his antique writing desk still held pride of place, and wing-backed chairs in sapphire blue velvet sat on a plush ivory rug.

She sat at the desk, smoothing her hands over the inlay. The smell of leather took her back. "I always loved this desk. I'd sit here to read to him. He'd sip tea and eat scones or shortbread. Occasionally, he'd ask me to reread a line or paragraph so he could grasp the meaning."

"*East of Eden* was one of the books you read to him, wasn't it?"

She smiled at the memory. "It was. We finished it two weeks before he died. How did you know?"

"He talked about it. Reading fiction was one of the few things we had in common."

Tayla glanced up. On the wall above the desk, a woodcut of a famous Tolstoy quote caught her eye. She read it aloud: "'If you look for perfection, you'll never be content.' Where did you get that?"

"I made it. It was one of Norman's favorite quotes. Not one he lived by, unfortunately." He watched her with the same intensity she'd felt the day he'd asked her to marry him—with questioning eyes and that hint of amusement. "What do you think? Of the cottage, I mean."

"It's beautiful." She swallowed hard, a physical reaction to how talking about Norman made her feel. "You've done a great job. You've never thought about moving in?"

"What, here? No. Too many ghosts from the past."

Tayla rose from the desk and walked through to the living room, Mitch following two steps behind. She stood back to admire the colorful artwork. "I love these Gauguin prints. They add a touch of vibrancy that lifts the whole interior. I've always been a fan of his work."

"Yeah? I found them rolled up in an old trunk in the spare bedroom. I love how he used bold color to offset the expressions of his subjects."

Tayla stepped forward and ran her hand over the frame of the first print. She hadn't thought of that before, but now Mitch mentioned it, she understood what he meant. "I miss him. Norman, I mean."

Mitch inhaled deeply, a sadness in his expression. It wasn't the first time she'd seen his vulnerable side. "Yeah. Me too."

"Thanks for the tour. He'd be impressed with what you've done, not just here, but with the orchard too."

"I'm not so sure about that. Norman didn't approve of my choices as a rule." He followed her through to the hallway. "At least he came to Massey for my graduation though. That was something."

"You went to university?"

"You sound surprised. Do you see me as uneducated, Tayla?"

Turning, she caught his wry smile. "Any man who quotes Tolstoy and understands Post-Impressionism is obviously educated. But education comes in varying degrees. What did you study?"

"Engineering."

"Norman told me you loved constructing bridges, dams, and tall buildings. But in my imagination, you were a cute little boy tinkering with that old-school Meccano set he kept in a box on his bookshelf."

"So, you imagined me as cute?"

Tayla looked his way. "Our imagination can play tricks when we don't possess all the facts, don't you agree?" And her imagination was playing all kinds of tricks right now. Ones it had no business playing. What would he taste like if they kissed, how would she feel wrapped in his arms?

He nodded, his gaze holding hers.

"Anyway, I should go." She broke eye contact. "Thanks again. I wished I'd had the chance to say goodbye. He was such a lovely man."

Mitch raised a skeptical brow as they stepped onto the veranda. Maybe now was her chance to talk to him about Cherry Grove.

"Actually, do you mind if we sit for a moment?" she asked. "I have something to say."

He pulled over a chair. "Sure."

Tayla sat on the love seat she'd sometimes shared with Norman. "It's about the sale. My sisters and I don't have enough money to buy Cherry Grove, and it's not profitable anyway. I've been to the bank, but they won't come to the party. If the sale doesn't go through, I doubt my parents will even have a roof over their heads by the time they return from Auckland. So, if there's any chance of you changing your mind…"

His hand went to his chin, where he rubbed a finger back and forth. "You've had no other offers?"

"Not at this stage."

Seconds passed before Mitch released a sigh from deep within his chest, as if clearing his thoughts and energy. "I still can't see it working."

"Why not?" Tayla said bluntly. "Have you met someone?"

He hesitated again, seemingly unwilling to elaborate. "From our contact so far, I doubt anyone would believe us."

Now it was her turn to stare. "How one behaves is all down to attitude. People act out their lives to some extent every day of the week. I'm sure I could play my part in this game of pretense."

He raised a brow like before, but this time, he added a huff.

"What? You have no faith in my ability to live a lie if it will save my parents from financial ruin?" Tayla asked.

"Not a lot."

"So, the marriage offer was just a front, was it? Are you waiting for the bank to foreclose so you can pick up Cherry Grove for next to nothing?"

"See, that's what I mean right there." Mitch sat forward, his hands helping him prove his point. "You don't know me, so stop pretending otherwise. It's obvious I pissed you off over that credit card mix-up, but let it the hell go. Learn to play nice, and we might have a deal. Keep acting like a prissy stuck-up snob, and all bets are off."

Tayla sat back, reclaiming her personal space. She crossed her arms over her chest and held his gaze. He had to be kidding. "You are the rudest man I have ever met."

"Yeah, well, some people bring out the worst in me. Now, if you'll excuse me..."

With that, Mitch stood, picked up Mr. Edward, and bounded down the steps, leaving Tayla glued to the seat, a 'but' dying on her lips.

She watched until he disappeared behind the lime trees, his words harsh in her ears, then took the steps two at a time and ran all the way home. No one had ever talked to her like that, and if Mitch wanted all bets to be off, she would happily oblige.

After a shower, Tayla made herself a sandwich and while she ate, surfed the internet again for realtors specializing in orchard sales.

By evening, a sudden cold snap gave the air a distinctly autumnal feel. Tayla never knew how to describe this conundrum —coolness wrapped around the warmth of late summer. Because in Clifton Falls, warm days often stretched well into the calendar months of autumn, and this year looked like being no exception.

And along with the unseasonable woodsmoke from a neighbor's fire came a stilled feeling of melancholy almost despondency. Tayla sat on the veranda, her hands curled around a mug of hot chocolate, and recalled their exchange with regret.

Prissy stuck-up snob?

She didn't want to be that girl. The one who held an eternal grudge because someone had misjudged her. And if she'd learned one thing from her relationship with Hayden, it was that things weren't always as they seemed.

Her hot chocolate finished, Tayla stood and walked through the house to the kitchen. She wondered if she should text Mitch an apology or just let the dust settle.

Deciding on the latter, she soaked in the tub until the water cooled, then went to bed, her life feeling devoid of purpose and direction for the first time in years.

1O

A GAME OF TOUCH

WHEN TAYLA PULLED into the sports grounds and saw the swarms of people milling around the field, she froze. Tim had called earlier, begging her to make up the numbers for his 'strictly social' touch rugby team after someone else bailed. Everyone played for fun, he'd said, and she'd probably spend the whole time on the bench anyway. Also, there'd be a band playing later and plenty of free beer. How exciting. *Not.*

Taking a deep breath, Tayla admonished herself for letting her sarcastic side rear its undisciplined head. She hadn't played touch rugby since high school, but how hard could it be? Like riding a bike, Tim reckoned.

She opened her car door and made her way to the pavilion, where Tim met her with a tight hug and his usual smile. "You ready for this?"

"I don't know about that."

He looked her up and down. "Well, at least you've dressed for the part. That's a plus. You look fabulous."

"Stop it. I wasn't going for fabulous. I'm channeling 'committed team member.'" She scanned the grounds. "Where do we go?"

Tim cocked his head toward his team. "And see the guys in red shirts over by the tree line? That's the opposition."

When Tayla looked in their direction, her gaze landed on a familiar face she'd never expected to see. And even worse, that face was staring at her. "You can't be serious! Mitch is on their team?"

"Yep. And the guy next to him is Luka O'Leary. They're both strong players. Mitch played rugby at provincial level before he screwed his ACL." As she went to turn away, Tim grabbed her by the arm. "I know you have a history with your fake husband-to-be, but—"

"I do not," she whispered with purpose. "I wish everyone would stop saying that. And I'm not playing touch with Mitchel Harrington, on or off the field."

Tim kept walking, his hand firm on her lower back. "History, schoolgirl crush, lust fest. Whatever you choose to call it, you had it all right. And I've never known you to be a quitter. Come on."

As they drew closer, Mitch and Luka strolled toward them. The men shook hands.

"Tim. Good to see you, mate." Mitch turned to Tayla and smiled as if their conversation at Norman's cottage hadn't happened. "Tayla, this is Luka O'Leary, a close friend of mine."

Luka offered a warm smile along with a firm handshake. "Nice to meet you, Tayla."

She returned the gesture. "You too."

"Right," Luka said, "I'd better go warm up."

As Luka jogged back to his team, words went back and forth between Tim and Mitch. Tayla hadn't realized the men knew each other so well.

Mitch looked Tayla up and down. "So you're joining the game?"

"Just filling in. I'm the bench babe."

According to Ruby, a moment was longer than a minute. Whereas a minute was sixty seconds, a moment was at least ninety.

Mitch stared for a moment. Long enough for her to prickle under his heated gaze.

"Nice," he eventually said.

With that one word branded on her skin, he also returned to his team, yelling, "Let's get this party started." He clapped his hands like he was amped up for a Rugby World Cup match against Australia rather than a 'friendly' game of touch. *Great.*

True to Tim's prediction, Tayla sat on the bench for the first three-quarters of the game, but then one of the other girls tagged her on. Tim had been right when he'd used the bike-riding analogy, and it didn't take long to find her flow. Mitch kept his distance as he concentrated on the game, but just as she was about to run across the line and score a try, he lunged forward to touch her. She stumbled, and before she knew it, he was on top of her—hard muscles everywhere—and she was eating a dirt sandwich.

"Harrington," the referee yelled, "what are you doing? Get off her."

Mitch sprang to his feet and helped her up, his eyes full of amusement. "Shit, sorry. Are you all right?"

With the wind knocked from her sails, she pushed his hand away, her breasts tightening behind the stretch of her sports bra as the force of his body lingered on her skin. She closed her eyes briefly, the sounds of whistles and shouts from across the field fading as she struggled to catch her breath—to calm her reaction. "I'm fine." *So not fine.*

She limped back into position, and as the referee blew his whistle, Tayla was ready to go. Or so she told herself.

They lost twenty-four to thirty-eight. It didn't sit well with Tayla. She liked to win, especially against the likes of Luka and Mitch— those 'accomplished at everything' types who strived for excellence and looked good enough to melt your panties off while doing it.

As she took a seat in the pavilion with her teammates, still stiff and sore from her encounter with Mitch, Tayla expected to hear his booming voice above the others around them. But he was strangely quiet. She wished she could say the same about his stare. That was as noisy as anything. Every time she glanced his way, that stare dared her to hold his gaze and not let go.

He rose from his chair and walked toward her. Certain men own a room; Mitch was such a man. People watched him, respected him, and his easy sexuality was constantly on display. He stopped at her side and crouched so they were at eye level, his half-smile holding her captive. "Can I get you a drink?"

Tayla held up her beer, her hand tight around the cool glass. "I'm fine. Tim just got a round in."

He pulled up a chair next to hers, uninvited. But that didn't matter. There was no stuffy ceremony in the Clifton Falls Sports Pavilion that evening. Over the next hour or so, her lovely neighbor, as her mother often called Mitch, engaged the table in relaxed conversation. Tayla downed one beer and then two more. By the time the band started, alcohol buzzed pleasantly through her veins.

Mitch turned to her now, leaning in close to murmur, "Do you need a ride home, or are you okay to drive?"

She closed her eyes for a second and inhaled, acutely aware of their nearby audience. "I'll just book an Uber."

He checked his watch. "I'll be leaving in thirty minutes. I'm happy to drop you off. Come find me later."

"Um…okay."

He moved away, and as she watched him slip onto the dance floor with a girl from another team, Tayla tried to ignore the feeling that it should be her dancing with him. Because, damn, the man could dance.

Of course he could!

"Yep. That's what I mean right there," Tim said.

She looked at him and frowned. "I have no idea what you're talking about."

"Liar. You two won't have to pretend on the day. Boom!"

Tayla sipped her beer as she snuck a peek at the man in question, his hands on his partner's hips as they moved to the beat. "There is no day. He's changed his mind."

"What the...? You can't be serious?" Tim's wide-eyed gaze shot to Mitch on the dance floor then back to Tayla. He leaned in close and whispered, "He's flip-flopped on you?"

"Well, to be honest, I flip-flopped first, so—"

"Stop." Tim held up a palm to silence her. "That's bullshit. I should talk to him."

Tayla grabbed him by the arm as he went to stand. "Don't you dare. I can fight my own battles, thank you very much." She chuckled as she let go. "But I appreciate the gesture of gallantry."

Thirty minutes later, Mitch sat perched up at the bar with not one but three women hanging off his every word. Tayla stood and said her goodbyes. But as she walked toward him, despite the alcohol warming her inside, that shy nerd with the goth obsession and slight stammer she thought she'd left behind at Clifton Falls High threatened to return.

Mitch set his water on the bar as his companions checked her out. "You ready to head home, babe?"

Babe? Seriously?

He remained poker-faced like she really was his 'babe.'

Two could play at that game. "I'm happy to call an Uber if you want to stay, *sweetie*."

He looked at her and grinned at their shared joke before turning to his friends. "Right, time for me to hit the road." With that, he stood, grabbed her hand, and led her out to his truck without saying another word.

Tayla sat next to him in silence, his presence filling the space.

And as he pulled onto the highway and headed for home, the alcohol-fueled attraction she felt for her very sexy, very attractive, and very cocky neighbor was at odds with her resolve.

"Did you enjoy the game?" he finally asked.

She turned to look at him. "I did. Except for the part where you literally took my breath away."

He laughed. "Unintentional, believe me. You played well, though."

"You sound surprised."

He shot her a sideways glance. "I was a bit. But then, I tend to judge a book by its cover, even though my grandfather advised me not to."

"Most men do, don't they?"

"Come on." He flicked her a sideways glance. "Not only men judge with their eyes. Women do it all the time."

"I bet they do," she murmured.

He chuckled at her response. She had no idea why he suddenly found her amusing. This was it, she thought, the sign she needed. The guy was trouble, and she should keep away. It wouldn't be fair to use him as a rebound from Hayden, the traitor. She certainly couldn't imagine Mitchel Harrington having an 'intellectual relationship' with any woman.

But then there was Cherry Grove.

He turned up the radio, tapping his fingers on the steering wheel to the beat. By the time they arrived at the house, the rain drifting in from the coast was pelting down with attitude.

She sat still, wanting to ask him a hundred questions, but too shy to voice even one. "Did you have a nice time in London?"

Lame, Tayla. So lame.

Mitch turned to face her and leaned his back on the door. "I did. Two of my sisters live there. They were both pregnant at the same time, and I'm officially an uncle now. Sam arrived before I was hardly off the plane, and Etta four weeks early, just before I left. My mother and stepfather were there too, so it was great."

"Family times are special. I love babies. I bet they smelled delicious."

He chuckled. "Not so much, but it was good to get away. I'd gone twelve months without a break. I hadn't realized how burned-out I was."

"Did you and Norman have a good relationship?"

Mitch hesitated at her sudden change of subject. "His depression was a problem when I was younger. I didn't understand how broken he was and took it personally. Some weekends he wouldn't come out of his room—not even to wave me off when I left on a Sunday. He put my mother through a lot, especially after I was born. I found it hard to forgive him for that."

"So, you're close to your mother?"

"Very. And Frank, my stepfather. I had nothing to do with Norman until I was sixteen. He called Mum out of the blue to ask if we could meet. I stayed for a few hours at first, and as I got to know him better, overnight. I hated those visits—that musty cottage full of books and old shit. But his link to my late father was the driving force, and in time, we relaxed around one another. The year I turned eighteen, I lived at Lime Tree all summer."

Tayla smiled. She'd always wondered about his relationship with Norman.

"How old were you when your parents bought Cherry Grove?" he asked.

"Fifteen. We lived in town before that. Dad worked as a produce buyer for Fieldmans. It was Mum who wanted to buy the orchard. Norman didn't want me to visit when you were there. He'd say, 'The boy's coming this weekend, so best you stay away.'"

"He always called me 'the boy.'" Mitch chuckled. "He was a grumpy old bastard, wasn't he?"

Tayla had never attached the word 'bastard' to Norman. "Misunderstood is maybe a better word."

Mitch shrugged. "Maybe. Still, when my Great-uncle Ken told

me about the conditions of his will, I was pissed off. Don't get me wrong. I loved Norman in my own way, but I still can't condone his treatment of Mum. The idea of a fake marriage to manipulate his conditions was a last-ditch effort to play him at his own game."

Even though she'd seen his vulnerable side after Norman passed away, Mitch's honesty now surprised her. He'd been kind to her in the days after Norman's death—offering books and records from his grandfather's collections, and asking questions about her relationship with the older man. And as he'd helped carry the coffin down the aisle of St Stephen's Presbyterian church, over eight years ago now, he'd looked directly at her, his eyes brimming with tears.

All the same, her younger self had been scared stiff of him. This large man, with his movie star good looks and beautiful, kind eyes, who'd later seen her as an opportunist unworthy of Norman's bequest.

"And you know what's funny?" His words dragged her back to the present. Why did he find everything so amusing?

"No, what?"

"On a good day, if I'd told him I'd contemplated a fake marriage to get the money, he would've patted me on the back, called me resourceful, and then chuckled about it."

Tayla smiled at the portrayal of Norman in a good mood. "He loved that word. Resourceful." She turned to face him, the confines of the Hilux feeling like a confessional. "What happened to the girl you were going to marry?"

He leaned his head back against the window. "She made a choice I couldn't condone."

"Are you still friends?"

He looked away. "Superficially. But betrayal has its own agenda when it comes to exes being friends."

Tayla agreed. She had no desire to be friends with Hayden. Ever. "Right. I'd better go inside. Thanks for the ride."

There was a stillness to him now, something she hadn't seen

before. Like he didn't want to leave. And if she were honest, she didn't want him to either.

"Thanks for the ear," Mitch said. "Apart from Ken, you're the only person who knew Norman as well as I did. It's been good to talk about him."

"He was very kind to me."

"And you to him. What's the story about him saving your life?"

"That was what started our friendship. I fell off my bike down by the mailbox and split my head open on a rock. Norman found me at the end of the drive, lying in a ditch and soaked in blood. He told me later that you'd made him get a cell phone, and the only thing he could remember was green for go and red for stop."

"It was a Motorola flip phone. I only added three people to his contacts—Ken, me, and your parents, but he refused to use it."

"Until that day. He called an ambulance, then Dad. I was in an induced coma for a while, with swelling to the brain. When I woke up, they'd shaved half my hair off. I was devastated."

"And here was me thinking that hairstyle was part of your goth fashion statement."

Tayla felt the heat creep into her cheeks. Not because she was embarrassed about her goth phase, but because he remembered what she'd looked like. "After the accident, that whole morbid obsession thing took hold for a while. I kept that hairstyle for ages." She reached for the door handle. "Anyway, thanks for the ride."

Mitch jumped out and rounded the truck to open her door, offering a rain-soaked goodbye. For a split second, she thought he might lean forward and kiss her, but he didn't. And as she navigated the slippery steps and stood on the veranda to watch him pull away, she'd wished he'd stayed. Followed her inside. Turned on the lights. Made conversation over the noise in her head.

She opened the front door and had just flicked on the hall light switch when a power outage plunged the house back into darkness. While she didn't usually feel uneasy when home alone, it was times like these that she mentally thanked her mother for having a house full of candles.

A few minutes later, with the kitchen shadowed in muted light, Tayla opened the fridge and pulled out a four-pack of cream donuts, a treat from Maisie's Bakery on Seaview Road. She dipped her finger into the jam and cream filling, then licked it off the tip with an enthusiastic "yum." Within a couple of minutes, the pack was two donuts down. Why did beer always make her hungry?

She reached for her phone when it dinged and took a bite out of donut number three as she glanced at the screen.

Mitch: You okay over there?
Tayla: Fine thanks. I have donuts. Or I did a minute ago. Oops.
Mitch: Yum! Donuts. Do you want company?
Tayla: Thanks, but the candles are glowing and door's locked. I'm used to being alone.
Mitch: How come? Didn't you have someone to keep you warm in Sydney?

She thought back to the nights she'd slept in Hayden's arms, and equally, how she'd ached for him when he didn't show. Those many nights when she'd craved human touch.

Tayla: Goodnight Mitch. Thanks again for the ride.
Mitch: Sorry I accidentally pushed you over BTW.
Tayla: Accidentally? Not sure I believe you.
Mitch: It's true. Goodnight *babe*
Tayla: Nite *sweetie*

Still feeling a little drunk, she wished she and Mitch didn't have that history Tim talked about.

11

HUMBLE PIE

TAYLA PULLED her car into a parking space outside Harper Realty ten minutes late for her appointment. As she took a seat opposite Andrew Harper's desk, her heart was still racing.

"Thanks for coming," he said as he sat in his chair.

"Sorry I'm late. I'm doing a locum stint at the hospital, and I couldn't get away."

Andrew's smile was warm and wide. "It's fine. What do you do there?"

"I'm a physiotherapist. I specialize in sports injuries. Anyway, Ruby said you might have a backup contract for Cherry Grove."

"I do. It was floating around a while back through another agent, but your father wasn't interested."

That was news to Tayla. But then, her father wasn't one to discuss business with his daughters. "Why's that?"

"To be honest, it's more of an opportunistic offer than a realistic one. But as we're not privy to the deal Mitch made with your parents, we don't know what we're up against. Still, considering the state of the orchard, its location, and Barry's ill health, it's worth a look. With Cherry Grove landlocked by Lime Tree Hill, it

66

tends to put most prospective buyers off, and that's before they've even seen the place or the financials."

Andrew was right. The orchard was in a state, especially compared to the slick operation that was Lime Tree Hill. But every time someone mentioned it, Tayla couldn't help but take it as a direct criticism of her parents. That hurt more than she let on.

He slid the sale and purchase agreement across the desk toward her. "Take a look."

Tayla scanned down the page, stopping at the scribbled figure with its attached zeros. It was a lot lower than Mitch's offer; however, Mitch's offer had a tight string attached. A marriage. Or at least, it did.

She looked up at Andrew, keeping her expression neutral. "Is there any room for upward movement?"

"We won't know unless we try."

"Who are the Stone and Pip Group?"

"A local company run by Chris Stone. They own orchards all over the province, growing apples and stone fruit for the high-end export market. Ruby mentioned a possible problem with Mitch settling. I thought we'd start the ball rolling just in case. What date is settlement due?"

"Three weeks, Thursday."

"Okay. How about you take a few days to mull it over? In the meantime, Chris is keen to meet up tomorrow, suggested we discuss it over dinner if you're free. But don't hold your breath for a higher offer. The guy's pretty cut and dried when it comes to business."

The following morning, Tayla awoke to a drizzly dawn. She snuggled down in her bed, rolled onto her back, and surveyed her surroundings. She'd experienced so much in this room. Written poetry, shared secrets with her diary, hidden under the covers with erotic novels—even shared her first awkward kiss with a boy from school who came to help her with a science project.

Mitch popped unbidden into her thoughts. He might be hot as the Sahara and able to charm a snake out of a basket, but their cozy chat in the rain aside, the man was ruthless when it came to serving his self-interest. And to think she'd once considered him boyfriend material; dreamed of his kiss, his touch. She shuddered at the stupidity of her hopelessly romantic teenage self.

Tayla drifted back to sleep and woke again around eight, surprised to see the sun streaming through the windows. She'd go for a run later, but first, she needed to call Ruby about the Chris Stone update.

Mitch wandered along the banks of the river with Edward in cold pursuit. The pug never hurried for anyone, but the pace gave Mitch time to ponder. Thinking back to the game of touch, he cracked a grin at the thought of Tayla lying on the ground with him on top of her.

At first, seeing her in those skimpy shorts, sporty tank, and high ponytail, Mitch had made an assumption he had no business making. But his opinion had soon changed. Light on her feet and a fast runner, she'd definitely held her own on the field.

He opened the gate and strolled over to the Whitman homestead, a small brown paper bag in hand. The sight of her feeding chickens and collecting eggs in the henhouse slowed his stride. In contrast, Edward ran on ahead to greet her.

"Edward. Here boy." She crouched to pet him. "Hey, beautiful boy. What are you doing here, fella?"

"Afternoon, Tayla."

She stood to full height at the sound of his voice. "Mitch. What can I do for you?"

Her frostiness caught him off guard until he remembered she'd been pretty buzzed the night before. "I guess a pat and a hug like you gave Edward is out of the question, so I'll settle for a coffee." He offered her the bag, then reached down and picked up the basket of eggs.

She looked inside at the berry pie dusted with powdered sugar. "What's this for?"

"It's humble pie." He flashed his best boyish smile, the one he kept for special occasions. "An apology, for landing on top of you when I tripped."

She brushed past him and walked toward the house. Mitch followed. The days were cooler now, and he noticed goosebumps on her arms. He doubted he was the cause, but it didn't hurt to dream.

"I'm not sure I believe you."

"It's true," he said. "My foot caught on a clod of dirt. My knee's still stiff."

"Come in." She held the door open. "So you've been baking?"

The kitchen seemed bigger without Barry and Jean, and it smelled faintly of lavender. He missed their casual chats over the fence. "Not me, Maisie's Bakery. But they made it especially for you."

"Is that right?" She opened the fridge to put the pie away and grabbed a bottle of milk. "Thanks. I love berry pie."

"Yeah? Me too."

"Have a seat. Have you seen anyone about your knee?"

"Not yet." Sitting at the island, he struggled to take his eyes off her. With her delicate features and dignified persona, she fascinated him more than anyone had in a long time.

"Would you like me to take a look?"

He stared at her for a moment. "I don't think that's a good idea, do you?"

"Why not, don't you trust me?"

"It's not that." He fought to suppress a smile. "It's just...well, I'm sure you understand."

A blush crept across her cheeks. She'd obviously caught his drift.

"So, what's on your mind?" Tayla turned her back and reached into the cabinet for two cups. The next time she glanced his way, the blush was gone. "Surely you didn't come over here just to bring me pie?"

"I hear you've had another offer."

"Not *another* offer. *An* offer. Your offer is no longer valid, remember. Anyway, how do you know? I only met the realtor yesterday."

He shrugged. "Word gets around. Especially when it spews from Chris Stone's toxic mouth. He thinks it's in the bag."

"Really?" She motioned to the coffee machine, obviously surprised he knew it was Chris Stone who'd made the offer. "What would you like?"

"Espresso, thanks."

"I take it you're not a fan of Mr. Stone." Tayla lifted the dome from a cake stand on the counter and placed two chocolate chip muffins on a plate. She slid it across the island toward Mitch.

"You could say that. Sure, he runs a slick operation, but that doesn't mean I want him in my back yard. I don't like the way he does business, and the feeling's mutual."

Tayla popped a coffee pod into the machine, then put a cup on the drip tray. "You may not have a choice."

Mitch looked at her and frowned. "No, but you do."

"So, what do you suggest? That we forgo the sale because you don't like the guy?"

"Your father won't be happy. Chris has made him offers before. Insulting ones. Barry can't stand him."

"This whole sorry business keeps getting worse."

He leaned forward, searching for the right words as he peeled the paper case from the muffin and took a bite. "I've been thinking about what you said the other day. Maybe we could pull off the marriage thing…if you promise to play nice."

"If *I* promise to play nice? Where's the note?"

He cocked a brow. "Note?"

"The note where you ask me to go steady."

Mitch caught her slight smile. "Very funny. Look, the SPG spray the shit out of their fruit. That alone could affect our operation, not to mention spray drift entering the river. We can't let that happen."

"Don't you ever tire of doing the right thing?"

He frowned. If she only knew how many times he'd screwed up in his life, his assessment of her after Norman died being one of them. "I don't always do the right thing. Offering to buy Cherry Grove on a drunken handshake is a case in point. But when it comes to organics, I want to do my bit."

Tayla pushed his coffee across the counter then started making her own. "So, you're out to save the planet?"

"The planet will save itself. Whether humans survive *on* the planet is another question. If we don't do something about the pesticides, plastics, and manmade fibers that flood our food chain and waterways, we're in trouble. And forgive me for sounding preachy, but we're literally shitting in our own nest."

"Is that why you always wear cotton and wool?"

His hand around the coffee cup, Mitch leaned back and smiled. He enjoyed making conversation with interesting people, Tayla included. She held his gaze, listening intently. And when she spoke, she wasn't afraid to voice her opinion, those dainty hands animated as she made her point. "For someone who pretends not to notice, you're very observant."

She shrugged. Lifted her coffee cup and took a sip. "What's the real reason you and Chris Stone don't get on?"

Mitch frowned at her candid question. He rubbed his index finger across his stubbled jaw, suppressing a smile as he recalled the summer he'd spent with the now Ella Stone. "What, apart from him wanting to get his greedy hands on my operation? Let's just say we once had a personal conflict of interest."

She waited for him to elaborate, but he wasn't about to tell Tayla that Chris's wife had been his first.

"So, what do you think?" Mitch asked. "Should we take the bull by the horns and go for it?"

Tayla picked up the other muffin, breaking a piece off the top with her delicate fingers. "Can I trust you to be discreet?"

"In what way?"

"My parents think the world of you, but they're also very conservative. It would break their hearts if they thought you were cheating on me." She hesitated. Popped the piece of muffin into her mouth and chewed. "Unfortunately, you have a reputation around town as a bit of a man-whore."

Mitch chuckled. "That's just a filthy rumor. Someone's trying to ruin my stellar reputation."

"From what I've heard, you've ruined it all by yourself."

"Lies, all lies. And, it works both ways, sweetheart."

"Please don't call me sweetheart. You make me feel like a secretary from *Mad Men*."

"Well, as our relationship is purely business, the insincere use of the term of endearment suits you." He realized by the look on her face that she didn't appreciate his sense of humor. "I thought you were keen."

"That was before you nearly squashed me by slipping a tackle into a game of touch."

"I've already apologized for that. I promise to be good from now on if you promise to tone down the snob fest."

She picked up his cup along with her own and rinsed them in the sink. Was this where she'd lose her cool, tell him exactly where he could stick his bull horns?

"Come on, Tayla. Let's move on. We can't let your parents down this late in the game."

She turned to face him. "It's not me that's letting them down."

"I get that, believe me. I'm not the heartless guy you think I am."

"No? Don't pretend this is about us doing the right thing. This is you, out to settle some petty vendetta against Chris Stone. Now, I don't mean to be rude, but I have a dinner date."

He stood, wondering who she was meeting. "We're running out of time, so don't hold my balls in a vise for too long."

"Seriously?" She sighed, shaking her head. "You think I'm deliberately trying to make you uncomfortable?"

"Maybe." Mitch walked to the door, then turned back. "Thanks for the coffee." He lifted the glass dome from the cake stand and grabbed another muffin. "These muffins are so good."

12

BABYCAKES

HAND OUTSTRETCHED, Chris Stone stood as Andrew and Tayla approached the table. Dressed in a navy blue suit and flowery shirt, he was much younger than Tayla had expected. She guessed he'd be in his early to mid-thirties, with a full smile and clammy palms. He looked her up and down, his gaze inappropriate for a business meeting.

During dinner, Chris held the floor, criticizing the state of the orchard and making no apologies for his low offer. As he finished his spiel, Tayla wondered if the guy actually believed his own BS.

"You do realize the Whitmans have an offer pending?" Andrew said. "We're simply putting out feelers."

"Sure. But if you have no joy, I'm happy to do you a favor and take the place off your hands." Chris leaned back in his chair, his expression smug. "I'd hate to see your parents go under for the sake of a few hundred K."

Andrew frowned at Chris before glancing down at his phone as it pinged. "Sorry to bail, but the wife's on edge. Thanks for the meal, Chris." He rose from the table and turned to Tayla. "I'll call you tomorrow."

"Thanks, Andrew." Tayla stood as he walked away, wishing she could leave as well.

"His wife's pregnant and about to drop," Chris explained as he looked around the restaurant, checking out the other diners.

"Yes, he mentioned that earlier." Taking her seat again, Tayla waited for Chris to return his attention to her. "Getting back to Cherry Grove, would you change it to organics in line with the other orchards in the area? It seems to be a growing trend."

Chris threw back his head and laughed. "I'm all for saving the planet—that's why we follow industry standards and guidelines when spraying, but a man has to make a buck. While that may not interest your 'convenient greenie' neighbor, Harrington, someone's got to grow decent fruit."

"Are you saying Mitch's fruit is inferior?"

"The guy's clueless. Sure, he's had some good years, but the global demand for organics is waning. I can't see him lasting much longer, to be honest. But you didn't hear that from me."

The urge to defend Mitch hit Tayla full on. "Surely the demand for organics is on the increase? It certainly is in Sydney."

"Maybe among the born-again vegan set. It's like a damn cult with some of those people."

Tayla held her annoyed tongue. Chris Stone obviously fancied himself as a bit of an expert on growing fruit, born-again vegans, and charming the fairer sex.

Yeah, right.

"I understand it's Harrington who's ahead of me in the race for Cherry Grove. Personally, I don't know where the money's coming from. Still, he's a trust fund baby. I'd watch him though."

"Meaning?"

Chris leaned forward, ready to part with his not-so-secret secret. "He's got a high profile, I'll give him that, but his reputation with the ladies could do with a bit of a spit and polish."

"Sorry? I don't follow."

"Let's just say the guy sleeps with anyone in a pretty dress and heels." His eyes shot to her chest as he raised a brow. "Although, to be fair, you're probably not his type."

Obviously. "Well, we're not here to gossip about my parents' neighbor. Thank you for your interest in Cherry Grove. There's a lot to think about."

Chris signaled for the waiter to top up his wine. Tayla stared out the window while processing his assessment of Mitch. She tried to imagine what it would be like to have lovers fall at your feet. Did women leave their panties in Mitch's mailbox, complete with a phone number attached?

"Oh, and one more thing." Chris smiled, displaying a row of overly white teeth. "If our offer's successful, we plan to demolish the house to make room for extra trees. Maybe we'll donate it to the fire service for a training exercise. Reduce demo costs. Or else, with the house on its own title, we could probably flip it and make a buck that way."

Tayla felt the blood drain from her face at the thought of her beloved family home going up in flames. She kept her expression neutral while inside she raged at the insensitive jerk in front of her. What would her parents say if they knew she was being wined and dined by someone they despised—trying to do a deal behind their backs? She looked down at her unfinished dessert, her appetite lost along with their conversation. "I'll talk to our lawyer. You'll have a counteroffer by the end of business tomorrow."

He downed his wine in one go. "I don't do counteroffers, baby-cakes. Best price first and last is my motto."

Babycakes? "Well, thank you for dinner."

"My pleasure. I've always got time for a pretty face." He checked his watch as they stood. "But just a heads-up. Don't hold your breath where Harrington's concerned. If his offer was uncon-ditional, you wouldn't be here. Am I right?" He leaned inappropri-ately close to her ear and whispered, "Let's have dinner again soon —a little deal sweetener?"

Tayla stepped back, her hands clenched at her sides. "I don't think that's necessary."

Chris's eyes crawled over her again. "I'm surprised your old man didn't accept our offer months ago. Still, I knew he'd come to his senses. How's he doing? I might give him a call tomorrow."

"My father's not well enough for calls at the moment, and I'd prefer we keep this between ourselves."

His eyes on her the whole time, Chris gave his credit card to the waiter, who scanned it and handed it back. "Yeah, maybe that's best, all things considered."

The hair lifted on the back of her neck. Did the guy think they were having a private moment? "And, Mr. Stone?" He looked up from slotting his credit card into his wallet. "Don't call me baby-cakes. Not now, not ever."

Back home, Tayla sat on the veranda with a cup of peppermint tea, weighing up the pros and cons of a fake marriage to Mr. Billboard. The burden of her parents' predicament felt like a cloak of duty. One about to smother her.

But every time she recalled Mitch's response to her offer to look at his knee, she smiled. He didn't want her touching him. Was he worried what would happen if she did?

Her phone chimed, and she picked it up and unlocked it.

Ruby: How did your dinner date go? Is he open to a counteroffer?
Tayla: 'I don't do counteroffers, babycakes.'
Ruby: He called you babycakes? No way!
Tayla: Yep!!! And he kept staring at me like I was a piece of meat while he twisted his wedding band. The guy's a dick.
Ruby: Did you tell him to go f@*k himself?

Tayla: Almost. And he plans to take a match to the house so he can plant more trees. Imagine what Mum and Dad would say. They'd be devastated.

Ruby: The bastard! So what's our next step?

Tayla: *Sigh* Persuade Mitch Harrington to marry me.

Ruby: Are you sure?

Tayla: No. He called me a prissy stuck-up snob.

Ruby: What is it with these men and their name-calling? Surely you wouldn't give him the time of day after that?

Tayla: Fortune favors the brave.

Ruby: Chin up @prissybabycakes. You've got this.

Tayla: I need a pretty dress. If I have to do this, I want to do it in style. Do you know any amazing dressmakers?

Ruby: Yes!!! I'll be in touch.

THE TERMS

WITH THE SALE date looming and Chris Stone's backup offer in the mix, Mitch wanted Tayla's decision. Not that he blamed her for running hot and cold. That same sharp temperature change hit him every time he thought of the marriage. It was one thing to manipulate Norman's wishes but another to feel comfortable about it. He picked up his phone, pushing those thoughts aside as he typed his message.

Mitch: Can we meet for lunch? The Spinnaker Cafe @ 12:30?
Tayla: Is that absolutely necessary?
Mitch: Yes. But hey, your call.
Mitch: And do me a favor. Ditch the attitude. I'm trying to enjoy my day here.

He admonished himself as he waited for her reply. There was no need to be rude. He imagined her at work, torturing her patients with those sexy hands of hers. Ever since she'd suggested looking at his knee, he couldn't help wondering how good her massage technique might be. Maybe one day he'd find out.

Tayla: Fine. See you then.

When Mitch parked outside the café at the agreed time, Tayla was already seated, sipping a coffee and looking gorgeous. Her sunglasses firmly in place, she watched him mount the steps.

As they made small talk and perused the menu, the term 'out of your league' slammed into his thoughts. He wondered if she was about to change her mind again. If she did, was there any point trying to convince her when he wasn't convinced himself?

He waited until the server took their order before asking, "So, what's the verdict?"

"I have terms."

Mitch leaned forward, his gaze drifting to the outline of her lacy bra underneath her blouse. *Get a grip.* He liked a girl with terms. It showed strength of character. "Of course you do."

"Okay. That's number one. Don't try to marginalize me for having an opinion."

Here we go. "Noted. Two?"

"I want to stay in my parents' place. Alone."

"Separate houses?" He huffed and shook his head. "Sorry, but if the deal goes through, I've already promised it to one of my managers."

"Well, where do you suggest I live?"

"Let me see? With me at Lime Tree Hill? I'll be away for a week or two in November. That should give you a bit of a breather."

"November's months away."

Mitch shrugged. They probably wouldn't last until mid-winter, let alone spring, but it was good to plan ahead.

"Is there a spare room in that shed of yours?"

Noticing the blush on her cheeks, Mitch suppressed a grin. She was stunning up close. Fresh and clean and sexy. The type of girl who could easily slip under his skin. But her fierce determination impressed him the most. With Barry unwell, the realities of packing up their family home, and her return to Clifton Falls, she had a lot on her plate. But she always handled herself with such dignity.

"What, no snuggling together under a crisp set of cotton sheets? That's not much fun." He laughed at her shocked expression. "Anyway, it's a loft, not a shed. And yes, there's a spare room. It even has a bed. Number three?"

"You're a surfer, aren't you?"

"I am."

"I want you to teach me."

Mitch leaned back in his chair, his arms crossed as he studied her, keeping his reaction low-key. "What, to surf? Are you a strong swimmer?"

"Not really. But I've been taking swimming lessons in Sydney. At the Icebergs Pool."

"Do you have a board?"

"Not yet. Will you help me pick one?"

"Sure." Learning to surf was the last thing he'd expected as a condition. He'd tried to teach Prue once, without success, but he wasn't averse to teaching Tayla. It might even be fun. "Why surfing?"

He noticed her hesitation.

"Our family spent a lot of time at the beach in the summer when I was a kid, but I never enjoyed swimming in saltwater. The waves scared me. The day after my sixth birthday, we were at the beach with friends. Lisa and Ruby promised to look after me while the adults set up the picnic. Dad insisted we stay in the shallows. But everyone got distracted, and I suddenly found myself out of my depth. I got caught in a rip and nearly drowned. According to family legend, when Dad realized what was happening, he screamed my name at the top of his lungs and ran into the waves. A surfer helped him pull me ashore. They had to resuscitate me, and I spent a night in the hospital."

"Shit." He reached for her hand and squeezed it, the gesture so natural, he didn't even think about it. "So how do you feel now when you're in the surf?"

"Nervous on a good day, terrified the rest of the time."

He frowned. "But you swim in the river?"

Color rushed to her cheeks as she pulled her hand back. He had seen her that day and she knew it. "Only by the grapefruit trees, where the current evens out. I can wet my hair, but not my face."

"So why do you want to learn to surf if you're afraid of the open water?"

She hesitated. "When I was in high school, being a surfer chick was a prerequisite for membership in the popular club. I was never that girl. It's not that I want to relive those teenage years, but sometimes, when everything else seems impossible, focusing on one goal gets you through. Do you know what I mean?"

"Sure. I get that."

"When I lived in Bondi, I walked along the beach most days. No matter the weather, surfers were always out, some of them for hours. I'd sit in the sand and watch, wishing I had the guts to join them. And despite what happened when I was a child, waves have always fascinated me."

"Yeah, me too. I'm happy to teach you, but we should wait until summer. It's no fun learning in the cold. Anything else?"

She took a deep breath. He was fairly certain she wanted to add another condition, but if she did, she wasn't ready to voice it. "Not right now."

"Are you sure?"

She pressed her lips together and gave a tight nod.

"Right. Where should we have the ceremony? There's a small chapel twenty minutes' drive from here. It's off the Eastern Pacific Highway just past Petrie Bay—"

"I'd prefer not to do it in a chapel." Tayla's expression saddened as she looked at Mitch across the table.

To him, this marriage was a way to honor the deal he'd made with Barry. Tayla had much more at stake. Her family would be adversely affected if Cherry Grove didn't sell, and he was mindful of that fact. If she'd received a decent offer from a third party, Mitch would have forfeited his deposit. But until now, he'd thought Ken might see reason and release the funds so the sale could proceed. He now realized that unless he married, the money would never be his.

"Okay. Where do you suggest?"

"On the beach…just before sunset. Petrie Bay's fine. I love it there. What about Sunday of next week if we can arrange it?"

"Sure, suits me. I'll pay for your gown. Just let me know how much."

"You mean we have to get dressed up?"

Her playful smile took him by surprise. "My sisters would disown me if we eloped with no pictures to show for it. Also, we need a license three days before and two witnesses. Luka will be mine."

"The guy from touch rugby?"

"That's him. What about you?" Mitch wondered if she had many friends in Clifton Falls, then remembered how close she'd seemed to Tim the night of the game.

"I'll ask Tim. I'm sure he wouldn't mind doubling as the photographer."

"Good. I have a friend who's a jeweler. Text me your ring size, and I'll take care of the wedding bands. Any preference in gold color?"

"Doesn't really matter as long as it's fine."

"Okay. And what day do you want to move in?"

She held his gaze, a flicker of trepidation in her expression. And in that moment, he wanted to reach out and tell her she didn't have to take the fall for everyone else's mistakes. That she'd be safe with him.

"After the wedding works best for me."

"After the wedding it is."

When Tayla entered her family home later that afternoon, there was a feeling of despondency about it. Like it knew it would be empty soon, knew it was time for her to pack. She stood in the large walk-in pantry and looked around at the many jars of preserves, small cake tins piled high, and packets of pasta and rice and baking goods. She was just about to grab a box and make a start when her text alert chimed.

Tim: Do I have to take my best suit to the cleaners?
Tayla: Yes. Wedding is Sunday next week, subject to celebrant availability. I'll need you from 3:30 on.
Tim: What? Thanks for the notice.
Tayla: You love spontaneity.
Tim: I do. And remember to have a practice.
Tayla: Practice?
Tim: A smooch rehearsal. You don't want to share your first kiss in public, do you?
Tayla: Oh. I hadn't thought of that.
Tim: Go on. You know you want to!!!
Tayla: As if.

Her phone still in her hand, Tayla left the pantry and flopped down on the sofa. Tim had a point. Kissing Mitch for the first time in front of Luka, the celebrant, and Tim would be awkward. But asking for a practice kiss—absolutely humiliating.

Tayla: I'm chewing my lip…
Tim: Ha-ha. I would be too if I was about to marry Mitch.

14

TO THE LETTER

MITCH GLANCED up when Tayla knocked on his open office door. With her hair in a messy knot, freckles fading across the bridge of her nose, and her lips bare, she looked breathtakingly carefree.

"Hi. I'd like a quick word if you're not too busy?"

He stood. "Sure. Come in."

She inched inside. Hesitant.

He strolled over and closed the door behind her. She remained standing, her fingers fiddling with the keys in her hand.

"I was wondering if we could maybe have a practice."

"Practice?" He frowned. "What kind of practice?"

"It's just…" Tayla glanced away. "What happens when we get to the 'kiss the bride' part? I don't want it to be awkward."

Mitch rubbed the back of his neck, wanting to smile at her request. But she was deadly serious, so he'd be the same. "Okay."

"And please don't be a dick about it. I'd rather our first kiss be in private, that's all."

"You do realize there will only be the five of us?"

"I know, but the celebrant has to think it's legit, or she may refuse to marry us. Or revoke it. Or…anyway, you know what I mean."

"Good point." He'd wanted to kiss Tayla that night they played touch rugby. But now, with her suggestion hanging in the air, Mitch unexpectedly felt nervous. And apart from his first time, in the back seat of Ella Stone's car, he'd never been nervous around women. "Shall we go upstairs?"

She chewed her bottom lip and shook her head. As he stepped closer, she whispered, "Here's fine."

Mitch took the keys from her hands and placed them on top of the filing cabinet behind her. He'd longed to touch her hair ever since that first day in Simon's office. To smell and taste her. But as his hands held hers, she inhaled sharply and trembled.

He dipped his head to meet her gaze. "Are you sure?"

Tayla nodded, keeping her focus downward. Mitch cupped her face, and as he brushed a kiss against her lips, she stilled. He pulled back, caught her hesitation, then bent down again, kissing her longer this time. Her response surprised him, the slow pleasure and inviting warmth of her mouth. Just as he went to deepen the kiss, a knock on the door pulled her away with a jolt.

"Hey, Mitch," Ned called. "Someone's here to see you."

He looked over his shoulder, mumbling, "Shit" under his breath. "Okay. Thanks."

A red-faced Tayla picked up her keys and opened the door. Before he had time to react, she darted from the office. He watched her stride past the conveyer belt, the taste of her fresh on his tongue and his jeans a little tight at the fly.

As Mitch went to go after her, he noticed Ella Stone sitting on the bench outside his office. He frowned. "Ella. What can I do for you?"

"Mitch." She stared after Tayla hurrying across the packing shed and onto the driveway. "I hope I wasn't interrupting anything."

His gaze flicked toward Tayla. "Nothing that won't keep."

"Is she a client?"

Mitch turned to look at her. There was no point in being secretive. "No, she's my girlfriend. Fiancée actually."

Ella stiffened. "Fiancée? But that wasn't Prue Preston."

"No, Prue and I finished months ago, remember?"

"I'm sorry. I should have called first. I didn't realize you were seeing anyone—and engaged again so soon. Wow. You don't mess around, do you?"

Mitch wasn't about to elaborate, but he wanted to nip her interest in the bud. "We've been keeping it under wraps. How can I help?"

Ella narrowed her eyes. He could tell she was itching to ask more, but instead said, "I'm after some advice. I'd like to try mandarins on a block we've just purchased. I was hoping you could help me with the organics side. But first, I could murder a coffee. Shall we go upstairs?"

He hesitated. Spending time with Ella anywhere seemed a bad idea. But in the loft? "Sure. Come on up."

She followed him to the bottom of the stairs. "Or a glass of red would be even better."

Mitch stood on the balcony, a strong cup of coffee warming his hands. Autumn was his favorite time of year—when the memory of summer faded, and the days were clear and calm. Winter was the main season for citrus, but the mandarins and limes started earlier, meaning there'd be pickers everywhere soon. Oranges and grapefruit followed, and the thought of the upcoming season excited him.

His gaze moved to the Whitman homestead, his thoughts on Tayla and their practice kiss. The best kiss he'd had in a long while. What would the next few months bring between him and his timid, yet often fierce, bride-to-be?

Harmony? Chaos?

Hearing his phone ding, he strolled inside to check it.

Luka: What's up? Keen to watch the game?
Mitch: Why not? Beats floating up shit creek without a paddle.
Luka: Great. I'll be there soon with a paddle and some beers.

Luka arrived half an hour later. He kicked off his shoes and dropped onto the sofa. Mitch grabbed a bag of chips from the pantry and chucked it to him.

"Thanks, mate." Luka opened the bag and helped himself to a handful. "What's happening up shit creek?"

"A lot. I want to show you something before the rugby starts."

Luka checked his watch. "Don't ask me to move from this couch. I've had a busy day."

"As if. And stay where you are." Mitch picked up the carved wooden box on the coffee table and opened the lid. He took out the top envelope and handed it to Luka.

"What's this?" Luka asked, sitting up straighter.

Mitch took a seat in the chair opposite; Edward settled at his feet. "The last letter Norman ever wrote me. My grandfather was quite the letter-writer in his time. Take a look."

Luka removed the fragile paper from the envelope and unfolded it. As he scanned the page, he frowned, then read aloud:

"Dear Mitchel,

If you're reading this, it's because I'm gone. I apologize for the type. I prefer to write in real ink, as I believe it adds a romance to the script that a ball-

point or typewriter cannot. Sadly, my
penmanship is not what it used to be, so
I'm sitting at my old Olivetti. At least
this way, you'll understand my intention.

We've had our struggles over the years. I
know you resented me for my treatment of
your mother, and for that, I apologize
profusely. I let my pride stand in the
way of acceptance. It's one regret of
many, but losing my wife and son left
such a gaping void, I lost myself as
well.

I've met a girl who's stolen my heart.
You will know who I mean. With her unique
style and poise, she isn't easy to
ignore. And while I have never so much as
looked at another woman since your grandmother passed, this one is different. She
takes my soul by her gentle hands, gives
it a tug and brings it back to life.

She visits me often. We laugh, and sometimes we cry while watching sad movies.
She bakes for me and reads in the most
beautiful voice I have ever heard. Lying
in bed, listening to her narrate the
words of Steinbeck brings a lump to my
throat.

Still, we're from different times, and my
love for her is purely platonic. I have
attached a page to my will. Please honor

it. I want her to finish her education
without having to worry about money. As
for my other stipulations, you may find
them controlling, but I have my reasons.

What was once mine is now yours. Make the
most of it. Leave the rat race behind and
tend the land. Build a wonderful home,
fill it with kids and laughter - surf,
eat beautiful food, find a balance. And
know this: Whatever you decide to do, if
you're happy and proud of your achieve-
ments, you have my blessing.

Some men are oat sowers, and some aren't.
You have many oats to sow, but when
you're finished with the bountiful
harvest your good looks and charm
provide, look to the girl next door. If
we lived in a society where elders chose
life partners for their offspring, she
would be my choice for you.

Your loving grandfather,
Norman."

Luka folded the letter and returned it to the envelope. "Wow.
The guy didn't ask for much, did he? Judging by your shit creek
comment, I take it the wedding's all go?"

"I'd decided against it when I was in London. Seeing Liz and
Ally settled and happy, I felt guilty about living a lie. But Chris
Stone's been flashing a wad of cash under Tayla's nose. Imagine
having that jerk set up shop in my backyard. And, his offer's a low
one."

"I don't blame you. But a fake marriage?" Luka took a can of beer from the six-pack in front of him and pulled the tab. He swigged. "Mind you, I can see the appeal. If you have to marry a stranger, you'll never tire of that view over the breakfast table."

"Piss off." Mitch chuckled. "It's a calculated business strategy, not a lust match. And Tayla's hardly a stranger."

"If you say so." Luka shook his head. "Norman, wherever he is, must be clapping his hands in glee. But what will Prue say?"

"Who knows? She doesn't want kids, did I tell you? 'Not now, not ever, Mitchel.' That's what she said the day we split."

"Didn't you discuss it before your engagement?" Luka had never warmed to Prue, and while he kept his opinion mostly to himself, his body language spoke volumes.

"We did. I got the impression we were on the same page. Looking back, we weren't even in the same book."

"And now Tayla holds the solution, does she? Have you sorted a prenup?"

"Not yet."

Luka grinned. "You sure as hell don't sweat the small stuff, do you, mate?"

"Yeah, well, the last time I dotted the i's and crossed the t's, the love of my life cheated on me. Who knew threesomes were her thing?"

Luka sipped his beer. "I'm sorry, but Prue was never the love of your life, and you know it. Nice enough girl, but…"

Mitch shrugged. Luka had a point, but that didn't mean their breakup had hurt any less.

"Are you sure you know what you're doing?" Luka continued.

"Nope. Norman always called me impulsive. Seems he was more intuitive than I gave him credit for. And just because Tayla's beautiful doesn't mean she'll be easy to live with."

"She's got a kind smile."

"Yeah, I may have seen it once or twice. Anyway, are you on board?"

Luka huffed out a sigh. "When and where?"

"Sunday of next week, Petrie Bay. And we have to look the part. Imagine what Mum and the girls will say if we don't have any decent wedding photos."

"So you're shouting me a new suit?"

Mitch chuckled. "Not in this lifetime."

"Come on. We need to match." Luka grabbed the TV remote and turned up the volume. "Right, enough wedding talk. The haka's starting soon."

Mitch sat on the sofa next to him and grabbed the chips. "Ella came to see me today."

"No way." Luka hit mute. "What the hell did she want?"

"A glass of wine and a shoulder to cry on under the pretense of advice. Chris is in one of his moods again. He thinks she's having an affair."

"Two words. Be very careful."

Mitch laughed. "That's three."

"Yeah, and three's a crowd. Add Chris Stone to the mix, and that crowd gets rowdy."

Mitch lay in bed after Luka had left, his conversation with Ella playing in his mind. Since they'd married, Chris's jealousy had made for a volatile union. A union Mitch wanted nothing to do with.

His thoughts turned to Tayla. How good she'd felt in his arms, and her hesitation as she'd asked for a practice kiss. He grabbed his phone from the nightstand and unlocked it. It was time to add a condition of his own.

Mitch: I have a condition.
Tayla: Which is?
Mitch: Another practice kiss.

92

When there was no immediate reply, Mitch placed his phone on the pillow next to him. He'd almost drifted off when his text alert chimed again.

Tayla: There's no need. The result was satisfactory.
Mitch: I can do better than satisfactory.
Tayla: I doubt that.

Mitch reread her text and laughed. *Satisfactory?* She clearly didn't rate him as a kisser. With his ego slightly bruised, he returned his phone to the nightstand, then pulled up the covers and waited for sleep.

15

THE PINES

WITH HER MIND on the wedding for most of the day, Tayla couldn't wait to leave work. The more she thought about it, the more that feeling of dread surfaced.

By the time she reached her parents' house, the air held a distinct chill, even with the sun shining in a cloudless blue sky. She'd walk the river track before dinner, but right now, she wanted to text Tim. Good old Tim. He'd always been her rock.

Tayla sat on the steps of the veranda and rummaged through her bag for her phone. Holding it steady, she gathered her thoughts.

Tayla: We had the rehearsal.
Tim: And?
Tayla: Um…well…
Tim: I knew it.
Tayla: Yep. Butterflies and moonbeams and starlight.
Tim: Not surprised one bit.

Tayla hit the blush emoji and pushed send. She sat on the steps a little longer, her thoughts still on Mitch and that amazing kiss. How could she be both excited and terrified at the same time?

During the days that followed, Tayla pushed the impending nuptials to the back of her mind. But at night, when her deal with Mitch, Hayden's betrayal, and her father's struggle with post-surgery depression consumed her, she went to bed before nine and waited for sleep to smother the blues.

They say time heals. But as her thoughts drifted between Hayden and Mitch, she wondered how long it would be before she had the guts to block Hayden on her phone. How long before the hurt of his betrayal waned.

Tim, in all his excited wedding-day glory, had organized every detail of her half of the affair. And as Tayla fussed with her hair and makeup on the 'big day,' she gave thanks for having a best friend who loved the pomp and pageantry of tying the knot—be it a fake elopement or otherwise.

Her two-piece nude-pink satin outfit came via a friend of Ruby's, a fashion blogger who'd designed and sewn the outfit for a photo shoot, only to have it rejected at the last minute. When Tayla first tried it on, she'd had her doubts. After all, with its full skirt of darted pleats falling from a wide waistband, and a form-fitting cropped-sleeve top that showed just enough midriff to make it interesting, the style could never be called traditional. But the more she'd looked at it hanging from the back of her bedroom door, the more she loved it.

Memories of her Sydney dress surfaced. Sleek and unadorned, the ivory satin had allowed little room for movement. And as Tayla's thoughts churned, she realized it matched the feeling of that day. Perfectly.

Now, as she slipped into her second wedding dress of the year, she wondered how Mitch would react to her radical choice. Would he even notice?

And what about the kiss? It was one thing to share a kiss in his office with the door closed and the blinds casting a discreet light across the room. But it would be quite another to kiss in front of Luka and Tim.

They hadn't seen each other since then, but the memory of that kiss lingered until she'd almost forgotten why she disliked him. And as she'd left the packing shed that day, hurrying home with her heart thumping in her chest, she'd failed to stop the chatter that was Mitchel Harrington. His smell, the way he kissed with passion, and the feel of his hands as he held her face—like she was precious to him. And those three small things amounted to one big thing. Trouble.

Tayla turned from the mirror when Tim knocked. "Come on, you," he called through her door. "We don't want to be late. He'll think you're not coming."

She opened the door and did a twirl, her hands shaking with nerves.

"Wow. Look at you. Now that's how a bride's done right there. Fabulous."

"Thanks." She held out her hands in front of her. "I don't know why I'm so nervous."

"Most brides are." Tim pulled her in for a hug. "But he'll show. You won't be left this time. I promise."

She frowned. "How can you be so sure?"

"Because Mitch Harrington is a man of his word. And while your reasons for doing this are as unconventional as that gown, I truly admire your courage."

Tayla swallowed the lump forming in her throat. If they didn't leave soon, she'd shoo Tim out the door, then lock herself inside the house until she came to her senses. "Thanks. I couldn't have done it without you."

Tim always smiled freely, but there was one smile he saved for the special people in his life, and that was the one he gave her at that moment. "Right, let's go take a peek through the lens. My fingers are itching to make magic."

Tayla followed him into the living room, her dress making magic of its own. "Who was at the door earlier?"

"A florist." Tim picked up an impressive bouquet of autumn wildflowers from the hall table and handed them to her. "Looks like your fiancé has a touch of the traditional in him after all."

Mitch going to the trouble of sending her flowers warmed her inside. "They're beautiful." She inhaled deeply. "And smell divine."

He pointed to the attached envelope. "There's a message."

Tayla removed the rough paper card from the envelope and read to herself as Tim repeatedly clicked the shutter.

Tayla,

Thank you for taking a chance
and trusting me to share this time with you.
And while I don't want to be a dick about it,
I just want you to know...
that practice kiss was perfect.

Mitch x.

A warm blush crept up Tayla's neck and face. She turned to Tim and laughed. "Put that camera down right now."

"No way. That's my best shot so far."

Two hundred yards from the Eastern Pacific Highway, a plantation of pine trees flanked the rock formations of the coast, like sentinels keeping watch over the bond between land and sea. Mitch had picked the spot, and when Tim and Tayla arrived an hour before sunset, apart from the odd seagull and a scurry of wild rabbits as they drove up the gravel road, the place was deserted.

Tayla stepped from the car, her skin taut with a sudden chill as she inhaled salt-filled air. She could do this. Mitch wasn't here yet, but that didn't mean he wouldn't show. Watching Tim set up his gear, she smiled. Her friend was passionate about everything he did, but photography had always been his greatest love.

For the next while, he directed the photo shoot with his usual flamboyant flair. And as she stood between the pines in her nude-colored sandals, the last of the sun's rays streaming through the branches and illuminating the satin of her skirt, Tayla felt strangely serene.

"Okay, face this way." Tim adjusted the lens. "Good, good. Look down. Drop the flowers to your side. That's great. Perfect. We've got this."

"What's the time?"

"Never mind." He clicked off another few shots.

"But the sun's about to set."

"Tayla. Stop." Tim lowered his camera and reached into the bag for another lens. "He'll be here. Come on."

She followed him across the stack of pancake rocks and looked out to the South Pacific Ocean. There was little to no wind, but the waves were loud and excitable. To the north, surfers bobbed on their boards—black dots in a vast sea of sunset hues—waiting for their turn in the lineup. And behind her, as the coast curved around the bay, the city of Clifton Falls dominated the distant vista.

Despite her fear of open water, Tayla loved Petrie Bay. When they were younger, she and Tim would meet at the beach at dawn and cook toast over an open fire while watching the sunrise and putting their world in order. They'd talk books and music, and sometimes, boys and how neither of them felt they belonged. It seemed like only yesterday.

Now her world was about to turn upside down. There'd be no order in the coming months. No sense of contentment as she packed up her family home and moved away from all she held dear. Her mother and father, Ruby and Lisa—her tiny Bondi apartment. All she could do was take a deep breath, brace herself, and hope she landed safely on the other side.

"Tayla?"

"Yes." She looked up, her hand shielding her eyes from the sun.

Tim cocked his head toward the car driving down the road. "Look."

16

THE KNOT

TIM'S CAR was empty when they stopped beside it. As the celebrant cut the engine, Mitch leaned forward and peered through the windshield. "Do you see them?"

"There she is." The celebrant pointed to the rocks. "Right. Let's do this. We're fifteen minutes late as it is."

Once out of the car, Mitch strolled toward her, adjusting his tie as Luka and the celebrant followed a few steps behind. The closer he got, the faster he walked. But as she turned, he stopped. With her hair falling in burnished waves around her shoulders, the fading light catching the folds of her dress and the surf crashing over the rocks behind her, she took his breath away.

The significance of what they were about to do slammed into him like a sucker punch. "This is for you, Norman, you romantic old bastard," he murmured under his breath.

Tayla smiled shyly, and as he regained his senses, Mitch stepped forward, one hand outstretched, urging her to join him. She lifted her skirt and navigated the rocks to where they'd stand in front of the celebrant. When she reached his side, he took her hand. It felt as cold as ice. For a moment, he wondered if she had a warm heart under that facade of indifference.

"Sorry we're late. We got caught in a mob of sheep just past the orchard. They blocked the road for a while." He stepped back, taking in her outfit, the flowers, and how her complexion came alive under the late-afternoon light. She'd be uncomfortable with the attention, but at that moment, he couldn't take his eyes off her. "You look amazing. That dress is perfect."

A blush bloomed on both cheeks as she pulled her hand from his. "Thank you. I like your suit. And thanks for the flowers."

It wasn't much of a compliment, but he'd take it. And as she stood in front of him, preparing to recite her vows, it was the first time he'd considered a different outcome from this sham of a marriage. The first time his fascination for her hinted at something more than the physical.

"Are you doing okay?" he murmured.

"Yes, fine." Tayla looked back at Tim, who stepped forward to take her bouquet. Mitch took both of her hands in his, and as he rubbed his thumbs over her knuckles, he sensed her relax.

The ceremony was brief and efficient. There were no hand-written vows, no romantic love songs. Just the two of them 'repeating after me' while Tim viewed them through the lens and Luka stood to one side, the rings in the breast pocket of his suit.

Mitch had been on edge all day, constantly second-guessing their decision, and as he held the ring at the tip of her finger, ready to slide it into place, his hands wouldn't stop shaking.

By contrast, when it was her turn to place his band, she did so with purpose. And when he looked into those soulful eyes, her expression softened as she smiled for the second time that day.

"By the power vested in me by the laws of New Zealand, I now pronounce you husband and wife." The celebrant beamed. "Mitch, you may kiss your bride."

There was no hesitation on his part. He leaned in and kissed her gently, his lips confident against hers. Her reluctance was evident, but at least she kissed him back. What more could he expect?

Luka moved forward, pulling everyone into a group hug before the celebrant said her goodbyes.

Mitch looked at Tayla. "Shall we FaceTime my in-laws? Tell them the news?"

Tayla frowned. "What, now?"

"No time like the present."

Luka laughed. "This, I have to see."

"No way." Mitch grinned at Luka and Tim. "Bride and groom only. We'll meet you guys back at the car."

And as he held her hand and led her away from the men so they could call her parents in private, Mitch thought the day couldn't have been more perfect.

Except...it wasn't real. He had to keep sight of that, always.

Little Brown Barn hummed with warmth and atmosphere as they walked through the door. If Tayla felt out of place among the Clifton Falls smart set, she didn't let it show. Maybe to her, dining in a crowded restaurant in her wedding garb was the most natural thing in the world. The waiter ushered them to their table, and when Mitch pulled out her chair, she smoothed her satin skirt and sat, ignoring the stares of the other patrons.

Mitch loosened his tie and perused the menu, smiling at the handwritten descriptions. *Earth mushrooms dancing in fields of green. Hand-crafted butter, fresh from the pat. Lovingly churned ice cream flirting with skillfully fragmented honeycomb shards.* It sounded pretentious, but as he knew from experience, the food here was anything but.

He turned to Tayla. "What are you having?"

"I can't decide." She closed the menu. "You order for me."

He stared at her in disbelief. Last week, Tayla could barely make eye contact. Now she wanted him to choose her wedding dinner. She faced Luka, engaging him in conversation about his work and family. When the champagne arrived and Tim proposed a toast, she responded with enthusiasm, leaning into her friend and hugging him.

Meanwhile, the enormity of what they'd done hit Mitch in his increasingly nervous gut. He ordered the twelve-hour shoulder of lamb with rosemary jus—a sharing plate for two. When the waiter placed it before them, along with an array of delicious vegetable sides, his new wife looked at him and declared, "Perfect." And with that, she tucked straight in.

He, on the other hand, couldn't find his appetite.

17

LIME TREE HILL

IT WAS JUST BEFORE eleven when they arrived at Lime Tree Hill. As Tim and Luka pulled away from the packing shed that was now her home, Tayla stood in the middle of the drive and watched the taillights fade to black. She had to stop herself from picking up her skirt, sprinting through the tree rows, up the veranda steps of her family home, and locking the door against the world. *And* her new role as Mrs. Harrington.

"Coming inside?" Mitch asked.

She studied the flowers in her hand: blush roses, stock, and cosmos, coiled between flamboyant branches of goodness knows what, and tied up with string. "I want to visit Norman's grave. To lay my flowers."

"What, now? I'm not too keen on cemeteries at night."

"No, tomorrow. Will you come with me? I'm not too keen on cemeteries period."

"Sure." He unlocked the door. "Tim dropped off your things earlier. I put them in your room."

"Thank you." Tayla followed him up a narrow flight of stairs, the skirt of her gown rustling with every step. Ever since her return from Sydney, she'd tried to imagine how this man lived—how he spent his evenings above the packing shed. Was there endless dust and noise from the operation below, or would his home be like any other?

Once upstairs, she relaxed. The interior came alive under industrial lights—and reminiscent of a European train station, a large vintage-looking clock hung from the ceiling, ticking away unsteady minutes.

"Wow, it's much bigger than I imagined."

"Yeah, it takes up a third of the shed's length." Mitch put his keys on the kitchen island and took the bouquet from her hands. He grabbed a vase from the cabinet under the kitchen sink, placed the blooms inside, and filled it with water.

"The bedrooms are this way." He cocked his head toward a short hallway.

Once again, she followed him with reluctance, the swish of her skirt reminding her why she was here with a man she'd once resented with a passion.

"This is my room."

Tayla peeked through the doorway. His bed was enormous but neatly made, with a navy linen duvet and pillows in various shades of dusky blue. Above the bed, a string of light bulbs twisted around a wooden support beam, and from a basket by the balcony door, Mr. Edward watched them with one uninterested eye.

"Does Edward sleep with you?"

"Not normally. I'll shift him to the office before we go to bed. It's off the living area." Mitch opened an adjacent door and motioned for her to enter. With a charcoal feature wall and a similar string of lights, this room mirrored his. A rust-colored duvet covered the bed, and on the floor, a flokati rug grounded the space.

"This is lovely, thank you."

Mitch nodded. Frowned. "I want to say something."

She waited. His tone suggested they were about to have a

heart-to-heart. She had a sudden thought he might want to sleep with her.

"You'll always be safe here, Tayla."

She held his gaze for a second. Her new husband knew the score. Knew she didn't feel safe around him. Not because she feared for her physical wellbeing, but because she feared for her heart. A heart that, until recently, had belonged to another. "Thank you."

"It's just… Sometimes I question your impression of me. I know we had our differences in the past, but we're both adults now and while we're living together, I hope we can get along without too much drama."

Differences was not how she'd describe what went down after Norman died. To her, it was more like an inquisition, but each to their own. "Of course. I'm sure we'll make it work. And I appreciate what you've done for my parents." She fiddled with her ring finger. "And thanks for the ring. It's stunning."

"You're welcome." He shifted his stance. "The bathroom's across the hall. I have an en suite, so please make yourself at home."

"Thanks."

"Right." He went to say something more then stopped. Was he about to invite her to his room after all? "There is one small problem." Tayla waited for him to continue. "My housekeeper, Valentina, comes in after school once or twice a week. She knows to be discreet, but it might be better if we share a bed. Looks more legit that way."

"You want me to sleep with you? In your bed?"

"That's what married people do. They sleep together."

She stared at him in disbelief. "Not this married person. That wasn't part of our arrangement."

Mitch studied her for a moment, a knowing half-smile coming into play. The kind of smile she'd no doubt remember as she lay in bed later. "Yeah, maybe you're right. It could complicate things."

He turned to walk away then paused. "Still, you know where to find me if you change your mind."

Tayla shut the door behind him and flopped backward onto the bed. *No way!* She lay there for a while, struggling to muster the energy to undress as his invitation played on loop in her head. She shivered at the thought of sleeping with him. Although she liked to sleep naked, she wouldn't be doing so under Mitchel Harrington's roof. Sharing his space reminded her of having a sleepover at a friend's house, one who wasn't really a friend.

Finally forcing herself to move, she crossed the room and opened the closet door. It was full of hangers, and on the top shelf, two spare pillows and a blanket. But there was something else. A surfboard decorated with a large blush pink ribbon rested against the mirror, and next to it, a full-length wetsuit in two-tone charcoal and teal blue. She pulled the wetsuit off the rail and held it up for size, then sat on the bed—the smell of the neoprene tickling her nostrils as she marveled at her new husband's thoughtfulness and wished she'd got something for him as well.

Happy wedding day.

Tayla admired her ring, a diamond-studded Russian wedding band that sparkled under the lights above. A perfect mix of function and charm, the ring of three interlocking bands—symbolizing the past, present, and future—was so very different from the one Hayden had picked for her.

Hayden. He'd been in her thoughts most days since she'd returned from Sydney, but today, not so much. Time must be doing its thing. She removed the ring and placed it on the nightstand. To her surprise, her left hand felt naked without it.

Tayla pulled her phone from her bag and unlocked it, her fingers immediately connecting with the keys.

Tayla: I'm sorry.
Mum: What are you doing still awake? And why are you sorry?

Tayla almost dropped her phone. She hadn't expected her mother to answer. Sitting on the edge of the bed, she closed her eyes briefly, the weight of regret heavy on her chest as she recalled her father's tearful reaction when they told him the news. He'd insisted they were tears of joy, but that made the lie even worse.

Tayla: I eloped.
Mum: Yes, we know darling. Isn't FaceTime marvelous? How was your meal at Little Brown Barn?
Tayla: Delicious. That place is top class. But I was nervous, so I overate.
Mum: Nervous?
Tayla: It's not every day you elope.
Mum: Of course. But don't be sorry. We always thought you'd take the unconventional route. Anyway, we'll talk tomorrow. Goodnight Mrs. Harrington. Say hi to your new husband.
Tayla: Goodnight. Love you both xx

Weary to the bone, she lay back on the bed and wondered if her *husband* was still awake. She thought back to the kiss on the rocks and how much she'd enjoyed it. The kiss that sealed the deal and wouldn't leave her lips.

18

SHARING SPACES

MAINTAINING a long-held belief about someone when their actions have you questioning everything about that belief was not an easy task. As a teenager, Tayla had been scared stiff of Mitch after his accusation. Every time she saw him that summer, her stomach tied itself in knots. Now, the more she got to know him, the more his persona softened that memory.

After a large breakfast, Mitch left the loft, Edward lagging behind. When she'd thanked him for the surfboard and wetsuit, he'd looked genuinely pleased with himself, as if he wanted to please her as well.

Tayla studied the space. A large sectional sofa flanked by two leather chairs dominated one end of the room, and against the back wall, a dartboard waited for someone to hit the bullseye.

Mitch had told her to make herself at home, so she opened the fridge to look for juice. There was none, but it was full to the brim, and the pantry was the same. Jars of nuts and seeds and interesting grains lined the shelves, along with olive oils and an incredible array of spices. It seemed Mitch was quite the home chef.

She opened the door to his office and peeked inside. Full of books and files, it was much bigger than she'd expected, with two computers on the desk and a large leather sofa against one wall. She wondered if he ever snoozed there on a sunny afternoon. It looked so comfortable, she wanted to lie down herself. But she should unpack and box up her dress for the dry cleaners.

Back in her room, Tayla checked her reflection in the mirror on the wall. She ran her fingers through her hair, untangling a few knots at the ends as she contemplated getting it cut—nothing drastic, just to shoulder length. Hayden had loved her hair. He'd wrapped his hands around it when they kissed. And she'd reveled in that feeling of being held so tightly that he'd never let her go. Never let her fall.

Funny how the mind can play elaborate tricks when you want something badly enough.

She made a mental note to check out the salons in town.

Later, as Tayla walked through the packing shed, past a young man standing at the conveyer belt grading fruit, she thought of Norman. How proud he would've been of Mitch and Lime Tree Hill's transformation. 'The boy' was now a man, leaving his mark on the world with a gentle hand.

They'd arranged to meet at two, so Mitch could take her to the cemetery. True to his word, he pulled up right on the dot. When she climbed into the Hilux, she was impressed by how spotless he kept it for a work vehicle. But everything about him was meticulous. From his well-pressed jeans and shirts to his home and office, it was clear her new husband liked order. Just like his late grandfather.

"How's your morning been?" he asked as he drove down the driveway.

Surreal. "Good." She turned to him and smiled. "Thanks for doing this…coming with me."

"No problem." Mitch made a left at the highway. "Ned and Maggie want us to call in for a drink around five."

"Both of us?"

"Yes, both of us. We're a couple now."

"Well, not really, but…"

He chuckled. "Did you give this any thought before you decided to marry me, or did you think life would carry on regardless?"

"Of course. I know what I have to do."

Mitch glanced her way. "Good."

The small cemetery was less than a hundred yards from the chapel Mitch had suggested as their wedding venue. He stopped in a deserted parking spot overshadowed by a row of blue gums. Despite the warm autumn day, the sky was overcast, with sheets of misty rain blanketing the coast.

Tayla turned to fetch her bouquet from the back seat and was surprised when Mitch opened the door for her a few seconds later, offering his hand to help her down. His scent enveloped her—a mix of cologne and whatever he used to launder his clothes. Probably some kind of eco-friendly liquid with hints of lavender and tea tree.

They walked across the park-like grounds together, Mitch with his hands in his pockets, Tayla clutching her bouquet for dear life. Once again, she compared the neat little posy she held in Sydney and the wild, flamboyant arrangement Mitch had picked for her. Stopping when he did, she spied a small plaque in front of them.

"This is it." He looked at her, his expression unusually solemn.

Tayla wanted to reach for him, to pull him into a hug. But instead, she crouched beside the grave and placed the wilted bouquet on the grass in front of the plaque. They stood in silence for a moment before she asked, "What sort of relationship did you have with Norman before he died?"

Mitch rubbed a hand over his chin. "Fractured, I guess. He was a control freak and the most narrow-minded man I've ever met.

Once his depression took over, I hardly ever saw him out of that plaid dressing gown. Mum never warmed to him."

"Why was that?"

"He treated her badly early on. Never thought she was good enough for his only child. Mum fell pregnant when she was barely nineteen. Norman refused to let them marry. They did anyway, but he never acknowledged her. He thought she'd trapped my father."

"What happened to him…your dad?"

He indicated to the left. "He's there, and that's my grandmother's grave to the right."

Tayla's heart felt like it was beating out of her chest. She'd asked him to come, giving little thought to his feelings or connecting the three similar-looking plaques. When she'd attended Norman's funeral, no one had ever mentioned he'd been buried between his wife and son. "I'm so sorry. I had no idea."

"It's okay." Mitch shifted his attention from her to his father's last resting place. "My grandmother was driving my father into town when she had some kind of blackout at the wheel. The car crossed the center line and collided with a milk tanker. They both died at the scene. He was twenty-two, she was forty-eight. Norman never got over it."

Tayla crouched down again and read part of the inscription on his father's grave. *Nicholas Harrington. A life cut short...* She looked up. "He told me he was a widower and that he'd also lost a son, but he never talked of the circumstances. How old were you?"

"Just turned two. Too young to remember him, but Mum kept his memory alive. My stepfather couldn't have been a better dad though. He loves me like one of his own. In fact, he was often a lot tougher on the girls than he was on me."

Tayla pulled two roses from the bouquet and handed them to Mitch, who placed one each on the grave of his father and grandmother.

"Norman taught Tim and I to dance, did you know that?"

"Seriously?"

"We'd decided to go to the school ball together," Tayla recalled. "Norman offered to teach us the waltz. The night of the ball, we called in to Lime Tree on the way. When he saw me in my gown and without the goth makeup, he got so emotional that he cried. It was the first time he'd ever let me hug him." Tayla's eyes pricked with tears. She turned away, embarrassed by the sudden rush of emotion.

"Hey." He rubbed a hand up and down her back. "It's okay."

"Sorry, it's been such a difficult time lately." She blinked hard, wiping her fingertips along the rim of her lower lashes. "Norman was a good friend to me."

"You were one of the few people who ever got through to him in his later years."

"Maybe because he saved my life."

"Maybe."

They rode home in silence, but the journey back to the orchard was anything but quiet for Tayla. What would Norman have said about her marriage to Mitch? About their deception? The thought of going to Ned and Maggie's played on her mind. It seemed too early in their marriage to act out the lie. She needed more time to get used to the idea.

Upstairs, she rummaged through her closet for something to wear, choosing an olive-green crossover style dress with a tie around the waist, and espadrilles with ankle straps. When she entered the living room, Mitch had changed also, into a white linen shirt and black jeans. *Tight black jeans.*

He looked her up and down without a word, then turned and grabbed a bottle of wine off the counter. And as she followed him down the stairs, she couldn't still the butterflies in her stomach.

"I should have made something to take."

"Don't worry, Maggie will have nibbles. She loves to cook."

He checked his watch. "We'd better take the Can-Am or we'll be late."

"You mean the four-wheeler?"

He grabbed a set of keys off a hook in the garage. "Yeah. Looks like that pretty dress has plenty of room for movement." He lifted the lid of the hold and placed the wine inside. "Hop on."

Tayla climbed on, surprised at how comfortable it was, and as he sat in front of her, she grabbed the hand grips and held on tight.

He took off toward Ned's, increasing speed as they rode along the river track. With the wind in her hair and Mitch at the wheel, she wanted to lean into his back, feel the warmth of him and forget about the part she'd agreed to play.

"Shit." Mitch slowed as he reached the gate. "Looks like we have a staff party in progress."

Tayla looked at the cars parked all over the driveway. "Should we come back another time?"

Mitch hopped off. "No, I think we're the guests of honor." He offered his hand and helped her down. "Come on Mrs. Harrington. It's show time."

"But you said it was a quiet drink." She stood on the drive and ran her fingers through her hair.

"Yep. Looks like our hosts had other ideas." He looked at her and smiled, then reached out and brushed a lock of hair from her face. "Take a deep breath. You'll be fine."

Tayla's heart fluttered. He offered his hand, and she took it. And as they walked through the door, she felt her apprehension vanish as Ned and Maggie welcomed her warmly.

"What's all this?" Mitch asked Ned as he accepted two glasses of champagne and handed one to Tayla.

"We couldn't let the staff find out through the grapevine." Ned tapped the side of his glass with a teaspoon. All eyes looked his way. "Everyone, may I present Mr. and Mrs. Harrington. Congratulations, you two. May your days be filled with love and laughter."

Tayla looked around the room and smiled as everyone lifted their glasses in a toast then yelled, "Speech, speech."

"Wow, when Ned asked us to come over for a drink," Mitch said, "I didn't expect it to be a full-on party, but thanks, Maggie and Ned, for hosting this impromptu gathering. As you all know by now, Tayla and I took a trip to Petrie Bay yesterday and came back married. While I was going to tell you all soon, this is a nice way to do it. So thanks for coming, guys, and please enjoy your evening."

"Right," Ned said. "I better put the steaks on the grill. Go show off your wife. She deserves it."

Mitch put his arm around her waist, and as they weaved their way into the crowd, he introduced her to so many people, she didn't know how she'd ever remember their names.

As the evening progressed, Mitch stayed by Tayla's side until she went to help Maggie with the dishes.

"You realize we're going to have to do this all over again when Jean and Barry get home," Maggie said as they stacked the dishwasher.

"I was just thinking the same thing. Thank you, I've really enjoyed my night."

"Well, Mitch has been like a son to us. It's the least we could do."

"There you are." Mitch looked around the kitchen, his gaze settling on Tayla. "I came to help, but I guess you're all done."

"We are," Maggie said. "Time to take Tayla home."

"Yes. I have work tomorrow, and I'm a little tipsy. And, I have to get on that four-wheeler."

"Do you want me to go home and get the car?" Mitch asked.

Tayla looked at him and smiled. "Where's the fun in that?"

With goodbyes over, she climbed on the Can-Am behind him, wrapped her arms around his waist and held on tight. And as Mitch pulled away, Tayla rested her head between his shoulder blades and smiled.

He stopped outside the garage door, and as he climbed off, she missed the warmth of his back. She sat for a moment.

He offered his hand. "Are you okay?"

"Um...yeah, great." She looked skyward. "Wow, look at those stars. It's such a beautiful night. I could just sleep here."

He chuckled. "Come on. Let's get you to bed."

"But weren't we going to call your folks?"

"Maybe tomorrow. I think someone's had one glass too many."

"And...I ate way too much. Man, Ned cooks a great steak, doesn't he?" She giggled as he helped her down. "I won't be able to do up my jeans if I stay here much longer."

In the kitchen, Mitch poured her a glass of water and handed her two paracetamol. "Here, you better take these."

"Thanks, but I'm fine, really." She threw back the pills and drained the glass. "I'm off to bed. Goodnight."

"Sleep well."

She went to step away but turned back. "Hey, Mitch?"

He looked up from putting her glass into the dishwasher.

"That was a great night, wasn't it. Neat people, amazing food and wine." She paused. "I like it here."

He flashed an amused smile. "I'm glad."

She pointed toward the hallway. "Anyway, time for bye-byes."

"'Night, Tayla."

Making her way to the bedroom, Tayla glanced at her phone as it pinged. She flopped on the bed. It was late. She wanted to sleep. Wanted to rest her head between Mitch's shoulders as she drifted off.

Lisa: You really do pick your moments, don't you?
Tayla: ???
Lisa: You go off on a whim and MARRY the boy next door when Dad's out of action. Don't you think that's a MEGA shellfish move on your part?

Tayla: Mega shellfish? You mean like oysters or scallops? ROTFL.

Lisa: Stupid phone. You know exactly what I mean. Brat!

Tayla: I do. And point NOT taken. Go to bed. You're grumpy and SHOUTING.

Lisa: Yes because I'm MAD at you. You can't just go off and get married without telling anyone. And to Mitch!! Rebound much.

Tayla: Oops. I didn't get that memo. Naughty Tayla. Goodnight. Love you xx

Tayla threw her phone onto the bed and giggled. She was officially a brat. A married brat. "Wow. Way to go me."

She thought of Mitch, lying in bed next door. Had he received a similar text from one of his sisters, telling him what a naughty boy he'd been? If he did, would he think it was funny too? And was he thinking of her arms around his waist as they rode home along the river track under the stars?

She hoped so.

19

TULLOCH POINT

TWELVE DAYS. Tayla had survived a week and a half under Mitchel Harrington's roof without wanting to pack her bags. They'd tiptoed around each other with stilted conversation, but when she'd discussed it with Ruby, her sister's advice was, as always, on point. Think of your time at Lime Tree Hill as a sabbatical, she'd said, a time to take stock and regroup after Hayden. A safe haven of sorts.

The sabbatical part she understood. The safe haven, not so much. In Sydney, Tayla had grown accustomed to having people around. It meant she didn't have to think too deeply. Just wander along the beach, sipping coffee as she watched the world go by.

However, the solitude of her new home didn't quite gel. Or maybe it was Mitch that she didn't gel with. Mitch, with his powerful presence, deep voice, and structured routine. A man who knew what he wanted out of life and how to get it.

As she dressed, Tayla thought fondly of Cherry Grove. The house would never again experience the conversations and laughter of the Whitman clan, and she had to accept it.

It was Friday morning. The week before, Mitch had invited her to join him on a trip to his family home to celebrate his sister Sydney's twenty-third birthday. Tayla had agreed, but as the day approached, her anxiety rose to the surface. She'd never been to Tulloch Point, the small Bay of Plenty town where his family had an avocado and kiwifruit orchard. Andrea and Frank were still in London, but she'd be meeting his friends and youngest sister for the first time.

Tayla walked into the kitchen, stopping at the sight of a teenage girl rummaging through the fridge. She placed two apples on the counter.

"May I help you?"

The girl glanced over her shoulder at Tayla. "Sorry. I didn't realize anyone was home. Aren't you guys going to Tulloch Point for the night?" She turned and wiped her hand down her jeans before offering it to Tayla. "I'm Valentina. Mitch's cleaner. But please don't call me Val. I can't stand it. I usually come after school, but we have a sports day and I don't need to be there until lunchtime."

Tayla nodded and smiled. "Of course. I'm Tayla."

They shook, Valentina's handshake warm, her smile welcoming.

"I know. I mean, he told me you'd be here. And congratulations. I can't wait to see the photos. I bet Mitch looked amazing in his suit. There's something about seeing a guy in a different light. Like when they're always wearing jeans and a tee, and suddenly, they're rocking a three-piece suit, shiny shoes, and a crisp white shirt. I love a guy in a suit, don't you?"

The smile widened. "I do. How old are you?"

"Sixteen." She caught Tayla's expression and giggled. "But I don't have the hots for your husband. He's too old for me. It's the clothes I'm interested in, not the man. I want to study fashion design and build my own label. I'm saving for a sewing machine. What was your dress like? Please don't tell me a puffed-out meringue. I couldn't bear it." Valentina paused for a breath.

"There wasn't a meringue in sight. Do you want to see a

picture?" Tayla unlocked her phone and pulled up the photos. "Here."

Valentina held the phone in one hand, zooming in and out with her thumb and forefinger. "Wow…seriously cool. I've never seen a wedding dress like it. Is it a skirt and top? I love high necks. The top's lighter than the skirt?"

"Just a shade, but I flashed my tummy every time I moved, so that wasn't ideal."

She looked up. "Way to go, you. Better than flashing your boobs. You're stunning."

"Thank you."

"I bet you felt it too. And look at Mitch and Luka. Awww. Too cute." Her eyes narrowed. "Wait, are those the pancake rocks at Petrie Bay? I love it there. It's just by the pines?"

"Yes. I love it too. It has a certain intimacy about it."

"It's spiritual. A place where angels go to heal. If you listen closely, you can hear them singing."

Interesting.

Valentina giggled at Tayla's expression. "That's what my grandma always says. She's into all that touchy-feely stuff." She handed back the phone. "Why did you sleep in the spare room? Are you guys fighting?"

Blunt as an old knife. "Mitch snores when he's overtired, and I'm a light sleeper."

Valentina nodded. She put her empty plate in the dishwasher before stuffing the apples into her bag. "I'd better finish up. I don't get paid to talk. Thanks for the breakfast. I'd love to see your wedding album when you get it."

They left just after one, and as Mitch drove away from Lime Tree Hill, Tayla wondered what they'd talk about on their five-hour journey. Being tongue-tied around men wasn't new to Tayla; she'd spent her teenage years too nervous to initiate conversation with most of the boys at school. But with counseling, she'd learned to curb that anxiety, to ride with it, not fight against it. Still, the feeling came and went, and sitting next to him, she struggled to relax.

As it turned out, she needn't have worried. Mitch liked to stream audiobooks when driving. And as they headed along the scenic route toward the Rata River Valley, Tayla found herself so engrossed in the story, she almost forgot the reason for their trip.

Having stopped just once along the way, they arrived in the coastal town of Tulloch Point right on dark. As Mitch pulled into the sweeping circular driveway and cut the engine, Tayla sat up straight and inhaled sharply. She wanted to listen to the rest of the novel, but that would have to wait.

An old villa stood before them, all lit up ready for a party. With smart paintwork and an iron roof, the house reminded her of her parents' home, right down to the wrap-around veranda and rambling roses bursting with late-autumn blooms.

"This is it. The Dobson homestead. It's a pity Mum and Frank aren't here." Mitch glanced her way; that look of empathy making an appearance. "You ready?"

It was showtime. She hadn't learned her lines but put on her happy face despite her inner turmoil. "Yes. I think so. Does your sister live here alone?"

"She does—just until the nomads return. But Frank's keen to stay in the UK for a while, so I have no idea when that will be."

Tayla busied herself in the truck while Mitch grabbed their gear. But when he opened her door and offered a hand, she couldn't delay the inevitable any longer. He looked at her with warmth. She suddenly wanted another kiss—practice or otherwise, she didn't care. But it seemed the pancake rocks kiss was the last one they'd share.

Dressed in light blue jeans, a plaid shirt, and ankle boots, a live wire of a girl with masses of curly dark hair bounded down the stairs and jumped onto Mitch's back. "Mitchel!"

Tayla stepped to the side as he wrestled her to the ground. "Get off me. What are you, twelve?"

His sister?

She dusted herself off, a throaty laugh filling the country air. "What time do you call this? The party starts in an hour. I need you to light the fire pit while I get changed. And you're the short-order cook, so I hope you brought your apron."

"I had to work this morning." He smiled. "You knew this."

"You always have to work."

"Not true, and"—he turned to Tayla—"Tayla, meet your sister-in-law Sydney, aka CeCe."

Sydney looked at Tayla for the first time, her arms crossed and her expression unreadable. "So, you're the wife?" She opened her arms and grinned. "Bring it."

When Tayla inched in for the hug, Sydney whispered, "Welcome to the family. I like you already."

Tayla pulled back. "Thank you. It's lovely to meet you, Sydney."

"My friends call me CeCe. What were my parents thinking, naming me after an Australian city?"

"You know you were conceived there, don't you?" Mitch said with a grin.

"That is an urban legend I prefer to ignore. And you'd better behave yourself. I still haven't forgiven you for not inviting me to your wedding."

"Luka was best man, so…"

"Yeah, I got that memo. He's more important than your sister, is he? The spineless bastard."

"Of course not." Mitch chuckled and turned his attention to Tayla. "Come on. I'll show you to our room."

As Tayla caught the 'our room' comment Mitch threw so casually across the driveway, CeCe linked arms with her. "Then you can help me decide what to wear," CeCe said. "Let me warn you though, I may look, smell, and talk like a girl, but I hate dresses with a passion."

Tayla glanced over at Mitch, standing at the back of the truck, their bags at his feet. He raised his eyebrows and mouthed, *"Good luck,"* and then with a chuckle, shut the lid of the tray before following them inside.

A short hallway separated Mitch's old bedroom from the rest of the house. French doors led to a garden courtyard, and through a side window, avocado trees covered the landscape.

CeCe turned to Tayla. "Right. I'll leave you to get settled." She pointed across the courtyard. "My room's the one on the end. See you in a bit."

As CeCe left, Mitch placed Tayla's bag on the luggage rack. She frowned at the queen bed. *Great.*

"Are you ready to play your part in this game of pretense?" he asked.

She caught his slight smile as he repeated her words from the day at Norman's cottage.

"You mean we have to share a bed?"

"CeCe will be asking all kinds of questions if we don't."

Tayla grabbed her phone from her bag, annoyed that the heat blooming on her cheeks would reveal her embarrassment. "Um... I'll just go help her with her outfit." She went to walk away, desperately in need of some fresh air and distance from her *husband* after all those hours on the road together.

"Tayla?"

She turned. Mitch seldom used her name, but when he did, she liked the way it sounded.

He stepped toward her. "Just relax. This is purely business, remember?"

"Of course."

Tayla walked across the courtyard to CeCe's room, her thoughts scrambling for order. *Purely business.*

She knocked before letting herself in and was amused when she came face to face with CeCe in nothing but a lacy bra and panties. "So, what have you decided?"

"I don't know." CeCe sighed. "And you know what? I hate birthday parties but I'm determined to enjoy this one, and I want to look the part." She pulled over a chair and motioned for Tayla to sit. "I'm so glad you came."

"Thanks for inviting me."

"In all honesty, I was shocked when Mitch told me you guys had eloped. So were the rest of the family." CeCe opened her wardrobe and pulled out several tops and a pair of jeans. "Did you have a thing for each other back in the day? Wait, don't tell me you made one of those marriage pacts?"

"I did, but not with Mitch. It was with my best friend, Tim. We were in our senior year of high school—both single—so we thought, gay, straight, it could work once we were over thirty. And to answer your other question…no, I was only seventeen when I met Mitch."

"I still don't get it. How come no one knew about you?"

Tayla shrugged, eager to shut down the third degree. "We'd both just come out of relationships, so—"

"Rebound romance. I love that trope in movies. Not that movies and real life often have much in common, but it doesn't hurt to dream."

"Do you have a boyfriend?"

"Not right now." CeCe's expression saddened. "I decided to up my standards a long time ago. Although, I did have an epic meet-cute moment once. And I mean *epic*."

Thoughts of Mitch drifted away, and she smiled. Tayla loved a juicy meet-cute story. "And?"

CeCe laughed. "Never mind. Enough boy talk. I'd better decide what to wear or I'll be late for my own party."

Despite her supposed aversion to dresses, by the time Tayla helped CeCe get ready, she looked like a girl from a country music video. All prettied up in a floaty floral dress and cowgirl boots, and with tiny rosebuds woven through her hair.

And the next time Tayla saw Mitch, he was manning the grill, drinking beer, and talking BS with half a dozen guys. When he glanced her way and offered a private smile, the flutters in her stomach didn't surprise her. Not one bit.

20

BIRTHDAY BLUES

MITCH mentally braced himself as Prue strolled toward him. They'd spoken earlier, and his lack of interest surprised him. There was no longing, no lust, no regrets. She'd talked about her new boyfriend, Otis—who he'd known since they were kids—but Mitch hadn't mentioned Tayla. At the end of their conversation, she'd wished him well, insisting there were no hard feelings and that he shouldn't feel guilty. Not that he had anything to feel guilty about. Prue had instigated the breakup. He'd simply pulled the pin.

She stopped at his side. For a second, he thought she might kiss him, but she didn't. "Are you all right?"

"Fine, why?"

Swaying a little, she took his arm and moved him away from the crowd around the fire pit, her breath thick with alcohol. "It's just... I know I made a mistake, but I never expected you to run off and marry someone else on the rebound. To tell you the truth, I was devastated when I found out. I always assumed we'd get back together."

"It's been over six months, Prue. People move on."

"Maybe, but you must admit, she's hardly your type."

Mitch knew she was trying to bait him, but after a few beers, he wasn't as sharp as usual. "What makes you say that?"

"I dunno. I just never imagined you being interested in some nerdy girl-next-door type with a flat chest and designer threads. I'll bet the sex is as boring as her overpriced outfit."

Mitch remained silent for a moment. With Prue, verbal retaliation was never a good idea, especially when she'd been drinking. But self-respect and an overriding sense of protectiveness toward Tayla meant he wouldn't stand by and say nothing.

"I'll say this only once." He stopped to clear his throat, his jaw tight with discomfort. "Tayla is my wife. I won't allow you, or anyone else, to come between us, understand?"

"But—"

"And you can gossip and disrespect people as much as you like, but that kind of destructive behavior won't do you any favors. My relationship with Tayla has nothing to do with you. We're over, Prue. And to be frank, our days were numbered anyway."

"How can you say that?"

Mitch took a swig of his beer. They'd been over the reasons way more times than he cared to count. "You can't cheat in a long-term relationship and expect to carry on regardless. It's a pity you let your secretive narcissistic side out of its cage because I'd hoped we might stay friends, but I'm done here."

"How many times do I have to say I'm sorry? This isn't who you are. You don't cut people off because of one mistake. I still love you."

Mitch frowned. He'd passed the point of offering a verbal comeback, so he turned and walked away.

The bench seat was slightly damp when Tayla sat at the table on the veranda. She stared up at the stars, clear and bright, and wished she was anywhere but here. Although Mitch had been far from inattentive, she still felt uncomfortable mixing with large groups of people, especially as the new sideshow in town. Mitchel Harrington's wife. The woman he'd eloped with. *The rebound.*

Earlier, Mitch had joined her on the makeshift line dancing floor, standing behind her and guiding her with whispered words if she fell out of step. At one stage, he'd placed both hands on her hips, and that one touch had set her imagination on fire. He'd left the dance floor after the next song, but whenever she'd glanced his way, he was watching her, his smile soft and reassuring. And as he gave a speech after CeCe cut her cake, she'd felt proud on his behalf. He didn't talk about his sisters much, but they obviously shared a strong bond.

His ex had turned up—an uninvited guest. CeCe had pointed her out to Tayla when she arrived. Tall and voluptuous, with flat-ironed hair that fell around her face in a silky mane, she'd make any women under five foot six feel like a pixie.

So, what had gone wrong between them? He'd never offered any details, and although it was none of her business, Tayla was still curious. And judging by the way people were staring at her, so were his friends.

Tayla checked her watch. It was almost midnight, and she could hardly keep her eyes open. But by the sound of the raucous laughter coming from inside, the party was still in full swing. She glanced over her shoulder as footsteps echoed toward her.

Without invitation, Prue pulled out a chair and plonked down opposite her. "Mind if I join you?"

Too late. Tayla offered her hand. "Tayla Whitman."

Prue ignored the gesture. "Do you actually know who I am?"

"Yes. Prue, isn't it?"

Nodding slowly, Prue held Tayla's gaze. "By all accounts, I should hate your guts, but that's not my style. So, you didn't take his name. How does Mitchie feel about that? He's such a traditionalist, my Mitchie."

My Mitchie? "I haven't really seen that side of him."

"I have to say, the news shocked me." Prue cocked an artistic brow. "But I know why he did it. Married you, I mean."

Tayla remained silent. Had Mitch and Prue had the same agreement? Maybe theirs hadn't been a love match after all.

Prue reached into her clutch purse and pulled out a pack of cigarettes and a lighter. Cigarette clenched between her lips, she flicked the flame. Her first inhale was deep and dramatic. "I don't normally smoke, only when I've had a few drinks. Helps calm the nerves." She offered Tayla the packet.

"No, I'm good."

Prue looked Tayla in the eye, hers bloodshot and heavily rimmed with kohl. "I guess you are. That's why he married you and not me. I'd been a naughty girl. Too naughty for Mitchie."

Tayla stood. She had no intention of getting into a catfight with Prue, the ex. "I should go. It's been a long day."

"Sit down. I've not finished talking yet. And if you want me to play nice, you'd better listen to what I have to say. Because Mitchie hates scenes. And when it comes to scenes, I'm an expert." She lifted her beer bottle as if in a toast. "Especially with the help of this."

As Tayla sat back in her chair, she felt Prue's gaze crawl over her skin.

"He'll never love you like he did me, understand?" Prue continued. "Said so the last time we talked...that he'd always love me, no matter what. This *marriage* has spite written all over it. Boys are silly sometimes, aren't they?"

Prue flicked cigarette ash onto the tongue and groove deck of the veranda. "So, don't be a bitch about it, Tayla *Whitman*. Walk away. Give the guy a chance at happiness, because he sure as hell can't be happy with you." She took a drag and blew the smoke out of the corner of her mouth. "Shit, you've only known each other five minutes. What do you even talk about? What prep school you attended? How rich he is?"

Silence stretched between them while Tayla mustered her

courage. "Actually, I've known Mitch for years, and my relationship with him is none of your business."

Prue took another drag of her cigarette then swigged her beer. "Maybe, but you're not his type. Not even close. If you were, you'd be in there"—she cocked her head toward the living room—"feeding him cake and stroking his ego."

Feeling sick to her stomach, Tayla held Prue's gaze with steady eyes. She thought she'd learned how to deal with confrontational bullies a long time ago. Then again, it was easy to tell guys to get lost, your husband's ex-fiancée, not so much.

"So, one piece of advice." Prue pointed at Tayla. "No matter how well you think you're doing around his friends and family, you will always be the bitch who stole my fiancé. You think you're so clever turning up in *my* town, with *my* man, rubbing *my* nose in your shit, but you don't belong here."

For the second time, Tayla stood. "This conversation is over. And do yourself a favor. In future, learn to keep your mouth shut."

"Prue, what the hell's going on?" Mitch's voice boomed across the veranda before Tayla had even noticed he was there.

"You did this," Prue yelled, her finger stabbing the air in his direction. "You expect me to sit here and listen to her bullshit without defending myself? Not going to happen."

"Tayla, go inside." The words were uttered without even a glance in her direction as Mitch focused on Prue.

As she entered the house through the kitchen door, Prue's words followed her every step: *spineless bastard...how could you? I will never forgive you...ever!*

Tayla walked down the hall and into their room. Fighting the rush of humiliation and close to tears, she sat on the edge of the bed.

CeCe knocked on the open door. "Are you okay? You're white as a ghost."

Tayla sucked in several rapid breaths as CeCe sat beside her. "I just need a minute."

"What happened?"

Waiting tears spilled onto her cheeks with no shame. "I'm sorry. My dad's unwell, I've spent weeks packing up our family home, and wine makes me a little fragile. I'm sorry you had to see me like this."

"Let me guess. Prue? What did she say?"

"Nothing complimentary. And Mitch walked in on the tail end of it. I shouldn't have come."

"For what it's worth, I never thought they'd last the distance. She's just pissed because he married you and not her." Tayla sniffed as CeCe handed her a box of tissues. "Here. Shall I go get you some cake?"

Tayla smiled through her tears, trying to calm her racing heart as Mitch entered the room. "No, thanks. I'm good."

He addressed CeCe. "Give us a moment, would you?"

"Sure. I'd better go say my goodbyes anyway. Then I'm off to bed. I have a headache ready to pounce." CeCe squeezed Tayla's hand, and as she rose from the bed, Tayla wished she would stay so she didn't have to deal with Mitch on her own.

"Thanks, CeCe," Tayla said.

He waited for his sister to leave the room then sat beside her, so close his leg touched hers. "You okay?"

Not trusting herself to speak in case the tears returned, Tayla nodded.

"I'm sorry you had to see that side of Prue. She was way out of line."

She glanced toward the door. "I should help CeCe clean up before we go to bed."

Mitch smoothed his hand over her hair and tucked it behind her ear. She closed her eyes for a second against the intimacy of his touch. "Stay there. I'll give her a hand. See you in a bit."

21

TWISTS AND TURNS

CURLED UP UNDER THE DUVET, Tayla struggled to fall asleep as she rehashed her encounter with Prue. And as the house creaked its secrets into the stillness, a part of her wished Mitch would join her.

They'd been physically close before—during their practice kiss and at the wedding ceremony. So why did sharing his bed worry her? Her nerves strung tight, she was just about to check the time on her phone when the door opened and closed with a whispered click.

Listening as he unbuckled his belt and unzipped his fly, she stilled. He slipped into bed behind her and lay on his side, so close his breath lightly caressed her skin.

She wanted to turn around and ask how he was, to reach out and trace her fingers over his chest and down the contours of his abs, until his skin warmed her touch...

"You still awake?" he murmured.

"Only just. I'm overtired." She glanced over her shoulder. "I'm sorry I ruined your night."

"You didn't ruin my night. But it's late, and I'm a little drunk, so I'd rather leave the debrief for now."

Hugging the edge of the bed, Tayla pulled the duvet tighter. He might not want a debrief, but she couldn't stop thinking about his world and how little she knew of it.

He moved closer, and as she shifted, searching for comfort, Mitch nuzzled into her hair and whispered, "Goodnight." Then he rolled over and fell asleep.

———

With Mitch burning like a furnace beside her, his body too close for comfort, Tayla slept poorly, then woke with a fright, uncertain for a moment of her surroundings. She looked around the room for any sign of him. But there were no jeans on the chair, no watch or phone next to the bed, no warmth on the sheet beside her.

She flung back the covers and placed her feet on the floor, loving the texture of wool underfoot. When she drew back the curtains, muted sunlight washed the room with warmth and uncertainty. With its white on white palette, iron bed, and lamps that hung from the ceiling over each nightstand, the room held no mementos of his childhood. For some reason, Tayla found that sad. Sitting on the edge of the bed, she wondered what kind of boy he'd been. Ambitious, sweet, kind?

With no signs of life in the house, Tayla donned her running shoes and went for a jog along the coastal road, timing herself for thirty minutes before heading back to the orchard under the threat of rain. The solitude allowed her time to think. Although, to be fair, she'd had plenty of time for wayward thoughts lately. Too much time.

Although there was no point in giving weight to Prue's insistence that Mitch was still in love with her, their conversation had helped Tayla separate fact from fantasy. Mitch wasn't hers and never would be. She was merely a visitor to his world.

When she walked into the kitchen, hot and sweaty after her

run, CeCe sat at the table, her head bowed over a cup of black coffee.

"Good morning," Tayla said. "How's the head?"

"I need a new one. This one's in pain." CeCe sipped her coffee. "How come you're up and about so bright and early?"

Tayla checked her Garmin. "It's after eleven. I needed to blow out the cobwebs."

"Where's Mitch?"

"I have no idea. He was gone when I woke up."

CeCe studied Tayla over the rim of her cup. "Have you called him? What if he's lying under a bush somewhere?"

"He's a big boy. I'm sure he's fine." Tayla grabbed an apple from the fruit bowl. Did Mitch's family know about the conditions of Normans will? She turned to face her sister-in-law. "I just don't want to be that wife. The needy nag who has to keep tabs on her husband." *And one who lies to people.*

"That's fine normally. But add a dash of Prue to the mix, and all hell could break lose."

Tayla bit into the apple, catching the juice with the back of her hand as it dripped down her chin. She was just about to shut down the conversation when Mitch strolled into the kitchen. He dropped his keys, wallet, and phone on the table.

"Where have you been?" CeCe asked.

"Having brunch with Otis. He's not in a good space."

CeCe cocked a questioning brow. "Was Prue there?"

Ignoring his sister's question, Mitch addressed Tayla, his expression warm, caring. "Sorry I didn't text, babe. My phone's flat." He leaned in for a quick kiss, taking her by complete surprise. "I might go for a run. We need to be away by three." With that, he walked down the hall and disappeared into the bedroom, closing the door behind him.

Tayla: Hey. How are you? In a better mood?

Lisa: A bit. Aren't you in Tulloch Point?

Tayla: Yep, in the truck waiting for Mitch. What's new?

Lisa: I'm still in shock about the wedding TBH.

Tayla: Me too.

Lisa: I had a tiny crush on Mitch back in the day. Now he's my brother-in-law. WOGE?

Tayla: I never knew that. What does WOGE mean?

Lisa: *Eye roll*. What On God's Earth. And you knew.

Tayla: Honestly, I didn't. Wait. You haven't slept with him have you?

Lisa: Very funny. I wasn't even on his radar. When do we get to see the photos?

Tayla: Soon. Talk later xx

Mitch said little as they drove away, less as they passed the town limits sign, and nothing as they joined the main highway south. Tayla stared out the window. The straight roads gave way to twists and turns as they hit the mountains, and the story streaming through the speakers seemed to do the same. Twisted and turned.

Right on dusk, they pulled into a gas station complex comprising of the usual: a restroom, a small convenience store, and several fast-food outlets.

He cut the engine. "I need to fill up."

"Okay. I'll just go to the restroom."

When Tayla walked back onto the forecourt, Mitch and his pickup had vanished. She sat on a seat outside the convenience store, looking around for any sign of him. Nothing. She fished in her bag for her phone, then realized she'd left it in the truck. The minutes ticked by. She was just about to walk inside to look for him when a familiar voice said, "Do you want something to eat?"

Relieved, she shook her head, overwhelmed by the trip, the restless night before, and Prue's cruel tongue. "Where did you disappear to?" she asked, managing a small smile.

"I needed to check the tires. You sure you're not hungry? They do great burgers here."

"I might just grab a juice. I'm still full from lunch."

Mitch narrowed his gaze and studied her. She waited for him to comment on her lack of appetite, but instead, he turned and walked inside. Tayla followed two steps behind.

She sat at a small table in the harshly lit interior while Mitch went to order. When he returned, he tucked into a double cheeseburger and large fries like he hadn't eaten in days. She sipped her vegetable juice, suddenly hungry as the smell of deep-fried food wafted across the table.

He studied her for a long moment. "So, are you going to tell me what happened with Prue?"

Until now, Tayla had seldom seen Mitch in a negative mood. He seemed more the 'glass brimming to the top and overflowing' sort. "I introduced myself, Prue told me exactly what she thought of me, and when I stood to walk away, she said if I didn't hear her out, she'd make a scene. You know the rest."

Mitch leaned back in his chair. "Prue reckons you gave just as good as you got."

Full of second-rate juice and worry, her stomach lurched. "Is this why you're angry? Because you think I encouraged her?"

"I'm tired and a little hungover, not angry." He sighed. "Look, I don't blame you for what went down, but I don't understand why you didn't walk away sooner."

"Oh, I wish I had, believe me." Tayla picked up his fries and started to eat. "She's a bully."

"I know what she can be like, and I trust you to be discreet. But that discretion doesn't apply between us."

"Surely that discretion works both ways?"

He took back the fries. "Meaning?"

"A little heads-up would've been good. But you just went about your night without even a thought for how I might feel."

He nodded, picked up his coffee and sipped it. "I didn't expect her to be there, but Otis is a family friend. I had no idea they were even together, neither did CeCe. Look, Prue can be an abrasive drunk, but despite everything, she's not a bad person. She does have a habit of lashing out when she feels threatened though."

"Yes, I got that vibe." She looked him straight in the eye. "But then, she obviously still loves you and says the feeling's mutual. That doesn't make my position an easy one when I'm around your family and friends."

"I understand."

Tayla noticed he didn't address her comment. Never said he didn't love Prue. Did his friends see her as the bitch who'd stolen another woman's fiancée, as Prue had so eloquently put it?

She reached for the fries again. "Do any of your family know about the conditions of Norman's will?"

"Just Mum and Frank. But I haven't discussed the purchase of Cherry Grove with them in depth. They're curious about our marriage, but it's no one else's business. As long as Ken's satisfied, it's all good."

Was it? All good? Living a lie where the truth would never be told? "And what about Prue?"

"She knows Norman left me the orchard but not about his final condition. I wasn't marrying her to get the money, so the subject never came up. She wasn't interested in my business affairs."

"She probably thinks I married you for your money. In a way, she's right, isn't she?"

With a shrug, Mitch grabbed the now almost empty pack of fries and helped himself to the last few. "It doesn't matter what she thinks, or anyone else. We both had our reasons."

"Maybe, but no matter your reason for marrying me instead of

Prue, I'd like to try to get through the next few months without any more drama." Tayla stood. "I'll be outside."

Mitch followed her through the door and into the truck. "Hope you enjoyed my fries."

She clicked her seatbelt into place, then looked at him. "I did. Thank you."

22

LAST MOVE

For the next few days, overwhelmed by packing at Cherry Grove and busy shifts at the hospital, Tayla kept her distance from Mitch as her feelings for him struggled for order. He didn't seem to notice. Even when she left the loft early and arrived home late, he never asked where she'd been. By Friday, she'd transferred most of the smaller items, one box at a time, to her parents' condo in the retirement complex.

That same day, Mitch left for Tulloch Point just after breakfast. An invitation to join him was refused. Visiting Tulloch Point no longer held any appeal, and anyway, she had too much work to do at the house and full shifts at the hospital the following week. Even so, she couldn't help but wonder if he'd gone to visit Prue.

The removal company arrived at ten on Saturday morning. Several hours later, the only thing she needed for her parents' new home was a bunch of flowers and some food for the fridge. But with no word of their return, the flowers and groceries could wait.

Back at the loft, Tayla trudged up the stairs. She fed Edward, then flopped down on the sofa and flicked on the wireless speaker, losing herself in moody music as memories of her teenage years at

Cherry Grove floated over the tree rows, up the stairs, and around the room.

The sound of her phone ringing brought her back to the present. *Mitch.* She picked it up and moved to his office so she didn't have to turn down the music. "Hello."

"Hi. How's Edward? He seemed a bit off when I left."

I'm fine, thanks for asking. "He's okay, eating well. I might let him sleep in my room tonight."

"Lucky dog. Is everything else all right?"

She frowned at the 'lucky dog' quip. "Yes, I think so."

"So, you're not out on the town tonight?" His voice softened.

"No, not tonight."

"Okay…well, I'll probably be home Tuesday." She could hear people calling him in the background, but he hesitated before continuing, "Text me if you have any problems. See you then."

Tayla opened her mouth to carry on the conversation, but he'd already hung up.

The following day, with Valentina in tow, Tayla returned to Cherry Grove to finish the cleaning. By late afternoon, apart from the carpet, the house was spotless.

It wasn't until Monday evening, as she stood on the balcony off the living room and gazed over the orchard to her family home, that the enormity of the move hit her. The evening had stilled, and the realization that she would never again sleep in her old bedroom, make pancakes in the kitchen, or soak in the clawfoot bathtub filled her with a lonely sadness. That loneliness didn't come from being alone; it came from her own inability to ask for help when she needed it. Her inability to let go.

Noticing vehicle lights on the side road, Tayla wondered if it was Mitch. But as the car drew closer, she realized it was only Ned. The wave of disappointment that crashed over her was puzzling. After all, she meant nothing to him, and he meant nothing to her. But when Mitch texted the following morning to say he was staying on for a few days, that disappointment intensified.

The week passed without incident until Thursday. On her way home from the hospital, Tayla sat at City Beach, picking at the teriyaki chicken and rice from the Japanese restaurant on Seaview Road. As usual during these reflective times, Hayden entered her thoughts. His betrayal had played out in front of her very eyes. How could she have been so out of tune with their relationship that she'd failed to notice?

Tayla removed her shoes and walked to the water's edge, hitching up her skirt as the swash rushed at her toes. Taking a series of deep breaths to calm her nerves, she contemplated her fears and regrets and life at Lime Tree Hill until she felt numb inside.

When she pulled up outside the packing shed and saw Mitch's white Hilux parked in the garage, Tayla stayed in the car for a moment, gathering the strength to face him.

The door to the loft stood open, and as she climbed the stairs, she heard Mitch on the phone, his tone jovial and light. Looking up from the couch, he smiled briefly when she placed her keys on the sideboard. As she opened the fridge to grab a bottle of juice, he stood, moved to his office and shut the door.

Standing at the sink, Tayla poured the juice into a glass and took several gulps, her throat dry from the salty teriyaki. Mitch returned to the room a few seconds later. He offered a curt 'hello' before inquiring about her day, Edward, and her father.

With the pleasantries out of the way, he asked her to sit for a minute. He wanted to get something off his chest, he told her. Something important. They sat at the table, the remnants of his dinner pushed aside, and as Tayla studied him across an open newspaper, he leaned forward, entwining his fingers in front of his lips. She noticed a tightness to his jaw and how his eyes narrowed. He looked as exhausted as she felt.

"I did a lot of thinking on the way home this afternoon." He held her gaze, waiting for an acknowledgment perhaps. But over the years, she'd learned not to preempt conversations that started with 'I did a lot of thinking.'

"This whole thing," he continued. "You and me...well, anyway, I'm finding it frustrating, to be honest, and I don't know how to make it right."

She didn't want to react but felt herself frown as he spoke.

"You've had so much on your plate lately, and I'm sorry I haven't had time to help with the packing, but we'll get stuck in tomorrow." He studied her as if waiting for a reaction. "It's just, with the move from Australia, your father's illness, and the crap I've put you through, do you think you need to talk to someone? A counselor maybe?"

Tayla pinched the bridge of her nose. She'd had counseling before, so wasn't opposed to the idea, but she had Ruby and Tim to talk to. And besides, they'd only been married a few weeks. How had he reached this conclusion when they'd scarcely spent any time together?

"I don't want you to be unhappy here."

"I'm fine. Just a little tired."

"Were you in a relationship in Sydney?"

Tayla hesitated. She didn't understand this sudden interest in her past. "For a while. Why?"

"You seem to be missing someone...something."

Silence stretched between them.

"Is it still too raw?" he asked.

"A bit." She forced a tight smile. "It's harder when you didn't see it coming."

Mitch nodded. "How long were you together?"

"Too long as it turned out. But it's all good." She rose from the table and returned the juice to the fridge, swallowing lumps of emotion as tears trickled over her lashes. "I might go to bed. I'm sorry me living here hasn't worked out the way you planned. Goodnight."

"Tayla?"

Leaving Mitch with his questions, Tayla shut the bedroom door and flopped down on her bed. She hadn't brushed her teeth or removed her makeup, but she didn't want to go out there again, not while he was still up. She stood and reached into her gym bag for a wet wipe to rub over her face and hands. Not ideal, but it would have to do.

With the curtains and window open, she lay on the floor, the cool breeze wafting over her as she watched the hazy band of the Milky Way fill the window frame. She sat up when he knocked.

"Tayla? Are you all right?"

"Yes, fine."

"Can I come in?"

"I'm almost asleep. I'll see you in the morning."

When Mitch didn't respond, Tayla wondered if he'd given up and gone to bed. She wanted to open the door, to have him hold her and tell her everything would be okay. But their agreement didn't include touch. Or empathy. Or companionship.

"Okay. Sleep well."

Her mouth parched, Tayla woke as she'd slept—still in her cotton dress. When she opened her closet, panda eyes stared back at her from the mirror, and her cheeks looked tight from lack of moisturizer.

Mitch had left for work by the time she entered the kitchen, which meant she didn't have to face him over breakfast. Edward moved to her side and lay down, openly loving her with those big brown eyes. "Hey, boy. Are you happy here?" He blinked and rested his head on his paws. *Too cute.*

As she drove to work, her thoughts struggled for some

semblance of order. She frustrated him, that's what he'd said. Did he want her to move out?

Later that afternoon, as her last patient left, her mother called with unexpected news. "They're taking your father back into the operating room. He's not doing so good, they're not sure why."

Tayla struggled to focus on her mother's words as she hurried down the stairs. "What? I thought you guys were almost ready to come home." Knowing the risks involved in two surgeries in a row at his age, she went to say more but stopped herself. Her mother needed support, not more reasons to worry. "I've just finished my shift. I'll be there as soon as I can."

"Okay, darling. But only if you have time."

"Of course I have time. What did the doctor actually say?"

Her mum sighed down the phone. "She said it could just be a failed stent. I knew something was wrong. He's been so uncomfortable. Too scared to come home. Anyway, how's Mitch?"

What could she say? That her husband was concerned for her welfare, her state of mind. "He's fine. Busy as usual. Anyway, I'll text you my flight details. Talk soon."

When she arrived home, Mitch was nowhere in sight. She called his phone, but his voicemail kicked in after several rings, and she didn't have the energy to leave a message. Right now, her father was her priority.

Tayla dragged her full suitcase down the stairs and caught a ride with one of the staff, who dropped her at the airport an hour before her seven-thirty flight departed. As she waited to move through to the departure lounge, she called Mitch again to the same response. "Mitch Harrington. Leave a message."

ICE QUEEN

MITCH SAT in his Hilux at Petrie Bay, his mind on Tayla and her recent preoccupation. Her tears the night before had him wondering what, or who, had made her so sad. He understood her concern for Barry, but something else was troubling her.

He picked up his phone and brought up her number. The call went straight to her voice mail. When Luka pulled up beside him, Mitch left the cab and unclipped his surfboard from the roof rack, thoughts of Tayla slipping away. "Are you ready to hit these waves?" he asked.

"Yep. More than ready." Luka untied his board. "How's married life?"

Looking to the horizon, Mitch searched for the right word. "Complicated."

"Yeah? Want to talk about it?"

Mitch zipped up his wetsuit and secured the back flap. "Nope. Nothing a bit of chilly saltwater won't cure."

"I thought you guys would've sorted out your differences by now."

"Yes, me too. But there's nothing straightforward when it

comes to Tayla. She's complexity in motion. The proverbial ice queen."

"Yeah, I've met a few ice queens in my time, believe me."

Mitch laughed and slapped Luka on the back. "I bet you have."

"Anyway, how's CeCe?"

"You know, still pretending everything's okay." Mitch hesitated. He and Luka rarely discussed his sister. They'd agreed long ago to leave the past where it belonged. "Running the orchard's too much for her, but she's determined to see it through. That's why I went to Tulloch Point last weekend—to give her a hand. She needs more staff."

"Any word of Andrea and Frank coming home?"

Mitch closed the door of the Hilux and locked it. He hid the keys on top of the tire. "Nope, they're loving the travel. But I wouldn't be surprised if they decide to sell up and move back to Clifton Falls when they do come back. Mum loves this area."

"What will CeCe do then?"

"No idea." Mitch chuckled. "She'd probably move here too if it wasn't for you."

"Piss off." Luka flashed a wide grin. "Is she seeing anyone?"

Flashing a wide grin back, Mitch picked up his board. "Dunno, mate. You'll have to ask her that one yourself."

"Yeah, right."

The wind picked up around five, bringing with it a bank of storm clouds drifting in from the east. With the water cooler than it had been in weeks and the waves dumping him several times, Mitch only lasted an hour before calling it a day.

When he parked outside the packing shed, Tayla's car was in its usual spot. He bounded up the stairs, expecting to see her lounging in front of the TV with Edward, a glass of wine in hand and her feet on the coffee table.

But the loft was empty.

Thinking she might be over at Cherry Grove, he grabbed a headlamp and summoned Edward to heel before strolling through the tree rows to the old homestead. The new tenants were arriving soon, and he hadn't organized the move. Still, it wouldn't take long once the removal guys got stuck in.

As he walked up to the veranda, the house stood in darkness with no signs of life. Mitch let himself in, calling her name as he made his way down the hallway and into the living room.

He flicked on the light and froze. The room was empty. Every stick of furniture. Every book. Every knick-knack. All gone. He checked the kitchen cabinets and pantry, all cleaned out and spotless. Even the stovetop, oven, and refrigerator were sparkling clean. On the kitchen counter sat a basket overflowing with wine, preserves, honey, and crackers with a small card that read: *Welcome to your new home.*

The thought of Tayla packing up the house on her own with everything else she had going on, had him shaking his head. And as he stood in the muted light of the dining area, he felt like a complete and utter bastard.

Heading back to the packing shed, a niggling doubt consumed him. He took the stairs two at a time and, once inside, checked her room. The nightstand, where a small stack of paperbacks and a water bottle usually sat, was clear. And in the closet, most of her clothes were missing. Had she left him already?

Mitch pulled his phone from his pocket and checked the time. It was now after seven. He called her again and this time, she answered.

"Tayla? Where are you?"

A sharp intake of breath. "I'm at the airport, about to board a flight to Auckland. I tried to call you. Sorry I didn't leave a message."

That 'utter bastard' feeling washed over him for the second time that evening, and for a fleeting moment, Mitch wanted to protect her with whatever means he had. "Auckland? Is everything all right?"

"Dad's back in the operating room." She hesitated, and he assumed by the sound of a flight being called that she was in the departure lounge. "Um…sorry, I'm having trouble thinking straight. He should be out by now. But we've heard nothing. They don't know what's going on."

"Shit. Luka and I went surfing this afternoon, so my phone was in the truck."

"No problem. I'm not sure how long I'll be gone."

Mitch moved to the office and sat at his desk. "Okay. Is there anything I can do?"

"No…but thank you. I have to go. They're calling my flight."

"Tayla—"

She cut the call.

He stilled as his screen saver flicked through the half-dozen wedding photos Luka had sent him from his phone, staring while the images merged from one to another. Dressed in that stunning pink gown and with her hair flowing as free as the waves behind her, she really was the most beautiful bride.

His beautiful bride.

Minutes later, as he was about to pack a bag to make the long drive to Auckland himself, she phoned back.

"Sorry to bother you again, but I forgot something." She didn't wait for a reply. "The carpet cleaner's coming tomorrow. Can you open the house for him?"

"I was there just before. Everything's packed. How did you get it all done by yourself? I told you I'd help."

"Valentina helped me." She sounded exhausted, her voice soft and laced with a quiver. "Anyway, it's all set now apart from the carpet. The window cleaner came today."

"Do you want me to drive up?"

"Dad can't have any visitors at this stage."

"It was more to support you."

Silence filled the space where words should have been. "There's no need," she eventually said, then went quiet again. "But thanks," she added as a polite gesture.

"Well, can I do any unpacking at your parents?"

"No. Everything's ready for their return. But that may be weeks away now."

———

Thoughts of Tayla consumed Mitch every day. He called her cell phone most mornings, but she seldom answered. Every night, he'd receive a brief text of a few generic words such as *Dad's stable* or *Dad's had a reasonable day.* His attempts to engage her in text conversation mostly went unanswered.

He ate alone, struggled to concentrate, and woke during the night, wondering how she was coping. In the evenings, after a nondescript dinner, he'd sit in front of the TV, staring blankly at the screen as he waited for her daily text update. With close friends and a supportive family, Mitch was unfamiliar with this state of loneliness. Now he struggled to comprehend the emptiness eating him up inside.

As he readied for bed the following Friday, he picked up the phone and called her again. He wanted to hear her voice, to reassure her everything would be okay. But what could he say that didn't sound trite? Barry might be out of immediate danger, but he knew the risks as well as she did.

"Hi, it's Tayla Whitman. Please leave a message after the tone."

"Hey. Just checking in. Call me."

Mitch woke with a start several hours later. Fumbling with the lamp switch, he grabbed his phone off the nightstand with his other hand and hit answer. "Tayla?"

"Mitch, it's Ella."

He sat up, leaned back on the headboard and checked the time.

Shit.

"Mitch, are you there?"

"Ella? It's two in the morning. Where are you?"

"Downstairs."

The following day, Mitch sat at his desk with his head in his hands, exhausted after talking to Ella half the night. She and Chris were having problems again, and while he knew not to get involved, he felt sorry for her. She'd asked for a brandy to calm her nerves, but the more she topped up her glass, the more suggestive she'd become. Just before dawn, he'd left her to sleep it off on the sofa and headed back to bed. When he walked into the living area for breakfast a few hours later, she'd gone.

Now Tayla was the only woman on his mind. He'd tried Ruby's landline earlier, but an answerphone kicked in after eight lonely rings.

"Are you in the office, boss?" Ned popped his head around the door. "Crikey. You look like you've been up all night. Missing the wee wifey, are we?"

"Yeah, something like that."

"She's a cute little bundle." Ned thought for a moment and smiled, showing a neat row of false white teeth. "A kind soul, but troubled."

Mitch nodded at Ned's perception. "Yeah, it's not an easy time for her. Let's hope Barry recovers, and they can move forward with their retirement."

"You did well there, boss. Don't blow it, eh?"

Mitch laughed at the older man and shook his head. "What are you, a freakin' mind reader or something?"

"I've been called worse," Ned said with a wink. "But a marriage must be worked at from the get-go. A little flirting, movie nights. Play your cards right, and you'll have her pregnant in no time."

As an image of a pregnant Tayla flashed into his mind, Mitch couldn't help but smile. "Speaking from experience, are we?"

"You young fellas think you have this romance business sorted, but I still like to lie with my woman. Keeps me young and sprightly."

Mitch pictured Ned's frail wife, Maggie—eighty if she was a day—snuggled up on the couch next to an equally frail Ned as they ate popcorn and watched movies. He burst out laughing. "Anyway, Casanova, what are you doing here? You realize it's Saturday, you're supposed to have the day off."

"Yeah, I know. But we may have a problem with the grapefruit."

"What sort of problem?"

"I'm not sure yet, but it looks like someone's been helping themselves."

24

OTHER PEOPLE'S SECRETS

As HER FATHER'S post-surgery recovery stretched into two weeks and then three, Tayla settled into Ruby's guest room, while her parents stayed in the granny flat at Lisa's.

Mitch texted most days and called every morning, leaving voicemail messages of concern as if he were her real husband and she a devoted wife. But Mitch and her father were close neighbors —friends—so his concern was genuine, of that she had no doubt. However, she still didn't understand why he'd paid a hefty deposit on a property when he knew the sale going ahead depended on him fulfilling a condition of marriage. It made no sense.

Then again, men and their black and white rationale had never made much sense to Tayla, Hayden being a prime example. Why had he insisted they marry a few weeks before his baby was due?

It was rare for Tayla and her father to be alone together at Lisa's. But when she called in that afternoon, she found him sitting in a chair, flicking through a magazine, the rest of the family nowhere in sight.

"Hi." She kissed him on the cheek. "Where's Mum?"

"Getting her hair done."

"Wow, that's a big step in the right direction."

"It's about time she had a little pampering. She's been with me every day for weeks." Barry rearranged the blanket in his lap while Tayla made tea.

"Actually, I'm glad we're alone," he said as she placed the cup of tea on an occasional table next to him. "I wanted to talk to you about the orchard." A trembling hand pointed to a chair in the corner of the room. "Pull up that chair."

Tayla had always had a strong relationship with her father, but they'd seldom talked about the business. She still wasn't sure why he'd given her power of attorney. After all, she was the youngest and didn't even live in the same country.

She pulled the chair over and sat in front of him. "I've sorted everything out with the accountant. All the bills are paid and the rest of the money's in the bank."

"Yes. I spoke to him the other day. Your mother still doesn't realize how bad things were. I'd like to keep it that way. You know how she worries."

"Okay."

"I always thought we'd trade out of it. When Mitch made his offer, a huge weight lifted off my shoulders. I headed home with a spring in my step, knowing we'd have enough money to clear our debt, buy the retirement place and still have a small nest egg."

She nodded but remained silent.

"But there's something I don't understand," he continued.

Tayla's already tight gut tightened a little more.

Her father held her gaze. She remembered he'd done this when she was about to get into trouble as a child. It still had the same effect. "Last I heard, Mitch was engaged to that Prue what's-her-name. Next thing, you've left Sydney, Hayden's out of the picture, and Mitch is at my bedside asking for your hand."

Tayla frowned. "He asked for my hand? When?"

"He called in on his way to the UK. I wasn't thinking straight at that stage, so I didn't pay him much heed. Not long after, you guys have eloped, and your mother's all excited over the wedding photos."

Her father leaned his head back and closed his eyes for a second. He'd always been physically strong, and it broke her heart to see him so frail.

"So why the hurry?" he continued. "You're hardly the spontaneous type."

She struggled to keep her gaze steady. "That's true, but sometimes life takes you on an unexpected twirl. You either embrace it or miss the opportunity."

"Yeah, well, I've always said, fate can't be contained or explained." He hesitated. "You know, I never liked that Hayden guy much when we met him in Sydney that time."

Tayla suppressed a smile and sipped her tea. "Now you tell me."

"He's just a bit...superior. Mind you, I always thought you'd end up with Tim."

She chuckled. "Dad, you know Tim's gay, don't you?"

"What does that even mean these days? Lots of people swing both ways, as you young ones say. I thought when you went to the school ball together, well..."

"Tim was never my boyfriend. He's like a brother to me."

His eyes bright, he reached for her hand. "I just want you to be happy, sweetheart. To wake up in the morning wearing a smile and go to bed at night knowing he gets you. Do you know what I mean?"

"Course I do."

"I remember what young love is like. Your mother and I, we never played the hard to get game. Never pretended. I bet you can't wait to go home. It's been what—three weeks?"

"Yeah. It will be good to get back." She reached forward and pulled him into a soft hug, his once muscular frame now wasted on his bones. "And please don't worry. Mitch is a good man—he's kind and considerate."

"Yes, he is. So, tell me this, what happened with the surgeon?"

Sometimes Tayla wondered the same thing. *What indeed?* "Let's leave that conversation for another day, shall we?"

"Only if you sneak me one of those cupcakes from the pantry. I need fattening up."

Ruby's house was unusually quiet when Tayla returned from Lisa's. Even the toys, which covered the family room floor on a good day and totally overtook it at other times, had vanished. But the best part of walking into Ruby and Noah's home that evening was the delicious smell wafting from the kitchen.

"It's so peaceful. What's the story?" Tayla dumped her bag on the floor beside the kitchen table.

"The girls are in bed, Noah's at the gym, and *we* are going to relax with a glass of wine and a bowl of linguine followed by a silky panna cotta. How does that sound?"

"Wonderful." She kicked off her shoes and took a sip of the shiraz Ruby had poured for her. "Dad looked good today. Better than I've seen him in ages. He even wanted a cupcake with his cup of tea."

"I thought the same when I saw him yesterday." Ruby raised her glass. "To Dad." They clinked. "And to many more years of sharing him with Mum. Are you ready for tomorrow?"

"Yes, I think so. I thought Mum and Dad might come with me, but when I mentioned it, he got a bit emotional."

"I'm not sure he can face going back to Clifton Falls just yet. I think their money troubles worried him more than we realized." Ruby handed her a bowl of steaming hot pasta, and as they sat at the table, she asked, "Does Mitch know you're coming home?"

Home? "Not yet." Tayla sighed as she twirled the linguine around her fork. "I might stay at Mum and Dad's new place for a few days. Clear my head a bit."

"So, things aren't going too well?"

"I have no idea. He's...complex."

"Well, whatever happens, you did the right thing. You know that, don't you? I doubt Dad would've survived if they'd lost the orchard."

"He asked me today...about our marriage."

Ruby's eyes widened. "What did you say?"

"As little as possible."

"You can't tell him. You know how proud he is. He'd be devastated." Ruby sipped her wine. "That settlement was all he looked forward to for a while there."

"I know. But it's a heavy burden, knowing my marriage to Mitch may be the only thing that kept Dad alive. Still, tides turn, don't they? He saved me once, twice if you count my bike accident. Returning the favor was the least I could do."

"Sorry. I didn't mean to dump that on you. You did the right thing, and I can't thank you enough."

They ate in silence for a while, the wine and Rumer's sultry voice helping Tayla relax until Ruby said, "Has Mitch ever talked to you about that inheritance fiasco?"

"Never. And I don't want him to. He made his position clear at the time." Tayla narrowed her gaze at her sister. "Why's that?"

"I was just wondering. You've never been one to hold a grudge, but is that the other reason you dislike him? Because of Norman's will?"

"Pretty much. I thought I'd grown out of the teenage petty-grievance stage. But when I returned from Sydney, my life tipped upside down, and sat in Simon Harrow's office, listening to my now-husband—"

"Mr. Billboard—"

"Yes, Mr. Billboard, calmly say he couldn't settle. Well, it all came flooding back."

Tayla stood and cleared the plates. After stacking them into the dishwasher, she removed the panna cotta from the fridge and handed one to Ruby, along with a jug of berry coulis.

"What actually happened?" Ruby asked as she poured the coulis onto her dessert. "With Norman's money, I mean."

"Do you remember when Mum and Dad used my university fund to pay the mortgage that year the big hailstorm destroyed the cherries?"

"Yes. I didn't really get it. I always thought we were well off."

"Me too. Anyway, a few months before Norman's death, he said he had a gift for me, one I was to accept graciously when the time came. According to Mum, he'd told them he wanted to help with my education costs. He was about to pay for my first semester when he died. Anyway, he left a note attached to his will, witnessed by one of his carers. But because the bequest wasn't legally documented, the executor of his estate refused to honor it."

Tayla paused to lick panna cotta off her spoon. "It's rumored his estate was worth millions of dollars, and Mitch was his only heir. So why would he go against Norman's wishes? Not that I expected anything, and I'd be the first to acknowledge Norman was as eccentric as they come, but he wanted me to have that money. Apparently, Mitch had other ideas. When I was working at the supermarket during summer break, he'd strut in without a care in the world, asking how I was. It made no sense."

Ruby drained her wine. "You're right about that."

"Anyway, Mum and Dad must have kicked up a stink because not long after I started at AUT, the money came through and kept coming every year until I graduated." Tayla noticed Ruby's expression. "What?"

"Oh, sweetie."

"What?" Tayla repeated.

"And Mitch has never mentioned it?"

"No. Why?" Tayla waited, fiddling with the stem of her wine glass, but Ruby hung back. "Okay. Am I missing something here?"

Ruby frowned. "I'm not supposed to tell you, but this wine's loosening my already chatty tongue." She sighed. "Mitch gave you that money. It was the great-uncle, Ken or whatever his name is, who tried to stop it."

Tayla covered her mouth with her hand as the significance of Ruby's disclosure held her in a tight grip. "No, that can't be right."

"I was there the night Mitch came to see Dad. They went into the office, and a while later came out and had a beer together. Mum was at her book club, so I quizzed Dad after Mitch left. He didn't want to tell me at first but was so relieved he couldn't contain himself."

"And you've waited until now to tell me?"

"Dad swore me to secrecy. When you and Mitch married, I assumed he'd told you. But he certainly didn't want you to know back then."

A wave of panic washed over Tayla as her long-held grudge resurfaced. Her feelings for Mitch had always been complicated— the crush and the grievance—and now what was Ruby saying? That this particular grievance was ill-founded? "But why would he do that? Give me the money?"

"Because, according to Dad, Mitch knew how much Norman loved you. He wanted to respect his grandfather's wishes, even if the bequest was scribbled on a scrap of notepaper."

Tayla poured herself another half glass of shiraz and took a gulp. All this time, she'd resented the wrong man. Her perception had drifted way off course, and she'd failed to listen to her gut when it tried to tell her that maybe she'd got it wrong.

"But why would Dad keep it from me all this time?" Her voice rose an octave. "To protect me?"

Ruby shrugged. "You're his baby girl."

Tayla stilled as she looked at her sister. "Shit, Ruby. This changes everything."

"I thought it might."

25

THE RETURN

TAYLA WALKED from the terminal and climbed into a waiting cab. The air, crisp and cool, felt like home, but she reminded herself that the word 'home' had many connotations. She had no home. Not now.

Decorated in various shades of tedious sage green and gray, her parents' condo at the retirement complex was pleasant enough. Still, she struggled to imagine them—with their vibrant personalities—living in such a small space after the large rooms and sweeping veranda of their family villa.

Mitch had called her several times that week, but they'd played phone tag as usual. If she were honest, she enjoyed listening to his messages. That rich voice, laced with care as he asked after her day, somehow helped her sleep.

However, being back meant she couldn't ignore him any longer, especially given Ruby's revelation. And despite the little white lie that she'd told her father, the thought of seeing Mitch filled her with apprehension. Because her husband—with his amused stare, pin-up body, and that sexy voice—was tiptoeing his way into her heart, one voicemail at a time.

Tayla had spent hours mulling over Ruby's words, questioning her sister's recollection of events. But the more she thought about it, the more it made sense. Mitch was doing the right thing by carrying out Norman's wishes.

Picking up her car and a few belongings from the orchard was Tayla's first step. If she left now, Mitch would be working, and she might not have to face him. Her Uber arrived ten minutes later, and she hurried out the door, her luggage still in the spare room.

When she arrived at Lime Tree Hill, Edward lay in the sun on the grass at the base of his kennel—a sure sign the king of the hill was in residence. She crouched to pet him, those big eyes looking up at her as he cocked his head to the side.

As she climbed the stairs and tiptoed down the hall, Tayla could hear him talking on the phone in his office, chuckling the way he often did when on a call.

In her bedroom, she noticed a duffel bag on the floor and a pair of women's boots against the closet door. Mitch had company.

"Hi, you're back. Welcome home."

She jumped. "Shit, you gave me a fright."

"Sorry." Mitch leaned against the doorframe. His arms crossed and his smile soft, he stared at her. "Your hair looks good."

Tayla ran her hand through her shoulder-length bob. She hadn't been sure about it at first but was used to it now. "Oh. Thanks. I needed a change."

"How's Barry?"

"Improving. They'll be home soon, all going well. He said to say hi."

Mitch intensified his gaze, nodding as if he'd heard what she said while his mind rehearsed his reply. "You should have texted. I would've picked you up from the airport."

"I caught an Uber. Actually, I thought I might stay at Mum and Dad's for a few days. You obviously have a guest."

"Yes, CeCe. She's visiting a friend, but she'll be back for dinner."

Tayla looked around. "Where are my things?"

"In our room. I'll go grab your suitcase."

Our room? "Oh, it's still at Mum and Dad's."

Mitch didn't miss a beat, but his frown said it all. "I have to make a delivery after dinner. We can pick it up then." He hesitated. "Or am I missing something?"

"I don't want to be a burden."

His face softened. "We have a deal, remember? And you're no burden." He started to walk away but turned back. "It's nice to have you home."

Home? There seemed little else she could say but, "Thanks."

As Mitch left the room, Tayla failed to understand her reaction. She'd planned to collect a few things and go. But as exhaustion overtook reason, returning to the retirement complex no longer appealed.

Tayla stepped into his bedroom and shut the door. *My Cousin Rachel* sat on the nightstand, along with her box of tissues and alarm clock. In the closet, her clothes hung on the right-hand side with his hanging opposite. She hesitated before peeking into the drawers. The few bras, panties, sweaters, and leggings she'd left behind sat neatly in place. Beautiful lingerie had always been her weakness, and for some reason, the thought of Mitch touching her smalls prompted an amused smile.

Late-afternoon sun washed the room with a soft glow. Tayla opened the sliding door onto the balcony. And as the scent of freshly cut grass drifted up from below, she drew the net curtains, slipped out of her dress, and lay on Mitch's bed in her slip and underwear. Resting her head on the pillow, she told herself it was just for a minute.

A mix of his bodywash and cologne lingered—the faint scent of familiarity—and as Tayla covered herself with the throw, she recalled their wedding day. The anticipation while waiting on the rocks, his smile when he caught sight of her, and how she'd been the focus of his attention for several hours. Those sublime make-believe moments where fact blended with fiction.

Was that what she was doing? Living a fictitious dream? Because, even though she feigned disinterest, the way he'd looked at her as he stood in the doorway, filled her thoughts as she drifted off.

"Tayla?"

She woke with a start, struggling to focus on Mitch who stood at the foot of the bed.

"Dinner's almost ready. I thought I'd better wake you."

"Thanks." She pulled the throw around her shoulders, aware of his gaze flicking to the blush pink satin covering her breasts. "I was out cold."

Mitch's warm smile caught her off guard. "CeCe's just finishing the salad." With that, he turned and left the room, shutting the door behind him.

She'd almost forgotten how incredibly handsome he was. How his looks unnerved her. The image of billboard Mitch flashed into her mind—half-naked, tight boxers, strong arms and shoulders. How would it feel to be held in those arms? Desired until all rational thought vanished?

Telling herself to get a grip, Tayla used his en suite to freshen up before slipping into her dress. As she entered the kitchen, the curtain rose once again. Fantasies with her husband in the lead role would have to wait.

It was showtime.

"Hi, you," CeCe leaned in for a hug. "I hope you like veggie lasagna."

"Love it. It's good to see you again." She glanced at the table, set with a basket of rolls, a large green salad, and various condiments. "What can I do to help?"

162

"Nothing. Sit and tell me about your dad." CeCe held up a bottle of wine. "Vino?"

"Please. And Dad's doing much better, thanks for asking. He's been pretty down in the dumps, but that's to be expected after what he's been through. It turned out one of his stents had failed. Bent almost in half." Tayla peered into the office. "Where's Mitch?"

"Downstairs, feeding Edward. He said you've been away for three weeks. That must have been tough."

"It was cathartic, to tell the truth. I haven't spent a lot of time with my parents over the past few years. We reconnected—shared lots of laughs and a few tears. And Ruby and Noah, my sister and her husband, have two little girls. They're two and four, so I loved being with them."

"Cute. I love kids."

"Me too."

They sat at the table, the aroma of tomatoes, basil, and garlic stirring her hunger.

"I've really missed Mum and Dad since they've been traveling," CeCe said. "Not that I'd tell them that. They worry enough about me as it is."

"Who's worrying about whom?" Mitch strolled into the kitchen. He walked straight up to Tayla and pecked her on the lips. Twice.

"Excuse me," CeCe said with a smile as Tayla struggled to compose herself. "Tayla and I are trying to have a private conversation."

He looked at Tayla and grinned. "Are you just?"

"Yes, and it's girl talk," Tayla said, her mood playful to match his sister's as her lips tingled from his touch.

"Right, this lasagna's done resting." CeCe handed Mitch a large knife. "Mitch, you do the honors."

As she watched Mitch serve a huge slice of lasagna onto her plate, Tayla struggled to understand the change in him. He'd barely said a word to her before she went to Auckland. Now he was attentive and charming. The perfect husband.

And while they ate, he looked at her as if he were a man in love with his wife, playing his part in front of CeCe with care. Because she wasn't privy to their secret. Or if she was, she didn't let on.

26

WATERFALL IN MOON SHADOW

AFTER PICKING up Tayla's suitcase and dropping off a crate of limes at a local café, they headed out of town along the Eastern Pacific Highway just after nine. In contrast to their dinner conversation, when Mitch had questioned Tayla about her father and her stay in Auckland, they drove in silence until they reached the billboard.

"I see you're still up in lights."

"Yeah, I wish they'd take the darn thing down. I can't believe the flak I'm getting because of it."

"Well, it does catch your eye."

He chuckled, sending her a sideways glance. "Really? I wouldn't have thought you'd dare look."

"Not at you, obviously, but the other three are worth a quick peek."

"That's not very nice. Make you blush, do I?"

"In your dreams. Tim did a great job of photoshopping in those abs though."

He huffed. "Listen to you. You're getting your spark back."

"I have no idea what you mean. But while I'm in this supposed 'spark zone,' why did you move my clothes? Couldn't you just tell CeCe I use the spare room as my dressing room?"

"My loft's too small for you to have your own dressing room, Princess. And I've had several overnight visitors while you've been away. Also, I didn't move them, Valentina did. I thought rummaging around in your panty drawer might be a bit weird."

Princess? Flicking a glance his way, Tayla caught his smile. It seemed he found her embarrassment amusing. She looked out the side window, the thought of a pair of her lacy panties dangling from his index finger making her cheeks impossibly hot.

"Have you ever seen the falls under a full moon?" he asked.

"No, never." Tayla frowned as Mitch passed the Lime Tree Hill sign.

"Let's do it. It's only a fifteen-minute drive."

"Won't CeCe be worried?"

"We're not kids, Tayla. We could stay out all night and sleep under the stars, and she wouldn't bat an eye."

"Of course, it's just…"

"Besides, Luka said he might try to catch up with her tonight. I want to give them some space."

"Luka? I got the impression she disliked him."

"Yeah. There's gallons of water flowing under that shaky bridge." He chuckled. "But it's not my tale to tell. I'm sure she'll fill you in at some point."

As they drove farther inland, Tayla tracked the moon, wondering if Luka was the guy from CeCe's meet-cute story. Because Luka—with his warm smile, streaked blond hair, and olive skin—was definitely cute.

They pulled into an off-road parking spot near the track leading to the swing bridge. Mitch took two small headlamps from the glove compartment and handed one to her. While she'd visited the falls many times as a teenager, she'd never been there at night. She opened the door and stepped out onto the gravel, the full moon lighting up the sky.

Mitch headed down the narrow track, and she followed, stopping when they reached the swing bridge. With its short drop onto the rocks below, she was nervous enough crossing it in the daylight, never mind at night. But as Mitch reached for her hand, she took that first step onto the deck.

"You okay?"

He let go, and she grabbed the cables on either side. "I've never felt safe on this bridge, even when I was a kid."

He turned and walked backward, shining his headlamp at her feet. "You'll be fine. It's thirty steps at the most. And we're only a few feet off the ground."

She stepped forward. "I'm okay. You can turn around."

He hesitated, and when she flipped her headlamp to his face, he flashed his amused smile. "But I'm enjoying the view."

What? He turned anyway.

Safely on the other side of the bridge, Tayla followed him up the half-dozen well-worn steps to a lookout point. And, there before them, flowing like a bridal veil, the Clifton Falls hit the pool below with an unusually quiet rumble, while the moon watched from the midnight-blue sky above.

"We haven't had much rain here lately." Mitch leaned on the railing in front of them. "That's why she's a little shy."

"She?"

"Well, she wears a veil, is mysterious and beautiful, so the feminine fits, don't you think?"

Tayla smiled at his reply. Mitch was in tune with his feminine side. Who would have thought? She took a deep breath, filling her lungs with the dampness of the surrounding native bush. And as she turned off her headlamp and looked skyward, a sense of freedom hit her with a jolt. "It's so peaceful."

"Yeah. One of my favorite places on the planet. This is what life's about, don't you think? These moments?"

"You're right. We're so lucky to live where we do."

"So you're okay with being back?"

Tayla looked at him, unable to read his expression in the darkness. "For now."

He grabbed her hand. "Come on. Let's go to the bottom and feel the water."

"But it will be freezing."

"Yeah. Too cold for a skinny dip, that's for sure. You'll have to keep your clothes on for a change."

She stopped still. "What's that supposed to mean?"

Mitch chuckled. "Not a thing."

The air had cooled dramatically by the time they returned to his truck, and as Tayla climbed into the cab, Mitch grabbed a blanket from the back seat and passed it to her.

She lay it over her legs and looked at him. "Thanks. I'd like to say something before we go back," she said, her hands busy in her lap. "About Norman's will."

Mitch shifted in his seat and leaned his back against the door. "Sure."

"I always thought it was you who held back the money Norman left for my education. I've only just found out the truth."

He glanced away, his fingers tapping the steering wheel. "Who told you?"

"Ruby. We'd had a couple of wines and conversation flowed, as is often the case after the second glass. She assumed I knew."

Shifting his gaze back to her, he nodded but remained silent.

"I just want you to know it meant everything to me. If it weren't for you, I'd still be paying off my student loan. But there's one thing I don't understand."

"What's that?"

"Why did you do it?"

"It was what the old man wanted. You made his life more tolerable, and he loved you for it."

Tayla smiled at the memory of her elderly friend. "I loved him too. I'm sorry I misjudged you. Turns out, I blamed the wrong man."

Mitch shrugged. "Unfortunately, Ken can be just as pedantic as Norman was, maybe even more so. That's why he didn't want you to have the money. It wasn't personal. And apology accepted."

"I never expected anything. From his estate, I mean…" Tayla searched for the right words. "Now I know the truth, I want to pay you back."

"What? No way. It was your money."

"It's just, while I appreciate what you did, I don't want you to be at a financial disadvantage because of me."

She waited for him to address her concerns, but instead, he went to start the engine, then stopped with a second thought. "Why didn't you want to come back?" He turned to face her again.

"When?"

"Today. You left your stuff at your parents' place without even telling me you were home."

She leaned back on the headrest and sighed. "Everything got on top of me… I wanted a few days alone to get my act together. Mum's running on auto pilot, Dad's struggling with depression, Lisa thinks I was selfish for eloping, and Ruby keeps singing my praises because we did. On top of that, you said you found living with me frustrating. I got the impression I'd passed my use-by date."

Silence stretched before them. "I didn't say I found living with you frustrating."

"Um, I think you did."

"I said, I'm frustrated when I'm around you."

A frown creased her brow. "Semantics."

"Is it?" Mitch slipped his arm along the back of her seat, leaned toward her and whispered, "Did you hear what I said? Or only what you wanted to hear?"

"You said…" Realization dawned on her. She tensed.

"Look me in the eye and tell me you've never thought about us." He moved closer, his fingers twisting a lock of her hair. "Us, married with benefits. Maybe that was your final condition. The one you couldn't voice because you were afraid I'd say no."

Fierce heat crept up her neck and face. He was right. Back then, she'd feared his rejection. She still did. "And would you have? Said no?"

"At the time. Mixing business with pleasure is never a good idea." They shared a look. "Besides, you didn't like me much at that stage."

"So why consider it now?" Unsure of what his response would be, Tayla braced herself.

"Because I think you like me more than you let on. But something's holding you back, am I correct?"

My virginity.

"Look," Mitch continued, "if I've crossed a line, I apologize. If not, take your time. I'm happy to wait."

She sat up straight and fastened her seatbelt with unsteady hands. "We should get going."

27

WHAT IF?

THEY RETURNED to Lime Tree Hill in silence. Tayla mentally played with her words all the way, wanting to agree to his suggestion but concerned at what would happen if she did. There'd be no going back once they took that step, and if it didn't work out, how could they continue living together?

Mitch pulled into his usual parking space outside the packing shed. He left the Hilux without a word but smiled as he held the door open for her. Upstairs, one dim light glowed above the dining table, and CeCe had gone to bed. Mitch grabbed a bottle of water from the fridge, unscrewed the lid, and took several gulps.

"You take my room." He screwed the cap back on without looking at her. "I'll sleep in the office."

"I'm not putting you out of your own bed. I'll take the office."

"No, you won't."

She huffed a sigh. "Fine. We'll share then, shall we? Do you have any extra pillows?"

Mitch frowned. "What for?"

"We could put a couple between us."

He looked at her in disbelief. "Are you serious? If you don't want me to touch you, just say so. But what are you afraid of? That you might enjoy it?"

Without waiting for an answer, he stormed toward *their* bedroom, pulling off his T-shirt and chucking it into the laundry room as he passed.

Tayla stayed in the kitchen. She picked up an orange from the fruit bowl. Put it back. This long day was about to become an even longer night. Thinking about it, the extra pillows did seem a little petty. After all, they'd shared a bed at Tulloch Point, but the closer they got physically, the more complex their *purely business* arrangement was becoming.

Ignoring the urge to sleep in the office, Tayla followed his energy down the hallway and into his bedroom. When Mitch strolled in from the bathroom, wearing nothing but his boxers, she couldn't resist a sneaky peek. Tim's photoshop skills hadn't been needed after all. Those abs looked just as good as the billboard version. The thought of touching them scared her to death.

"Bathroom's free." Mitch climbed into bed and switched off his bedside lamp. He punched his pillow into shape. "Goodnight."

In the bathroom, Tayla sat on the lid of the toilet seat as she considered his suggestion. Marriage with benefits. *Sex!* Because that's what he meant. She already enjoyed the benefits of marriage to Mitch—living in his home rent free at his insistence. A few groceries that weren't available at the farm gate store her only contribution to the household expenses.

And now Mitch was offering a solution to the lonely nights and her need for touch. There was no doubt she was tired of being a virgin—and not just a virgin, but a timid one at that. But did she have the confidence to accept his proposal?

Back in the bedroom after a quick shower, she sat on the edge of the bed. She removed her panties but kept her slip on, then lay in the dark—the satin cool against her skin as her hands relaxed at her sides.

A shift in his position and the rhythm of his breathing told her he was still awake.

"I'm sorry I shut you down before," she said. "Up at the falls, I mean."

He rolled onto his back. "Don't worry about it. It's no big deal."

"It's just, I thought you wouldn't be interested."

Mitch remained silent, but his sigh filled the void.

"What if I don't live up to your expectations?" she murmured. "Or...or you don't enjoy kissing me. Or touching me. I don't want things to be awkward and weird between us."

He turned to face her, resting his arm in the space between their pillows. "Things have been awkward and weird between us since that day in Simon's office. But, full disclosure, I'm definitely interested, and I suspect you feel the same way."

Every muscle in her body tightened under his gaze. "That may be true, but—"

"Tayla, stop. Let's forget I mentioned it, okay? You're over-thinking it."

She placed her hand next to his, the outline of his torso highlighted by the moonlight flooding through the net curtains. He kept his gaze steady as he reached for her hand.

"I don't want to forget you mentioned it," she whispered. "But...I want to slow it down."

Mitch lifted his other hand, brushing it across her cheekbone before tracing her cupid's bow with his index finger. She closed her eyes and sucked in a breath.

"Okay." He pulled her toward him and touched his lips against hers. As she opened her eyes, his smile engulfed her.

He leaned in again, his hand cradling the back of her head, guiding her as he kissed her once, twice. And as the third kiss built, Mitch moaned softly into her mouth. When he pulled back, the only thing between them was Tayla's insecurities.

"But if you really want to slow it down"—he traced his fingers back and forth across the neckline of her slip, almost touching her breasts—"you shouldn't kiss me like that...or come to bed in this tiny slip. It's been on my mind all afternoon."

On his mind? "I hate sleeping in pajamas."

Mitch tapped her playfully on the nose. "Yeah, me too. I'm gonna go now. Before the brakes fail." The covers came off with a flourish. He grabbed a pillow and stuffed it in front of himself as he walked out the door. "Goodnight."

Tayla sank back into the bed with a grin as she imagined what that pillow covered. She recalled their kiss. Warm and gentle and breathtaking. Mitch kissed as he lived. Dripping with confidence and in total control.

Tayla woke to the sound of the shower running and the sheets warm on the opposite side of the bed. She'd stirred when Mitch had crept into the room in the early hours. But as she'd drifted back to sleep, the warmth of his body comforted her; his presence now etched in her memory. The type of memory that offered a small smile.

Mitch returned from the en suite fully dressed—his hair wet and combed away from his forehead—and picked up his belt from the chair. As he threaded it through the loops of his jeans, he asked, "How did you sleep?" His hands worked the buckle, but his lazy, take-me-now eyes focused on her.

Tucking the top sheet under her chin, she broke eye contact, hyperaware of her breasts tightening as the cotton brushed against her skin. "Great, thanks."

"Sorry I invaded the bed, but Edward was snoring."

"No problem. Actually, I enjoyed the warmth."

Mitch smiled as he opened the curtains. Outside, mist shrouded the hills surrounding the orchard. He turned, searched for eye contact. "I won't be home tonight, and CeCe's leaving after breakfast, so you'll have the place to yourself."

"Of course. Poker night."

"Yeah. And I'm coaching a high school rugby team now the season's started." He headed for the door, then turned back. "I'm making scrambled eggs. Want some?"

Tayla wondered how he could be so casual about breakfast after last night. Once he'd left, she'd stayed awake thinking of him. Fantasizing. And when she stirred around dawn, she'd wanted to reach out and kiss him again. Feel his hands on her face, his arms around her. Make sure he got the message. "Thanks. I'll just jump in the shower first."

CeCe poked her head around the bedroom door. "Morning, you two. Did I hear scrambled eggs mentioned? Any bacon?"

Mitch smiled at his sister. "You know processed meats are bad for you?"

"Surely bacon doesn't count, does it?"

He looked at Tayla. "Bacon?"

"Just one rasher, thanks."

"Scrambled eggs and bacon times two." Mitch shook his head and chuckled as he left the room.

"And sourdough toast," CeCe yelled down the hallway after him.

"How was your night?" Tayla asked as CeCe sat on the bed.

She dropped her shoulders and let out a heavy sigh. "Why does life have to be so complicated?"

"I ask myself that very same question almost daily." Tayla hesitated. She didn't want to pry, but if CeCe needed someone to talk to, she'd be happy to oblige. "Do you want to talk about it?"

"Nah. I just want to crawl under a rock and hide, but I'll have breakfast first. No point in rock crawling on an empty tummy." She jumped off the bed. "See you in a bit."

28

FROM SYDNEY WITH SORROW

FOR TAYLA, Wednesday night had a stay-at-home kind of vibe. But every Wednesday since she'd lived at Lime Tree Hill, Mitch had left the house at three in the afternoon to head into town for the night. And just like previous weeks, when Tayla awoke the following day, his bedroom door was open and his bed as he'd left it the morning before—neatly made.

She stood on the balcony and stared out over the fruit-laden trees. As she squinted against the rising sun, movement in Norman's cottage caught her eye when someone switched on the light in the kitchen. Shivering, she walked inside and locked the sliding door behind her.

Later, when she drove past Norman's on her way to work, Tayla noticed a man on the veranda. Although she was too far away to make out his features, he seemed familiar. Maybe she'd introduce herself later. See if he needed anything.

As she turned onto the highway, she saw a woman pushing a baby stroller toward Norman's gate. She stopped on the grass verge and waved. Tayla waved back. When she glanced in the rearview mirror, the woman hadn't moved and didn't until Tayla reached the bend. Prickles caught the back of her neck, and as she headed south, she wondered why the sight of the woman with the baby affected her in that way.

When she arrived home from work, Mitch was in the kitchen cooking dinner. He turned from the stove and smiled, as he usually did when she entered a room.

Since he'd proposed his sex without sentiment idea, the air between them had changed—to an awkward, elephant-in-the-room type of air. Would he make another move, or had he changed his mind?

"I saw someone in Norman's cottage this morning," she said as she placed a small box on the counter.

"Yes. A couple from Sydney. They booked while you were in Auckland. Whats in the box?"

Sydney? "Oh, I bought you some brownie, from Fig Leaf."

He smiled. "Thanks."

"Have you met them, the couple I mean?"

"Briefly. They seem pleasant enough." Mitch turned back to the pan and added more stock. "Hayden and Anna. Can't remember their baby's name."

Tayla stiffened, inhaled. Her words coasted on a breath as she fought to calm her racing heart. "How long's dinner?"

"Twenty minutes, max." He stopped what he was doing. "Are you okay? You look shattered."

"I'm fine. I'll just get changed."

Tayla shut the door to her room and sat on the edge of the bed, her face in her hands. *Shit!* Hayden, Anna, and their baby boy were playing happy families in Norman's cottage. And she couldn't do a thing about it. How dare he taint Norman's sacred space by turning up uninvited! What was the man thinking?

Of course, she knew the answer. He hadn't gotten over her leaving the way she had. Now he was here to prove his controlling point. Protect his pride.

Back in the kitchen, she made a beeline for the fridge. "Would you like a beer?" she asked Mitch as she opened it.

"Yeah, why not. Rough day?"

In no mood to talk, Tayla passed him a Heineken then grabbed a glass and poured herself a wine. "Not the best." She took a gulp. Then another. "Yours?"

The afternoon was bleak as Tayla drove from the hospital to the orchard the following day. Before her trip to Auckland, blue-sky days had lingered from late summer into early autumn, something she'd almost taken for granted. But as she traveled along the Eastern Pacific Highway, misted sheets of rain hugged the horizon, and her mood darkened along with the sky.

Hayden invaded her thoughts. Questions, theories, and possible solutions jostled for position in her mind until she felt sick to her stomach. Should she go see him, text, or wait for him to make contact? Because one thing was clear. His visit wasn't some random coincidence. He would have meticulously planned it, and he'd know exactly what he was doing. Letting her stew in her anxiety until he was ready to make his move.

As she approached the packing shed, her eyes narrowed at the sight of Hayden talking to Ned. Even with his back to her, Tayla knew it was him. She could tell by his stance.

She parked in her usual place, and as she opened the door and stepped out, Hayden turned, his smile warm as always, and his expression just as bright as the last time she saw him. He was casually dressed. Jeans: black. Boots: brown. Shirt: blue.

Taking a sharp breath, she walked toward them.

"Here she is," Ned said warmly, as if Hayden was a long-lost friend paying a visit. "I was just telling Hayden you'd be home any minute. I'll leave you two to catch up."

"Thanks, Ned." Tayla pulled her bag onto her shoulder and watched Ned walk away. She turned but didn't meet Hayden's gaze. "You'd better come inside."

He followed her up the stairs without a word. It wasn't until she'd closed the door that she addressed him again. "What on earth are you doing here?"

"We needed a break. Your cozy cottage was available." He rubbed the back of his neck. "And anyway, how else was I supposed to see you?"

"You're not. That's the whole point of a breakup. We're done. No further contact necessary."

Hayden closed his eyes and pinched the bridge of his nose. The gesture was so familiar, and yet, she couldn't remember the last time she'd seen him do it. "Yes, I got that memo. Aren't you going to offer me a drink?"

"I don't want you here, understand?"

He sighed. Paced a few steps back and forth. Stopped. "Look, I'm sorry I hurt you, I truly am. But I still love you, Tayla. You know I do."

"You don't treat the people you love the way you treated me. That's not love. That's—"

"So you punish me by hooking up with some random farmer you've only known five minutes? Where did you find each other? On some country dating app? Did you swipe right and end up in a dead-end orchard? What the hell do you talk about? Oranges and lemons? Because this stunt has lemon written all over it."

She twisted her wedding ring around her finger. "You're in a relationship and have a new baby. What do you want me to say?"

"That you'll come home. Anna and I, we've always had a strong physical connection. But intellectually, we're poles apart. She's nothing like you. We don't talk books and philosophies and art, we…"

"Fuck?"

Hayden stared at her, his expression one of shock. "See, that's what I mean. Six months ago, the f-bomb wouldn't have left your lips. You meet this country hick, and you're all over it. You've swapped brains for brawn? And I bet you're not the only woman he's *fucking*, so why choose him over me?"

Tayla pulled out a chair from the dining table and sat. "You made that choice, not me."

"Don't make me out to be the villain in all this. Do you honestly think this step backward is the right direction for you? What about your dreams?"

"My dreams are just fine."

"Are they? So, tell me this, have you invested in property? Started your thesis? Learned to surf?"

His questions didn't warrant a reply. Hayden had a bucket list a mile long, so who was he to judge?

"Have you even been in the water?" he continued as he joined her at the table.

"Whether I have or not is none of your business. I hadn't even realized how your pressure for perfection was slowly suffocating me."

He huffed. "Life isn't a game of chance. You build your place in this world by sticking to the rules, not by drifting along on some whimsical cloud."

"Yes, so you've always said. We've both made our choices. Let's just move on, shall we?"

Hayden sat forward in the chair, his head between his hands. He looked up. "I've tried, but I can't."

"You left me at the altar, Hayden. In the sweltering heat. With no one but an anxious photographer and a celebrant whose look of pity I'll never forget." Tayla swallowed hard, her throat dry as she spoke. "And all because you didn't have the decency to pick up the damn phone. And you know what? I hated you for that. Hated you with a passion I never thought I was capable of. How could you have stooped so low…left me at the chapel like that?"

"Because Anna went into labor. There were complications. What did you expect me to do? Excuse myself to call my needy girlfriend?"

"*Needy!* I thought you were dead," she yelled. "That you'd been in an accident. One text. That's all I expected. Just one text."

"I'm sorry. But please, hear me out." He reached for her hand, but she wouldn't engage. "Anna and I have agreed. She likes her own company, always has. I annoy her if I'm around all the time. She's happy for us to go back to how we were."

"Anna knew about me?"

"Not at the start, no. But she wants to explore other options when Theo's older, so—"

"And is that what you want? A lover in one house and a part-time wife in the other? Unbelievable." Tayla's hands shook. She needed air, a drink of water…Mitch. "I'm married now. It's done. Please leave."

EAVESDROP

MITCH HAD SPENT most of the morning in town, looking at a property with Luka. They managed to ignore the topic of CeCe until they had a beer with lunch. With a little alcohol in his veins, Luka wanted to talk. It seemed nothing had changed between his sister and best friend. They were still jostling for position on the outskirts of each other's lives, much the same as him and Tayla.

He couldn't work out where Tayla stood. She seemed conflicted, unable to decide whether she was open to his invitation. Maybe he'd misread the signs. *Slow it down?* They were already parked at a stop sign. But when he thought about it, his verbal foreplay technique had left a lot to be desired. 'Let's have sex. Marriage with benefits; no emotional attachment necessary.' *Shit.*

Just as he pulled into the driveway, his phone rang. He hit the call icon on the steering wheel. "Ned, what's up?"

"Where are you?"

He eased his foot off the gas pedal. "The bottom gate. Why?"

"Tayla has a visitor, and it's not sounding pretty. Do you want me to go up? See what's going on?"

"No, I'm on my way."

Mitch parked in the garage and joined a concerned Ned outside the packing shed. "Who's with her?" he whispered.

"Some fella in a rental car, Hayden someone, a friend of hers from Sydney. They were hollering back and forth before, but it's been quiet for a bit. You want me to hang around in case I need to show him who's boss?"

"That's the guy who's staying in Norman's old place." Mitch looked toward the now silent loft. "I'll be fine."

"Okay, I'm off home. Call if you need me. He seemed happy to see her, but Tayla didn't give much away. See you in the morning."

"Yeah. Thanks."

Mitch stood for a moment, watching Ned walk toward home. The packing shed was quiet when he entered; the staff had gone for the day. He took the stairs one at a time instead of the usual two, stopping on the top riser as snippets of a conversation floated through the door.

Hayden was speaking. "...by taking off and marrying some hippy organic farmer?"

Tayla replied, but her words were muffled.

"We'll make it work," Hayden continued. "You can live in the terrace. It won't be any different from before."

"Why would I want a relationship with another woman's husband? A man who sneaks away to visit me between daddy duty and sleeping with his wife?"

Mitch shook his head; murmured an obscenity under his breath.

"It's how half the world lives," Hayden said. "Monogamy is an overrated concept maintained by religious dogma, and I, for one, don't buy into it."

"Good for you," Tayla said. "But even if I were single, I wouldn't come back after what happened. You don't deserve me. And I'm done."

Mitch had heard enough. He straightened his stance, took a deep breath, and strode through the door. He addressed Hayden. "What are you doing here?"

Tayla stood and moved to Mitch's side as Hayden eyed him up and down. "Sorry, I should introduce myself properly. I'm Tayla's fiancé."

Mitch scoffed. "As if, mate. Tayla's my wife, and I heard her say she didn't want you in her life."

Hayden stood and puffed out his chest but kept the table between him and Mitch. "When?"

"Just now, when I was climbing the stairs to my home."

"Home? Is that what you call this tin shed?" Hayden frowned at Tayla. "You can't possibly be happy here. I'm not leaving without you."

"Tough, because I'm not going anywhere."

"Okay, both of you calm down," Mitch said. "If Tayla really wanted to be with you, I wouldn't stand in her way. But it looks like she's picked me, and I'm damn happy about that."

Hayden ignored Mitch and addressed Tayla again. "I don't even believe you're married."

Mitch crossed the room to his office and returned with a framed wedding photo. He lay it on the table in front of Hayden. "There. Proof enough for you?"

Paying no attention to the picture, Hayden's eyes stayed on Tayla. "We fly out at four thirty the day after tomorrow. Anna would like to meet you. It might help you understand what the three of us could have."

"Let's get something perfectly clear," she countered. "I am not meeting your wife. Not now, not ever. Understand?"

Mitch walked to the door and held it open. "Okay. That's it. This little reunion is over."

Hayden stepped toward Tayla, his expression showing a sadness Mitch understood only too well. "Please, just think about it overnight." He turned, brushed past Mitch, and bounded down the stairs with Mitch a few steps behind. Outside, the men stood on the drive, eyeing each other.

"It seems you're quite the flavor of the month." Hayden pulled his car keys from his pocket and pressed the fob. "But it won't last. She'd never had a relationship before me, did you know that? That's why we work. I don't expect her to live in my pocket every minute of the day, or do my laundry and cook my meals. She's better than that."

"Look, Hayden, I'm an easygoing guy, but you're trying my patience to the max. I'm asking you, man to man, to leave her alone. With her father's illness and sorting her parents' affairs, she's had more than enough to deal with lately. And if you think you can come over here and throw your weight around, you can piss off back to Sydney right now."

"So you scored yourself a virgin bride on the rebound, did you? Bully for you. Shit, she didn't waste any time, did she?"

Virgin bride?

"Well what do you expect her to do? Live on her own while she shares you with your wife and kid? What kind of love is that?"

"You're telling me you don't play around?" Hayden scoffed. "That you don't have any outside interests?"

Mitch clenched his fists at his side. He wasn't a fighter, but he wanted to deck the guy. "Shit, mate, you really do have a screwed-up sense of reality. But, hey, each to their own."

"I'm not your mate, and I can't imagine you giving her the intellectual stimulation she needs."

"My wife can get intellectual stimulation from her friends and family any day of the week. But the type of stimulation I *do* give her isn't so easily quantified. If it weren't for your little boy, I'd have the cops come and remove you from my property right now. I want you gone by ten tomorrow morning. And don't you ever come over here again."

"But we're booked until Saturday."

"Tough. What part of piss off don't you understand?"

Her hands shaking, Tayla stood at the sink sipping a glass of water. Ever since leaving Sydney, she'd dreaded meeting Hayden again, but now she had, his demeanor seemed so out of character that she'd hardly recognized him. And as he'd stood in front of her, in need of a shave but still dressed as impeccably as ever, the knowledge their life had been based on a lie was all she'd needed to cut him adrift.

He'd always been a proud man, brimming with confidence in every aspect of his life. From his knowledge of the arts to his bedside manner and the way he presented himself, Hayden was well-respected. Not only by his friends and colleagues, but by his patients too. If summing him up in one word, 'wonderful' would fit perfectly.

So what caused a 'wonderful' man to lead a double life? Was it greed? Excitement at the prospect of being caught? She'd never know. That part of her life was over, and while Tayla hadn't realized it at the time, it had ended the day he'd left her at the chapel.

The sound of footsteps ascending the stairs filled her with dread. Apart from the once, Mitch had never asked her about her life in Sydney. Now he'd heard snippets of their conversation. Had he heard Hayden say he still loved her?

Tayla turned as he opened the door, the glass of water still in her hand. She tried to read his expression. His height and the broadness of his chest and shoulders made her feel small insignificant. And as Tayla stared at Mitch across the kitchen, she wished he'd scoop her up in his arms and hold on tight until her racing heart slowed.

He strode across the living room and into his office without saying a word. He was angry, and rightly so, but she'd never expected the silent treatment. Although, when she thought about it, that had been his reaction when he was angry with Prue as well. Closed off.

Tayla sat at the table for several minutes, wondering if she should approach him. She recalled his words from the night they traveled home from Tulloch Point: *discretion doesn't apply between us.* She stood, walked to the office door, knocked and entered.

He sat on the leather couch, his head in his hands, filtered sunlight hitting the wall above him in horizontal bands. She sat side-on next to him. "I'm sorry," she murmured. "I had no idea he'd pull a stunt like that."

He looked up. "You knew he was coming?"

"No, not at all."

"But you knew he was here. I told you two days ago."

"Yes, but I decided it was best to ignore him."

"Come on! The guy flew over from Sydney to see you, and you thought if you buried your head in the sand, he'd just disappear? Does his wife know about your little affair?"

"Please don't pretend you know the details, because you don't."

He held her gaze for a moment, then rose from the couch and sat at his desk. "When I phoned you that day from London, were you with him?"

"No. I went to sort out my apartment. He didn't know I was there until after I'd come home."

"But you've kept in touch?"

"Not lately."

He leaned forward in his chair. "You told me you were single. When did you two break up?"

"When I left Sydney."

Mitch nodded, his attention focused as he waited for her to elaborate. She didn't.

"You'd better start from the beginning. And before you tell me it's none of my business, when a guy barges into my home and causes a scene that can be heard from downstairs, it's my business."

"I agree. But you seem to think I'm an adulteress, and that couldn't be further from the truth."

"I never said that. But why don't you enlighten me? Just so we're clear."

Tayla went to stand, then thought better of it, her hands gripped together as she took a deep breath. By the time she'd finished, she'd told Mitch almost everything. Almost.

"So you didn't realize he was still with his wife, is that what you're saying?"

"I had no clue. Their divorce was finalized in January of last year." She twisted the wedding band on her finger, the same finger that once held Hayden's engagement ring. "He said they were long over."

"What kind of relationship did you have? Were you happy?"

"Cognitive...intellectual might be a better word. We were friends. And yes, I was happy. Content."

"Friends with intellectual benefits." She noted the sarcasm in his tone. "That's a new one."

Shaking her head, Tayla struggled for composure. When she'd told Ruby and Tim, the process had been different, like narrating a movie trailer for a life she'd never lived. Now she felt as if her heart were slowly being torn open and stuffed with cotton balls. She didn't want to continue. Didn't want to tell Mitch the worst part—about the dappled light in the chapel, the forced smile of the photographer as he'd told her how amazing she looked, and the minutes ticking by as she held an anxious breath

Tayla rose from the sofa and moved to the window, her focus on the farm gate store. She couldn't see the Cherry Grove homestead or Norman's cottage from the office, which was just as well. Mitch stayed at his desk, saying nothing.

Overwhelmed and choked with emotion, she didn't look at him as she continued, "He proposed last Christmas, in the Blue Mountains, and suggested we elope sooner rather than later." She stopped and took a breath, hot tears threatening to fall. "Turns out, on the day of our wedding, his wife went into early labor. I caught a flight to Auckland to be with Dad the following day. You know the rest."

"Are you saying he called off the wedding on the day?"

Tayla turned from the window. "He didn't call it off." She moved to the chair in front of his desk and sat, her hands trembling in her lap. "He didn't turn up…didn't call or send a message. He just left me waiting…all dressed up with nowhere to go. Fairytale over."

"He left you at the altar?"

She nodded. "When I found out about the baby, I understood why he couldn't contact me. Anna was in bad shape; they had to operate afterward. I'm not an uncaring person but finding out he'd lived a double life was the hardest thing I've ever had to deal with."

"Do you think he still loves you?"

"Who knows. When I returned to Sydney that weekend, I went to his house while he was at work, to collect some things. The moment I placed my engagement ring on his kitchen counter, a weight lifted. He was furious when he realized I'd been there and hadn't made contact. But what was the point? He's a very persuasive man. I didn't trust myself to be around him."

"So how did you feel when you saw him today?"

Tayla fixed her gaze on his. The air in the office was warm and slightly stuffy and she needed a drink of water. "Okay…once you came home." She caught his expression, wondering if he understood that her feelings for him were changing by the day. "I feel grounded here, does that make sense?"

"Not trapped?"

She shook her head.

VIRGIN BRIDE

THE HOUSE SEEMED empty without her, almost desolate. Mitch closed his magazine, put it on the nightstand, and clicked off the bedside lamp. He lay back, his fingers interlaced behind his head as he imagined the scene at the chapel in Sydney. Tayla, sitting in her wedding dress, waiting for a man who would never show.

His mind raced, the unease nothing to do with their contract, but rather, his growing feelings for her. That chemistry between them. Because, as much as she'd kept her distance with that air of indifference, Hayden's visit meant the pieces of the puzzle had slipped into place. He'd left Tayla at the altar, the jerk. How could he do that to her? And what about his 'virgin bride' comment? Surely Tayla wasn't still a virgin?

Slow things down.

Just as Mitch picked up his phone to check his texts, the bottom door opened and shut. He closed his eyes, feeling a release of tension as Tayla climbed the stairs. She went to her room without a word, and a few minutes later, the shower turned on. By the time she'd finished in the bathroom, he'd almost dozed off.

He rolled over to face her when she knocked on his door, the dim light from the hall washing her from behind. Dressed in a tank and skimpy sleep shorts, she carried a small pack of tissues in her hand. "Can I come in?"

"Sure. Are you okay?"

"I'm a bit fragile, to be honest."

Tayla moved to the bed and sat cross-legged on top of the duvet. His heart raced at the sight of her, and as she draped the throw around her shoulders, he sat up and rested his back on the headboard, so they were face-to-face.

He inhaled, struggling to focus. "Have you been at yoga all this time?"

"No. It finished about an hour ago, but I went for a walk along the boardwalk."

"I don't like you walking by yourself at night."

"I needed to clear my head. It was full of what-ifs and maybes." She fiddled with the hem of the throw, twisting a snagged thread with her fingers. "Anna called me this morning."

"Who, the wife? Did you talk to her?"

"Not for long. Well, she talked, I listened, then hung up on her. She's...loud and brash. Hayden's such a gentle man—traditional and articulate. They don't seem to fit somehow. It was weird; even weirder when she said that monogamy threatened her independence."

"She's in favor of his extended family suggestion?"

"Apparently. Seems I'm the only one who's not. I guess that's me—old-fashioned Tayla. She said they have strong sexual chemistry, but she doesn't want a full-on relationship."

"Does that make you sad...knowing they have that chemistry?"

Frown lines tracked across her forehead. Mitch waited for her to reply, to confide.

"It's something we never explored. We were waiting until after the wedding."

Hayden's 'virgin bride' comment flashed through his mind again. "So, you guys never...?"

Tayla shook her head. Broke eye contact. Mitch wanted to

reach out—to hold her—but it wasn't the right time. He didn't want to confuse her. She had to come to him on her own terms.

"I don't know why. Maybe he didn't love me after all."

"I doubt that's true," he said gently. "He flew from Sydney to woo you back. I'm sure he loves you a great deal."

"Or the thought of me perhaps—pure and untouched." She pulled a tissue from the pack and blew her nose. "Looking back, I can't believe I went along with it...our 'intellectual relationship' as he called it."

Mitch wanted to ask the obvious question but decided against it in case he'd misinterpreted her meaning. Surely she'd had boyfriends at university? He'd heard of the born-again virgin movement, thought it was ridiculous. You were either a virgin or you weren't, but maybe Tayla had been celibate since meeting Hayden.

"When he turned up unannounced, I was terrified. Not of him, but of my own feelings—scared I'd look at him and that love-light filter would be as strong as ever."

He waited. When she didn't continue, he took his cue. "And is it?"

"No." She looked at him now, the half-hearted smile on her lips not making it to her eyes. "In a way, that shocked me. That feeling of being free from his...control is the wrong word, but I'm tired and can't think straight."

Having felt the same way when he finished with Prue, Mitch understood. "I get it."

"Anyway, I'd better go to bed. Thanks for the ear. I'm sorry I've been distant, but those first few months I questioned every decision I'd ever made, wondering why I wasn't good enough. And as the weeks passed, I sometimes forgot the person I'd spent months investing my time in wasn't there anymore."

"You mean Hayden?"

Tayla nodded.

"I understand. It took me a long time to get over Prue."

"What happened…with you and Prue?"

"Same shit, different scenario." He leaned his head back and sighed. "I thought I'd miss her much more than I did…I do. And I did at first. Now, I'm just relieved it's over."

"Are you saying that she cheated?"

"Yeah, and spectacularly. It seems threesomes were the flavor of the month back then. Luckily, I didn't know the other two guys. I tried to get over it—forgive her—but in the end, I'd lost that trust."

They stayed silent for a few moments. Mitch wished she would slip into bed with him, for them to make love and shut the world out for a while.

"If you want to go back to Sydney, I won't stand in your way. Now the sale's been finalized, I can tell Ken you've got work commitments there."

Tayla buried her face in her hands. When she finally looked at him, he knew he'd said the wrong thing. It hadn't occurred to him she might want to stay, no matter what she'd told Hayden.

"Thanks." She stood and folded the throw, then placed it over the end of the bed. "But I need to be here for Mum and Dad."

He reached out, offering his hand. "Hey, come here."

Tayla glanced toward the door, her hesitation giving Mitch a small ray of hope. She looked back, shaking her head. "I'm sorry. I can't. Not tonight."

―――――――

Freedom. Such a strange concept. Something people often longed for from the security of a stable yet stale relationship. But freedom comes in many forms, and without love and friendship, freedom easily slips into loneliness.

Tayla returned to her bedroom and shut the door. She'd known that Hayden would crash back into her life at some stage. He seldom took no for an answer. And while waging a vendetta wasn't his style, Hayden had no difficulty in getting his point across.

She'd once seen herself in the same vein—articulate and self-contained—and with a determination to make the most of her freedom, Tayla had wanted for nothing. She'd shopped, eaten, and breathed city life. Traveled to Bali for yoga retreats, gone to concerts and stage shows, lived the dream.

Life had been full, but when she'd let the mask slip, empty all the same.

Self-assuredness aside, she'd wanted a romantic relationship for years. Longed to marry and have children, to lie in bed on a Sunday morning in the arms of her man after a wild night of heady pleasure.

And when her Sydney girlfriends had complained that most men had one-track minds, she understood. She thought about sex too. A lot. Longed for it, marveled at the concept. After all, sex was arguably the strongest instinct known to mankind. And when you're denied something, you crave it more. Much like being on a crash diet.

Hayden had called in that morning to drop off the key, full of apologies and solutions. He and Anna had it all planned out. Tayla just had to play her part. Toe the line.

Hell no to that!

Her heart had raced as he'd tried to kiss her goodbye. Not with excitement but alarm. When she'd pushed him away, he'd thrown his hands in the air and stormed off. She'd rarely seen him sulk, but when she had, he'd done it well.

Now Mitch had set her free before they'd had a chance to visit his marriage with benefits suggestion. Set himself free as well, she suspected. Not that she blamed him. Tim always said that it can take six months to get over a bad breakup. If you hadn't moved on in six months, it was time to stop the pity party and see a shrink. As usual, Tim was right. And while Tayla hadn't reach that milestone yet, she'd moped around long enough, dragging her baggage behind her.

But when the dust settled, she knew her feelings would still be the same. She didn't want Hayden and Anna and a stepchild. She wanted Mitch.

Hello, freedom, you old bastard of a friend.

QUIET REFLECTION

Two DAYS after Hayden and Anna's departure, Tayla took the river track to Cherry Grove for a stroll around her mother's garden before sunset. With the sale finalized and the tenants not yet in residence, it gave her time to let go. When she reached the house, pruned rose bushes and lavender trimmed into tight balls ready for spring greeted her. That was how Mitch operated—everything done with an efficiency Tayla had never mastered.

Sitting on the steps of the veranda, she recalled the many nights she'd lain awake in her room, wishing for a boyfriend, her imagination running sexually wild. Fueled by stories from her sisters and peers, she'd dreamed of nights where stolen kisses and hushed tones would lead to messy, passionate sex in the back seat of some boy's borrowed family car.

But her dreams remained just that. Figments of her overactive imagination. Because for Tayla, no boy ever showed an interest. By the time she'd met Hayden, she'd resigned herself to a life of what her Great-aunt Annie had referred to as spinsterhood. That barren existence so earnestly portrayed in historical novels and movies. It was either that or submit herself to the pick-me-at-any-cost scenario. Where sex was offered to and by jerks with no thought or feeling—until the booze wore off.

When Tayla met Mitch in Norman's sunroom in her eighteenth year, she hadn't realized he was 'the boy'—the grandson who'd come and gone like a proverbial ghost from Norman's life. A man in his early twenties, he'd seemed so unavailable then. With his height and bulk and inquisitive eyes, he was as handsome as any man she'd ever met. She'd babbled on about groceries and library books and insisted there must be some mistake when Ken told her Norman had passed. But Mitch had remained silent as he'd looked upon her with pity.

Or had he simply shared her pain? After all, he'd lost his grandfather that weekend. A grandfather he seemingly loathed and loved in equal measure.

And now they were married—albeit a marriage of convenience. Mitch had suggested they become lovers without ties or commitment. Lovers without love. And while she'd imagined being with him in those times of quiet reflection, she'd never in a heartbeat considered he might reciprocate the notion.

Later, she climbed the stairs to the loft and slipped into the bathroom for a shower, leaving him to work undisturbed in his office. As the water soothed her skin, the billboard flashed through her mind. It wasn't there any longer, replaced two days earlier by a new BMW advert. She missed it. Missed his smile even more than those perfect abs. And the longer they stayed together, the more she'd liked the comfort of Mitch watching over her as she drove toward Lime Tree Hill after work.

She imagined having sex with him. Was he a lights-on or a lights-off kind of guy? Would he take care of her needs or simply use her as an outlet for his frustrations? Had he been with anyone else since they'd eloped? Would sex with him be a moment of tenderness or a time of regret? Questions flooded her thoughts until she had to shut them off along with the water.

As she walked back into the kitchen for a glass of juice, he called to her.

When she popped her head around his office door, he sat forward in his chair and steepled his hands in front of him. "You okay?" It reminded her of their wedding day, when he'd demonstrated his caring side with such thoughtfulness. A side she'd seen more and more of since then.

"Fine. I just needed a walk. I had a call from Mum earlier. They're coming home this weekend. It will be strange seeing them crammed into their new place."

"Yeah, but their move couldn't have come at a better time. Imagine if they still had the orchard. Barry wouldn't have coped with that."

"You're right, but it's still the end of an era."

"Do you miss the house?"

"Yes, a lot, actually. It was always so full of life. Lots of noise —everyone talking at once sometimes."

"I appreciate what you did…the sacrifices you made so I could buy the orchard."

She swallowed the lump forming in her throat. "Thank you. But we both made sacrifices, didn't we?"

Mitch stood and walked toward her, offering a soft smile. He took her hand and gave it a slight squeeze. "I guess we did."

Was this their new normal? Touching hands and knowing smiles? Seduction without emotion?

Her hand slipped from his and she looked away. "You know what, I don't feel like cooking. Let's go into town and I'll shout you a takeout. We could eat at the beach."

"Sure, sounds good." He gestured for her to go first. "I'll grab some beers while you get your jacket."

They sat at the northern end of City Beach, two bento boxes on the picnic table in front of them. Mitch reached into the cooler bag and pulled out a couple of bottles of craft beer. He flipped the lids with an opener from his key ring, and for a moment, the differences between him and Hayden made her smile. Mitch, with his large hands and gravelly voice, had a bottle opener on his key ring. He offered her a beer much as Hayden would have offered her a fine wine and explained the bouquet as they sipped.

Tayla focused on the water, a fishing boat—a dark dot against the sunset—catching her eye. She inhaled; the smell of miso soup, seaweed salad, and tempura vegetables making her hungry after days of little appetite.

"Did you see Hayden before they left?" Mitch asked as he tucked into his meal.

"Briefly. He came over to drop off the key, then stormed off in a huff when I wouldn't let him kiss me goodbye. He texted later to apologize though."

Mitch didn't reply, conveying his thoughts with a slight shake of his head.

"I won't be going back to Sydney to live. Although, I do have to sort out my apartment soon."

He stopped eating. Put down his chopsticks.

"I know I've been withdrawn," Tayla continued. "But after everything that's happened and returning to Clifton Falls, I've struggled to pull myself through the mist. Do you understand what I mean?"

Mitch kept eye contact, sipped his beer. "Sure."

Tayla moved rice around with her chopsticks while her thoughts found order, the other hand holding her jacket tight against the wind. "Still, I'm over the worst. When I saw Hayden the other day, standing in the driveway talking to Ned as if he belonged, I despised him for his insensitivity."

Mitch reached over and fastened the jacket tab around her

neck. Such a small gesture, but intimate. Caring. "Do you still love him on a deeper level?"

She finished her mouthful of food. "It's taken me a while, but no. Seeing him in a different light the other day—that pleading, blame-shifting shit-show he put on—helped snip that last thread of doubt."

"But you still haven't blocked his number?"

She grinned. "It's on my to-do list."

Mitch chuckled. He picked up a piece of chicken with his chopsticks and took a bite. "I'm sorry I screwed up, with Cherry Grove, I mean. I've put you through a lot of crap."

"We did what we had to do. Hayden could have told me about Anna, but he chose not to. He lived a double life and thought I'd never find out. I've never considered myself gullible but, maybe I'm not such a good judge of my own character."

Mitch raised his beer. "To gullibility. May we both smother it under the weight of regret."

Tayla glanced his way and laughed. Some days, he said all the right things. She clinked her bottle against his. "I'll drink to that."

"May I ask you a personal question?" Mitch said after a moment.

"Depends."

He touched her hand, rubbing this thumb back and forth across her knuckles. "You said you guys didn't have a sexual relationship, Just how experienced are you?"

His bluntness surprised her. Apart from Ruby, no one had ever asked about her sexuality outright. She didn't reply.

"Sorry, it's none of my business," he said. "You don't have to answer."

They ate in silence until their bento boxes were empty. Tayla stood and stuffed the bottles and boxes into a bag for recycling. "I'm going back to the truck. It's freezing." She paused, her expression flirtatious. "And to answer your question, I'm not experienced at all."

Mitch picked up the cooler bag and followed her across the boardwalk. As he opened the truck door for her, she smiled her thanks. Once inside, he went to start the engine, then stopped.

He looked at her. "You're still a virgin?"

She hesitated. Exhaled. "Not by choice."

"Shit, seriously?" He leaned back in his seat, the keys still in his hand. "Don't you ever…wonder about sex?"

"Of course." She giggled, as she often did after a beer or two. "I'm not asexual, I've just never had the opportunity. That must sound strange to a guy like you, but not everyone's out there doing it all the time."

He grinned at her words. "But you're still open to us sleeping together?"

Tayla nodded. "I won't lie, I'm scared stiff of taking that step. I never had a boyfriend at school or uni. When I moved to Sydney, I went out all the time—quiz nights, speed dating. I still didn't meet anyone I felt a connection with. When I finally met Hayden, I hadn't been on a proper date in four years."

"I don't get it. Most guys would jump at the chance of dating you."

She shot him a wry smile. "Maybe it's the prissy stuck-up snob vibe that puts them off."

Mitch threw his head back and laughed. "I still can't believe I said that."

Tayla loved the sound of his laugh. Warm and throaty and teasing in its message. "Is that an apology?"

He leaned across the cab and kissed her on the cheek. "No."

ANTICIPATION

DRIVING HOME, Mitch tried to imagine a life sheltered from the usual teenage heartache and breakups. No necking in the back seat of a car, no fumbling with blouse buttons and jean zippers as sexual desire overtook all sense of reason. He'd had that, not as frequently as his friends thought, but his experiences had been rich and varied.

So how could he make the experience rich and varied for Tayla?

By the time they hit the highway, he'd devised a plan, the songs streaming from his phone in coincidental sync with his state of mind. The sun had set hours before, leaving the air frigid with the threat of a frost. When he drove past the orchard gate, Tayla shot him a sideways glance, then closed her eyes, her fingers tapping against one another in time to the music. She seemed to sense where they were going, as if their thoughts were somehow transcribed on the same page. That erotic narrative of a lovers' dream.

Petrie Bay was deserted when Mitch pulled in beside the thicket of pines, close to the spot where they'd recited their vows. He cut the engine. She stared straight ahead, as did he until she spoke.

"Why are we here?" she whispered.

"You know why." He tipped her chin with his finger and claimed her with a fragile kiss. She pulled back, understandably nervous. Shit, he was nervous for her—for himself. But he wanted her to experience the anticipation of wanting something so badly, she could hardly think straight.

She looked down, her hands fiddling with a button on her jacket. "I don't want my first time to be in the back seat of your truck. That would be so wrong at my age."

Mitch chuckled. "Duly noted. But a little necking while parked at a deserted beach on a winter's night is a rite of passage all of us should experience, even if it's only once."

He jumped out and rounded the truck to open the door for her. Tayla took his offered hand, and as he helped her down, she pressed against him. When he opened the back door, she climbed inside without hesitation.

She turned, her hand reaching for his. And as he cradled her face in his other hand and kissed her, he willed himself to slow it down. To build that anticipation over days until she thought of nothing but him. What he'd do to her. How she'd respond.

They kissed again, cautiously at first, and then with fevered intensity as he cupped her breasts and squeezed with gentle pressure, making her nipples peak beneath the cashmere of her sweater.

"You're a beautiful kisser," Mitch whispered, his voice husky in the dark.

"Am I?"

He nuzzled her neck, gently sucking the delicate skin. "You kiss like you've kissed many men and picked the best technique."

Tilting her head to one side, inviting him to continue, she murmured, "And you kiss like you know what you want and are determined to get it."

Mitch pulled back. "Determination is a prerequisite to success in my book. I want us to be a success, even if you only rate my kissing technique as satisfactory."

"I didn't mean it that way." She giggled.

"No?" Weaving his hand through her hair, he inhaled the smell of lightly spritzed perfume and fruity shampoo. "I love that sound. You don't often laugh. Why is that?"

"Is that how you see me? As solemn?"

"Sometimes. I know you've had heaps going on, but…well, there's a lot to be said for living in the moment." He traced his index finger down her nose, over her cupid's bow, and stopped at her lips, swollen under his touch.

"I didn't think you'd want to…" Tayla said.

"What? Have sex with you?"

She nodded.

"Seriously? Why wouldn't I? I blame that practice kiss. I felt drawn to you before that if I'm honest, but until I've kissed someone, I never know if the chemistry is really there or just an illusion. Those flutters in your belly, everything tightening with an anticipation you can't ignore."

Tayla shot him a sly grin. "So that happens to guys as well?"

"Sure. But maybe we're cockier about it. Well, I was back in the day. I like to think I have more self-control of late."

She glanced down at the bulge in his jeans, before flicking her lashes his way.

Mitch threw back his head and laughed. They kissed again, her hands in his hair gently tugging against his scalp. Slow, sensual kisses that built in intensity until he had to pull the pin. It had been months since he'd slept with anyone. When they made their deal, he'd told himself he could handle celibacy, but now he questioned where that fanciful notion had come from.

Pulling back, Mitch broke the kiss, his expression a mixture of amusement and affliction. He reached over her and opened the door. "Let's go get our feet wet before we head back."

With their shoes left strewn across the cab floor, they walked along the shore in silence. Reassuring her with his touch, Mitch pulled Tayla toward the water, his headlamp lighting the way. As they reached the swash, she stopped and hitched up her dress to above her knees. "It's freezing."

His back to the water, he stood and cocked his head. "You look puzzled. What are you thinking about?"

Shivering, Tayla stepped back until her feet were firmly planted on dry sand. "You. And anticipation."

In contrast to their drive to Petrie Bay, they talked freely on the way home. After the intensity of their make-out session, the distraction gave Tayla time to relax. To breathe. Mitch didn't seem breathless. Not one bit. She struggled to understand how he could be so casual when her insides were screaming to speed things up.

Once he'd parked in the garage, Mitch reached over and rubbed the back of her neck, the sexual tension at his touch instant. "We should say goodnight here," he said. "If we don't, there's no way I'll be able to hold back."

She leaned across the seat and kissed him. "Goodnight."

He pulled her closer, his hand stroking her hair. "Sleep well. You know where I am if you need me."

They climbed the stairs without words or connection. But when they stepped inside, he pressed her against the wall and kissed her breathless, his knee forceful between her legs.

"I thought you said—"

Mitch held up his hands and stepped away. "Life's heaps more fun when you buck your own rules. And I want you to remember one thing."

"What's that?"

"Attraction is mysterious. It doesn't always make sense, so relax, nothing's under control." Mitch inclined his head toward his office. "I have to check my emails. I'll see you in the morning."

She watched him walk across the living room, her lips tingling with want and her thighs clenched. "Okay. Goodnight," she said. But he'd already shut the office door.

Back in her room, Tayla sat on the bed with her head in her hands. Should she shower, eat chocolate, or jump online to order a vibrator? A discreet cylinder, one that hung from a neck chain.

Anticipation.

She'd wanted to take things slowly. But since they'd kissed with much more passion than their practice or the chaste 'kiss the bride' attempt—the pace felt more like torture.

On hearing the shower running in his en suite, Tayla's imagination shifted to a naked Mitch—one hand braced against the wall as he calmed his frustration with an eager fist, steaming hot water, and a series of murmured f-bombs.

In bed, she read for a while but found herself unable to concentrate as she willed Mitch to open her door. But as she snuggled under the covers, anticipation in her every thought, her sense of inadequacy deepened. Romance novels and movies aside, Tayla knew little about sex. Apart from a couple of times when Hayden had slipped his hand between her jean-clad thighs, no one had ever touched her in that way. What if she didn't please him? Would he show his disinterest or persevere?

And what if Mitch didn't please her?

For the next few days, Mitch crept into her bed in the early hours of the morning, but even though the lessons kept coming, there was never any suggestion of full-on sex. That feeling of him, half-naked and warm at her back as he cuddled her awake, was the best part of her day. And every morning, when he held her in his arms, she ached for him to slip inside of her, longed to feel his hands cup her breasts, his lips soft on her nape.

But on the fourth morning, his invitation to shower with him added another dimension to their increased intimacy. In some ways, Tayla wished she had the courage to invite *him* into the shower, rather than the other way around. But until they took that final step in the dance, she wanted him to lead.

They stood under steam-covered light, his biceps and the swell of well-defined pecs glistening with bodywash. Tayla had never showered with Hayden. Too tempting, he'd said. Now, with Mitch's hungry eyes watching her and his growing erection in her peripheral vision, she turned in hesitation, resting her arms above her head as he ran a soapy sea sponge along the length of her spine.

"Does that feel good?"

She leaned her forehead on the wall, closing her eyes as he crouched behind her and washed her butt and legs. "So good," she whispered.

"I'm glad. Some women are so self-conscious about their bodies. They can't relax when they're naked."

Despite being teased about her flat chest in high school, Tayla had never felt self-conscious about her body. It was what it was. A body that stayed fit and lithe. She looked over her shoulder at him and flashed a half-smile. "You think I'm relaxed?"

"Probably as much as I am. So that would be a no."

"If I wasn't a virgin, would you hold back?"

Mitch dropped the sponge and slipped his hand around her waist. His lips found her ear. "I thought that's what you wanted, to take it slow."

"It is, but—"

One hand slid between her legs, firm on her inner thigh. Tayla closed her eyes, held her breath as his body brushed against her.

"You want more?"

"Yes." She rested her head against him, the word a whisper to herself.

He gently slipped a finger inside. "How much more?"

"Oh...there. Just there!" She moved against him in a rhythm formed by instinct.

"You want me to make you come?" he asked, his breath hot on her ear, his erection hotter against her butt.

"I—"

A loud banging on the entry door made them both freeze. "What was that?" she whispered.

Mitch listened for a moment.

"Boss? Are you there?" Ned's voice boomed from the living room. "There's a problem with the conveyer belt. You'd better come take a look."

"What the hell?" Mitch removed his hand slowly. "Does the guy have no boundaries?"

"Didn't you lock the door?"

"No. I never do." He slapped her playfully on the butt, cut the water, then reached for a towel and wrapped it around his waist. "I have to go. Raincheck?"

"What? No!"

With Mitch gone, Tayla rested her head on the tile wall, lightly banging against it several times as she cursed under her breath. Maybe Mitch had planned it all along—told Ned to interrupt so his lessons of love held drama, want, and intrigue. *Men!*

"Just shoot me now," she murmured under her breath as she turned the water back on. She hadn't even rinsed the conditioner out of her hair.

Ruby: How's work going?
Tayla: Good. Busy. Just grabbing a coffee.
Ruby: Have you done the deed with that hunk of a husband yet?
Tayla: Currently experiencing frustration overload.

Ruby: What's wrong with the guy? You need to catch that train.

Tayla: We're standing on the platform. At my insistence.

Ruby: I feel guilty now.

Tayla: Why?

Ruby: Noah and I…we've done it 3 x in the past 24 hours. Blush. Blush.

Tayla: TMI! Take your finger off the keypad. Now!!!

Ruby: Just saying!

Coffee break over, Tayla slipped her phone into the pocket of her uniform and chuckled. Some days she had no idea what she'd do without Ruby. And after that shower, and those hands, and that last kiss on her nape, Tayla had definitely needed a good dose of Ruby's humor.

"What are you grinning about?" one of the nurses asked as he strolled into the clinic.

"Nothing much. Just an amusing text from my sister about husbands."

"Speaking of, how's Mitch?"

It seemed every other person she worked with knew she was married to Mitch, even though she'd never discussed him at work and hadn't taken his name. "He's well. Busy as usual."

"I nursed him after he tore his ACL. He's a nice guy."

Fighting to keep her face straight, Tayla tried to rid her mind of the shower scene and just how *nice* Mitch could really be. "Yeah, I think so too."

33

STAR RUBY

MITCH CAME in from the orchard to find Tayla settled on the balcony in one of Norman's old wicker chairs, a throw and wheat bag warming her stomach, and her copy of *Jamaica Inn* on the table. He bent down to kiss her. "Hey, are you okay?"

"Just a little time-of-the-month discomfort."

His hand stroked her hair. After Ned's interruption, the day had dragged as snippets of Tayla naked in the shower frequently flashed through his mind. "Do you need me to buy you tampons?"

Her lips twitched. "Um, no, but would you?"

"Course I would." He sat in the chair beside hers. "That's what husbands do, isn't it? Oh, and before I forget, the guys are coming at the end of the week to remove the cherry trees at your parents' place. I hope it won't upset everyone too much."

"Not at all. What have you decided to plant?"

"Star Ruby grapefruit. It's a Californian variety."

"Yum. I love grapefruit." Tayla shifted in her chair, pulling the throw tighter around her. "I'm glad you're turning it into a profitable unit. Dad will be pleased."

"We'll leave those two trees by the henhouse for us." Mitch

caught her smile. It was a little flirty, intimate. He kept seeing her like this—in varying shades of light—and when he thought about it, the adult Tayla wasn't so different from the teenager who'd stolen his grandfather's heart. Warm, kind, considerate to a fault. "Dinner smells good."

She went to stand. "It's all ready."

"You stay there. I'll dish up. Shall we eat out here?"

"Sounds good. And I picked up a bottle of wine on my way home. It's in the fridge, and so is the salad."

"Great."

When Mitch returned with the chicken and spinach pie, Tayla was staring out over the orchard toward the river. Putting their plates on the table, he wondered what she thought about in these times of quiet reflection.

She took a seat across from him and inhaled. "Yum. I'm so hungry."

"You start. I'll grab the wine."

They ate between sporadic conversation for the first half of the meal, but as the wine warmed his blood, Mitch asked, "How come you never had a boyfriend before Hayden?"

Tayla shrugged and finished chewing. "I was too shy to approach guys, and worse on the odd occasion one approached me. The longer I stayed single, the more it became the norm. Boys never sat next to me in class, or gave me their hoodie, or asked me out. I didn't ride around in cars or live at the beach all summer. I read, worked at the supermarket, and hung out with Tim." Tayla smiled at the recollection. "I guess you gave your hoodies to lots of girls."

"Nope, I never even knew that was a thing."

"Really? I had this friend, Ava. She was sweet and popular, but she lost her virginity to an older guy with a Harley when she was barely sixteen. She wore his hoodie to bed every night in the winter. He'd drop her off at school on his way to work. I was so envious. I went through a phase of wanting a boyfriend with a Harley too, even had a poster of a guy on a Harley on my bedroom wall."

"And what happened to Ava?"

"They got married and moved to Western Australia after she fell pregnant at eighteen. I remember one day at school, she told me about their sex life. I spent the entire lunch hour with my eyes as wide open as my mouth." Tayla chuckled. "Apparently he was quite the lover. We still keep in touch."

"Do you ever feel you missed out?" Mitch served himself another slice of pie.

"Not really. I may have been painfully shy, but I was content. Some of my friends had no interests apart from boys and makeup and clothes. I found it rather shallow. But then, Lisa didn't call me 'Tayla Superior' for nothing."

Mitch chuckled. "Do you get on with your sisters?"

"Mostly. Ruby's hilarious; she always makes me laugh. Lisa can be a tad judgmental. She told me I was mega-selfish for marrying you."

"Yes, you said that." He frowned. "Did it upset you?"

"No. It's just the way she is. She doesn't ask for details, just jumps to conclusions."

"And would you tell her the reason if she asked?"

"Probably not." Tayla reached for another helping of salad. "She loves to gossip. Not maliciously, but if she knew, so would everyone else on the planet."

Mitch topped up her glass, and then his own. "I have a motorcycle."

"What?" Her eyes widened. "You do not."

"I do. A Ducati. It's over in the shed by Ned's place, currently in pieces while I wait for a part."

"Will you take me for a ride when it's back together? I've never been on a motorcycle."

Mitch leaned over the table and kissed her. "I'd love to."

Dinner over, he picked up her book, removed the bookmark, and started to read aloud.

34

ELLA STONE

UNTIL NOW, Tayla had never fully understood the power of anticipation. Sure, she'd anticipated events in the past, many times. But the expectancy of what was soon to happen in the bedroom above the packing shed clouded her thoughts, making everything else pale into insignificance.

During the days following 'Showergate,' Tayla walked the beach every afternoon after work. Sometimes she'd hitch her dress up so she could wade into the cool surf, each time willing herself to take those few extra steps. But no matter how hard she tried to distract herself, thoughts of Mitch—his smell, his touch, his taste—were ever-present.

And now, it was Wednesday. With Mitch away for poker night, Tayla called Tim to ask if he'd meet her at the Surf Life Saving Club around five.

He arrived a few minutes after her, already wearing board shorts and a rash top. "So we're going for a swim?" Tim said as he opened the car door for her. "You do realize it's still winter?"

"But it's been such a beautiful day. The water can't be that cold."

"Did you bring a wetsuit?"

Tayla sighed. "No. I meant to grab it, but then Mum called, and I forgot."

"Just as well I brought a spare. I was at Petrie Bay yesterday. It's freezing." Tim opened the back door and grabbed the wetsuits. "Has Mitch given you any lessons yet?"

Tayla wanted to say yes, but Mitch hadn't mentioned surfing lessons again. "Not yet."

"I thought that was one of your conditions."

"It was, but we've been busy." She shot him a sly smile.

Eyes wide, he stared at her. "Doing what?"

She laughed. "Orchard stuff. He's replacing the cherry trees at Mum and Dad's with grapefruit this week."

"So you talk business together, do you?"

"Sometimes. You know how passionate he is about organics."

"I do." Tim flashed a wide grin. "Even so, it sounds to me like he wants you to be a real couple. Shit, you'll be having babies soon."

Chuckling, Tayla snatched the wetsuit out of his hands, and as she stripped down to her bikini and tugged it on, her body bumped with the cold. "I'm pretty sure you can't get pregnant just from kissing." She put her hand over Tim's mouth as he went to say more. She didn't want the third degree. And anyway, there was nothing else to say.

"Come on," she said, removing her hand. "I'll race ya. Go."

When she entered her bedroom later that evening, a red hoodie with 'Ducati' printed on the front sat folded on the end of her bed. Frowning, she read the attached Post-It-Note.

T
You want to wear my hoodie, babe?
M xx

Tayla smiled as she pulled on the hoodie and studied herself in the mirror. With the length and huge fit of it, she looked ridiculous. But it was warm and snuggly, and although she'd never seen it before, well-worn and smelled faintly of Mitch.

She moved through to the bathroom and turned on the shower, eager to wash away the salt and sand. The wetsuit's buoyancy had provided a level of security, and with Tim's encouragement, she'd dipped her shoulders under the swell twice without feeling rooted to the spot.

Small steps, significant gains.

Sleep was difficult to find that night. The loft was isolating without Mitch, and even though Tayla had lived alone in Bondi and loved it, she wondered how she'd feel when it was time to leave Lime Tree Hill. She enjoyed being part of someone's world. Part of a couple.

Most Thursdays, Mitch texted her around lunchtime, asking when she'd be home. But that Thursday, there was no text. When she walked through the door that evening, the place was a mess. Dirty dishes toppled out of the sink, and files and stacks of papers covered one end of the dining table.

She knocked on his office door to no answer. By the time Mitch bounded up the stairs, she'd cleaned the kitchen and made a start on dinner.

He picked up the remote and turned down the music. "Thanks for cleaning up. Sorry, the day got away on me," he said without offering her the usual hello kiss she'd come to expect.

"Is everything okay? You look exhausted."

He stood at the table, gathering files and papers. "I feel it too. Someone's stripped half our avocado trees."

"Who would do that? Aren't they too young to ripen?"

"That's what I can't fathom. The pricks must know that. What the hell were they thinking?" He ran a hand through his hair, not bothering to look at her, then sat at the table and shuffled through a file in front of him. "And now someone's laid a complaint against us with the OCA. We have a large export order ready for Japan, so it's bad timing."

"What's the OCA? Is it serious?"

"The Organic Certification Association. And yes, it's serious. They've ordered an audit of our practices. I've nothing to hide, but we'll be tangled up in sticky red tape for a while."

She wanted to go to him, to massage the tension from his shoulders, but his body language told her to stay back. "Will it affect your other exports?"

"Maybe." He stood and grabbed his jacket off the back of the chair. "Anyway, I have a meeting in town. I'm not sure when I'll be home."

"Do you want me to keep you dinner?"

"No. I'll grab something later." He kissed her on the forehead. "Don't wait up."

On the drive into Clifton Falls, Mitch berated himself for his own stupidity. He knew better than to engage with Ella, but when she'd arrived at the loft, upset after an argument with Chris, their history had tugged at his heartstrings. They'd met a few times after that night—for lunch one day and the odd coffee. But every time she quizzed him about converting part of the Stone and Pip Group's holding to organics, he couldn't help but doubt her sincerity.

Ella had always run hot and cold with Mitch. Whenever she and Chris had a major fight, she'd gravitate his way, arriving at the orchard in the early hours of the morning, or texting him throughout the night.

Now it was his turn to arrive at her place uninvited.

Ella pulled the door open, her perpetual smile firmly in place. "Mitch! I was just thinking about you."

Really? "Is Chris here?"

"Not right now." She stilled for a moment, offering a small frown. "Is everything okay?"

"I've had better days."

She stepped back in invitation. "Come on in. I have a new pinot you should try."

Mitch hesitated. Sharing a wine with Ella while she was home alone was not a smart move. But he stepped inside anyway, the aroma wafting from the kitchen making him realize how hungry he was. He followed her into the family room, removed his jacket, and stood while she checked the casserole in the oven.

"Please, sit. What do you want with Chris?"

"I thought he might be able to shed some light on why I'm being investigated by the OCA." He pulled out a chair at the breakfast bar and sat.

"What? When did this happen?"

"I received the email this morning. The inspector arrived not long after."

Her arms crossed, Ella rested her butt against the kitchen counter. "And you think Chris is behind it?"

"It fits his style. Has he mentioned anything to you?"

She held his gaze. "Don't get angry with me. It's not my fault."

"He's your husband. I don't need this kind of bullshit in my life. Doesn't the way he conducts business ever play on your conscience?"

"I'm not him, Mitch."

"No, but you're a director of the company. If he's meddling in my affairs as a 'concerned' competitor, surely you should've been informed."

"You don't even know if it *was* him."

"Who else would it be?"

"Prue? A jealous ex of your wife's?" Ella poured him a glass of wine, then topped up her own and slipped into the seat next to his. "Are you okay otherwise? I don't often see you upset."

"This investigation's a big deal. I could lose my main market while they search for something that doesn't exist. I have nothing to hide, but the inconvenience is huge. Especially at this time of year."

"I'll talk to him."

Mitch inhaled deeply then released the breath. He didn't need Ella acting as an intermediary between him and Chris. "No, it's all good. I'll call him tomorrow."

"He's in Auckland at a conference until the weekend. Why don't you stay for dinner? I'm sure Tayla wouldn't mind you spending a night in town."

The hairs on the back of his neck stood to attention. Ella had always been forward, but not usually as blatant as this. "Am I missing something?"

She leaned back in her seat, her fingers sliding up and down the stem of her glass as she spoke. "I'm not happy here."

That wasn't news to Mitch. Ella constantly thought the grass was greener. "Then leave. You've talked about it long enough."

She pulled a face. "Ouch. Don't hold back, will you."

"Look, I don't mean to be unkind, but I can't do this. Whatever we had ended years ago. At your insistence, I might add."

"So what? You don't even want to be friends now?"

"How can you sit there, basically inviting me to your bed, and have no qualms about who gets caught in the crossfire? This"— Mitch waved his hand between them—"you and me. It's not gonna happen. Ever."

"We were good together. Don't you remember that last night?"

"Come on, Ella. We were eighteen. I'm in love with my wife now. Differences aside, I suspect you feel the same way about Chris."

"Does Tayla feel that way about you?"

Mitch often asked himself the same question. He had no idea. "You'd have to ask her."

"I don't get it. You've never been one for rash decisions, but one minute you're licking your wounds over Prue, the next you've married the girl next door. So what was the deal? You take his youngest off his hands, and Barry Whitman thanks you with the deed to Cherry Grove? This whole sorry business has nepotism stamped all over it."

"Wow. You always have an uninformed opinion, don't you?"

Ella shrugged. Sipped her wine. "I saw her yesterday. Tayla." Her words sounded like an afterthought. A need to substantiate her judgment. "Down at City Beach with Tim, the photographer, frolicking in the water like freshly baked lovers. I didn't realize he swung both ways."

Mitch wondered how Ella knew what Tayla looked like. To his knowledge, they'd never been introduced. "They're friends. He has a partner."

"Yes, don't we all." She leaned forward, placing her hand on his thigh. "Sometimes, I wish society allowed us the freedom to enjoy alternatives; that's all I'm saying."

"Society has nothing to do with it." He lifted her hand from his leg and pressed it against her chest. "It's what's in here. I have no desire to invite a third person into my marriage."

"Well, by the way your wife was acting at the beach, it seems she's as bored with you as I am with Chris."

Mitch stood and reached for his jacket, leaving his wine virtually untouched on the counter. "I'll see myself out."

Mitch: You alone? Eaten?

Luka: All alone, and no. Are you in town?

Mitch: Yep. Shall I bring food?

Luka: Naan bread from Singh's. I have a curry on.

Mitch: Perfect. See you soon.

35

INDIFFERENCE

MITCH SLOWED as he turned into the driveway, the living room lights visible when the loft came into view. Once parked, he sat in his truck for several minutes, mulling over Ella's words, her blatant invitation, and with a touch of envy, the thought of Tayla and Tim at the beach together. He'd promised to teach her to surf but had been so tied up in his own world lately that he'd neglected to see how his preoccupation might seem to her.

He'd admitted to Ella that he loved Tayla, and once the shock of that admission sank in, Mitch realized it was true. He was in love with her. Not in the way that sexual energy takes over your soul, but that easygoing, relaxed love that's so much more than lust alone.

Even so, the physical need was a heady mix of anticipation and desire, and as he climbed the stairs, Mitch knew it was time. He didn't want to wait until he lost her through his indifference—or to some other guy who did seduction better. Maybe he'd left it too long already.

Mitch checked the clock as he opened the door. Ten after ten. Tayla lay asleep on the sofa, the TV humming just above mute in the background. He picked up the remote and switched it off. She stirred as he stepped closer, stretching her arms above her head, her cleavage visible through the gap in her bathrobe.

"What's the time?" she asked, her voice low and husky.

He crouched beside her. With her face fresh from sleep and lips softly smiling, she looked beautiful in her innocence. "Bedtime."

Tayla clasped her hands behind his neck. Her affection for him had grown over the past few weeks, and when they kissed, she relaxed under his touch. "I didn't think you'd come home tonight. I haven't kept you any dinner."

Taking her hand in his, he pecked her on the mouth. "It's fine. I went to see Luka. He fed me."

"He's a good friend." Her concern showing in her expression, she brushed a lock of hair from his forehead. "Is everything okay?"

"It will be soon." He kissed her again, but this time with increasing urgency. Grabbing fistfuls of his shirt, Tayla pulled him closer, the need of her touch matching his in a way they'd never explored. Different from the restrained make-out kisses they were used to, this kiss would break down that final barrier between them. A lovers' kiss. And when they let go, the memory would be etched on their hearts forever.

"I'm so pleased you're home," he whispered.

She frowned. "Where else would I be?"

"I don't know." Mitch snuggled into her neck. "And I don't care. I need you." Unsteady fingers raked through her hair as emotion welled in his chest. "You're here. That's all that matters."

Kissing her gently, he pulled her closer, her body tight and ready beside him. They stayed that way for a moment, connecting with touch, words lost in an air of want. He longed to bury his face between her breasts—her thighs—for her to tremble as he entered her and call his name as she came. But instead, he pulled back, tugging his shirt over his head with both hands. He wasn't about to make love to his wife for the first time on the living room sofa.

Mitch lifted her, and she instinctively curled her legs around his waist. As he walked to the bedroom, she pressed her lips to his neck. Those warm lips caressing his skin; that was it for him. His knees weakened, and when he placed her on the bed, he stared, the sight of her illuminated by the soft light spilling from the hall mesmerizing him.

He stilled, drinking her in, then sat beside her, easing off her robe while his heartbeat hammered in his chest. "Are you sure?" he murmured, struggling with his belt buckle. "Because if there's any doubt, any hesitation, stop me now."

"Don't you dare stop. Not this time."

"When did you get so bossy?"

"It's those lessons of love you've been giving me. I'm over the theory."

He laughed. "Lessons of love? Is that what we've been doing? More like lessons in frustration."

"Just be gentle," she whispered, her expression suddenly pensive as she held his gaze with wide-open eyes. "Okay?"

Mitch studied her—graceful and elegant, and her skin fair without that tinge of summer warming it. Was she worried he might hurt her, that she wouldn't enjoy it? He'd felt that way when he lost his virginity, too. Scared and excited and nervous as hell. Cupping her face, he smiled down at her. "You know what?"

Tayla shook her head.

"There's a little performance anxiety going on in my head right now too. First time ever."

Her teeth scraped across her bottom lip. "Do you want a massage? I'm good with my hands. It's my field of expertise."

Mitch watched her unzip his fly. She slipped her hands into his boxers, his body stiffening with pent-up anticipation under her touch. He closed his eyes, tipping his head back as she ran her hand down his length. "*Shit!* Knock yourself out."

"Tell me what you like."

His eyes still closed, Mitch sucked in a breath. "I like...our connection. *Shit, Tayla...*seeing your keys on the sideboard after work…knowing the wait is finally over." He moved into her rhythm. "And I really like…what you're doing to me right now."

"You do?"

"Oh yeah."

He placed his hand over hers. This night wasn't about him. "Slow down. It's been a while, and I'm losing control here."

Sitting back on his haunches, Mitch briefly closed his eyes and inhaled sharply, the throb of his erection almost unbearable. When he opened them, Tayla smiled up at him, both hands cupping her breasts. He lifted one hand and tenderly kissed the delicate center of her palm, then did the same with the other as she watched him with lust-filled eyes.

Mitch lay beside her, and she turned toward him, her hands caressing his chest as he slipped his arm around her waist and pulled her closer. They kissed, the husky groan in her throat all the encouragement he needed.

He brushed a hand over her breasts—small and perfectly round under his touch—his fingers doing their work until she arched her back, her breath hitching from her lungs in short, uneven pants. Her reaction amazed him. He'd expected her to be timid and reserved, but it was Tayla who guided his hand downward. And a few minutes later, when she came under his touch, it surprised them both.

Mitch reached for a condom from the nightstand drawer and put it on. Holding her with care, he entered her gently, stilling several times to catch himself as his need for release threatened to overtake his resolve. "Does this feel okay?"

She nodded. Held his gaze. Rocked into his rhythm. "Amazing."

They kissed again—the smile in her eyes his cue to proceed as she wrapped her legs around his waist and held on tight.

Mitch smoothed her hair away from her face with a gentle touch. "That flush on your cheeks…so damn beautiful."

"You make me feel so desired, watching me the way you do."

"I never want to look away. Haven't for weeks." His lips found her earlobe, neck, collarbone. "But I can't hold on much longer."

To his surprise, her release was as vocal and intense as his, and as they lay back on the bed, both panting for breath, all he could think was *fuck*. He turned his head to look at her, her hand resting at the base of her throat where his lips had been moments before.

"What's going on in that busy mind of yours?" he asked, unsure if he wanted a truthful answer. What if she hadn't enjoyed it? Although, she hadn't faked it. Of that, he was sure.

Tayla reached for his hand, her fingers warm as she traced back and forth across his knuckles, her touch featherlike against his skin. She sighed, closed her eyes, and whispered, "That was the most intensely beautiful moment in my entire life. Thank you for being so patient."

Rolling onto his side, Mitch propped himself up on one elbow, smiling down at her as he relaxed. He brushed a lock of hair from her face then kissed her—not passionately like before, but with appreciation, admiration. "Thank you for trusting me to be your first. I'm honored."

Her hand cupped his cheek, her face still flushed and her eyes wide. "So…was it okay? For you, I mean?"

He leaned in again, his lips soft against hers, then pulled back. "You were amazing. Was it what you expected?"

"Kind of. I didn't think it would be so intense…so all-consuming. Ned could have been banging on the door for ages, and there's no way I would have noticed."

Mitch laughed. He loved her playful side. Loved the look and smell of her, the delicate feel of her body under his, her enquiring mind. "Me neither."

"How does it feel for a man, you know, when you come?"

"Well…"

As the moon traveled across the sky, Tayla had stayed awake for a while longer, her thoughts in overdrive as she listened to Mitch breathing beside her. How had it come to pass that this man, Norman's grandson, was her husband—her lover? Was it fate or circumstance that brought them together? She'd imagined this night many times, but never in her wildest dreams had the fantasy matched the reality.

Making love to Mitch brought with it a new level of understanding. The intensity of losing yourself in the touch of another—the euphoria, and afterward, that feeling of pure contentment—was akin to a spiritual experience. The memory of his energy and power over her, and how she'd given herself to him without restraint, would stay with her always.

She'd expected it to hurt, and at first it had a little. But as they'd synced in beat and rhythm, the pain vanished. She'd also thought it would be over quickly, but there had been no haste as she released herself into his giving hands. Afterward, she'd wondered if Mitch would roll over and fall asleep straight away. But they coiled around one another as if bound together by an invisible cord, and talked until he drifted off.

And now, as the dawn chorus made a racket beyond their open window, she recalled the details—every kiss, every whispered command—and she wanted to reach over, take him in her hands and beg for more.

"Hey." He stirred, his breath puffing across her neck. "How come you're awake so early?"

Tayla looked at him over her shoulder and smiled. "Just thinking."

"And what's the verdict?"

"What do you mean?" She turned in his arms to face him.

He kissed her on the forehead. "In there. Do I still pass the test?"

She cupped his face. Kissed him. "I'm not sure. I might need you to repeat it before I award an A-plus."

Mitch chuckled. "So, you're giving me the opportunity to up my performance?"

"No. Just to match it."

He pulled her closer and whispered, "I like you, wife. A whole lot."

"I like you too, husband."

FLIRTING WITH INDECISION

WHEN SHE'D FIRST MOVED to Bondi, Tayla had walked past the Icebergs Pool at least three times a week. Sometimes, she'd lean over the rail of the boardwalk, watching swimmers glide through their lengths with ease, and wonder if she'd ever have the guts to learn to swim.

It had taken two years for her to find that courage and another year before she could comfortably swim in the outside lane, closest to where the waves crashed over the pool wall. But by the time she'd left Sydney, Tayla still hadn't ventured into the surf itself.

Mitch teaching her to surf had been a condition of their arrangement. But as the winter months slipped into spring, her board leaned against the garage wall, the bow still attached, and her wetsuit hung unused in the closet where he'd left it.

Tayla had never mentioned that condition again, and given his preoccupation with the business, she hadn't wanted to push the point.

So when he arrived home early the following Saturday and suggested they 'take her board for a spin,' she wasn't prepared.

The weather flirted with indecision: cold one minute, warm the next. And as Tayla sat in his truck, their boards strapped to the rack and wetsuits strewn across the back seat, that familiar panic held her in its tight grip.

Mitch pulled into a parking space south of Petrie Bay, where a cliff face calmed the easterly and the surf was soft and slow. As she watched the Pacific amble into the shore, she let out a sigh of relief.

He turned to look at her and reached for her hand. "Are you ready?"

Her mouth dry as she squinted against a brief flash of sunlight through the clouds, she picked up her water bottle and took a sip. "I'm kind of nervous to tell you the truth."

"That's understandable." He smiled. "You think I'll be a tough teacher?"

She took another sip. "Maybe we should go. I'm just wasting your time."

Mitch leaned over and kissed her before tapping her on the nose. "I enjoy wasting time with you." He opened his door. "Come on. It's the perfect day for it."

They donned their wetsuits without a word, then walked to the shore, their fingers entwined. Standing knee-deep in the water with her arms crossed over her chest, Tayla watched Mitch dive under. He resurfaced with a flick of his head. "Shit, it's cold." His hand outstretched, he waded toward her. "Come closer. I've got you."

Tayla stepped forward, the sand beneath her slipping through her toes as the waves receded. He held her around the waist and walked backward, guiding her past the breakers with steady steps and calming words. By the time she stood chest-deep in the water, she didn't know what took her breath away more. The cold water, fear, or Mitch protecting her with his body.

"You're doing great." He pulled her against him. "Wrap your legs around my waist. We'll tread water through this next swell and let it flow around us. I'll still be able to touch the bottom once it passes, so don't worry about being out of your depth."

She wrapped her arms around Mitch's neck as the swell lifted him off his feet. "I can't."

"Yes, you can. Breathe through it." He moved toward the shore and set her down. "What are you afraid of? That I'll let go?"

Tayla braced herself against a breaking wave. "No, it's just…"

"I won't let go until you're ready, I promise."

His words were a practical statement of their present situation, but Tayla couldn't help but think of the wider picture. He wouldn't let her go until she was ready. But would she ever be ready? Their association had a time limit; she hadn't expected it to last beyond a few months. And yet, here they were. Dancing through the waves of the make-believe world they'd created.

"Right." He took her hand. "Ready to go deeper?"

———

They'd stayed at the beach until late afternoon and arrived home tired and content, their skin polished by salt and intermittent sunshine. Tayla hadn't put her head under, but as they'd stood in the water, her arms around his neck and their bodies close, Mitch couldn't have been prouder of his wife.

Despite the twilight chill, they'd eaten filo-wrapped chicken parcels on the balcony while soft music and easy conversation flowed. He'd watched Tayla animated as she told a funny story with a twinkle in her eye. And at that moment, he'd wanted nothing more than to pick her up and take her to bed, to feel her lean legs wrapped around him, to lose himself in their rhythm. Because, while she'd been a virgin when they married, her new enthusiasm for him knew no bounds. And to Mitch, that was the best feeling in the world.

But first, he had some urgent work to attend to.

He looked up when Tayla knocked on his office door. She wore another satin slip, pearl white with lace trim and shameless darts pointing to her peaked nipples.

"What are you doing?" she asked.

He rocked back in his chair, enjoying the sight of her. "Just running some numbers."

"Come to bed," she said, her voice husky, her smile full of an invitation he couldn't refuse.

"Ask me again." He closed the lid of his laptop.

"I want you to come to bed...so we can make love and try something new."

A slow smile moved into play as he cleared his throat. "I'll be there in a few minutes. Keep the slip on."

Tayla walked toward him and leaned over his desk until her face was inches from his. "Only if you wear those tight boxers from the photo shoot."

"Come here." He tried to grab her by the wrist, but she pulled back.

She turned and walked away, and as he jumped from his seat and ran after her, she took off into the bedroom. They fell together onto the bed, Mitch on top, both of them laughing. It reminded him of the touch rugby game, but this time, she was his to have—willingly. He wrapped her in his arms and kissed her over and over, her mouth minty fresh, her scent wafting around him.

"Where do you want me?" he asked.

"On your back."

Mitch rolled over and lifted his arms above his head while Tayla tugged off his T-shirt. She straddled him, grinding against him as his erection strained beneath his fly. He moved to unbuckle his belt, but she stopped him. "Let me."

"I thought you never looked at me on the billboard."

Her hands went to work, and as she pulled down his zipper, he lifted his butt so she could remove his jeans. She admired his boxers. They weren't the ones he'd worn in the photo shoot, but they were just as tight. "Every woman in Clifton Falls looked at you on that billboard. Ogled you even."

He grabbed her butt with both hands and squeezed gently.

"*Every* woman ogled me? Including you?"

"Oh yeah, including me." She kneeled back, taking his boxers with her, her eyes widening at the sight of him.

Mitch placed his hands behind his head, grinning as his erection freed. "What are you going to do to me?"

Tayla crawled forward. Cradling his face in her hands, she kissed him before whispering, "Sit on top, but backward."

"Reverse cowgirl?"

She lifted her arms so he could remove her slip. "Yes. Reverse cowgirl."

He laughed deep within his throat, his hands around her waist. "Have I died and gone to heaven?"

"No, you're very much alive."

The next day, Mitch sat in his office, his eyes glued to the screen in front of him as he wondered what on earth was going on. Ever since they'd opened the larger premises, Lime Tree's farm gate store had enjoyed a string of four- and five-star reviews. But as he scrolled through the latest dozen or so, they were all one star, each a variation on the others. Rude staff, overpriced produce wilting on the shelves, out-of-date eggs and milk, stale ciabatta.

Weeks ago, when several of the grapefruit trees were stripped bare, Mitch had put it down to petty theft. Then they'd lost hundreds of avocados, stolen so early that there was no chance of them ever ripening. But when the complaint to the OCA had surfaced, he'd really started to worry. And now this.

"Shit!" He picked up his phone and hit Luka's number.

"Mitch. What's up?"

"What's the name of that private detective you play water polo with?"

"David Wong. Why?"

"Lime Tree Hill is under attack."

37

MOOT POINT

With Mitch away at his usual Wednesday night poker game, Tayla pulled into the retirement complex for a dinner date with her dad while her mother played bridge.

Jean greeted her with a warm hug and a smile when she walked into the room.

"Where's Dad? I just called in to see what he felt like for dinner."

"He'll be home soon. He's down at the center, playing mahjong with his cronies. It gets him out from under my feet. But you choose. You know he's not fussy." She narrowed her eyes. "You look tired. You're not pregnant, are you?"

"What? No! Of course not."

Her mother moved into the kitchen and poured two glasses of lemonade from a jug on the island. She handed one to Tayla. "Why did you say it like that? I know your generation thinks you can have it all, but don't leave it too long. Your eggs aren't getting any younger."

Moot point. "Obviously, but I'm only twenty-six." Tayla sipped her drink, the sourness making her wince, as did living a lie. And while her mother didn't need to know everything about her life,

Tayla hated keeping secrets from her parents. It was time to change the subject.

"I have to hop over to Sydney to sort out my apartment. If you guys are okay without me for a couple of weeks, I might go in the next few days." She took a bliss ball from a jar in front of her and popped it into her mouth, the sweet taste of dates and almonds settling her nerves a little.

Having spent all afternoon mulling over her options, she couldn't shake the feeling that returning to Sydney was something she should do sooner rather than later.

She needed that closure.

"We'll be fine. What about Mitch? Is he going?"

Tayla thought of Mitch, lying on the bed with his hands behind his head as he watched her dress that morning, that lazy gaze of his washing over her. Of his gentle touch and not so gentle release. "Probably not."

"He could do with a break. And you could too. Your feet have hardly touched the ground since you came home. Mind you," her mother continued, "without your help with the orchard, I don't know where we'd be now. And as for Mitch, I'm glad you've found each other. But...what are you so afraid of?"

Tayla looked up from screwing the lid back on the jar of bliss balls. "What do you mean?"

"With Mitch. I get the impression you're holding your breath, waiting for something bad to happen."

Her mother was right. That's exactly what she was doing. Holding her breath, marking time, putting her life on hold. "I've always been cautious; you know that."

"Let go a bit, eh? What's the worst that can happen?" She smiled at Tayla. "He loves you very much. The way he looks at you, with that warmth in his expression."

Tayla had to stop herself from rolling her eyes. Her mother was too cute. "You're such a hopeless romantic."

"You should try it sometime. Relax a little. There are no guarantees in this life, so we might as well have fun while we're here."

The loft was still when Tayla walked upstairs later that evening. She glanced up at the oversized clock, its steady tick reinforcing the feeling that something wasn't quite right. She'd just flopped down on the sofa when the phone rang in Mitch's office. Thinking it might be him, she ran to answer it.

As she picked up, she glanced at the screen saver of his desktop computer. A photo of her in her wedding dress, standing on the pancake rocks at Petrie Bay, a soft smile on her face, filled the screen. *What on earth?*

"Lime Tree Hill, Tayla speaking."

"Hi."

"Who is this?"

"What? You've forgotten what I sound like already?"

She tightened her grip on the handset. "Hayden? Why are you calling the landline?"

"Because you won't return my calls."

"I can't talk right now." Tayla sat at the desk, spellbound, watching as the screen saver flicked from one frame to the next—all wedding photos, all of her.

"Please don't hang up. I just... Oliver died. Yesterday. He was hit by a car while out riding his bike."

She swiveled in the chair, away from the screen, her hands shaking. "Oliver? No! I'm so sorry."

"Yeah, me too.

"Are you okay?" It was a stupid question, asked without thought. A knee-jerk reaction to news no one ever wants to receive. Of course he wasn't okay. Oliver had been Hayden's closest friend.

"I need you, Tayla. My life's falling apart. I don't love her like I do you. And now Oliver's gone. Just like that."

"Hayden, please don't—"

"I can be in Auckland next weekend. Fly up to meet me. We'll talk, visit the museum, eat some decent Kiwi food."

"I can't, you know that," she murmured. "I'm sorry for what you're going through, but—"

"You really do love him?"

"I wouldn't be here otherwise."

"Is that the truth, or are you scared to turn back?"

"Please don't do this. Tell me more about Oliver. What did you do the last time you saw each other?"

The call lasted longer than she'd expected as they reminisced about their friend. By the time Tayla sat the phone in its base, it was after ten and the loft had that lonely winter feel about it.

Tayla sat forward in Mitch's chair and watched the slideshow, warm tears trickling down her cheek as she struggled to pull herself together.

Memories of her life with Hayden and the bond of old friends filled her thoughts. She'd never see Oliver again, or stroll along the boardwalk on a Sunday morning. And if she stayed in Clifton Falls, she'd probably never again stand on Bondi Beach with her toes gripping the sand against the tide. Never take those surfing lessons she'd paid for.

Would she ever conquer her fear of the open water?

Tayla wandered into the kitchen and pulled a carton of frozen yogurt out of the freezer. As she ate, she thought of Oliver. His slow smile and quick wit. While she hadn't known him well, they'd struck up an instant rapport the first time they met. He'd been easy to talk to. Reserved and polite, but engaged and interesting, very much like Hayden.

Dessert over, Tayla was about to have a bath when her phone lit up with Mitch's number. She'd called him earlier to no reply, but now, after her conversation with Hayden, she was all talked out. Her finger hit *Accept* before she had a chance to stop it.

"Hey. Sorry I missed your call." He sounded tired, preoccupied, as was often the case lately. "What's up?"

"Actually, I wanted to run something by you, but we can talk about it tomorrow night if you're home."

"Tell me now. I have a few minutes."

"Oh, okay. I might go to Sydney for a couple of weeks, just until my next contract starts. My tenant's moving out, so it seems a good time to tidy up a few loose ends. What do you think?"

While Tayla waited for his reply, she wanted to fill the void but remembered to practice the pause.

"Right," he finally said. "When do you leave?"

"As soon as I can arrange a flight."

"Okay. Fine." Mitch's tone was flat, annoyed. She wanted him to say he'd come with her. That he couldn't bear for them to be apart. But possessiveness wasn't his style.

"I have three weeks off, so it's perfect timing before you leave for Milford Sound."

"Maybe you're right." She could hear music in the background as someone called out to him, and his muffled reply. "I have to go. I'll see you tomorrow. If you're still here."

He cut the call.

She sat at the kitchen island, her head in her hands. *Men!*

———

Tayla woke with a fright and sat bolt upright. Hearing a car on the driveway, she checked the alarm clock on her nightstand. It was after midnight.

The downstairs door opened and closed, and as Mitch walked up the stairs, she snuggled under the covers and waited. He didn't come in straight away. She heard him talking to Edward, the fridge open and close, and a few moments later, the light in the other bathroom switch on. She wondered why he was home. It was the first Wednesday night he'd spent at Lime Tree since she'd lived there.

Tayla rolled onto her side, and as he entered the room and slipped into bed beside her, her whole body tensed with anticipation. She still couldn't get over how sensual she felt whenever he was near. Although she'd never been attracted to the muscly type, when Mitch curled in behind her, one arm slipping under her pillow and the other pulling her close, that sense of belonging—of being safe—had her swallowing a lump in her throat.

"Hey. How come you're home?" she whispered.

"I missed you. Needed a hug." He inhaled deeply, his face nuzzling into her neck. "You're everything that's good in my world, do you know that?"

Tayla turned in his arms. He cradled her face with gentle hands and kissed her, his erection stiffening between them.

"About Sydney," he said, his voice soft and his tone sincere. "You don't have to ask my permission to live your life. I'm not your keeper."

"I know that, but I didn't want to make plans without telling you."

He kissed her again and pulled her closer. As usual, her response was swift and strong. That flutter in the pit of her stomach, the tightening of her breasts, and the way her hands reached for the silky warmth of him without thought or control.

It had started to rain—soft patters on the iron roof and a light trickle down the windowpane. And in the distance, a muffled clap of thunder announced the onset of the forecasted storm. They kissed. Touched. Smiled. Mitch's hand slipped between her legs, holding her hostage, her release at his control.

A security light flicked on with a gust of wind, casting a shadow across his face. Closing his eyes, he murmured her name under his breath.

Mitch reached for a condom and watched her roll it on, a half-smile playing on his lips. Tayla tightened her grip around his erection as his breathing quickened, thoughts of Sydney pushed aside as she fell under his spell.

"You don't know what you do to me." He rolled her onto her front and lifted her butt into the air. "I need to be inside you."

It was her new favorite position, and as she braced herself against him, Tayla closed her eyes tight and let him take her hard and fast until she could no longer think straight. She called his name as she came, and moments later, he collapsed on top of her, his face in her neck as he too let go.

3 8

WHISPERED HESITATION

THE FIG LEAF, a vegan eatery on the waterfront, was fast becoming a favorite haunt. The following day, as Tayla walked into the café for a slice of their famous tahini caramel brownie, she thought of Oliver. He loved brownie. Incredibly fit and fastidious about his diet, it was the one treat he'd allowed himself whenever she and Hayden met him for coffee.

Just as Tayla was about to leave with the tiny treat box in hand, she spied Mitch on the other side of the room, dressed in the shirt she'd bought him for his birthday. As she watched, a tall, elegant woman with a slick blonde bob and full lips walked from the restroom and joined him at his table. Wearing wide-leg pants, the color of pumpkin spice, and a black blouse unbuttoned to show a delicate amount of cleavage, his companion was so poised and stylish that Tayla couldn't take her eyes off her.

Any other day, Tayla would have gone over to say hello. However, a whisper of hesitation stopped her. She observed their interaction for a moment. Running her fingers through her hair, the woman laughed at something he'd said. She then leaned forward, and when the server approached their table, she barely looked away from Mitch.

Tayla took a deep breath and walked out the door. If he wanted her to know he'd had lunch with another woman, he'd tell her. If not…well, it was none of her business. And yet, as she crossed the street to her car, her stomach tied in a tight knot, she couldn't get the image of the other woman out of her mind.

With thoughts of Mitch crowding her head for much of the afternoon, Tayla left work early and stopped at City Beach to unwind before going home. As she walked barefoot along the shore, she questioned her reaction to the sight of her husband having lunch with his friend.

When she'd found out about Hayden and Anna, the emotions that overwhelmed her hadn't so much included jealousy. Hurt and anger and denial—that's what had consumed her. But seeing Mitch with the stylishly dressed woman that afternoon had certainly had an effect.

When she arrived home around six, Mitch was working in the packing shed office. She poked her head around the door. "Hi. How was your day?"

Still dressed in the same shirt from earlier, he looked up, preoccupation dulling his expression. "Not bad, yours?"

"Great. What time will you be finished?"

"Actually, don't worry about dinner for me. I have to shoot into town. I'll grab something later." He glanced at his computer screen then back to her, his hand still on the mouse. "Did you book a flight?"

"Not yet. I'll look after dinner."

She stayed in the doorway, trying to gauge his reaction, but it wasn't immediately evident.

"Okay."

"Also, full disclosure, Hayden called yesterday."

Mitch gave a small nod and continued to study her. "So that's what going to Sydney's about? Hayden?"

And there it was. The reaction. Maybe Mitch was the possessive type after all.

She paused, determined not to rise to his annoyance. "One of his close friends was killed in an accident. He called to let me know."

"So he reached out to you. Isn't that what his wife's for?"

"I knew Oliver too." She crossed her arms over her chest. "I had a right to know."

"Fair enough. How come you didn't mention it last night?" The coolness in his mood persisted. A side of him she wasn't familiar with.

"Because I wasn't expecting you home. We just talked, Mitch."

"And yet, as soon as he calls, you're off to Sydney."

"To tie up loose ends. I want to bring my scooter home, and I still have a few things in my apartment."

"Fine." He stood and grabbed his jacket off the back of the chair. "Anyway, I have a meeting in town. I'm not sure what time I'll be home."

Tayla followed her moody husband out of his office but she didn't wait for him to lock the door. And as she climbed the stairs to the loft, Edward two steps behind, she wondered if his reaction was simply another stage in their relationship.

That of the jealous lover.

Standing at the kitchen window, Tayla watched his truck speed down the drive and turn right onto the highway. He hadn't even registered when she'd told him about Oliver. He'd been too busy being jealous of Hayden.

Well, he could stew all he liked. There was no point in standing on the sidelines of life, waiting for something to happen. She'd told CeCe she didn't want to be that clingy girl, and she was determined not to be.

Later, with the lights dimmed and Mr. Edward tucked up in the office, she grabbed an orange from the fruit bowl and sat at the island, peeling the fruit with her fingers. While she ate, yesterday's conversation with her father played in her head as the dishwasher hummed through its cycle. They'd discussed the tale of Hayden—sordid and otherwise—and also her parents' dire financial situation and the insulting offer Chris Stone had tabled last year as he'd tried to get his hands on Cherry Grove. When they'd said their good-byes, her father couldn't hold back the tears.

As soon as she heard the Hilux pull up outside, Tayla went to bed and lay there waiting, unable to get Oliver or the scene at Fig Leaf out of her mind.

Mitch showered in the other bathroom, as he often did if he thought she was asleep. By the time he tiptoed into the room, eased back the covers and slipped in beside her, she'd almost dozed off. He cradled a hand on her hip, the weight of his touch reassuring. "You're still awake?"

"Only just."

"I'm sorry about this afternoon." He snuggled closer. "For being callous about your friend."

Tayla turned. Warm tears surfaced, and she blinked them back. "He was a good guy, always happy to see you."

His strong arms encircling her in his warmth, Mitch kissed her with tenderness. "Do you miss your Sydney life?"

No one had ever asked her that. Not even Ruby. "Sometimes. Maybe I'm just a city girl at heart."

"Maybe you are." His words held a note of inevitability—a resignation she couldn't process. Would this be the point where he gave up on her?

"Dad and I had a talk last night."

Mitch smoothed a lock of hair from her cheek, his touch gentle. "How did that go?"

"Okay. He still doesn't want Mum to know about the orchard." She swiped away a tear. "I felt bad not telling him about us. He just wants me to be happy, and yet, I'm deceiving him, aren't I?"

"We both are to an extent. But our marriage is our business. What does it matter if we took an unconventional path?" He kissed her tenderly. "And I want you to be happy too, but you're not quite there yet, are you?"

The scene at Fig Leaf flashed before her again. "I honestly don't know."

39

NEW SOUTH WALES

Springtime was Tayla's favorite season, and as she waited for Ruby's flight to land in Sydney, a pang of nostalgia for the city she'd once called home surfaced.

That aside, and despite the traffic, every day in Bondi Beach was a good day. Except, she missed Mitch. Although they talked most evenings, that unsettled feeling in the pit of her stomach never went away.

Their last day together had gone well, but as they'd driven to Clifton Falls Airport, Mitch fidgeting beside her, doubt had cast its shadow. Tayla hadn't asked him about his lunch date. Oh how she'd wanted to. But as she'd snuggled in his arms in the early hours of the morning, she hadn't had the courage to deal with that uncertainty before she left.

And when he'd held her and kissed her without restraint in the middle of a terminal full of travelers, she'd barely kept it together.

Shifting in her chair under the harsh lights of the arrivals hall, Tayla mused over the value of independence. Mitch was right. Before her return to Sydney, it had been months since she'd spent time alone. The realities of their marriage and relocating her parents had kept her busy and focused, but now the time had come for Tayla to regroup, decide her next move, her new path.

She stood as Ruby rushed toward her, a smile from ear to ear. They hugged tightly until Ruby pulled back. "You do realize they're forecasting a hot day? You told me it was pleasant."

"It is. Come on." Tayla took Ruby's case and wheeled it out of the terminal and across the parking lot to her waiting van.

As Tayla unlocked the door, Ruby chuckled. "What on earth are you driving?"

"I borrowed it from my neighbor. I couldn't pick you up on my scooter, now could I?"

"It looks like Postman Pat's mail van, but the flower model."

"They use it for their florist business. Just jump in before we get stuck in rush hour traffic."

All the way back to Bondi Beach, Tayla struggled with the stick shift while Ruby talked nonstop. By the time they pulled up outside her place, Ruby had given Tayla a rundown on the whole family and many of her friends as well.

Ruby stepped from the van and stretched her legs, her sight on the two-story apartment block in front of them. "Don't you get lonely on your own?"

Every day. "The owners are just next door if I need them. And there's always the noise of the surf to keep me company."

"Sounds like heaven."

"Yes, except...I'd forgotten what it was like, not having someone to share my life with. I miss him."

"I'm sure he feels the same way." Ruby followed Tayla inside. "I might have a quick shower to wash off the travel dust. I didn't sleep well last night. I was worried about being away from Noah and the girls for the weekend."

"Go right ahead. Then we'll hit the market."

Sydney's sky flushed with a brazen hue as the sisters walked toward their table in a bustling café on Campbell Parade. Tayla had been there with Hayden several times, and as she stepped through the door, the sound of the other diners humming around them, she'd paused to suck in a breath.

Their wine and food ordered, Ruby started the conversation. "Has Mitch mentioned coming for a visit?"

"No. He knew you were over for the weekend, so... Anyway, I'm sure he thinks I've come to see Hayden, so he's probably pleased to be rid of me."

"Does that worry you?"

Tayla shrugged. It did, but she was determined not to dwell on it.

"Have you talked to him about you and Hayden?" Ruby asked.

Tayla paused as the waiter served their wine. After thanking him, she continued, "Not a lot. Communication isn't a strong point for us. Especially when he's busy with the orchard."

"Well, he doesn't have that on his own. Noah hardly talks when he's bogged down at work. When he's really stressed, he's not even interested in baby-making practice."

"You said you weren't having any more kids."

"We're not," Ruby replied with a wide grin. "But we've never stopped refining the process."

"I see you still take your job as Ruby Tuesday's communications officer way too seriously."

"Only with you, Tayla Tilly." Ruby giggled.

Tayla sipped her wine. It was fruity and a little tart, just the way she liked it. "Mitch is so different from Hayden in that respect. We used to talk everything out."

"Except that one time when he didn't mention the baby business before your wedding day."

"Yes." It wasn't funny, but Tayla suddenly found the whole situation amusing. The limo, the chapel, the celebrant's expression as she'd hurried Tayla out the back door. She giggled. "Except that."

Tayla paused as a hot waiter, sporting a man bun and a twinkle in his eye, served their mains. Ruby kicked her under the table, and as he walked away, the giggles started again.

"Anyway"—Ruby stopped to compose herself—"returning to the subject at hand, what are you afraid of? That Mitch doesn't love you? Because if he doesn't, tough titty."

"Tough titty? Who says that?"

"Excuse me." Ruby cut into her chicken. "I'm trying to impart words of wisdom here."

Stabbing a potato with her fork, Tayla smiled. "Go ahead."

"But if he does, and you're timid and unsure, that doesn't make for an equal partnership. And equilibrium is the key to a successful relationship, don't you agree?"

"Yes, but—"

Ruby pointed her knife at her sister. "Stop right there. Do you want to be a 'yes but' girl all your life? Let's break it down. What's your main concern?"

Taking a calming breath, Tayla sat up straighter. "I can't stop thinking about him…you know, in that way. Being apart makes it worse. I even dream about him sometimes."

Ruby leaned across the table and whispered, "Sex is your main concern?"

"It's okay for you. You started young. I had no idea what I was missing. Now it's as if we have a connection that I can't explain or comprehend."

"Excuse me. I was a perfectly respectable eighteen when I started," Ruby said, her lips twitching at the corners. "So, I take it he's good in bed?"

Heat crept up Tayla's neck and face. She had no comparisons to draw from, but even so… No man made love to a woman the way Mitch did without knowing a thing or two. "Don't be nosy."

Ruby laughed. "He's good. In fact, by the look of that blush on your cute little cheeks, I'd say he's *exceptionally* good."

"We've only been intimate for a short time, but it's like I'm a different person. Guys never noticed me before, but since I've... well, I can feel it—that interest from men. Weird, don't you think?"

Ruby lifted her glass toward her lips but stopped halfway. "Doesn't that make you curious?"

"About what? Sleeping with someone else?"

Her sister shrugged.

"No, I couldn't think of anything worse."

"Yeah, I'm the same. Imagine showing your bits to another man." Ruby raised her wine glass in a toast. "Congratulations."

"For what?"

"You, my baby sister, have finally fallen in lusty love."

Tayla clinked her glass against Ruby's, unsure of how to respond. All this time, she'd convinced herself she wasn't falling in love with Mitch. But lust? Tayla was definitely in lust with her husband. Maybe 'lusty love' was just another term for sexual chemistry. "I have, haven't I? That's crazy!"

Tayla climbed off her scooter and removed her helmet before strolling down the path and up the steps to her front door. A pair of running shoes to the left of the mat puzzled her. Her sister had left two days before, and anyway, they were much too large to be Ruby's. Once inside, she checked out the tiny living area, then tiptoed to her bedroom and peeked around the doorjamb.

Mitch lay naked on the bed, a sheet draped across his lower back, a paperback face down on the pillow next to him, and his rounded butt on full display. He stirred and rolled over, the filtered glow through the shutters casting ribbons of sunlight across his chest. Her eyes widened at the sight of his erection tenting the cotton sheet. She stared as he flashed his lazy smile.

"You're home." He sat up and propped the pillow behind his head, seemingly without a care in the world.

Tayla stayed glued to the spot. "What are you doing here?"

He laughed. "Visiting my beautiful wife."

She stepped forward. "Why didn't you tell me you were coming? Everything's almost packed, the fridge is bare, and I need a shower." She paused for a breath. "And how did you get in?"

He held out his hand. "Hey. Come here."

She sat beside him, bursting into tears as relief washed over her. "I can't believe you're really here."

Cradling her face in his hands, he kissed her with care. "I missed you. Your landlady thought me turning up on your doorstep unannounced was so romantic that she didn't hesitate in letting me in."

"Mavis has always been too trusting. You could have been anyone."

"I showed her a picture from our wedding. She ended up scrolling through the lot. Anyway, I thought you might need a hand."

"Thank you," she whispered. "I should go shower."

Mitch shook his head. "That can wait." He reached for the top button of her blouse, his eyes never leaving hers as he set each button free. "It's hot, let's get you naked. I'm so horny, I can't think straight."

She wanted to crawl onto his lap, take him in her hand and guide him inside her without foreplay or words or restraint. But instead, she stayed still while he undressed her, his hands warm against her skin, and his pupils dark as he watched her.

They lay on their sides, the need to reconnect fierce between them. Although Mitch had undressed her gently, that's where his hesitation ceased. He took her mouth with his, and she moaned, the salt of her tears drying on her cheeks.

He was there, and she'd never imagined how totally absorbing reunion sex could be. "I don't want you to sixty-nine me."

His head fell back, and he laughed. "Tayla Whitman, I've missed you so much. No sixty-nine. Got it."

She giggled. "It's been a long day. And I need you inside of me. Now."

Two fingers slipped into place. "I love it when you boss me around."

She rocked against him, desperate for release. Watched him. Smiled. Tensed.

"Let go." He tugged hard on her nipple, and that, coupled with the sensation of his fingers curling inside her, had her arching toward him. "Have you missed me?"

"Mitch...please."

He stilled. "I asked you a question."

"More than missed..." She paused on a shaky breath as he entered her. "Oh, you feel amazing. So. Amazing."

They stayed in bed for a long time afterward, the fan above them ineffectual against the humidity, and the ever-present rhythm of the waves three short blocks over barely audible.

"Are you still mad at me?" she asked. "For coming here?"

"I wasn't mad about you coming to Sydney." Mitch brought her hand to his lips and kissed the center of her palm. "But I admit, I was jealous *and* pissed off about Hayden. There's nothing I can do about it if you still have feelings for him, but..."

"I don't. But even though I struggle with what he did to me, I still care about him. Does that make sense?"

"Sure. That doesn't mean I trust the guy."

"But you trust me?"

"I trust you to be up front with me. I think the intimacy of our relationship warrants that, don't you?" He squeezed her hand. "Have you seen him?"

Tayla shook her head. "He doesn't know I'm here." Her mind flashed back to Fig Leaf. She'd almost managed to put the sight of Mitch and his companion out of her mind, to see it as an innocent lunch between platonic friends. But sometimes, in those pre-dawn moments when insecurities crept across her mind, she wasn't so sure. "And are you always up front with me?"

Mitch sat up and rested against the headboard, a frown tracking across his forehead as he rubbed his jaw. "I try to be, but some things might slip my mind."

She pulled the sheet over her naked breasts. Was now the right time to bring up the woman in the pumpkin-spice linen pants? "Like what?"

"I'm sorry I've been preoccupied lately, but someone's stirring crap back home, and I'm not sure who."

Maybe not. "Do you mean with the audit thing? You said it was sorting itself out."

"Yeah, it is, but we still had to dump most of last month's exports on the local market, which meant a sharp drop in revenue. But the orchard's almost debt-free, so we'll cope. It's nothing for you to worry about."

"But I want to support you." Tayla snuggled into his chest, sincere in her concern.

"You do support me. More than you know. It's been lonely at home without you."

She nodded. It had been lonely in Sydney without him too, especially after Ruby left. "Sometimes, I feel like we're on borrowed time…that I'm living someone else's life."

"We have the here and now." He pressed a kiss to the top of her head, his fingers tracing up and down her arm. "That's all we can be sure of."

He was right. Life could change with a conscious thought, in an unplanned moment, or because of a choice made by another. She knew that, but contentment sometimes nudged that thought sideways.

"Mitch?"

"Yeah."

"Did you ever think this would happen, you know, before we were married?"

He pulled her closer. "I knew our growing attraction could complicate things, for sure. That first kiss in my office stayed in my head for weeks."

"It really was an amazing kiss. But you said you weren't looking for a connection."

"Yeah, but I've never been one to hold back if a shift in focus is warranted. I love the connection we have."

"Me too. I'm sorry I misjudged you in the beginning. I thought you were ruthless and a player. But actually, you're a big softy. Romantic too."

He pulled back to look at her, his eyes bright with amusement. "Are you falling in love with me, Mrs. Harrington?"

She reached up and kissed him. "Maybe…just a tiny bit."

"I'm falling in love with you too, and more than a tiny bit."

Tayla closed her eyes, his chest smooth under her cheek. She'd once thought people put too much emphasis on the L word, but his declaration warmed her inside more than she'd ever expected it would. "Doesn't it worry you, how we came together?"

"Not one bit. The journey may have been unconventional, but the destination suits us both, and I'd like to settle here for a while. See how it goes."

"Me too."

"Great. Now, we need to get up, before that hand you're rubbing over my abs moves closer to another round." Mitch let her go and pushed himself off the bed. As he stood naked before her, she tried to maintain eye contact, but she couldn't resist a little peek at his pecs, his abs, his…

"You hungry?" he asked with a grin as he followed her line of sight.

She shot him a cheeky smile. "Starving."

He headed into the bathroom and turned on the shower. "Great, because after that emotional workout, I could murder a huge steak and fries, followed by a dainty crème brûlée, and washed down with a glass of cold beer."

"I know just the place. I love dainty crème brûlée. And it's my shout."

40

SURFING THE FEAR

MITCH HAD STAYED with Tayla for the rest of the week while she arranged for her Vespa to be shipped, and packed her remaining few things.

They'd booked into a B&B for the last two nights, and both evenings, strolled along the Bondi shoreline, hands entwined as easy conversation flowed. Afterward, they'd dined at a nearby eatery, then walked home again, eager to make up for lost time between borrowed sheets and tender moments.

Without the hum of the packing shed, the workers coming and going, and Ned calling in for cups of tea, their time together had felt like a honeymoon. Like lazy Sunday mornings spent in bed enjoying mind-blowing sex while drizzle dampened the earth. Exactly how she'd imagined honeymoon sex to be.

Now, back at Lime Tree Hill, the days blurred into each other as Mitch slipped into his work routine, and Tayla started her second stint as a locum at Clifton Falls General. However, when the weekend arrived, he relaxed again. So when he suggested a surfing lesson, despite the overcast day, Tayla took a deep breath and agreed.

They drove to the northern end of Petrie Bay, to the spot where a local surf school held lessons. With the Pacific calmer than usual, the waves rolled quietly into shore, and her stomach didn't flip as much as she'd expected. They'd had a few lessons since their return, each one building on the next as her confidence increased, but she still hadn't ridden a wave.

He cut the engine and took her hand, his gentle squeeze reassuring. Independence aside, Tayla enjoyed being part of a couple. That comforting feeling of someone having your back.

"Ready?"

Tayla nodded. She could do this—would do this—no matter how long it took to stand on that board.

When she first entered the water, those familiar feelings surfaced. But as they waded through the breakers, she reminded herself of everything he'd taught her so far. *Chin up, one foot forward, ditch the head trash.*

"Right, let's go over what we did last time," Mitch said.

Her first few attempts were a disaster. She spent more time off the board than on it. And as Mitch offered advice in his usual calm manner, displaying the patience of a saint, Tayla wished he'd step away for a while and leave her to it. She'd never been a team player, preferring to learn on her own terms and in her own time.

"You're too far back, and the nose is lifting. Find your sweet spot on the board when you paddle out. Let's try again. Once you hit white water, stay prone while you paddle in to get used to the feeling. Don't try to stand yet, okay?"

Tayla lay on the board while Mitch held it for her. "Okay."

"And remember to lose yourself in the landscape and ditch the head trash. You've got this." He pushed her forward.

She followed his instructions. Found her sweet spot and made it to the shore several times without incident while Mitch stood waist-deep in the water, watching her.

"Okay. That's good. You want to try to stand now?"

Standing up was all she'd thought about for the past half hour. She squinted against the sun. "I'll try."

Mitch waded beside her, staying close as she paddled out to find that perfect stretch of white water. He kept talking, his instructions precise, but often distracting.

Tayla stood on the board, barely finding her balance before the wave threw her off. She hadn't even lasted a few seconds. As saltwater rushed up her nose and into her throat, strong arms grabbed her from behind and pulled her upright. Although the water was only chest deep, by the way her heart raced, it felt like a twenty-foot swell.

Mitch dipped his head to meet her gaze. "You okay?"

She nodded, trying to catch her breath, a sudden cool breeze biting at her face.

"You're doing great, but you were looking down again," Mitch said. "We've discussed that, and your front foot's still too far back. Let's go again."

"There's just so much to remember."

"It's all about muscle memory, you get that, don't you?"

"Yeah. I get it." She wanted to add, 'It's my field, remember?' But it wasn't his fault she couldn't master the board. And it wasn't fear messing with her head, more her desperation to succeed.

She tried a few more times, the results always the same. Mitch watched intently, pointing out where she was going wrong as any good coach would. Once, he raised his voice in frustration, and after that, her resolve increased.

I can do this. I can do this. "I'm going again."

"No, you're not. It's time to get out."

"I don't want to get out. Just once more!"

Mitch stood tall, his arms folded over his chest, reinforcing his point. "No." He stretched the word out. "You're tired and cold, and if something *does* happen, you won't have the strength to fight it. Listen to your body and you'll be fine. Ignore the warning signs and you're screwed."

"I'm fine. I'm going again." She went to paddle away, but he grabbed hold of her board and pulled her back.

"You want to learn to surf, then know when to call it quits. Stop being so pigheaded and get your pretty butt out of the water."

"Fine." Tayla leaned forward on her board, turned, and paddled swiftly toward the shore. Smart people say you should never ask your husband to teach you to drive. It seemed surfing lessons fell into the same category.

Cold and upset, Tayla reached the truck before him. She'd tried her hardest but still couldn't master the gentle white water, let alone something bigger. By the time Mitch joined her, she'd peeled her wetsuit half off and was towel drying her hair.

"What's got up your nose?" he asked.

"What, besides saltwater, sand, and you? Nothing!"

He chuckled. "So, it's my fault, is it, Princess?"

"I wanted to try again. But you're the coach. And don't call me Princess."

"Fine." He tugged down his zipper. "Find someone else to stand in the freezing water all afternoon if I'm so hard to deal with."

"I will. Tim's offered, more than once."

"You want Tim to teach you? Knock yourself out."

Tayla dropped her bikini top at her feet and pulled his hoodie over her naked chest, then peeled off her wetsuit and flung it onto the tray of his truck. She wrapped a towel around her hips and waited in the front seat, her arms crossed and face tense.

They drove home in stony silence. The sun had dipped behind the hills, and her skin bumped with the cold. She couldn't wait to have a hot shower and warm up. When Mitch parked outside the packing shed, she flung open the door and stormed off without a word.

Standing in the shower, Tayla wondered why she was mad at Mitch instead of herself. As usual, he didn't come inside straight away. Having an orchard meant there was always something to check on, but maybe he was giving her space to calm down.

She'd just washed her hair when he opened the shower door

and slipped in behind her. She had to step aside as he positioned himself under the flow from the showerhead, his body hard against hers. She turned, and despite her annoyance, the sight of him naked and engulfed by steam almost took her breath away.

Mitch glanced down at her, no trace of softness in his expression.

"You're taking my water," she said.

"Get over it." He squeezed shampoo into his palm and started washing his hair, not bothering to look at her. "You're trying my patience, so I guess we're even. You need to learn to do as you're told."

"I can't believe you said that when you know my history. You're so insensitive."

"I'm not being insensitive to your fear. But when I told you to get out, you didn't listen. There's plenty of time to be perfect, but no, you want to surf like a pro without learning the basics first."

"I got out when you said."

"Yeah, and you're still mad about it. If you want me to teach you, you have to do as I say, understand?"

"I don't *have to* do anything. You men, you're all the same." Tayla seldom raised her voice, but she wasn't opposed to a little agitation creeping into her tone. "It's always about you."

"Hey." Mitch lifted her chin with his hand, his dark eyes staring into hers. "Let's get one thing clear." He bent and kissed her, his tongue firm against hers, then pulled back. "I'm not like any other man you'll ever meet, and you're not like any other woman I'll ever meet. And you know why? Because we fit. Understand?"

She understood, so much so that she struggled for a comeback.

Needy lips found the side of her neck—one hand on her breast, his touch wild and urgent. "So, let's cut the crap," he whispered, his breath hot against her ear. "Because the moment you dropped that scrap of fabric you call a bikini top and pulled my hoodie over your naked breasts, I wanted to pin you against my truck and fuck you until your knees buckled and your heart pounded in your chest. To make you breathless and wet for me until I controlled your thoughts *and* your body."

She tried to suppress her smile, the effect of his words immediate. *Like gravel on velvet.*

"It's not your hoodie," she said, her last attempt at defiance. "You gave it to me, remember?"

He gently pushed her against the wall. Another desperate kiss followed as he eased her legs apart with his. "I did. Now, I want something in return." He dropped to his knees and buried his face between her thighs, his hands pinning her hips against the tiles. He pulled back, looked up. "And I'm going to make you come so hard, you won't know what's hit you. If you don't want this, say so now."

"Yes!"

"Yes?"

Raking her hands through his hair, Tayla braced herself against his intention. "I want this…so bad."

When they'd left the beach, she could hardly speak to him. Now, with his hands holding her still, and his lips and tongue reducing her to a quivering mess, she forgot about the surfing lesson, his attitude, and finally, why she was even mad in the first place.

Mitch moved his lips and hands up her body, "You have perfect breasts. Small and firm and just begging to be touched."

She trembled, moaning his name softly, her legs turning to jelly and her heartbeat racing in her chest as he reached for a condom from the vanity drawer and rolled it on. He turned her to face the wall and rubbed himself between the cleft of her buttocks in hot, even strokes. And as he plunged into her from behind—thrusting harder with every stroke until they both came—she felt exactly how he'd said she would.

Controlled. Beautifully, utterly controlled.

Mitch collapsed against the wall and slid to the floor, taking her with him as the water streamed down on them.

"Wow." Panting for breath, Tayla stayed in his lap, her hands braced on his thighs. "That was… What actually was that?"

He wrapped his arms around her and chuckled. "Best make up sex ever. Holy shit!"

41

ARMS OF STEEL

WHEN TAYLA ARRIVED home from work the following Wednesday, she found Valentina in the laundry room doing the ironing. She popped her head around the door. "You're here late. Is everything okay?"

"Yeah, I have exams soon, so I'm trying to juggle my workload."

"I can take over the cleaning if you want."

Valentina stopped mid-press, stood the iron on its heel and frowned. "I need this job. I'm saving for my sewing machine, remember?"

"I'm not suggesting you leave, just take a few days off. We'll still pay you. Think of it as a bonus."

"Thanks, but has Mitch ever told you the story of how he hired me?"

Apart from the odd time, Mitch didn't often discuss his staff with Tayla. "I'm not sure."

"I was fifteen. Young, stupid. He caught me stealing oranges from the trees by the highway. Mum was sick with the flu. We had no money, hardly any food in the house, and I thought no one would miss them. I was scared stiff, but instead of telling Mum, he offered me a job. Now I get all the oranges I want, but I earn them."

Tayla studied the beautiful wild child in front of her, marveling at such pride and dedication in one so young. "I never knew that."

"Yeah, well, I've learned my lesson, and I'm thankful for this job."

"And we appreciate all you do for us."

Valentina grabbed another pillow slip from the pile and smoothed it onto the board. "I don't always get it right, but I try. Dad left when I was little…jumped the ditch to Australia. My relationship with Mitch is important to me."

Tayla nodded. She'd already worked that one out and suspected the feeling was mutual. "I understand. Right, I'd better get changed and hit the river track. Mitch is teaching me to surf, so I have to stay fit."

"Good luck with that." Valentina chuckled. "He sometimes coaches my rugby team. He's deadly behind that smile."

"Yep. I got that vibe the other day."

When Tayla walked into the bedroom, a pile of freshly pressed clothes sat on the chair. While putting them away, she found a cotton jacket and a blood-red G-string that didn't belong to her. Thinking they must be CeCe's, she returned to the laundry room and placed the folded jacket and panties on top of the washing machine. "These were in my pile."

Valentina looked up from her ironing. "They're not yours?"

Tayla shook her head. "No, not mine. Maybe CeCe's."

"Or they might be Prue's from when she stayed while you were in Sydney."

Rational thoughts vanished as Tayla processed Valentina's words. She watched the iron glide over the cotton, steam rising off the board with a hiss. When she did manage to form a reply, she had trouble executing it. Seconds passed in silence.

"I'll give them to CeCe when she's here next. She can pass them on if they're not hers."

Valentina looked at Tayla, her eyes wide with alarm. "He didn't tell you, did he?"

"No."

"I'm sorry, but she stayed all the time before you guys were married, even a couple of times after they'd finished. She's a sales rep and travels a lot. Please don't tell Mitch I told you. He always says"—she made a gruff-looking face and lowered her tone—"discretion in all things, Valentina."

I wonder why? It was a cynical thought, one that normally wouldn't have entered Tayla's head. Who was this jealous person inside of her? "It's okay. Mitch doesn't need to ask my permission to have houseguests."

Valentina hesitated. "I didn't like Prue much at first." She folded a pillow slip and placed it on the counter before reaching for another. "She's such a drama queen, and they argued a lot. Yells like a fishwife, as Mum would say. But she was always kind to me. It was Mitch she was horrible to. Not that I saw them together often, but she'd roll her eyes at stuff he said. I hate that, don't you?"

"I do." Tayla picked up the jacket and panties and walked toward the door. Engaging in a conversation about Prue wasn't a smart move. "I'll leave you a bag of oranges on the kitchen counter. They're big and ugly but taste divine."

"Thanks. Mum loves oranges. And I'm sorry I have such a big mouth."

"It's fine. You weren't to know."

Tayla jogged along the river track until her lungs burned with determination and her mind screamed with regret. There had once been a time when she'd act before her thoughts had a chance to register. But after what had happened with Hayden, she'd learned to take a different tack. To step sideways and observe from a distance before making rash decisions. Or so she'd told herself.

Leaning over to catch her breath, Tayla checked her Garmin. And as she watched the sun dip behind the western hill line, she wondered where Mitch went on his Wednesday poker nights—and who he was with. She'd never thought to question if he really stayed at Luka's. But that was before she'd become invested in his world. Before he'd slid over her skin, claiming her with his arms of steel and hot mouth.

Tayla walked most of the way home, her energy only returning when she passed the lemon trees of the northern block, their blossoms fragrant in the evening air. She bounded up the stairs and made a start on dinner, already chastising herself for doubting Mitch's sincerity.

But by midnight, as her thoughts raced with whys and what-ifs, doubt settled in a vacant corner of her mind. Feet on the floor, she cradled her head in her hands and sighed.

Outside in the night sky, a brilliant full moon mocked her exhaustion. Inside, the noise in her head did the same. She picked her phone up off the nightstand and unlocked it. She didn't know why. Habit?

Or maybe she did.

Mitch: Thinking of you in bed this morning - my lips on your neck, your scent wafting around me...your touch... xx

---

As Mitch drove home from his meeting with Chris Stone the following day, an image of Tayla lying on their bed the day before came to mind. With the crinkled sheet covering her naked body, the line of her collarbone and the creaminess of her skin had taken his breath away. Apart from the few months that he and Prue were engaged, he'd seldom considered the term 'domestic bliss' and its connotations. But there were no other words for it. He was domestically happy.

Arriving at the loft before Tayla, Mitch entered his office to check his email. There was one from Ella asking if they could meet, and another from the police saying they had no leads on the avocado or grapefruit thefts. Not that he expected they would.

His phone rang. He picked it up and hit *Accept*. "Luka. What's up?"

"How did the meeting with Mr. Stone go?"

"Fantastic. I asked him about the OCA complaint, he denied any knowledge and called me out for filling Ella's head with organics bullshit. Then just as I was about to leave, he pushed me against the wall and threatened me to stay away."

"But the guy's half your size."

"Yeah, but he's strong. He used to box as a teenager." Mitch chuckled. "I was just waiting for him to take a swing."

"Those two are as bad as each other."

"Maybe. Mind you, Ella's been all business since I went to see her that night. Like butter wouldn't melt."

"I still don't trust her," Luka said. "Anyway, how's it going with your tenant in Seaview Road? Mike's interested, as long as he can move in early next year."

"Her contract's almost up, so she'll be out of my hair soon. If not, I might have to change the locks. So, hook me up. I'm keen."

"Perfect."

"It's been the year from hell having her in my life. But, anyway, I'm counting down the days. I should have trusted my gut."

"How did she take it?"

"I haven't told her yet. I'll get my lawyer to sort it out while I'm down South. She'll be out by the new year."

"Okay, I'll give him your details. The space will make a great café. Any problems converting the side room into a kitchen?"

"Shouldn't be. We'll take a look once she's moved all her stuff out."

"How's Tayla?"

"Great."

"She's a keeper that one. I'm glad you guys are happy."

Mitch chuckled. "Yeah, me too. Maybe Norman had a few clues after all."

"Say hi to her from me."

As Mitch strolled out of his office, still on the phone, he noticed Tayla heading for the bedroom. "Hey, I have to go. Talk soon."

"Hi." Mitch followed her into their room. "You're home already?"

The overheard words of his phone conversation screaming in her head, Tayla turned to look at him. Who had he been talking to? CeCe? Telling CeCe that she'd be out of his hair soon? Or Prue? And why say he'd change the locks when he never locked the damn doors anyway?

She swallowed hard and looked away. "I had a headache...so I finished early."

"Shall I get you some paracetamol?" He stepped forward and reached out to brush a lock of hair off her face.

"Thanks, but I had a couple at work."

"I've just been talking to Luka. He said to say hi."

Of course, Luka. "How is he?" Tayla liked Luka, but betrayal comes in many forms, and Luka would always be Mitch's friend, not hers. Even so, she would miss the friendships she'd made while living at Lime Tree Hill when it was time to move on. Those people in his circle—friends, family, the workers in the packing shed, and Ned and his darling wife.

"He's good. Are you sure you're okay?" He held her at arm's length so he could take a better look. "You're a little pale."

Pause, Tayla. Pause.

"I'll be fine. I might lie down for a bit."

He kissed her on the forehead, his scent reminding her of that night in the back of the Hilux at Petrie Bay. Her 'necking in the back seat' experience.

"Okay. I need to check an irrigation pump. I'll be half an hour at most. Don't worry about dinner. I'll cook."

Tayla lay on top of the covers and watched him leave, a tight ball of emotion grabbing her throat in a stranglehold. Had she missed the clues? Wanted their marriage to work so badly that she succumbed to false hope instead of facing cold hard facts?

Now she had to spend the next twenty-four hours pretending, then wait for the inevitable call from his lawyer as she played her part in their marriage lie. And what was there to sort out? Everything had been watertight from the beginning. She had no right to anything of his, especially not his stone-cold heart. Had she been no more than a convenience to him?

He'd played his part well—the caring husband with the good-guy persona and drool-worthy body. Her heart wide open, she'd lived in his home and slept in his bed, willingly giving him what he wanted—where and when he wanted it. But now, Mitch was counting down the days. *Year from hell!*

The door opened and Tayla stirred. She hadn't meant to doze off, but as she'd pulled the quilt around her, she couldn't stay awake. Staying awake meant rehashing Mitch's conversation with Luka. There'd be plenty of time for that next week while he hiked the Milford Track with 'the boys.'

He climbed in behind her and held her close as he peppered kisses down her neck and across her shoulder blades. She stiffened and closed her eyes again. The brush of his lips and his warmth was the best feeling ever.

"Are you ready to eat?" Mitch asked.

"What time is it?"

"Six thirty. I've made chili."

"Okay. I'll get up." She stretched forward but didn't make eye contact.

He pulled her back into his arms. "Not just yet. We've hardly had any time together lately. And I'm away tomorrow. Tell me about your day."

"Nothing much to tell. It was frantic, as usual. But I'm not sure if they'll have many hours for me after Christmas, though."

"Would you consider going into private practice?" Mitch moved his hand to the back of her neck, his touch soft and reassuring as he traced his fingers in lazy circles.

"Maybe, but I'm not making any major decisions at the moment."

"Yeah, I guess that's wise." He rose from the bed. "Right, let's eat. I still haven't finished my packing."

They ate dinner in uncomfortable silence. She didn't trust herself to speak. What was the point in confronting him about Prue? Or his phone call with Luka? Making a scene would only add to her humiliation. As he'd said, he wasn't her keeper, and she wasn't his.

After dessert, Mitch retreated to his office. She heard him on the phone to CeCe, laughing as they talked. Her life was in turmoil, and he acted as if the world were his oyster. Mr. Lime Tree Hill. King of his domain.

Tayla grabbed a throw off the sofa in the living room and stepped onto the balcony, where she sat in Norman's old wicker chair. She pulled her knees up to her chin and wrapped her arms around them, wondering where Norman's soul might be as she questioned her beliefs about life—and death. Could he sense her as his soul floated in another spiritual plane, away from ordinary people and their petty differences?

She inhaled deeply, the scent of lemon blossom wafting up from the garden below. It was her favorite smell in the whole world and had been Norman's too. He'd said that when he read a great book, he could smell the lemon blossom between the pages. And as she matured, she knew what he meant.

Thoughts of Hayden surfaced. Hayden with his double standards and walking contradictions, who crossed a line she'd never thought he'd cross...

"Come to bed."

The timbre of Mitch's voice startled her, pent-up emotion overtaking her resolve to stay strong. Looking up, she pulled the throw tight around her shoulders. "I'll be there soon."

He stepped forward and kissed the top of her head, his hand stroking her hair. "I'm gonna hit the shower. Don't stay up too late." He walked back inside and shut the sliding door behind him.

Tayla's feelings remained conflicted. She wanted to scream at him for the situation they'd agreed to commit to. Tell him she'd overheard his phone call. Found the jacket and panties. Knew Prue had stayed.

She wanted to pack her bags and leave.

And yet, despite her inner turmoil, part of her longed for his touch. The feeling of his muscular arms wrapped around her as he whispered how sexy and beautiful she was. How much he *loved* her.

She wanted him to care.

Tayla stayed outside until after eleven, gazing at the midnight-blue sky with its brazen moon. It intrigued her how some stars appeared in her peripheral vision, but when she looked directly at them, they disappeared. Was this a metaphor for life? If she examined her problems too closely, the solution was uncertain. But if she shifted her focus a fraction, everything became clearer.

When she slipped in beside him, Mitch was already asleep. She moved into his warmth, aware he was leaving straight after breakfast. Would this be the last time they shared a bed, reached for each other during sleep?

Tayla woke around dawn to the sound of Mitch in the bathroom. The temperature had dropped, and the air felt unseasonably cool. He slipped back into bed a few minutes later. As he moved over to cuddle her, she lay her hand over his like she always did when they spooned, desperate for that last thread of connection.

"Tell me what's wrong," he whispered. "Are you sad about being alone?"

She paused. Took a breath. "A bit."

"I've been thinking. With everything that's been going on, maybe you should stay with your folks while I'm away. Ned will look after Edward."

She closed her eyes tight. "Okay. But they're going on a road trip to Auckland tomorrow for Dad's checkup and to visit the grandkids."

"Even so, at least there you'll have people close by. That Mrs. what's-her-name from next door won't leave you alone."

"I guess. And her name's Hannah."

"I'm gonna miss you. So much." His lips found her neck in the darkness, and the intensity hit her head-on. And as she heard the foil wrapper of a condom tear, her whole body tightened. *Anticipation.*

She struggled to resist, and the world around her disappeared as he filled her senses. His words calm and reassuring. His touch commanding and seemingly sincere.

They kissed, hot and hard against one another, his desperation showing in dominance. He rolled Tayla onto her back, their fingers entwined above her head, and entered her without restraint. This was dawn lovemaking at its best. Where foreplay was the act, and the act foreplay, as he edged his release by careful variation of speed and intensity.

Mitch pulled back and sat on his haunches, his expression tender in the shadows of sunrise and uncertainty. He shook his head. "Fuck, you're so beautiful. What would I do without you?"

She stilled, watching with wide eyes as he stroked himself. A few months ago, she would have lowered her eyes in embarrassment, but she wasn't that girl anymore. After all, the erotic mind is not politically correct. If it was to be their last time, she wanted to make it count. Determined to stay in control, she held his gaze without shame.

Mitch moved off the bed and sat on the low slipper chair in the corner of the room. Tayla rolled onto her side, one hand between her legs. He enjoyed watching her touch herself; she liked it too. Self-pleasuring was nothing to be ashamed of and having him watch only added to the experience.

He offered his hand. "Come here."

She stood before him, just out of reach. He cocked his finger. "Closer."

Tayla stepped forward and slowly lowered herself onto his impressive erection. As she started to move, strong hands guided her hips with gentle pressure.

"Open your eyes," he commanded. "You gonna let me light you up?"

"Yes."

"Say it again," he hissed as he increased his hold on her hips, moving her now in expert rhythm.

"Yes! A hundred times, yes."

"No thinking now." He pumped harder. "Just feel."

Leaning forward, Mitch took her breast in his mouth and nipped. She arched her back and closed her eyes. Cried out. He groaned deep within his throat, his legs trembling beneath her as she let go—his release, loud and audacious, hers quieter but just as intense.

Tayla rested her head on his shoulder, panting for rhythmic breath while Mitch did the same. Stroking her hair as he softened inside her, he whispered, "I love you, Tayla. Always trust me on that."

Emotion rose in her throat, her eyes stinging with unshed tears. "I love you too."

The sob freed, uncontrolled and raw. Holding her with care, Mitch moved to the bed and lowered her onto her side. He covered her with the duvet and climbed in behind her. "Hey. Don't be upset. Everything will be fine, I promise." They clung together, finding their fit in that moment in time and staying that way until she stilled into sleep.

When she woke a few hours later, he'd eaten breakfast and was packed and ready to go.

42

MISSING YOU

ACROSS THE DRIVE, Luka and two other guys waited in Luka's pickup as Mitch packed his gear onto the tray. He shut the lid and turned to look at her. "Gotta go. I still think you'd be better off at your folks. I know Ned's close by, but…"

Lost for words, Tayla nodded. What could she say at this late stage in the game? If she'd wanted to confront him, she should have done so last night. Instead, she'd let him make love to her until his deception and the blood-red G-string lost their significance.

Then again, in her book, confrontation was overrated. Just like judgment and accusation and trying to win an argument. All pointless exercises.

Mitch cupped her face in his hands, his thumb brushing away the single tear trickling down her cheek. "Hey, it's okay. You'll be fine."

She sniffed. Bowed her head. Scuffed her feet in the gravel.

He drew her in for a hug and held her for several seconds.

"Hurry up, Mitch," Luka yelled out the driver's side window. "Just kiss the life out of her. We won't look."

"Right." He laughed, then kissed her softly on the lips, his fingers twisting in her hair. When he pulled away, his expression was full of warmth. "Don't miss me too much."

As Tayla watched them drive away, she held on tight to the notion that this didn't have to be hard. With Mitch away, she'd have time to reflect, to take that pause. She stood at the edge of the driveway, tears threatening to spill as Luka took a right onto the highway, her husband riding shotgun. In another blink, they were gone.

She stood for a while longer. When Ned approached from the packing shed, Tayla wiped her eyes with the back of a hand before greeting him with a forced smile.

"Is that hay fever affecting you again?" he asked.

Tayla laughed despite herself.

He put his arm around her shoulders. "Hey, come on. He'll be back before you know it."

How could she tell Ned what was really troubling her? Mitch might only be away for a week and a half, but missing him wasn't the issue. He wanted her out.

"I've just been down at the farm gate store." Ned handed her a large brown envelope. "The girls asked me to deliver this. It arrived for you a couple of days ago, but someone filed it beside the coffee machine, and they forgot all about it. I hope it's nothing important."

Tayla stared at the envelope in her hand: *Tayla Harrington, Lime Tree Hill*, scrawled in black lettering across the front. She never received mail, especially at the orchard, and if someone she knew had sent it, they would've addressed it to Tayla Whitman. "Thanks."

"Right. I better get this milk to Maggie. Don't be a stranger."

"I won't."

Back upstairs, she made herself an espresso, then sat at the kitchen island while the envelope lay in wait. She ran her fingers under the flap and pulled out several photographs.

The top one set the scene. It was of Mitch, walking along the beach with a woman—if Tayla wasn't mistaken, the woman from Fig Leaf. In the next frame, he rested his hand on her shoulder, and the next, they smiled at one another over coffee. As she flicked through the pile, each photo told the same story.

One of deceit.

She studied the prints again, frowning at the look on Mitch's face as he interacted with the woman as if they were more than friends. She turned them over, but there was no date stamp or any other information.

Tayla sat back in her chair, her thoughts in overdrive until a phone alert startled her. She stuffed the pictures back into the envelope and pressed the Messenger icon.

Hi. This is Prue Preston, Mitch's friend. I'll be in Clifton Falls on Wednesday next week and was wondering if we could catch up. I'd rather not come to the orchard. There's a seat on the boardwalk in front of the Scented Garden. Shall we say around 12:30?

Tayla reread the message. What could Prue possibly want to talk about? How much she loved Mitch and wanted him back? Prue had made her feelings perfectly clear the night of CeCe's party and had been blatantly unkind about it.

Hesitant, Tayla held her phone in a tight grip until another message popped up.

Please be there. It's important.

What on earth?

She moved to the living room, curled up on the sofa and stared into space. At some point, she'd pack a few things and drive into town, stay at her parents' place as Mitch had advised. But for now, she just sat. Existed.

Tayla moped through the day without accomplishing anything.

When her text alert chimed just on dusk, she considered ignoring it, but then her dad's face flashed through her mind. What if her mother needed her? She picked up her phone from the coffee table and unlocked it.

Mitch: Bumpy flight into Queenstown. Missing you already. You were beautiful this morning. I can't stop thinking about you…us. Anyway, we're off out for dinner. Call you tomorrow xx

Great!

With her thoughts in turmoil, it was two days before Tayla had the energy to haul a suitcase from the top shelf of the closet and pack her things. The room looked the same as the day she moved in, but so much had changed since then. Smiles, tears, moments of connection, and now…disconnection.

She'd spent those two days in consultation with her inner self. The jacket and panties she could rationalize, even the photographs —because when she'd studied them again with an open mind, the intimacy between Mitch and the woman wasn't necessarily sexual. But his phone call with Luka had become an all-consuming weight on her chest that she just couldn't budge.

And the more Tayla tried to dislodge that weight, the more stupid and naïve she felt. She'd trusted him and had done so completely.

Curiosity getting the better of her, Tayla replied to Prue with a confirmation of day and time, then second-guessed her motives, her reasoning.

. . .

True to his word, Mitch had called just like he said he would, and as the world spun around her, they'd spoken of the mundane—Mr. Edward, the orchard, the restaurant where he'd eaten dinner—as if he had no secrets and she had no doubts.

Tayla left Lime Tree Hill for Clifton Falls on the edge of dusk, but as she drove the Eastern Pacific Highway, nothing about the journey inspired her. Not the stillness of the ocean, nor the rolling hillsides bathed in the shadows of sunset, not even the apple trees bursting with maturing fruit that dotted the route. By the time she reached Seaview Road, one thought drowned out all others.

She still hadn't learned to surf.

The guest room at her parents' place was tiny, with just enough space for a double bed, nightstand, and a tub chair. And as she opened the window against the stale air, she felt confined. Suffocated. Rejected.

Even so, their condo felt more like home now. Family photos hung on the walls, and vibrant pieces of art enlivened the otherwise bland decor. She wished her parents were here. Her love of solitude seemed to have waned of late.

Tayla pulled a loaf of bread from the freezer and put two slices into the toaster. The only peanut butter in the pantry was the smooth type laced with sugar that her father loved, but it would have to do.

She slathered it onto the toast and had just taken a bite when her phone lit up with a text.

Mitch: Boarding the boat at Te Anau Downs in the morning. Cooler today. How are you and Edward?

She took another bite of her toast and moved to the dining table, unsure whether she should reply. Her fingers hesitant on the keypad, she typed her response.

Tayla: Fine. Moved into Mum and Dad's for now.

Edward's with Ned. He's his usual unaffected self. Edward,
I mean, not Ned.

Mitch: That's good. Have a peaceful sleep without me.
Miss you. So much xx

Tayla stared at his message. How long would it take to sleep
peacefully without him? Days? Weeks? Months? And what did
'that's good' mean?

The following day, Tayla returned to the orchard, and after a brief
visit to Maggie and Ned's to see Mr. Edward, she cleaned the loft
from top to bottom, removing all traces of her presence.

As she stood at the kitchen island, the insanely large clock
ticking away the minutes, she spied a rubber ball of Edward's
under the dining table and let her bravado slip. She thought of his
chubby, squat body and those pleading, nut-brown eyes, and knew
she would miss him terribly. But then, she'd miss many things
about this life she'd once scorned. Her husband. Her lover. Her
friend.

Earlier in the day, the office of Shand Shand and Harrow had
called to say Simon Harrow wanted to see her. *I'll get my lawyer to
sort it out.* She'd made an appointment for Thursday.

Later, Tim called to suggest they catch a movie, but Tayla
couldn't stomach acting the part of 'everything's okay.' She'd been
there, done that a thousand times, in a thousand different ways.

Life would be okay again, but first, she needed time to do its
thing. Her energy levels had plummeted, and without Mitch, her
days suddenly held no purpose.

Welcome to the final lesson of love—that of the lovesick
teenager.

Full circle right there.

Tayla entered his office and tugged the loft key off her key ring
then placed it on his desk. When she walked down the stairs and

pulled the door shut behind her, it was all she could do to get in her car and drive away.

In the days that followed, Tayla's plans to keep busy fell flat. She made it to work and home again, but apart from that, she could hardly bother to eat and shower. Even yoga took a back seat to her malaise.

That weekend, she opened her Facebook to see Mitch tagged in a post. She scanned the pictures from the boys' night out in Queenstown before they headed to the Milford Track. There were only a handful, but in the first, a grinning Mitch had his arm around some girl, and in the next, she was kissing him on the cheek with hashtags to match: *#oldfriends #freedom #finderskeepers*.

Tayla sat with her eyes glued to the screen. It seemed Mitch was celebrating his *#liberation* in style.

Tim: Where are you?
Tayla: At Mum and Dad's. They're in Auckland visiting the grandkids.
Tim: Why aren't you at the orchard?
Tayla: I have no idea. I'm confused.
Tim: You want company?
Tayla: Yes please.
Tim: Shall I bring wine or chocolate?
Tayla: Both.

43

THE SCENTED GARDEN

TAYLA LOVED THE SCENTED GARDEN. She'd taken Norman there once, on a rare day when he'd agreed to leave the house. They'd stayed just long enough for her to read a few chapters of *Rebecca* while he basked in the early summer sunshine. It was the last time Norman ever left the orchard.

She sat on the bench and checked her watch. Twelve twenty-five. Arriving early was a habit she'd mastered young after missing the school bus twice in one week. And as she watched full waves dump onto the shore, Tayla had no idea why she'd agreed to come.

However, the reason was obvious. The brown envelope and its contents. Tayla wanted answers and thought Prue might know something. She'd pored over those prints until she couldn't bear to look at them anymore. Speculated. Rationalized. They lingered on her nightstand while she slept, and lay fanned out over the break-fast bar as she sipped her morning coffee. It seemed her *husband* had more than one way to teach her the final lesson.

"Hi." Prue's greeting startled her. "Thanks so much for coming. I thought you might say no after what happened when we met."

Tayla glanced at her before turning her focus to the shoreline, a sudden breeze blowing wisps of hair across her face. "What's on your mind?"

"Mitch."

No shit.

"Also, I wanted to apologize for what happened at CeCe's party. I was hammered, but that's no excuse."

Prue was right. Alcohol was no excuse, but Tayla had agreed to the meeting; the least she could do was allow Prue to speak her mind.

"You know I stayed with him while you were away?" Prue said.

Tayla inhaled a shaky breath and handed Prue a brown paper carry bag. The evidence. "Your jacket and underwear."

She peeked into the bag. Frowned. "Um, these aren't mine."

Tayla scanned the Pacific once more, her hands clenched in her pockets, the brisk wind making her eyes water. "Oh? Maybe they're CeCe's." She took the offered bag from Prue, the paper cold in her hands.

"Nothing happened between us. Honestly."

Prue's declaration sounded sincere. Tayla relaxed a little. But then, why hadn't Mitch told her he'd invited his ex to stay?

"That night, at CeCe's birthday, I knew Mitch and I had reached the end of the road as soon as I saw the way he looked at you. When you guys were dancing, he couldn't keep his eyes off you. I was so jealous. I didn't even care that he was married. How screwed up is that?"

Tayla frowned. *What way?*

"I said some nasty things to him as well, and he shot me down. More or less told me my narcissistic personality would ruin my life. When I said I still loved him, he blew me off."

"Weren't you with someone then?"

"Yes, Otis." She smiled. "Solid, dependable Otis. He took me home and put me to bed, but I was so drunk, I puked all over the carpet. Anyways, the next day, I phoned Mitch to apologize. When he didn't pick up, I locked myself in the bathroom, curled up on the floor and cried until I had nothing left. Otis was mad as hell when he found me, and we ended up having a massive fight. He wanted us to be exclusive, and as usual, I couldn't commit. Turns out, self-sabotage is a mean bitch, one I know only too well."

Tayla settled her gaze on the horizon again, her hands rubbing together for warmth. "You don't have to tell me this."

"Please, I want to. I didn't stay with Mitch because I wanted him back. I needed to talk to him, to explain. Why I cheated, why I didn't want kids, and why I ended up drowning my sorrows in booze every day."

Prue reached down, picked up a shell and ran her thumb and forefinger over the smoothness. "I lost a baby...when I was just sixteen." She threw the shell toward the waves, but it landed at her feet. "Fell pregnant to a boy from school. I thought we were going steady. Of course, he ghosted me after I told him. My little boy died inside of me at thirty-three weeks. I had to be induced. Turned out, he had a rare congenital deformity that affects the lungs."

Swallowing hard, Tayla reached for Prue's hand but didn't speak, allowing Prue to finish her story.

"I can't go through that again." Prue stopped, closed her eyes briefly, and took a deep breath. "When you hold your dead baby, a part of you dies as well. And the loneliness, the grief... Nobody has your back, in your mind anyway. My family and friends carried on regardless, as if he'd never existed. People said it was for the best. It let everyone off the hook."

"Except you," Tayla murmured, still holding Prue's hand.

Prue sniffed back a tear. "Yeah, except me."

"I'm so sorry. That must have been devastating for you."

"I'd never told Mitch, not until that day when I stayed at Lime Tree." Prue pulled a tissue from her pocket and blew her nose. "At first, I didn't think he'd let me stay. But you know what he's like... such a softy underneath. He talked about you. A lot. Said you read books together. That made me sad. I wish he'd read to me."

Tayla viewed Prue with newfound compassion. She loved it when Mitch read to her before bed and had sometimes wondered if he'd done so with his other girlfriends. Obviously not.

When Tayla met Prue at CeCe's party, she'd been quick to make assumptions about her, unfounded assumptions possibly. As Mitch had said, maybe Prue wasn't a bad person underneath.

"Mitch is a wonderful man," Prue continued. "He's a hopeless communicator at times, takes things for granted, but when he's in your corner, he'll be there through thick and thin. He loves you, just like Otis loves me. But we have to allow it. Have to let them in —you know what I mean?"

Tayla nodded. Prue was right, but now, the point was moot.

"We can't let our fears hold us back," Prue said. "Otherwise, what will we have in the end? Dissatisfaction? The certainty that we never did enough? Someone once told me I should dare to succeed. And that's my new focus."

Tayla blinked to stop a wayward tear from falling. "Thank you. I can't imagine how hard it must be to bare your soul to a stranger."

"I don't see you as a stranger. You have a kind soul, or you wouldn't be here. And I don't want your man—not anymore. I wasn't enough for him. I wish I could say I let him go a long time ago, but…well, it's only been a blink."

They sat in silence while a couple and their dog walked past.

"Otis asked me to marry him the other day."

Tayla shot her a sideways glance. "Did you say yes?"

"No. I'm not ready yet. Maybe one day. I'm still struggling to fit into my own skin. Do you understand?"

"Totally."

"He's pretty rough around the edges compared to Mitch, but he's loving and kind. He hates confrontation. That's hard for me. The need to fight overwhelms me sometimes. I get anxious and lash out until I calm down. Mitch couldn't handle that."

Prue stood and slipped her hands into her jacket pockets. "Anyways, I should go. Thanks for coming. Part of my recovery is making amends with people I've hurt. It's been hard, but I'm getting there."

"Before you go, can I show you something?" Tayla asked.

Prue sat back down. "Sure."

Tayla took the envelope from her bag and handed it to Prue.

She pulled the contents free, glanced at the photographs, then back at Tayla. "Where did you get these?"

"Someone left them at the farm gate store, addressed to me. I thought you might have sent them."

Prue shook her head and frowned. "That's not my style. And you don't know the woman?"

Tayla recalled the day she'd seen Mitch having lunch with the blonde at Fig Leaf. "No."

"She looks kind of familiar." Prue pulled a pair of reading glasses from her bag and put them on to study the top photograph more closely. "That's Ella Stone. They've been friends for years, although they dated back in the day. I'm sure there's a reasonable explanation. Mitch isn't a cheater."

"Yes." Tayla wondered if that was true. "I'm sure there is."

"But look." Prue passed the photo to Tayla. "She's carrying that jacket, the one in the bag."

Squinting against the sun, Tayla looked more closely at the jacket in the photo. It wasn't CeCe's. It was Ella Stone's.

"Give him a chance to explain. Mitch is a straight-up guy but can be preoccupied at times. Ask him a direct question, and he'll usually give you a direct answer." Prue returned the envelope to Tayla and stood again. "Right. I have a client meeting, so…" She picked up her bag.

"What do you do?"

"Sales, for a power tool company. It involves a lot of traveling, which suits me fine. But I'd be lying if I said it keeps me out of trouble. Hot guys everywhere." Prue laughed for the first time. "I'm glad you came. I really do wish you and Mitch well."

"Thank you."

Prue hunched her shoulders against the wind and walked along the boardwalk until she ducked behind the information center and disappeared from view. Tayla sat a little longer, and despite the unseasonably cool day, longed to strip naked and dive under the waves; to test her newfound freedom in the water. And as she watched beady-eyed seagulls squawking over the remains of a discarded lunch, a single thought prevailed.

Ella Stone. Chris Stone's wife?

44

THE SHARE

ALTHOUGH THE MUSTARD-COLORED WALLS, natural wood paneling, and carpet were well overdue for a makeover, Simon Harrow's office looked the same as it did ten months ago. And as she sat in front of his desk, waiting for him to join her, Tayla second-guessed why she was here. When Simon's PA had called, she'd assumed it was something to do with the divorce. But if that were the case, why hadn't Mitch said anything before he left?

But then, by his own admission, he disliked confrontation. Maybe he used Simon to do all his dirty work.

"Tayla, so sorry to keep you waiting." Simon hurried into his office, running his hands through his hair as if he hadn't had a chance to brush it. "Is Mitch joining us?"

"No, he's away. Sorry, your PA didn't say anything about Mitch coming."

"Oh, okay. No problem." Simon opened a file and removed the top pages. "Has he said anything about why you're here?"

I'll get my lawyer to sort it out. "No. He hasn't mentioned a thing."

Simon looked up from the file and rocked back in his chair. "I see. Okay, well, it's in relation to Norman Harrington's will."

Puzzled, she asked, "Norman's will?"

"At the time of his death, Mr. Harrington left the majority of his estate to his only grandson."

"You mean Mitch?"

"Yes. But there was one last provision that, until now, we couldn't finalize. Or disclose, for that matter."

As Tayla stiffened in her seat, Simon continued, "Besides his intention to cover the cost of your education, Norman left you one hundred and fifty thousand dollars. Payable on the fifth of this month."

Simon cleared his throat as Tayla stared at him in disbelief. "What? Why would Norman do that? And why wouldn't Mitch contest it?"

"His will stated there was to be no contesting by any party. Norman clearly indicated his intent. The signatures on the document include his brother, Kenneth Harrington, and two other members of the legal profession. The last and final condition is as follows." Simon picked up the will and cleared his throat again. "The inheritance must remain confidential until November fifth in Ms. Whitman's twenty-seventh year."

He glanced up. "It seems the education provision was made after the fact and attached to the original will as an adjunct."

November the fifth, the anniversary of her bike accident. "And Mitch knows about this?"

Simon had a nervous habit of smoothing his tie, but this time, he fiddled with the knot. She wanted to reach over and loosen it for him. "He does, as does your father."

Tayla sat in shock. Mitch and her father both knew and hadn't told her. "Seriously? Dad knew?"

"Norman told him before he died. But he was bound by a confidentiality clause, as was Mitch."

"This doesn't make any sense." While Tayla tried to rationalize her thoughts, Simon remained silent. She couldn't take the money. It belonged to Mitch.

"Mitch is the rightful heir to Norman's estate," she finally said. "All I did was be his friend. And while I'm grateful for what I received, you and I both know that money should stay with Mitch. He's given my family quite enough already."

"You might say that now, but the original investment is worth substantially more in today's market. I strongly recommend you take a pause and at least consider it."

There was that word again. *Pause.* "And how will Mitch afford to pay me out?"

"Norman set the funds aside months before his death. The money's been invested in shares and bonds as per his instruction. Under the terms of your prenup, the investment is yours, not Mitch's. Unless you renegotiate, it will go into the matrimonial property pot after the prenup has run its course. In the meantime, I advise you to seek guidance from your accountant."

Tayla was lost for words. The prenup had a lifespan of three years. When they signed it, Mitch and Tayla both knew their fake marriage wouldn't last much beyond Christmas.

"Look, take your time. It's a lot to absorb."

Simon and Tayla bandied words back and forth, his responses to her questions guarded and peppered with legal speak until she said, "Can I ask you something, off the record?"

"Sure. I may not be able to answer but go ahead."

"Is Ella Stone Chris Stone's wife?"

Tayla noted Simon's hesitation. For a lawyer, he wore his expressions freely. "Yes. The Stone and Pip Group is their company. They're big players in horticulture around the district."

"Of course. I met Chris when he put in an offer to buy my parents' place." She paused. Should she say more? "From what I gather, Mitch doesn't have much time for Mr. Stone."

"I'd say the feeling's mutual. The guy's an interesting character."

"Why's that?"

"Maybe you should ask Mitch that question." Simon stood,

signaling the end of their meeting. "Right, I'll await further instructions."

Tayla picked up her bag from the floor. "Thank you for your time. I'll be in touch once I've had time to think."

But as Tayla walked back to her car, thinking was the last thing she wanted to do.

When she'd left Simon's office, Tayla couldn't wait to talk to Mitch. But now, she didn't want to talk to him at all. Quite apart from the revelations about Mitch and Ella, and the phone call to Luka, he'd known about the money before they'd married. So had her father, and probably her mother.

Back at her parents' place, Tayla called Ruby to no answer. She'd just sat down to a grilled cheese sandwich when Ruby returned her call.

"You called, Mrs. Harrington?"

Mrs. Harrington? "I did. Do you have a spare twenty minutes?"

"Sounds serious. If you can condense it into ten, shoot."

Tayla shuffled her thoughts. With limited time, she'd concentrate on her visit to the lawyers. Her marital problems could wait until she and Ruby talked face-to-face. "I went to see Mitch's lawyer today. There is something else from Norman's estate."

"Go on."

"He left me one hundred and fifty thousand dollars in his will."

"What! And you've only just found out? Way to go, you."

"It was to be gifted to me on the fifth of November in my twenty-seventh year."

"Well, that's crazy right there. If it was your actual birthday, well okay, but—"

"It's the tenth anniversary of my bike accident. He didn't think like other people. According to Simon, Dad knew but had to keep quiet because of a confidentiality clause. Nothing makes any sense these days, Rubes. It's like someone's in the background playing the strings of my life, and I've only just realized it. Mitch, Norman…even Dad. They're all taking care of shy, impulsive Tayla's interests. But I'm not that girl anymore. I told Simon it should go to Mitch."

"What? Why on earth would you do that?"

Tayla had asked herself the same question as she'd left Simon's office. "Because he's done enough for our family lately. It's only fair."

"Even so, it's a lot of money. Probably more than you'd save in a lifetime. You could climb onto the property ladder with that kind of deposit. Have you talked to Mitch?"

"Not yet. He's still away."

"Of course. Swanning around Fiordland. I forgot. Anyway, I'll call you later tonight. Mum and Dad are coming for dinner, and I have to collect the girls from Noah's mother. If I'm a few minutes late, I'll get a big black mark against my name in her book of spells and naughty deeds."

Tayla laughed. "Behave."

"It's okay for you. You haven't even met your mother-in-law."

"I have on Skype. She's lovely." Tayla wondered if she would ever meet Andrea and Frank in the flesh.

"Yeah, so was Noah's mum in the beginning. Anyway, you'd better go eat some chocolate. You've had quite the shock. Love ya."

"You too. Thanks for the ear."

"You're welcome, but whatever you do, don't make any rash decisions."

Tayla went to say goodbye but stopped with another thought. "You know what really bothers me?"

"No, what?"

"If I'd known about the money earlier, Mum and Dad would still have the orchard. I could have paid off some of their debts."

"Maybe, but Dad was ready to bow out two years ago. And you know how proud he is. He wouldn't have accepted it. And Mitch was a beneficiary of the will, not the executor. He probably has no idea what the money's worth in today's market."

"Yeah, I guess. Anyway, bye, Ruby Tuesday. Love you."

Tayla ended the call and flopped onto the sofa. Ruby was right. Paying her parents' debts would only have been a short-term solution to a long-term problem.

So what would she do with the money if she kept it?

45

THE CHOICE

"HEY, BEAUTIFUL," Mitch said down the phone. "Where are you? I thought you'd be home by now."

Beautiful? Tayla stilled. She normally loved the sound of Mitch's voice. The way he enunciated his words with such deep clarity. Today, it had the opposite effect. She swallowed hard. "I'm still at Mum and Dad's. Are you home already? How was your trip?"

Her question stemmed from nervousness rather than genuine inquiry. She knew he was home.

"Great. Didn't you get my text? We caught an earlier flight. I tried to call you."

"Yes, sorry. I couldn't find my phone, so I went to work without it." Tayla flinched as she uttered the little white lie.

"What time will you be home?"

As her nerves tightened, she let her hesitation last a little too long. "With everything that's been going on, I might stay in town for now."

"Why?" He sounded genuinely puzzled. As if the phone call with Luka, his meetings with Ella Stone, and the G-string had never existed. "Is everything okay?"

"I went to see Simon Harrow on Thursday."

There was no reaction to her words. No pause, no sharp intake of breath. "Oh, okay. So you know about the will?"

"I do. What I don't understand is why everyone kept it from me until now."

"That's Norman playing master controller again. The guy liked to be the one pulling the strings."

She swallowed hard. "Anyway, don't worry, the money's all yours."

His hesitation told her he was catching her drift. "Tayla, what's going on?"

"It's not a conversation for the phone. Text me a time and place, and I'll meet you."

"I'm coming over."

"Mitch, no—"

"You'd better be there." He cut the call.

The drive from Lime Tree Hill took at least twenty minutes in rush hour traffic. As Tayla showered and changed into jeans and a longline sweater, she rehearsed what she'd say when he arrived. That she knew about Ella Stone, and Prue, and his phone call with Luka, and that she pulled her own strings.

But as he stood at the doorway, fresh from the shower judging by the way he'd combed his hair off his forehead, the need to reach out and hold him was so strong, it caught her off guard.

He followed her inside. "What's going on?"

"Would you like to sit down?"

"No, I would not like to sit down. What happened while I was away? It's that Hayden jerk, isn't it? He's back in the picture. You've decided to join his little threesome after all."

"Don't be ridiculous. This has nothing to do with Hayden. How can you even think that?"

He threw his arms in the air. "What then? I go on a trip I've been planning for months, and I come home to an empty house and no wife."

"You were the one who said I should move out. Told me it was for the best."

"What the actual fuck, Tayla! I meant for a few days…so you didn't have to be alone at the orchard. Did you honestly think I wanted you to move out for good? Why didn't you talk to me?"

Tayla wrung her hands as she avoided eye contact, her rehearsed words lost in his confusion. "Prue texted me when you were away, asked if we could meet up."

He huffed. Nodded. "And let me guess. She told you she'd stayed when you were in Sydney?" Mitch sat in her father's chair, his head in his hands. He looked up. "Nothing happened," he said softly. "If it did, I wouldn't be here. But she's going through some personal stuff and needed support. She asked me not to tell anyone where she was. I still care for her, even after what she did, but I'd never go back there."

"You should have told me."

"You're right. I'm sorry." He offered his hand, as he always did when he wanted her to sit with him. "So, we're good?"

Tayla shook her head. She wanted to take his hand, let him pull her into his lap, and kiss him until the noise in her head hushed. But if she reached out, letting go would be so much harder. "It's not only Prue. I thought we could do this, step from fantasy to reality, but…"

He looked puzzled. "Are you breaking up with me?"

"I heard you talking to Luka."

His puzzled expression remained. "Sorry, I don't follow."

"The day before you left. You told him that the contract's up soon, that I'd be out on my ear. That you'd get your lawyer to sort it out."

"Shit! Seriously? Why didn't you ask me about it?"

"What did you want me to ask? Why you pretended to care? Why you led me on? And I shouldn't have listened in on your private conversation, but you need to hush up when you're having a boys' talk with Luka."

"I need to hush up? *You* need to communicate. And now we're over because you assumed I was talking about you? Is that the gist?"

"I heard you."

"I don't doubt it. But my conversation with Luka wasn't about you."

"No? Everything you said related to us. Every single word."

"We were talking about my tenant. Her lease is up soon. She's behind in her rent, and I can't wait to get rid of her. Next time, ask the damn question."

"But—"

"Luka's friend Mike wants the building for an organic café. I'll take you there when it opens...*if* you're still talking to me." He stared her down. She'd never seen him angry like this, but maybe he'd change his tune when he saw the photographs. "What's next on your Naughty Mitch list?"

Tayla went to the bedroom and returned with the envelope. She sat on the sofa and placed it on the coffee table in front of him. Mitch frowned as he opened the flap and removed the photos, and he continued to frown as he flipped through them.

"Her name is Ella Stone," Tayla said. "She left her jacket and panties at your place. I assumed they were Prue's or CeCe's. But, if you look closely, Ella's carrying the jacket in one of the shots."

"I know who she is." Fanning the photos across the table, he shot her a questioning frown. "Are you having me followed?"

"What? Of course not. Do you honestly think I'd do that?"

"So, where did you get these?"

"They were left at the farm gate store for me." Her tone softened. "Are you sleeping together? You and Ella Stone?"

Tayla waited for Mitch to defend or deny, but he remained silent, one large hand rubbing his designer stubble, and his brows knitted together. Her stomach lurched.

"No. But we do have a history."

He stood and stared out the window to the outdoor chess set

across the green. She stilled, waiting for the blow he was about to deliver.

"We were both eighteen," Mitch said as he turned and leaned his butt on the windowsill. "Norman grew a few peaches and early apples in those days. I came to stay with him over summer break, so I could work at the orchard." He smiled at the recollection. "Ned ran the place back then. Norman just sat around in his plaid dressing gown, counting his profits on an old Casio adding machine."

Tayla remembered that adding machine. She'd seen it sitting in the same place on Norman's desk every time she went to visit.

"Anyway, I arrived at work one morning, and there she was. Ella McKenzie. The most beautiful girl I'd ever seen. I dreamed about her for days, but when I showed an interest, she turned me down flat with a swift flick of her lashes. That made me want her even more. I later found out she'd had the same boyfriend since she was fourteen."

"Chris?"

"Yep." He returned to the chair. "I couldn't stand the guy. Even back then, he was a smart-ass jerk with too much of his father's money to throw around. I didn't understand what she saw in him. Neither did any of her friends. Anyway, the week before Christmas, a group of us were at a party. He had sex with her cousin in the bathroom, and he wasn't discreet about it. Ella dumped him the next day." Mitch's expression was retrospective.

"We started dating a week later. By the time summer was over, I was so in love with her, I couldn't think straight. The night we said goodbye, she picked me up in her father's car, and we drove to the beach. She was an emotional wreck. Crying and saying how much she loved me. And when we made love, I cried too. I wanted to call Mum and Frank and tell them I'd decided to take a gap year. But Norman and I discussed it, and he persuaded me to go to university as planned. If it was meant to be, he said, Ella would still be there when I got back."

"And was she?"

He huffed. Smiled. "Turns out I'd unwittingly enrolled in Rebound 101, with Ella as the tutor. She wrote to me three weeks later saying it was over, and while she'd never forget me, she'd gone back to Chris. The guy's despised me ever since, but not only because of Ella. His family was interested in the orchard before Norman died, but the old man took an instant dislike to the Stones. Chris expected me to walk away once it was mine, so he made me a crazy low offer. I said I wasn't selling, and he took it personally."

"So, you and Ella are obviously still friends?"

"Not so much. She's interested in organics so came to me for advice. We've had several meetings."

"Then who took the photos?"

Mitch shrugged. "Who knows. Someone Chris hired? The guy's an asshole. But I'm not going to bullshit you and say the opportunity wasn't there with Ella, because it was. She wants an affair and makes no bones about it." He moved to sit beside her on the sofa. They sat face-to-face, the distinct inhale and exhale of his breathing audible in her ears; her rehearsed words diluted by his honesty. He reached for her hands, and his touch gave her strength. "But I don't want her; I want you."

"We married for the wrong reasons."

"Maybe we did, but that doesn't mean we can't have the right outcome. We fit...make sense. This thing we have, it's bigger than the both of us. Bigger than Ella and Prue and Hayden. It's even bigger than Norman and his need for control. Fate brought us together, and fate knows a shitload more than it ever lets on."

Tayla swallowed back the tears, desperate to stay in control. "This past year... I thought I was doing okay. But the whole Hayden thing. Moving from Sydney, Dad's illness, even the sale of Cherry Grove. I didn't want to step up, didn't know if I could. And now that it's over, I feel like I'm falling apart. The one thing I wanted the least is now what I want the most."

"And what's that?"

"You." She shook her head and whispered, "But you didn't pick me, Mitch."

"Of course I did." He reached out to smooth a tear from her cheek with his thumb. "Not traditionally, maybe, but why does that matter?"

She searched for a reason. "Because without that traditional foundation, it's hard to know what's real. I need time to get my head around that."

"I love you. That's what's real. And even if Ella and I were both single, she's the last person I'd want to be with. I can honestly say, there's been no one else since Prue and I broke up—physically or emotionally. I hope you can say the same."

He cupped her face with both hands and kissed her. She returned the kiss, putting aside her hesitation from earlier.

Mitch pulled back, his expression one of acceptance. "I'm gonna go now. I'll see you at home when you're ready. But take your time. I don't want you to have any doubts."

PAYBACK

MITCH PICKED up his phone and glanced at David Wong's name lighting up the screen. He hit *Accept*. "David. What's up?"

"Do you have time for a debrief this morning?"

He checked his watch. "Sure. I can be there in half an hour."

"Great. We've been over the CTV footage while you were away and finally found the needle in a haystack. It appears Ella Stone paid you a visit recently, but when she found no one home, she let herself in anyway. Also, that lead on the grapefruit checked out, and the reviews definitely came from an IP address linked to Mrs. Stone's mother. The avocados are proving more difficult, but it's just a matter of time before someone talks. Anyway, it's not looking good for the Stones, that's for sure."

Mitch grabbed his keys from the sideboard then bounded down the stairs and out the packing shed door. "What about the OCA?"

"It's not a crime to make a complaint to the OCA, but if it came from Chris Stone, he might get a slap on the wrist for harassment. Theft is a different story, as is home invasion. Anyway, I'll see you soon."

"Yep, I'm on my way. And, David, thanks."

"My pleasure."

The Stone and Pip Group owned a suite of offices on the southern side of Clifton Falls CBD, in an area known as the Exchange. After parking his Hilux next to King's Gardens, Mitch crossed the street and walked the couple of blocks to their office, the envelope tucked under his arm and a USB flash drive in his pocket.

It had been two days since David Wong's call. Time to make the Stones squirm.

Frigid air-conditioning hit him as he walked through the entrance. He'd expected the usual commercial space, with gray walls and austere furniture, so the fruit-tree murals and lush potted plants surprised him. He stopped at the front desk. "Is Ella free?"

The receptionist raised a brow as if he were her bodyguard. "Mrs. Stone is busy right now. If you give me a second, I'll check her diary. May I ask your name and the nature of your business?"

"Mitch Harrington, and it's personal."

The young man had no sooner looked at his computer screen when Chris's voice boomed across reception. "Mitchel." He stepped forward, his hands in his pockets and no warmth in his expression. "What can I do for you?"

"Nothing. I'm here to see Ella."

Chris nodded as if he'd been expecting him. He held open the boardroom door. "Come in. I'll see when she's free." Mitch hesitated before following him into the small windowless space, and as Chris walked away, he questioned why he'd come. Was he trying to prove a point before the police got involved?

"Ella's on a conference call," Chris said when he returned to the room. He stood at the head of the table. "She'll be here in a minute. Sit, please. How's that business with the OCA going? Are they still digging around in your chemical-free shed?"

"You tell me." Mitch remained standing. "You seem to know everyone else's business."

Chris smirked. "I told you weeks ago that I had nothing to do with it."

Annoyed by Chris's expression, Mitch slapped the envelope down on the table. "Did you send these to Tayla?"

Chris picked it up and sat, leaning back in his chair as he removed the prints. With his baby-faced features, loud floral shirt and bow tie, he seemed out of place in the head chair. Mitch watched his poker face with interest. "Well, well, well. The philandering husband caught in print. I'd love to take the credit, but—"

"Come on, who else would've sent them?"

Chris held Mitch's gaze with his piercing blue eyes. "Damned if I know. But I'll tell you one thing I *do* know. My wife never strays far. And do you know why?" Chris didn't wait for his answer. "Because Ella doesn't back losers; she just fucks them and screams their name as she comes. Why the hell she wanted to jump on the organics bandwagon and follow you in your oversized footsteps as she worshipped the ground you pissed on, I have no idea."

"You spineless bastard. Ever since you missed out on Cherry Grove, you've stepped up your personal vendetta against me. First the grapefruit and avocados, then the OCA, and now a shitload of fake online reviews." The heat rising in his blood, Mitch resisted the urge to bang his fist on the table. Justice couldn't come soon enough.

Chris moved to the drinks trolley and poured himself a drink. He took a sip. "I have no clue what you're talking about. But, hey, a man can only take so much when he finds out an archrival is screwing his wife. Maybe some other guy's out to prove his point. And as far as I'm concerned, you deserve everything you get. Why the hell Tayla married a loser like you, I have no idea. She seemed such a nice girl when we had dinner together, but then, there's no accounting for taste."

Mitch clenched his jaw, determined not to let the 'dinner' comment outwardly rile him. He had no idea Tayla had met with Chris. Why would she keep that from him?

Both men stilled as Ella stormed into the boardroom. She planted her hands on her hips. "Would you guys keep it down. I can hear you from my office."

Noticing the photos strewn across the desk, she frowned at Mitch. "You told him? About us? How could you?" Her back to Chris, she stepped toward Mitch and murmured, "I said I'd take care of it."

Mitch backed away, his mouth dry. She'd always played her parts well, and today was no exception. "There is no *us*, Ella. What the hell are you playing at?"

Ella turned to Chris. "I know how this looks, but he won't leave me alone." She lowered her tone, and when she spoke, she sounded like a whiny teenager. "I was gonna tell you, baby, but I didn't want to make things worse between the two of you. He means nothing to me."

"Bullshit." Mitch raised his voice. "You come to my door at two in the morning, crying your frigid heart out, and now you're saying we slept together? Unbelievable."

"You've been after me ever since you broke up with Prue," Ella hissed. "Then when I rejected you, you turned around and eloped with the girl next door. Chris is right—you really don't have much going on between the ears, do you?"

Mitch shook his head. Luka had warned him about Ella, but he'd always given her the benefit of the doubt. "This trouble at Lime Tree Hill, it's all about revenge, isn't it? I turned you down, so you're out for blood. You always did have a nasty streak."

Her nose in the air, Ella remained silent. It was the first time he'd ever seen her lost for words. He looked at Chris. "Who should I send the account to for the grapefruit and avocados?"

"Email it to the office. I'll make sure to dump it in the *trash* where it belongs." Chris smirked. "Now, if you'll excuse me, some of us have work to do." He stood and held open the door.

When Mitch turned to Ella, her expression was cold. "I want those fake reviews removed within twenty-four hours."

"I have no idea what you're talking about." As usual, her tone was measured. Controlled. "You come in here throwing around accusations with no proof. What's wrong with you? I thought we were friends."

Mitch held her gaze until she broke eye contact. "Fine. If that's the way you want to play it." He reached into his pocket, pulled out the USB flash drive, and slid it across the table. "You want proof, knock yourself out."

He looked Chris straight in the eye then checked his watch. "As of half an hour ago, the police have all the details, including CTV footage of Ella letting herself into my loft when my wife and I were out of the country recently. Plus a statement from one of your ex-workers who helped strip the avocado trees. Oh, and, that guy you offloaded my grapefruit onto, he's come clean as well."

Chris scoffed. "You're bluffing."

"I wish I was. I'm sick and tired of your underhanded attempts to destroy me." He glanced back at Ella, whose face was ashen, then walked to the door. "I'll see you both in court."

47

PERCEPTION

THE FOLLOWING DAY, Tayla pulled up outside her parents' condo to find Valentina waiting for her, dressed in her school uniform. Her smile lit up Tayla's afternoon, and she jumped out of the car to engulf the younger woman in a hug. Valentina belonged to Mitch's world. A world Tayla missed and longed for.

"Hi, you." Tayla stepped back. "I thought you'd finished school for the year?"

"I had my last exam this afternoon. English."

"How was it?"

Valentina scrunched up her face. "Not good. I'm a creative, not a nerdy academic, but I think I did enough to pass."

Tayla fished in her bag for her keys and opened the door. "Come in. Mum and Dad are at my sister's, so I'm house-sitting."

"Yes, so Mitch said." Valentina followed her inside and dumped her backpack beside the sofa. As her judgmental eye flicked around the space, Tayla had to suppress a grin. "But I call bullshit."

"Do you now?" Tayla moved to the sink and poured two glasses of water from the filter. She passed one across the island.

Valentina drained the glass and held it out for a refill. "Look, I get it. Boys, they're so freaking complicated. Always wanting to play lead guitar and expecting us to play bass. But you and Mitch, you make loving look like it's meant to be, and I don't see that often. I need you to succeed because if you guys blow it, what chance do the rest of us have?" Valentina's eyes misted with tears.

"Hey, come here." Tayla opened her arms, and Valentina gave her a half-hearted hug. "What brought this on?"

"I was at the loft yesterday, and when I looked in the closet, your stuff was still gone. It made me sad."

"Don't be sad, sweetie. We'll work it out." She took a pack of tissues from her bag and handed it to Valentina.

"So, what did he do? And don't say he cheated with Prue, because that's not who he is."

Valentina was right. Some men cheated, no matter what. Others, only if the opportunity arose, but many men wouldn't dream of cheating. Tayla now believed that Mitch was in the third category. "We just need some space, that's all."

"No, you don't. You need to be honest with each other."

"It's not that simple. Time is not only a great healer; it also helps to put things in perspective. It clears the mist."

"I get that, but Mitch is like a father to me. He's not really old enough to be my father, but he treats me with respect. He even pays my school fees at Immaculate Heart. Bought my uniform and everything. Did he tell you that?"

"He didn't, no."

"See, that's what I mean. What's wrong with you guys? Why don't you communicate? I was expelled from my last school. If it wasn't for him, I'd be running around with boys in cars and working in some fast-food joint."

Tayla smiled. With Valentina's creativity and free spirit, she couldn't imagine her flipping burgers for a living. "First, there's nothing wrong with working in a fast-food joint. Second, talking of food, are you hungry?"

"Always."

"Why don't you text your mum and ask if you can stay for dinner? I'll drop you home later. Or we could go out."

Valentina narrowed her eyes. "First," she mimicked Tayla, "I'm in my school uniform, duh. Second, I don't have the money for dinner out. And third, Mum's working until nine, so she might not get the text until her break."

"Okay, well, text her anyway while I find you something to wear. And don't worry about money. Norman's paying."

"Norman?" Valentina frowned. "Isn't he that dead guy?"

Tayla chuckled. Norman may have passed into the spirit world, but he'd be forever alive in her heart. "Only in body. He may even help with that sewing machine you're saving up for."

"Really?" She stepped up to Tayla and hugged her, then pulled back. "When we first met, I thought you were stuck up. But you're kind of neat when you relax a little."

"Thank you. I think."

"Can I wear those wide-leg striped pants and the black off-the-shoulder top?"

Tayla chuckled. "Sure."

Mitch: I have a bedtime story for you.

Tayla: Describe its plot in one word.

Mitch: Perception.

Tayla: Sounds interesting. Sweet dreams xx

Mitch: Don't go. What have you been doing today?

Tayla: Valentina and I went out for dinner. It was great. I met her mum when I dropped her off. She's lovely.

Mitch: Yes, she is.

Tayla: What about you? How was your day?

Mitch: Kind of lonely to tell you the truth.

Mitch opened the sliding door and settled himself in her chair, the novel in question on the side table. Staring at his phone, he wondered if she'd text back. He'd told Tayla to take her time. And while he understood her reasons for pulling back, the longer she stayed away, the more he questioned her need to do so. Granted, Hayden had betrayed her, but infidelity wasn't part of Mitch's nature—never had been—and he hoped he'd made that clear.

The memory of their last time together surfaced. How confident she'd seemed when he reached for her. And when he'd arrived in Queenstown to an overcast afternoon, he'd wished she was there. To share the sight of the snow-capped peaks, to smell that fresh mountain air, and to make love to in his hotel room overlooking the lake.

Mitch: I miss you. More and more each day.

He imagined holding her, kissing her until she moaned his name. Tayla had only to ask, and he'd jump in his truck, race into town, and take her in his arms.

But she never asked.

Tayla: I miss you too. But thank you.
Mitch: For?
Tayla: Giving me breathing room. You're a good man.
Night xx

48

UNDER THE DOGWOOD

THROUGH THE FRONT windshield of his Hilux, Mitch watched Tayla as she waited for her turn in the lineup. She paddled backward several times, moving to the end of the group as if she didn't have the nerve to take the wave.

Willing her forward, Mitch left the truck and strolled along the beach until he had a better view. The day was hot, and a light breeze stirred the pines. Instead of a wetsuit, she wore a high-necked black rash guard. Although her torso was completely covered, with her hair wet and athletic body glistening in the sunlight, she couldn't have looked sexier.

And he couldn't have been prouder.

Tim paddled close by, her partner of choice in the water now. It saddened Mitch. He wanted to be there for Tayla, but maybe she had to conquer her fear without him. As she moved down the lineup, her gaze scanned the shore. She noticed him. Waved.

Her board lifted with the swell, and while he struggled to read her expression, there was no mistaking the determination in her body language. She paddled forward into the pocket, generating enough speed to stand up.

When she glided along the wave, her feet, head, and weight

were exactly where they should be. He wanted to jump up and clap, to race into the water and pull her into his arms. Instead, he sat in the sand and watched from behind his sunglasses, wondering if she'd ever change her mind.

At one stage, he thought she might come and say hi, but it was Tim who made that initial contact.

"Thanks for the text," Mitch said as he continued to watch her. "She's doing great."

Tim sat beside him. "Out there, maybe. Not so much otherwise. I've never seen her like this…well, not since high school."

"I feel like we're caught in a whirlpool, being sucked away from each other."

"Whatever you do, don't give up. She loves you, man. She'll come back." Tim motioned to the waves. "You coming in?"

"Not today. My wife deserves her time in the sun without me cramping her style. I might go to the falls and lose myself under the veil." He slapped Tim on the back then gazed out over the water again. "You've done a good job. Look at her go."

Tim shot Mitch a sideways glance and grinned. "You did the groundwork; I just added some encouragement. She's been at the beach every day this week, spent more time in the water than out, but she keeps getting back on that board. Right. I'm going back in."

"Enjoy."

As Mitch watched Tim walk away, he murmured, "And that determination, my friend, is why I'm so in love with her."

Back in his truck, Mitch was just about to reverse when he noticed Tayla running up the sand toward him. He pushed the gear lever into park and cut the engine, his arm out the window. "Hi. I saw you take the wave. Well done."

She hesitated, shuffling her feet in the sand. "Thanks. It feels great."

"Tim tells me you've been living at the beach for the past few days."

"Yeah, pretty much." She glanced away briefly, shielding her eyes with her hand. "I was just wondering... It's Norman's anniversary tomorrow. Are you going to the cemetery?"

"Yeah, I thought I might. I have to carry on to Luka's parents' place after, but I'll be there around four thirty if you want to meet up."

"Okay. Sounds good. I'll see you then." Her smile gave him hope. He wanted to kiss her with every ounce of passion he could muster, but she didn't offer him the opportunity.

Mitch put his foot on the brake and started the truck, his gaze focused wholly on Tayla. The saltwater in her hair, that ridiculously sexy rash guard, those long lashes casting feathery shadows across her cheekbones, and her legs—muscular and tanned. She stepped back.

"You look good out there. I'm proud of you." Before she could reply, he reversed and drove away, the woman he loved a fading image in his rearview mirror.

It was right on four thirty when Mitch pulled into a park outside the gates of the cemetery the following day. Summer had turned humid, the sky dulled with an oppressive haze. He sat for a moment, his thoughts finding order as he watched Tayla crouch beside his grandfather's grave.

The days without her had been tough. Empty. As he'd walked the Milford Track, consumed by the majestic beauty of nature, it had never occurred to him that when he returned home, excited to see her and desperate to reconnect, she wouldn't be exactly where he'd left her.

He climbed out of his truck and walked toward her, his grandfather's last letter slotted in the back pocket of his jeans. She turned as he approached. "I thought you'd be waiting in your car," he said.

She stood to greet him, her smile soft as she leaned forward and kissed him on the cheek. "Yes. I've faced a few fears lately. Coming to the cemetery alone being one of them. I feel his spirit here. Maybe that doesn't make logical sense, but there you go. Besides, I needed to talk to him about the money. I still don't understand why he chose me."

Mitch stepped away to place bunches of lemon blossom and lavender on each grave: first his father's, then his grandmother's, and finally, Norman's. "Why is it so hard for you to accept that he loved you?"

She crouched down again and bruised a sprig of lavender between her fingers before inhaling the scent. "I don't really know the answer to that one."

"He talked about you sometimes. Usually after a glass or two of tawny port. He'd get quite a glow on and, believe it or not, could be amusing once he relaxed." He motioned to a park bench under a nearby dogwood tree. "Shall we?"

As Tayla sat, she lifted the hair off her nape and secured it with a band from her wrist. He loved her neck, the creamy skin flawless and soft. She liked to be kissed there, the effect always immediate.

"Whatever you decide about us," he said, "I want you to have the money. It's yours, not mine. Even when we married, it wasn't about the money. With Cherry Grove landlocked by Lime Tree, it made sense for me to buy it when your folks decided to sell. Also, I wanted to protect the river."

She nodded as she twisted her wedding ring, deep in thought. The fact that she still wore it gave him hope.

"Norman had few acquaintances, and even fewer friends," he continued "One of the only people who shared his grief, he shunned."

"You mean your mother?"

"Yes. Mum. She tried to reach out, but he wouldn't accept it. It made for a fractured family dynamic, something I found hard to understand until I matured. But Norman had a lot of time for you.

He said you never expected him to be anyone other than himself. That unconditional acceptance of who he was set you apart from the rest."

"There were days when I longed to join him in his solitude." Tayla smiled. "To lounge around in my dressing gown, eat shortbread, and simply be. He loved my shortbread."

"Yeah. I did too. He'd count how many were left in the jar. I remember when I arrived home drunk from a party once and inhaled six pieces in one sitting." Mitch chuckled at the recollection. "He was furious and didn't talk to me for a few days."

"I can imagine."

They sat in comfortable silence for a moment.

"Anyway, I have something for you. Here." Mitch handed Tayla the thick white envelope he'd pulled from his pocket. She looked at the inscription. *Mitchel Harrington.* It was obvious by her expression that she recognized Norman's fluid hand.

"What is this?"

"Read it."

Tayla turned the envelope over, opened the flap, and removed the letter. She unfolded it and scanned the text before flicking her sight to the top of the page. Mitch studied her expression with interest.

"*...I've met a girl who's stolen my heart. You will know who I mean. With her unique style and poise, she's not easy to ignore.*" Tayla caught his gaze and frowned. "Who does he mean?"

"Keep going. You'll see."

She read in silence, her expression alternating between amusement and concern. When she reached the last paragraph, she found her voice again and continued aloud, "*If we lived in a society where elders chose life partners for their offspring, she would be my choice for you. Your loving grandfather, Norman.*"

Tayla looked at Mitch and frowned. "Does he mean me?"

"Who else?"

After scanning the page once more, she folded the letter and returned it to the envelope. Handing it to Mitch, she asked, "When did you receive this?"

"It was in the top drawer of his writing desk when he died."

"Wow. I don't know what to say." She smiled sadly. "He struggled to sustain relationships in real life, but he loved fictitious romance. I remember when we binge-watched *The Bridges of Madison County* three times in the same week. Apart from Audrey Hepburn, he always said Meryl Streep was the most beautiful woman in film."

Mitch gazed across the cemetery toward the coast. He'd watched that movie with Norman too and had been so embarrassed by the bathtub scene that he'd made a beeline for the bathroom as soon as it started. "The old guy wanted us to be together," Mitch said.

"He wanted a lot of things that had no basis in reality."

Mitch took her hand. "I want it too. Being apart doesn't work for me, Tayla. And I don't want to pressure you, I just want you to know how I feel."

"Even when our relationship is based on a lie? You didn't choose me, Mitch. I don't want to be a convenience just because I crashed into your life through a set of circumstances neither of us planned."

"I get that. But my grandfather chose you, and for once, his perception was spot on. Norman may have been a pigheaded recluse, but he understood love and loss. His awareness never ceases to amaze me."

Tayla nodded her agreement, but it was clear she was still struggling with her doubts. Pressing her to make a decision right now would only push her away. He leaned over and kissed her on the cheek. "Don't stay away too long. It's lonely without you in my arms."

He stood, headed back to the Hilux and jumped inside. She kept eye contact as he peered through the windshield, her brows knitted together with concern. And as he shifted the gear lever into reverse, he remembered the leather jacket he'd bought her, wrapped up on the passenger seat, and wondered if she would ever share his bed again. Ever sit at his table.

Ever come home.

Throughout the following day, that thought stayed front and center in his mind, but when he walked into the kitchen after work, a large jar of shortbread sat on the counter with a handwritten note that said:

Your many acts of kindness have
never gone unnoticed.
Love you.
Tayla. xx

49

PANCAKE ROCKS

Mitch: Meet me at the pancake rocks. Sunday 5 p.m.
Mitch: And I know what you're going to say.
Tayla: What's that?
Mitch: You don't like to be summoned.
Tayla: I'll make an exception just this once.
Mitch: Good. Bring an open mind and jeans. And your leather jacket.
Tayla: Oh? Sounds interesting. Shall I wear a top? Underwear?
Mitch: *laughs*

WHEN SHE ARRIVED at Petrie Bay to find Mitch's truck nowhere in sight, Tayla's heart sank. Out on the Pacific, surfers dotted black in the blue, the swell lifting their boards up and down as they waited for their turn in the lineup. It had been a hot day, and she longed to join her superficial friends—those regular surfers she nodded hello to as she shared their waves. Fellow travelers on that out-of-your-head road.

Stepping from the car, she recalled the last time they were here: Mitch watching from the shore, his sunglasses firmly in place. And as if fate had waved its hand, he'd arrived at just the right moment. She'd never forget riding the wave successfully for the first time, or Mitch being there to see it.

Her parents didn't yet know about the surfing—she hadn't told them of the triumph or joy. The adrenaline. They'd nearly lost her at six, then again as a teenager, and those two events had forged their parenting style for the rest of her life.

She removed her sandals and walked across the sand, holding them with nervous hands. The burnished orange of her full-length linen dress offset her tan, and the float of the fabric around her ankles gave a sense of freedom that matched her mood. The jeans he'd mentioned in the text were in her car, along with her new leather jacket and a pair of Chucks.

Tayla had made her decision about their marriage when they'd met at the cemetery—before that, if she was honest. But right now, her bravado seemed misplaced; Mitch was still nowhere in sight.

With her stomach in knots, Tayla strolled up the beach. She sat on a large log of driftwood, watching as people passed—elderly lovers holding hands, kids joking with each other, and dogs walking their owners. The smoothness of the wood felt cool under the fabric of her dress, and although the wind had died down, the taste of salt lingered on her lips.

Apart from that one text, there had been no contact with Mitch since that day at the cemetery. Five lonely days. Tayla had seen him once, driving his truck along Seaview Road as she waited on her Vespa at an intersection. If he saw her, he didn't let on. But the next day, a package arrived for her at the hospital. When she pulled back the wrapping paper, a black leather jacket sat nestled in layers of tissue. The card with it read:

For those days when your Vespa just doesn't cut it.
Love always,

Mitch xx

Tayla had quickly tried it on, smiling as she inhaled the sweet smell of leather. But when she'd texted him her thanks, he hadn't replied. Even now, with the jacket sitting on the back seat of her car, his lack of communication worried her.

She checked her phone. Five twenty-three. She had no missed calls, no new messages. It reminded her of the day at the chapel when Hayden failed to show. Except without the heat and the wilting bouquet.

As she stood and brushed the sand from her dress, her sight drifted to the south once more. And there he was, standing in the very spot where they'd recited their empty vows. Dressed in a white cotton shirt and jeans rolled up at the ankles, he kept his hands in his pockets. Lying on the rock next to him was his leather jacket and a helmet. She stepped forward, increasing her pace until she reached him. Mitch held out his hand and smiled, and as she took that last step, he did the same.

"Hi." She stood on her tiptoes and kissed him. Then kissed him again as the tension left her body.

"That was nice." His eyes twinkled in the late afternoon light as he looked down at her. "I miss kissing you."

"Me too." They kissed once more, hands entwined as they renewed their connection. "You've got your bike running?"

"Yeah. And before we talk, I'd like to take you somewhere. Did you bring your jacket and jeans?"

"Yes, they're in the car." She looked over to the Ducati parked on the road verge next to her Subaru. "But are we going on the bike? I don't have a helmet."

"Here." He handed her the helmet. "This one's for you; mine's over there. Come on, let's get you changed."

Back at the car, Mitch helped her with her jacket and offered instructions on how to ride pillion. He climbed on first, and as

Tayla snuggled in behind him, she relaxed, the warmth of his back and smell of leather calming her.

Mitch took off slowly, the dust from the gravel road billowing behind them until they reached the Eastern Pacific Highway. She held on tight, scared but exhilarated as he changed gears and increased his speed.

When they reached the turnoff to Cherry Grove, he rode up the driveway and parked in front of the steps leading to the veranda. She climbed off the bike and stood in front of her old family home. Mitch joined her, removing his helmet before helping Tayla with hers.

"How did you enjoy the ride?"

His smile warmed her insides. "It was a bit scary, but I loved it. What are we doing here?"

"I want to show you something. Come on."

Her jacket hanging open, Tayla followed Mitch up the steps, her legs still a little wobbly from the ride. He unlocked the door, and as she followed him inside, she wondered where the tenants were. "It's empty. Have Will and Alexis moved out?"

"Yeah, they bought their own house in town, so she could be closer to her work."

Mitch opened the French doors onto the veranda, letting the breeze greet the room. And as Tayla scanned the space, devoid of laughter and color and oversized cotton-covered sofas, a pang of nostalgia surfaced. She missed this house more than she'd realized. Missed the ambiance of a home well loved and cared for.

Beyond the windows, rain clouds rumbled closer, and the scent of lavender from the garden freshened the air. Mitch turned to look at her, his eyes dark, his expression hopeful. He wore his hair a little shorter now, and if anything, he looked better than ever. Tayla basked in the visual form of him: his butt in tight jeans, the tattoo just visible below his rolled-up shirt sleeve, and impressive biceps straining against cotton. But mostly, she loved the way he communicated his mood with a lazy gaze and knowing smile.

Mitch walked toward her, hands outstretched. "Are you hungry?"

Returning the gesture, Tayla met him halfway, her hands slipping into his. "A little. When are your new tenants arriving?"

"I don't have new tenants." He led her outside to a small ironwork table set for two—with silverware, plates, wine glasses, and candles—and pulled out a chair.

She removed her jacket. "What's all this? It looks gorgeous."

"Sit, please. I have food. I'll just go grab it."

As Mitch walked away, she gazed out over the newly planted grapefruit trees toward Norman's cottage, and in the far distance, the packing shed where they'd shared their first kiss, their first touches of passion. She smiled at the memory.

Mitch returned a few minutes later, carrying a large platter of rice paper rolls, fresh herbs, julienned vegetables, and dipping sauces in one hand and a bottle of pinot grigio in the other.

She accepted the platter and placed it in the center of the table. "Wow, you've been busy. It's like a picnic."

"I can't take the credit for the food, but I did open the wine."

"Let me guess, the staff at the farm gate store made the platter to your specifications?"

He filled her glass. "No, Valentina did. She's a budding chef. Anyway, I want to say something before we start. Promise me you won't interrupt until I've finished."

Tayla nodded. Sipped her wine. Wished they could make love. "Okay."

He cleared this throat. "When I saw you in Simon's office that first day, I had no idea which sister you were. When Simon called you Tayla, I couldn't believe you were the goth girl with the half-shaved head who was also a beneficiary of Norman's will. I didn't like you much back then, but you still intrigued me. Weeks later, when we discussed the Gauguin prints, I wondered if Norman might have been onto something when he suggested we'd be good together."

He reached for her hand across the table and squeezed gently. She sat still, afraid of what he might say next.

"You've fascinated me for a long time. But my excitement for you, the real excitement, started the day we said our vows. When we arrived at Little Brown Barn afterward, I was so nervous, I could hardly eat a thing. And as we walked up the stairs that night, your skirt swishing on the treads, I wanted to pick you up and carry you to my room so I could spend the night making love to my beautiful bride."

Her brows knitting together, Tayla swiped away the tears threatening to flow.

"And that excitement's still there every time I hear your car come up the driveway. When you crack small jokes, and cry at sad movies. And when I see the way you are with the people you care about, I admire you so much. But our lack of trust, our jealousy, has damaged what we had. Unless we address those issues, maybe we can't find common ground."

Tayla looked away for a moment, pressing her lips together to halt the tremble, not trusting herself to reply. Although she'd heard his words, she couldn't quite grasp his meaning.

"I'm not going to pretend I wasn't jealous of you and Hayden," he continued. "When you went to Sydney, I didn't trust you to be faithful, and I had no right to expect you would be. All the time you were away, I imagined you with him—sleeping in his bed, eating out at fancy restaurants, and conducting your 'intellectual relationship,' but this time, with added intimacy. I thought you'd want to experience sex with other men. That you'd be curious."

"Why would you even think that?"

"Because you're a highly sexual person, and I wasn't sure if I'd be enough for you. So, I'm sorry I doubted you, but if I'm not enough—"

"I—"

Mitch held up a palm to stop her. "Just one more thing. I choose you…in every way, and I hope you'll choose me back. And before you answer, I have something for you." He pulled an envelope from underneath his placemat and handed it to her.

"Should I be scared?"

"Depends. Open it."

She lifted the flap and pulled out the document, her eyes widening with disbelief as she studied the deed with her name on it. "What is this?"

"Before we married, you said you wanted to live here, alone. I still think of this house as your home, and I'm sure you do too. So, I want you to have it. And whether you choose me or don't, this house and the two acres it sits on will always be yours."

"But you can't do that. That's crazy."

"Well, I hope we can live here together. If not, at least I'll know that wherever you travel or live or work, the Cherry Grove homestead will always be your home." He flashed her a wide grin. "We could be neighbors with benefits if you want."

She grinned back, cocked a brow. "I don't think so."

"Right. Let's eat, give you time to think about it." Mitch picked up a rice paper roll and dipped it into the sauce.

"I've done nothing but think lately. I need to say my piece while it's fresh in my mind."

He placed the roll on his plate.

"Thank you for this generous gift, but..." She shook her head, struggling for words, her mouth dry until she took another sip from her glass. "Anyway, I no longer have feelings for Hayden, but I was so jealous of Ella and Prue that I didn't trust you either. When I saw those photographs of you and Ella together, I cried every night for a week. I'm sorry for doubting you, but over the past few days, I've realized how far we've come as a couple. These moments, when we speak from the heart, are what matter in life. And while I appreciate your grand gesture, I don't want to live in this house alone. But we could live here together...if you'd like to."

He leaned over the table and kissed her. "There is nothing I'd like more."

"Also, I was thinking about telling Mum and Dad...about us and the orchard. But I don't want to cause Dad any more distress, so I've decided against it. What do you think?"

"Absolutely. I feel the same way about Mum and Frank."

"Good. That's settled. And there's something I've been meaning to ask you."

He waited.

"Who was the girl you were with in Queenstown? The one who tagged you on Facebook?"

Mitch frowned as he removed his phone from his pocket and scrolled back to refresh his memory. He chuckled as he handed her the phone. "This one?"

She nodded.

"That's Dani, Luka's sister. She's living down there at the moment. And before you ask, I've never slept with her. We've partied together occasionally, and hard. She's nothing like Luka, doesn't have a reserved bone in her body. Anything else?"

"Not right now."

"I have a question for you. Why did you have dinner with Chris Stone?"

"Who told you that?"

"He did."

"Andrew Harper set it up—when Chris tabled his offer for Cherry Grove. The man's a jerk. Called me babycakes."

Mitch flashed her a wide grin. "Whoa. I bet that didn't go down well."

"It didn't. That was the night I decided to reject his offer and marry you."

Low laughter bubbled from his throat. "Are you saying Chris calling you babycakes is the reason why you chose me?"

"Kind of." She shot him a knowing smile. "Anyway, let's eat. I'm starving."

He shook his head. "Hold on a minute. I have terms."

Tayla reached for a carrot stick and took a bite. "Of course you do. Go ahead."

"First, we don't sleep in your parents' old bedroom. That would be weird. Second, apart from our special things, we buy new beds, furniture, and curtains, so it's ours."

"Sounds good. Is that all?"

His hand on his chin, Mitch held her gaze, a slight smile coming into play. "We christen the Ducati. Tonight. Under the cherry trees. Naked apart from our leather jackets."

"Is that even possible?"

"Course it is. Not that I've ever made love on a motorcycle before, but I'm sure we can make it work."

"I don't know." She offered him a coy smile. "I was thinking we should stay celibate for a while, get to know each other better."

He folded his arms over his chest, his expression giving nothing away. "Tell you what, why don't you accept my terms as they stand, and we'll worry about getting to know each other later. How does that sound?"

She thought for a moment before offering her glass in a toast. "Terms accepted."

The End.

Thank you so much for reading *Lime Tree Hill*. I appreciate your support.

Book Two in the Reluctant Kiss series, *Reluctant Chemistry,* is now available on Amazon stores worldwide.

So if you're curious about Luka O'Leary and his history with CeCe Dobson, order *Reluctant Chemistry* today or download for free in KU.

. . .

Reluctant Chemistry.

**"I wish we could live like there's no tomorrow
and love like there is."**

He picked her up from the side of a dirt road.
Ankle: Sprained.
Mood: Agitated.
Interest: Piqued.

Oh, the romance of that balmy summer.
Floating on the swell at Sandwater Bay.
Eating plump white-flesh nectarines straight from the tree.
Singing along to Calvin Harris on the radio.
It was a summer fling, nothing more. Until…

An off-the-cuff remark from her father tossed them into turmoil.
Summer romance over.

He met her again a few years later, not by fortune or design, but
rather by a twist of fate.
Face: Elegantly beautiful.
Mood: Indifferent.
Interest: Elsewhere.

The second chance he never saw coming. He wouldn't drive away
this time.
Because…

One Reluctant Kiss Would Never Be Enough.

Welcome to Luka and CeCe's story.

**Buy Now at Amazon Stores Worldwide
or download for free in KU.**

MANY THANKS

Dear Reader,

As you may have guessed, I'm a Kiwi, so I often write about Kiwi characters living in Kiwi locations. And down here in New Zealand, some things are a little back to front and upside down compared to where you may live.

The school year goes from February to December, we have a summer Christmas, not a winter one, autumn (fall) is in April, spring in September, and kiwis (the fruit) are called just that—kiwifruit. We also drive on the left side of the road, and the legal drinking age is eighteen.

And, Kiwi authors love reviews, so if you enjoyed *Lime Tree Hill*, please consider leaving a short review/star rating on Amazon and/or Goodreads.

Thanks. Your reviews matter, and I appreciate your time.

Frances.

ACKNOWLEDGMENTS

When I wrote this book, the title, *Lime Tree Hill,* had been with me for some time. I wanted to set it in New Zealand because Mitch lives here—and, it's a great place. For this reason, I've decided to call the New Zealand-based books in the series 'A Reluctant Kiss,' while the 'Imagined Kiss' books are those set in London.

As always, there are many people to thank for their contribution along the way. My editors: Liz Dempsey from The Error Eliminator for your attention to detail. I couldn't do this without you, Liz. Emma Bryson, who helped develop the story. To Steven Novak, from Steven Novak Illustration, for the cover completion, it's great to work with you.

Thanks also to my beta readers: Jane, Laura, Samantha, Carole B, and Kate GS. Your feedback was, as always highly valuable. To Kate and Marjorie for your encouragement over our writing-group lunches. Abby-Lee, Louise, Hilly, Sharlene, Phil, Yvonne, Penny, Rachel H, Gemma, Jazz, and Sarah R—I'm so blessed to have you guys in my 'enthusiastic readers' tribe. Ben and Sarah, thanks for the books on surfing and for showing us around Bondi when we visited.

To the members of the Otago chapter of Romance Writers of NZ, you guys are a great support. I'm privileged and humbled to have you in my writing life.

To Kevin, thanks always for your enthusiasm.

Last, but by no means least, to my readers. My heartfelt thanks for taking the time out of your busy lives to read my novels. If you enjoyed *Lime Tree Hill,* please consider leaving a review on your book retailer's site and sharing the title with your romance-reading friends.

And if you 'Like' my Facebook page, you'll have a chance to win a copy of my next effort.

Happy reading,

Frances

ABOUT THE AUTHOR

Frances Cowie's journey to writing romantic fiction began after waking one morning with the story of an old pump house and three characters—Rose, William, and Jessa—floating around in her head. That story, *The Watershed,* was her first novel.

A country girl at heart, Frances resides with her husband in a small town in New Zealand's Southern Lakes area and has two adult children. For more information, including sneak peeks at upcoming projects, visit Frances online:

www.francescowie.com

ALSO BY FRANCES COWIE

Clifton Falls Companion Novels

The Watershed

Field of the White Snow

An Imagined Kiss - The London Series

The List Maker

How About Thursday

Hampton Lane

A Reluctant Kiss - The South Pacific Series

Lime Tree Hill

Reluctant Chemistry

www.ingramcontent.com/pod-product-compliance
Lightning Source LLC
Chambersburg PA
CBHW030413180626
46812CB00005B/1989